Dear Reader,
I hope you find
the times, places,
and people of
Scarlet Surrender
as fascinating as
I did while writing
this book for you.

All my best,

Sandra DuBay

FORBIDDEN ECSTASY

"No," she whispered, fearful, pleading. "Don't."

"I must," he answered simply.

Her small hands pried his larger ones from about her waist and she backed away. Silently, gracefully, like some sleek black jungle cat, Grey followed.

"Please," she breathed, one fragile hand outstretched as if to ward him off. "You mustn't."

"Tell me that you've never thought of me during these past seven years."

"I haven't!"

"Tell me that you don't want me—here, now, the way I want you."

"I don't want you!" she wailed, tears welling into her eyes.

He smiled, his eyes glittering. "Liar."

SANDRA DUBAY writes "wonderful escapist fiction. It fulfills all her readers' fantasies!"

—*Romantic Times*

LEISURE BOOKS

LEISURE BOOKS
by Sandra DuBay:

FLAME OF FIDELITY
FIDELITY'S FLIGHT
WHISPERS OF PASSION
CRIMSON CONQUEST
IN PASSION'S SHADOW
WHERE PASSION DWELLS
BY LOVE BEGUILED
BURN ON, SWEET FIRE

SANDRA DuBAY

SCARLET SURRENDER

LEISURE BOOKS ❧ NEW YORK CITY

A LEISURE BOOK

Published by

Dorchester Publishing Co., Inc.
6 East 39th Street
New York, NY 10016

Printed in the United States of America

1

New Orleans 1861

"Is he dead?"

The black-haired man strolled toward the little group huddled on the ground beneath the ancient trees known as the 'dueling oaks.' A pistol dangled from his fingers, its barrel still warm, the wisp of smoke at its muzzle indistinguishable from the mist that swirled around them, writhing like a living thing, its cold, grey tendrils weaving their serpentine way along the ground.

"Is he dead?" he repeated, relinquishing his gun to his second, who brought him the dark brown coat he'd doffed scarcely a quarter of an hour before.

One of the men kneeling beside the still, pale body nodded gravely. "He is."

The man's steely gaze shifted to the other man who knelt opposite the first.

"As his second, do you consider that you have

7

received satisfaction?''

"I do," was the reply, uttered between clenched teeth in fury and hatred. "Now for Christ's sake, go!"

Bending gracefully, the man slid the second, unfired pistol from his opponent's limp fingers. A case was produced and the pistol laid into the velvet-lined hollow from which it had been taken. With a brief, final glance at his fallen adversary, he started toward one of the carriages that stood, half-obscured by the fog, at the edge of the stand of oaks. His best friend, his second at the duel, followed.

They were well away before either man spoke.

"Do you think there will be reprisals?"

The duelist lifted his eyes to his friend's face. He cocked an arched, jet-hued brow and his full lips twisted into a sardonic smile.

"Reprisals? For what?"

"For what!" Valentine Phipps was frankly amazed. He'd known Greyson Verreaux for five years and knew from experience that there was little in life that daunted him. But this was carrying things a bit too far! "Good God, Grey! You just killed Lucien Bellechasse! There isn't a Creole in New Orleans who won't be outraged!"

"He's not dead."

"He's not . . . But the doctor said—"

Grey gestured impatiently, silencing his friend. "I know what the doctor said, Val. I should. I paid him enough to say it."

"Then it was all a charade?" The thought that he worried so for nothing sent a rush of angry indignation coursing through him.

"Not entirely. The charge in Bellechasse's pistol was all too real. After all, he was serious in his challenge."

"And the charge in your pistol?"

"Tow. Oh, he'll have a nasty bruise but nothing more."

"But the way he was lying there—"

"He fainted, I imagine. Lucien Bellechasse is not the bravest of men. I daresay Marie was behind the challenge in the first place. You know what they say about a woman scorned."

"So in essence, you were unarmed."

"In essence," Grey agreed blithely.

"He might have killed you!"

Grey's sideways glance was lazily amused. "I've seen Bellechasse shoot. It would take a miracle for him to hit anything smaller than this carriage."

"What will he say when he wakes up, do you think?" Val asked, the humor of the situation taking the edge off his irritation.

"First he'll be relieved to find he's still alive. Then, he'll realize what I came to understand some time ago."

"And that is?"

"That Marie Bellechasse, beautiful though she may be, is worth neither killing for nor dying for."

"She's a beautiful woman," Val pointed out with a sigh of admiration.

"Exquisite," Grey agreed. "But faithless."

Val chuckled, the corners of his brown eyes crinkling. "Considering that you were Madame Bellechasse's lover, do you think you should be the one to condemn her for faithlessness?"

Grey pursed his lips and cast a glance askance at his friend. "I wouldn't dream of condemning the lady at all if it weren't that she had four other lovers at the same time. One lover . . ." He shrugged, an eminently Gallic gesture he had inherited from his beloved Creole mother. ". . . so long as she is discreet no one is harmed. But lover after lover after lover? I cannot condone that."

"I don't think a woman should be unfaithful to her husband at all," Val decided.

Grey laughed. "There speaks the married man." He patted his friend's arm. "No need to worry on that score. Your Elizabeth is not the kind of woman who strays far from her husband's side."

"I can't tell you how relieved I am to hear you say that," Val jibed. "By the bye—Elizabeth asked me to invite you to dinner tonight."

Grey stared out at the tree-shaded streets of the Garden District. The skies were darkening with promised rain but even the shadows of a threatening cloudburst could not dim the beauty of the magnificent mansions springing up in that part of the city.

"Thank her for me," he replied, still gazing out the window, "but I cannot join you tonight." A smile quirked the corners of his mouth and a long dimple appeared in his left cheek. "I trust the young lady will not be unduly disappointed."

"Young lady?" Val feigned innocence commendably. "Elizabeth, you mean?"

"You know damned well I don't mean Elizabeth. I mean whatever young cousin or acquaintance your pretty wife has invited along to try and tempt me into the silken bonds of matrimony."

"She means well, Grey. She thinks you're lonely. She believes you need a woman to look after you."

"Too many try," Grey sighed.

"Come now. Marriage isn't the prison that you make it out to be. You know that. You were engaged once yourself."

Grey nodded thoughtfully. Valentine Phipps

was one of the few people who knew the story of his broken betrothal.

The carriage approached the iron gates flanking the drive that circled before the columned façade of Grey's home.

"You have a visitor," Val observed, nodding toward the carriage standing there.

Grey peered out. "Oh, Christ! It's Monique!"

"Ah, the fair Mademoiselle Bouladoux." Val laughed at the baleful glare Grey shot in his direction. "Surely you don't deny that she is beautiful."

"By no means. She's exquisite. Unfortunately, her temper is as extraordinary as her beauty." He pushed open the door as the carriage rocked to a halt behind the one belonging to his fiery quadroon mistress. "Will you come in, Val? I may have need of reinforcements."

The two men mounted the steps. As they approached the door, it swung open and Grey's butler, the venerable, imperturbable Merriweather, appeared.

"Where is she?" Grey asked.

Merriweather sighed. "Having demolished the petit salon, the mademoiselle is now wreaking havoc on the study."

Grey looked past him into the long, narrow hallway. "Thank you, Merriweather. I'll see to the mademoiselle. I suggest you find a haven out of range until she's left. Coming, Val?"

From the study near the foot of the stairs came a shriek of pure rage followed by a shattering crash.

Grey winced. "That sounded expensive."

There was a moment of silence and then:

"Grey?" A breathtakingly beautiful woman in flame-colored silk appeared. Her dark auburn hair, shaken loose from its pins, fell like a glistening cloud about her shoulders. Her eyes were a pure, glittering violet and her skin the color of old ivory.

"Monique, *ma chère.*" Grey made her a mocking bow.

From opposite ends of the hall they took silent stock of each other. Monique, bosom heaving with the exertion of having torn apart two rooms, glared, her purple eyes sparkling. She was the first to speak.

"You fought a duel this morning!" she spat. "Over that bitch, Marie Bellechasse!"

"Have a care, Monique," Grey cautioned. "Madame Bellechasse is a lady and not to be abused in that manner."

Monique trembled with fury. Always jealous, nothing roused her temper quite so much as being reminded of the difference in status between a quadroon, however beautiful, and the fine Creole and American ladies to whom Grey occasionally paid his addresses.

"You defend her!" she screeched. "To me! I'll kill you!"

Seizing an eighteenth-century vase of fine French porcelain, she flung it the length of the hall sending it shattering between the two men. But though Val ducked for cover, Grey merely watched the pieces rain down on the dark flowers of the carpet.

"I've seen your aim better, *chérie,*" he told her serenely.

Curls flying, skirts whipping about her legs, Monique charged up the hall. "I'll kill you!" she screamed. "I swear it!"

Grey caught her wrists and held her at arm's length. As Val watched from the doorway of the salon in which he'd taken refuge, Grey stepped this way and that trying to avoid the sharp points of Monique's shoes.

"I hate you!" she shrieked. "I hate you!"

Then, as quickly as it had begun, the storm had passed. Weeping bitterly, she cast herself into his arms. "I was so worried," she sobbed. "I thought you would die. I thought old Bellechasse would kill you."

"You should have known better," Grey soothed. "I would not die for the sake of Marie Bellechasse."

The exquisite, tear-stained face of his mistress turned up toward his. "Would you die for me, *mon cher*?"

Grey glanced, amused, at Val. "I would not die for any woman, my dear."

Monique jerked herself out of his arms. "*Cochon*! I hate you! I wish Bellechasse had shoot you!"

"Shot," Grey corrected. He himself had taught Monique English and her mistakes were growing fewer.

She waved a dismissing hand. "Shoot, shot. I wish you were dead!"

"Then I assume you will not be too disappointed when I tell you I cannot come to dinner with you after all tonight."

The fires of Monique's volatile temper, always simmering just beneath the surface, burst once more into flame. "What!" Balling her fists, she pounded on the hard wall of his chest. "Damn you! What is it? Another of your whores!"

The lazy humor faded from Grey's face. "Monique, I am growing weary of this scene. I think perhaps it is best if you leave now."

"No! I—"

"Monique."

A look passed between them that held a threat—a threat Monique could not ignore. There was, and had always been, a point beyond which Grey could not be pushed. She had reached that point now and she knew it. A step further could spell disaster, for she knew beyond all doubt and self-deception that she needed Grey Verreaux far more than he needed her. There would always be another Monique waiting in the wings—waiting to step into the envied position of mistress to the dashing, enigmatic Monsieur Verreaux—but she knew it would be hard for her to find another protector so exciting, so generous.

Shaking his head, Grey patted Val's arm. "I don't know about you, my friend, but I could use a drink."

Amid the destruction of the study, he found the brandy and two mismatched but miraculously intact glasses. With Val's help, he tipped a gilded Regency sofa back onto its dolphin-shaped legs and sank gratefully onto its green and gold silk cushions.

"That's not a woman," Val observed wryly, "that's a hurricane! She'll do you some harm some-day, Grey."

"It's happened. On occasion she manages a rather too well-placed kick and I find myself contem-plating a life of enforced celibacy."

Val winced sympathetically. "I say we send her against the Yankees. Might shorten the war." Grey smiled wanly and he went on. "At any rate, since you're not spending the evening with Monique, why not reconsider Elizabeth's invitation?"

Grey sipped his brandy and shook his head. "I can't. I wasn't lying when I told Monique I couldn't come to dinner with her. I've been invited to the home of Christophe Duclaux.''

"Duclaux! I didn't think he knew anyone existed outside Creole society. I thought he abhorred Americans.''

Grey shrugged. "The war threatens us all, Val. I don't think men like Duclaux can afford to cling to these petty prejudices any longer. If the South falls, the Creoles will fall along with the rest of us. Apparently, he's agreed to further our interests in France. He wishes to hire *Nightshade* to take him to Jamaica. He has a plantation there so his departure should not arouse undue suspicion.''

"But why hire a blockade runner? If his departure can be perceived as legitimate . . .''

"A precaution. It seems Ramsey has been spotted in New Orleans.''

"Randall Ramsey! Washington is getting suspicious that the South may try to enlist France on her side?''

Grey shrugged. "It may be a coincidence. It may not even be Ramsey. The reporters may be mistaken. But still, no one wishes to risk it and so Duclaux wants to be away as soon as possible.''

"Even if it means breaking his iron-clad rule against dealing directly with Americans?''

"I cannot imagine that his rule is all that iron-clad.'' Grey swirled the brandy in his glass. "After all, his wife is one.''

"Is she? It seems someone pointed her out to me once but that was just after Duclaux's parents died of the fever. She was in mourning—so heavily veiled that she might have been a beauty or a beast. I couldn't tell.''

"She's a beauty. A great beauty indeed.''

"You've met her?'' Val's interest was undeniably piqued. Though he was married, and happily, he was not so far from the carefree womanizing days of his bachelorhood when he and Grey cut a scandalous swath through the hearts—and beds—of women in every city through which they traveled in their restless wanderings.

"Yes, I've met her. I met her long ago." His smile was tinged with irony. "You mentioned my engagement in the carriage. Victoria Duclaux was my fiancée's cousin. On the night of our engagement ball, Amanda discovered me in Tori's bedroom—the circumstances were compromising, to say the least." If his broken engagement had caused Grey any anguish, it was not apparent now in the wicked glint in his eye.

"And Duclaux is willing to sail with you? I should think he'd rather kill you. The Creoles are a notoriously jealous lot when it comes to their women. You should have learned that this morning."

Grey nudged the fragments of a japanned box with his toe. "I sincerely doubt Tori has ever told him the whole story of her cousin's broken engagement. It's hardly the sort of thing a woman tells her husband."

"Even so. Do you think it's wise?"

"Perhaps not," Grey allowed after a moment's reflection. "But I think it might be damned interesting. And I'll admit I'm curious to see Tori again. She was only fifteen the last time I saw her. Beautiful, to be sure, but scarcely more than a child. She's a woman now and I confess I'd like to see how she turned out."

From a single glance, he could see that Val's misgivings had not been allayed. He patted his shoulder and his smile, though meant to reassure, was amused.

"Easy, my friend. Tori's grown, a woman now. A wife. She'll likely be as curious to see me as I am to see her, but that's the extent of it."

2

New Orleans Le Vieux Carré

"Christophe!"

The bell-like voice echoed through the grand upstairs corridor, reverberating between the Moorish arches and down the exquisitely carved staircase of hand-rubbed, honey-hued South American primavera.

"Christophe!"

Below in his study, Christophe Duclaux laid aside his pen and waited. It was only a matter of time, he knew, before his wife would appear in the doorway, pretty mouth pursed in vexation over some minor problem. She thought nothing of interrupting his work over some trivial matter which she should have been able to handle quite well on her own. Occasionally he found her habitual interruptions vexing. But for honesty's sake, he had to admit that he himself had made her dependent upon him. He had kept her a child long after she should have become a woman. He had willingly spoiled her—made her little more than a pretty plaything. He had not wanted to see her grow, mature, become one of the sleek, sensuous, sophisticated Creole ladies one met every day in the shops and salons of the Vieux Carré.

Had he wanted a wife like that, he would have married long before he did. Heaven knew he had had scores of beautiful Creole *mesdemoiselles* paraded before him by hopeful mamas in the days of his extended bachelorhood. It was not until he had set eyes on Victoria Barton—not yet sixteen—that he had felt the urge to marry. He had been mere months short of his forty-fifth birthday. A part of him had felt like a ridiculous old fool for having desired to marry a girl not even out of the schoolroom but he had had no choice. He had been determined to wed her, and even the hushed rumors of a scandal that prevented her from marrying in her native Virginia failed to deter him.

He had thought to take Victoria and mold her into his notion of the perfect wife. After all, it stood to reason that a girl so young would be unformed in nature and attitude. And indeed she had proved to be an amenable, obedient, even affectionate wife. The one thing he had not counted upon was her reserve. It was as though there was a wall about her heart—like the battlements of some ancient, impregnable fortress—and he had never been able to breech that wall. It had frustrated him beyond bearing in the early days of their marriage. He had pleaded with her to share the reason she could not open her heart but she would not. At last he had simply ceased trying to arouse her passion and contented himself with the simple pleasures of having her near him—with the pride that came from having such an exquisite young wife who would never betray him as so many of his friends' wives had their older husbands.

They had settled into a satisfactory, if unexciting, union. But beneath Christophe's cool, elegant exterior beat the heart of a passionate lover, and once he had ceased trying to find the fire, the answering passion he craved in his marriage, he had taken a mistress, Joséphine Morande. Only occasionally now did he feel any last, fading glimmer of desire to break through his wife's reserve and discover the true nature he felt sure she had locked away before he met her. He contented himself now with petting her, pampering her, spoiling her.

Even now, the smile on his lips was more one of paternal fondness than husbandly love as he heard the dainty fall of her satin-slippered feet descending the stairs. The enticing swish of silk preceded her into the room.

"Here you are, Christophe." Delicate blonde brows arched over sky-blue eyes. "I was calling you. Didn't you hear me?"

Christophe leaned back in his chair and gazed at his wife. As always, he was struck by the sheer, perfect beauty of the girl he'd married. She was delicate, his Victoria, almost to the point of fragility. But that delicacy was an illusion. He had learned—regrettably, after the wedding—that her exquisite form sheathed a heart encased in steel and the will to keep it that way. She was not a shrew or a virago—she was simply unwilling to open her heart to anyone no matter how noble his intentions. It was a fault her incredible beauty almost compensated for. He sighed in admiration. Her skin was as pale and soft and fragrant as the gardenias that blossomed in the courtyard, and her hair was a glistening champagne blonde that, when freed from its pins, tumbled like a shining waterfall to her hips. The sight of it being brushed, twining like a living thing about her maid's wrist, never failed to stir him. Her eyes were the blue of a perfect summer sky and were ringed with long, curling, silken lashes. To Christophe she looked like nothing so much as an angel in some cathedral painting; to gaze at her produced a feeling inside him not unlike that evoked by the viewing of some masterwork of divine inspiration.

"Christophe," Victoria Barton Duclaux prompted gently, "I'm ready to go."

He came back to himself with a jolt. "Go, *chérie*?" he asked, searching his mind for the memory of some engagement they had accepted. "Go where?"

Tori's beautiful eyes held a mild reproach and her full, pink lower lip jutted ever so slightly. "You promised to go with me to Madame Watier's to look at the hats."

"Ah, I am sorry, *chérie*, butI cannot go with you."

"But, Christophe!"

"I am sorry, *ma chère*. Business . . ."

"Business, business!" she pouted. "Always business!"

"The war . . ."

"I'm tired of the war!"

In spite of himself, Christophe chuckled. Holding out a hand to her, he gathered her onto his lap, cuddling her as she laid her head on his shoulder. His hand clasped hers amidst the billowing folds of her silken skirts.

"I fear you will grow more tired of it before it is over, my pet. Despite what some, less practical gentlemen think, this is a conflict that will drag on for years.''

"Years! Oh, Christophe! Surely not!''

"I fear so. And men like myself, men of business, must involve ourselves in the winning of this conflict. We must do so not only to defend ourselves, but to protect our way of life.'' He shrugged his shoulder beneath her cheek. "Do you understand, *petite ange*?''

Her hand, its heirloom wedding band nearly dwarfing her tiny finger, lay amidst the snowy folds of his silk cravat. "I suppose,'' she admitted, grudgingly.

Taking her hand in his, he lifted it to his lips. "Good. Why don't you take Louise to Madame Watier's?''

She shrugged. Her maid was not her favorite shopping companion, but she supposed it was better than staying home. "Perhaps I will,'' she agreed. "When we get back, I shall show you my new bonnets. Then you will be sorry you didn't come along! I intend to spend lots and lots of your money!''

Christophe laughed. "You know I do not begrudge you your pretty frocks and bonnets, *ma chère*. But I may have to wait until tonight to see them. I have an appointment to keep this afternoon.''

"An appointment?'' Tori repeated. Her voice was filled with unease. She wondered if he were going to Joséphine Morande.

Though Victoria, like most women of her station, pretended not to know that her husband kept a mistress, she had taken pains to catch a glimpse of the beautiful, widowed Madame Morande. That single stolen glimpse had been enough to shake her.

Joséphine was dark, exotic, delicate—and feminine to the tips of her fingers. Tori had not the slightest doubt she could make Christophe believe that the sole aim of her existence was his pleasure. While Tori bore for her husband no great passion—indeed, seemed incapable of opening herself to anything approaching it—she could not bear the thought of his seeking satisfaction in another woman's arms. She could not bear the thought of his going to his mistress and reflecting on the kind of woman he could have married had he not been dazzled by her pale beauty—so different from the dark, sensual Creole charms to which he was accustomed.

Victoria slid her arms about his neck and nestled more closely to him. "Don't leave me, Christophe. Please don't go."

Christophe caressed her as she laid her head against the soft cloth of his coat. When he kissed her, she yielded her lips sweetly, submitting silently as she had always done.

He closed his eyes, sighing. Submitting . . . It had always been her way during the seven years of their marriage. She had submitted to him, yielded to his desires as, no doubt, her mother had told her a good wife must. But he longed for more—needed more. Wearily, he released her.

"I must go, Tori. I am going to be late."

Tori clasped her hands in the whispering folds of her skirts. "And you cannot keep Madame Morande waiting?"

"Madame Morande?" he repeated, uncomprehendingly.

"I try to be the kind of wife you want, Christophe." She gazed up at him, blue eyes wide. "I do try."

Christophe felt his heart swell with affection for

the beautiful child-woman who was his wife.
"*Chérie, chérie.* I am not going to Joséphine's. I
have a business appointment. Honestly. You must
not worry. You are exactly the kind of wife I want.
That is why I married you, little goose."

Holding Tori gently, he felt a bittersweet
melancholy inside him. He truly had no desire to go
to Joséphine's and it was true, in this case at least,
that his appointment was business. That had not
been the truth at other times. But he would not need
the lovely Madame Morande at all if only Tori could
respond to him, open her heart to him, release all the
passion she had locked away, crushed like a rosebud
that never had the chance to blossom. Ah, well. He
had other, more pressing matters requiring his
attention just now. He had to change his clothes,
order his carriage, and go to his appointment—a
luncheon meeting with certain representatives of the
Confederate government who would explain what it
was they wished of him and why they had arranged to
put him in touch with . . .

He snapped his fingers in sudden remembrance.
"By the bye. Did I mention that we will have a guest
coming for dinner?"

"A guest? Tonight? Only one?"

"Only one. A gentleman. I intend to enter into a
business arrangement with him. He will be joining us
for dinner, and then he and I will retire to the study."
He tugged at one of her curls. "Perhaps you could
tell Cook to prepare the sort of meals you served
back home in Virginia. I am told Monsieur Verreaux
hails from there."

Tori blanched. She couldn't have heard him
right! "What did you say?" she demanded, a tremor
in her voice that puzzled her husband.

"I said, you might tell Cook—"

"No, no. The name of the gentleman—what did you say it was?"

"Verreaux. He is not a Creole. Or wait—I believe I heard his mother was. But he is not one of our—"

"Not Grey Verreaux!"

Christophe was confused and alarmed by her sudden pallor. "Why, yes. Greyson Verreaux. But surely you could not know . . ."

"My God. Grey . . ." Tori murmured. And there was no chill in the room that could have accounted for her shivering. "Grey . . ." she whispered again. For years she had refused to think of him, had exorcised the memory of his name, his face, his touch, from her conscious mind. By sheer force of will she had endeavored to forget him. She had thought never to see him again. And now . . .

"How do you know this man?" Christophe demanded.

Tori raised a trembling hand to her lips. "He was betrothed—briefly—to my cousin, Amanda Hunter."

"Why did he not marry her?"

Victoria busied herself straightening the fronds of a fern and studiously avoided his questioning gaze. "Please, Christophe. I do not wish to speak of it. Amanda has since married a distant relative and refuses even to hear Grey's name. It was a most distressing time for my family."

Some indefinable emotion Christophe had never seen flickered across her face; a shadow of remembered pain. It bewildered him and made him vaguely uncomfortable.

"Perhaps you would prefer to remain in your rooms while he is here?" he suggested, wishing, although he did not know why, that she would agree.

It would be the easiest course, Tori thought, the safest. "Yes," she assented softly. But she knew she had to see Grey again. "No."

"Yes. No. Make up your mind, Victoria. I will speak with you later."

Tori's nod was absent. "I'll go speak to Cook now, shall I?"

Christophe watched as she turned and wandered off in the general direction of the kitchen. He didn't like his wife's reaction to the news of their dinner guest's identity. Greyson Verreaux had a reputation for attracting and seducing married women. He had fought too many duels—including the one that very morning in which he had done both his opponent and his opponent's wife the grave insult of refusing to kill the cuckolded *mari*. He was not a man any husband would welcome as an acquaintance of his wife. Moreover, Grey's acquaintance with Christophe's wife had taken place before Tori's mother had brought her to New Orleans, fleeing the breath of scandal and rather obviously in search of a suitable husband.

Christophe's sable brows drew downward as he frowned thoughtfully. No, he didn't like the notion of his wife's knowing Grey Verreaux at all. Their meeting tonight would bear watching closely—very closely indeed!

3

"*Madame*?"

Tori looked up to find her maid, Louise, holding the ruby and diamond bracelet that had been Christophe's last anniversary gift to her. Absently she held out her wrist.

"What is the time?" she asked, and her whispered words trembled noticeably.

"Half after seven," the maid replied. She eyed her mistress curiously. Though Tori maintained a certain distance between herself and all the servants, Louise could not help feeling alarmed by the state of nervous anxiety Tori had been in since she came upstairs to begin preparing for their dinner guest. Louise frowned, uncertain of how near the unspoken boundaries of their relationship she dared to step. "Is something wrong, Madame?" she ventured at last.

Tori shook her head slowly and the jeweled clasp that secured the spray of silk rosebuds in her curls winked in the lamplight. "Nothing," she murmured, though her every gesture and expression belied the word. "Leave me now, Louise. I will call you if I need you."

The maid hesitated but there was nothing she could do. Dismissed, she left the room. Her last glimpse of her mistress was of Tori gazing absently into the ormolu-framed mirror of her dressing table.

Though she stared into the silvery depths of the glass, Tori saw nothing of the pale, strained woman reflected there. Her sights were set instead on a time long past. A time she had done her best to forget. A time shrouded in the mists of passing years and unforgotten heartache.

Seven years. Only yesterday it had seemed an eternity, but now it was but the blink of a tear-filled eye. She had been a child then, a happy child filled with hope for the future and lost in the rapturous joys and sweet sorrows of first love.

She had grown up happily on her parents' plantation, Barton's Landing, in Virginia. If she knew at all that her father, Henry Barton, was bitterly disappointed that his only child had been a girl instead of the longed-for son and heir, it was only a vague awareness of missing warmth. She was beautiful. At fifteen she gave every promise of surpassing all others to become the belle of the county—and that, to her father, was some small compensation. If more were needed to salve his injured pride, the most eligible beaux in all the county had begun to swarm around Victoria. When the time came, she would have her pick of some of the richest, noblest men in Virginia. What Henry Barton did not know was that his daughter had

30

already set her sights upon one man in particular—
Greyson Verreaux.

Grey Verreaux. If Tori could be said to be the
belle of the county, Grey was indisputably its beau.
The mere mention of his name caused a fluttering of
female hearts for miles around. And with reason. As
darkly handsome as Tori was brightly beautiful, he
was also the great-grandson of a French nobleman
who had come to the fledgling United States as an
aide to the Marquis de Lafayette. In spite of the
revolution that had torn France apart seventy years
before, Grey's French cousins had regained both
their titles and their estates and still held sway over
thousands of acres of prime land both in the French
countryside and in Paris itself. They were said to
frequent the court of Napoleon III.

Though not, perhaps, as attentive as some of
Tori's would-be beaux, Grey was unfailingly kind to
her, teasing and sweet. Though he made no overtures
that could be construed as the preliminaries of a
serious courtship, his every smile, his every
compliment, filled Tori with the hope that, when she
was old enough to be deemed 'marriageable' she
would become Mrs. Greyson Verreaux.

When he began to treat her more as a lovely
woman and less as a pretty child, Tori only too
willingly plunged into the throes of first love. But if
the emotions of womanhood were awakening in
Tori, so, all too soon, did an awareness of life's
harsher realities. The dawning came on an otherwise
carefree spring morning in the unlikely form of a
letter.

Octavia Barton, Tori's mother, lay weeping on a
chaise in the ornate boudoir that adjoined her bedchamber. Tori, summoned to her side, read the tear-
stained missive that was thrust into her hand.

"Dead!" her mother sobbed. "Poor Caroline! And Robert and Stephen as well!"

Trying without much success to block out her mother's voice, Tori read the letter. It seemed the ship carrying her Aunt Caroline and Uncle Robert Hunter—her mother's only sister and her husband—and their two children from England, where they had lived for the past four years, had gone down in a storm off the South Carolina coast. There had been few survivors. Of the Hunter family, all had perished except eighteen-year-old Amanda who, miraculously, had been rescued.

Octavia daubed at her eyes with a sudden wadded handkerchief. "She's coming here to stay with us. Did you read that part, darling?"

Tori nodded. "Didn't Uncle Robert have a fine home in Beaufort, Mama? And cousins in Savannah?"

"Of course he did. But you cannot expect poor Amanda to live in Beaufort alone, nor with cousins she does not even know. We are her closest family now. She must live here until she recovers from her grief."

Tori felt a rising sense of unease that was not at all relieved when her cousin arrived days later looking fragile and beautiful in stark black mourning and bemoaning most of all, it seemed to Tori, the loss of the elegant London wardrobe purchased just before her family's departure on their ill-fated voyage.

"So tell me, little cousin," Amanda said soon after her arrival, "who is the handsomest man in these parts?"

"Grey Verreaux," Tori said, sighing.

Amanda's mocking laughter made Tori blush.

"You sound as if you're in love with him yourself. Is that it, child? How sweet! Your first crush!"

Tori scowled. Though scarcely three years separated them, Amanda was so worldly, so sophisticated and knowing, that beside her Tori felt like the gauche little girl Amanda thought she was. "It's not a crush," she hissed.

"It's not? Why, Tori, it must be love!" Amanda smirked. "And does he love you as well?"

Tori flushed with anger. "I . . . he . . . when I'm older . . ." she hedged, wishing she'd kept her secrets.

"I see." Amanda swiveled on her dressing table stool. "Tell me, dear, is your Mr. Verreaux rich as well as handsome?" Tori nodded. "How old is he?"

"Twenty-nine."

"Don't you think he's a little old for you?" There was a distinctly feline purr to her voice that set Tori's teeth on edge. "Where is this wonder? When do I meet him?"

"He's gone away on family business just now. But he will be back soon."

"I see. And has he kissed you, this handsome, rich Mr. Verreaux?"

Tori's cheeks pinkened. How desperately she wished she could regale her smug cousin with tales of stolen kisses and lovers' trysts. She was tempted to lie but she knew Amanda would discover the truth all to easily. Shrugging, she affected an air of scandalized surprise.

"Of course he hasn't! I'll have you know Grey's not the sort of man to take liberties with a lady."

Amanda's snort was derisive. "They're all that sort of man, dear! If they're not interested in taking liberties with a pretty woman, they're either impotent

or . . ." In deference to Tori's wide-eyed, uncom-
prehending innocence, Amanda censured herself.
"Well, it doesn't matter what else they may be. But
let me assure you that a gentleman of fashion won't
buy a suit without trying it on. He's certainly not
going to choose a wife with less care."

Tori couldn't disguise her shock. "But no lady
allows a man to touch her before they are wedded!"

Amanda roared with laughter. "Gad! How
provincial!" She tossed her dark blonde curls and
eyed her young cousin from beneath disdainfully
lowered lashes. "Really, Tori, your parents haven't
done you any service by immuring you in this
backwater. I assure you, very few couples in
fashionable circles wed without first having discovered if they are compatible where it matters
most!"

"Have you?" Tori could not resist asking.

"None of your business, chatterbox." Amanda
turned haughtily back to her mirror. "Now go away
and leave me alone. I'm in mourning, you know."

Tori left her cousin's room and, though she was
eager for Grey to return, she could not stem the tide
of rising apprehension over his coming meeting with
Amanda Hunter.

"It's a lie!" she had screeched on the morning,
barely two months later, when the news of Grey and
Amanda's engagement was broken to her. "I won't
believe it!"

"Tori!" Octavia whispered, shocked.

"Grey wouldn't do this! I know he wouldn't!"

Amanda had looked inordinately pleased with
herself, saying nothing as Tori's dreams shattered
about her in the rose-walled parlor of Barton's
Landing.

"I hate you!" Tori hissed. "I wish you had drowned!"

"Victoria!" Henry Barton, her father, rebuked her.

In short order Tori was dispatched to her room where she wept long and bitterly over the betrayal of her treacherous cousin and the man she had loved.

It was growing dark when Augusta Paige—Tori's nurse since her babyhood—let herself into her room. Tori lay on the high, four-poster bed staring up at the sunburst of pink satin nearly hidden by the gathering shadows of twilight.

"Tori, darling, you mustn't take this so hard."

"It's unfair," Tori breathed. "Why should she have Grey? I wanted him to be mine, Gussie. Mine!"

"He offered for Amanda, darling."

"But I love him. And I thought he might . . . some day . . ." A fresh torrent of tears flooded her eyes. "Oh, Gussie! It hurts me so! I want to die!"

The old nurse gathered her charge into her arms and rocked her as she hadn't done in years. She sympathized with the child—she herself had once loved a man and had lost him to another. Even now, after so many years the pain was still fresh. She would have done anything—anything—to spare Tori this heartache. There was nothing in the world Tori could have asked for that her beloved Gussie would not have moved heaven and earth to try to obtain for her. But this . . .

"Tori, you must realize that Grey is a man, and like all men he is susceptible to the charms of women."

"But I am a woman, Gussie."

The nurse smoothed back a dampened curl from her charge's cheek. "Not yet, sweet. Not in the way that Amanda is a woman. You see, men . . . there are things that go on . . . A knowledgeable woman can make a man . . .''

"She seduced him, didn't she, Gussie?''

The nanny sighed. There was no point in lying to her. "Yes, child, she did.''

A sob caught in Tori's throat. "But I thought he cared for me! I thought that when I was older . . .''

"He may well care for you, Tori. And perhaps, if things had been different, when you were older, his caring might have turned into something more. But he met Amanda.''

Tears glittered in Tori's eyes. "He never gave me a chance, Gussie.''

"Tori, Tori,'' Augusta cooed, at a loss to find the words to comfort her. "Someday, when this pain has passed, you will see that love—''

"Love!'' Tori snarled, azure eyes glowing savagely. "I want nothing to do with love! I'll never love anyone! No one is ever—ever!—going to hurt me again!''

"You mustn't say such things,'' Gussie admonished. "Now, dry your eyes and have faith. One never knows what the future will bring.''

"If it doesn't bring me Grey,'' Tori vowed, "then I don't give a fig for the future.''

Tucking her into the big bed, Gussie kissed her pale, cool brow. "Sleep now, sweeting. Things have a way of working out.''

"What do you mean, Gussie?'' Tori demanded. "Do you think there's a way . . . ?''

"Hush now. I don't know. Just rest, and we'll see what tomorrow brings.''

But 'tomorrow' brought no changes and the month that followed was misery for Tori. The preparations for Amanda's engagement ball went forward, and Tori spent most of her time in her room or in the rose-covered gazebo at the end of the garden. It was there that Grey found her one morning not quite a week before the ball.

"So, this is where you've been hiding, Miss Barton," he said softly, his tone lightly teasing.

"I haven't been hiding," she snapped, longing desperately to run. But he stood in the doorway, stopping her there.

"I haven't seen you when I've come to Barton's Landing."

Her mouth twisted bitterly. "I'm surprised you noticed."

His jet brows arched quizzically. "Why are you angry with me, Tori? I thought we were friends, you and I."

"Friends!" Somehow that was worse even than his betrayal. "Is that all I was to you?"

"What is all this about?" he demanded.

"I thought you cared for me!"

"I do care for you. I—"

"I mean really care! I thought you loved me the way I love you! I thought that when I was older, you and I . . ." She swallowed hard to force back the tears she couldn't bear to shed before him.

The reason for her behavior at last dawned on Grey. "Oh, Lord," he murmured as he sank to the latticed seat. "Tori, if I've given you cause to think . . . if somehow I've led you to believe . . ."

She turned her back toward him. "How you must have laughed at me!"

"I never laughed at you," he vowed gently. "And I do care for you. But it's not . . ."

She swung toward him. "I don't believe you!"

"It's true." He took a step toward her but she backed away holding out a hand to ward him off. "Tori, listen to me. There are things you don't understand. You're too young. Too innocent."

"I understand more than you think I do!" Rushing at him, she tried to push past. He held her as she struggled wildly. "Let me go!"

"Tori, listen to me. Listen!"

"No! There's nothing you can say that I want to hear! I hate you! Hate you, do you hear me! I'll never forgive you! I'll hate you for as long as I live!"

Tearing herself free of him, Tori fled from the garden to take refuge in her room. But though she vowed she would never be done with hating Grey Verreaux, she could not keep herself from going to the window to watch him walk slowly—pensively, it seemed—from the garden toward the house. It was only when Amanda appeared and linked a possessive arm through his that Tori turned away.

The evening of the ball found Tori confined to her room with a feigned cold. She tried to close her ears to the sound of a waltz that wafted up the stairs. I hate him, she told herself over and over in a venomous litany. I hate him! But she felt lonely and unloved. She wondered why Gussie did not come to keep her company on this, the worst night of her life.

Had she but known, her old nurse was at that moment in the gazebo. She had been about to return to the house when footsteps on the path had caused her to shrink back into the shadows.

In the pale, flattering light that was half golden lantern light and half silver moonglow, Gussie saw Grey pull Amanda into his arms and kiss her hungrily.

Amanda drew back as far as Grey's encircling arms would allow and laughed teasingly. "We must go back."

"Why?"

"It's our ball, darling." She chuckled. "Gad! How I love the envy on those women's faces. I swear, they all hate me for stealing you! Tori most of all. Did you notice? They said she has a cold. It's a lie, of course, she couldn't bear to come to our ball."

"Leave Tori out of this," Grey ordered. Then, to escape the questions he could see forming on Amanda's lips, he went on quickly: "I don't want to go back. I want to make love to you."

"Here! In the garden? Grey! You must restrain yourself! In a few weeks' time we'll have one another whenever—"

"No! Tonight! I'll come to you, Amanda—in the early hours when everyone is asleep."

"You mean in Uncle Henry's house? Really, Grey! We've never dared that before! Surely you can wait. The wedding will be soon."

"Not soon enough!" He plucked one perfect, full-blown rose. "Put this on the table outside your door so I'll know which is your room."

"But, darling . . ."

He silenced her with a savage kiss before leading her back up the path toward the ballroom.

Behind them, her presence unsuspected, Gussie fumed. That brazen hussy! She was just like the little slut who had stolen Augusta's own beau nearly forty years before! Well, she didn't deserve Grey! Why, she was no better than the bitches in Henry Barton's kennels.

Gussie's old eyes softened as she thought of Tori, lying miserable and alone in her room while the entire county was downstairs celebrating her misfortune. The poor, sweet child. If only Grey could be brought to see the error he was on the verge of committing. If only he could be made to realize that Tori was the girl for him! Then, perhaps, dear little Tori would not be hurt as Augusta herself had been. If only there were a way to force Fate's hand . . .

She drew herself up in the fragrant darkness of the perfumed garden. It wasn't too late! Not yet. There might still be a chance to get Grey for Tori. There might just be a way to see that it was Tori and not that little Hunter trollop who became Mrs. Greyson Verreaux!

Gathering her billowing skirts, Gussie hurried into the house and waited impatiently for the ball to end and her opportunity to arise.

Finally, those guests who lived nearby took their leave and those who were staying retired to their beds. Gussie crept along the shadowy corridors to the table outside Amanda's room, where she found the rose Grey had picked. Snatching up the blossom, she lay the flower instead on the table outside Tori's room. Grey would come looking for Amanda's chamber—looking for the perfect rose that should be lying on the table outside her door. Instead he would find the girl who truly loved him—the budding woman who was fit to be his wife.

The room was pitch black. Gussie had drawn the draperies, shutting out the light of the waning moon. Tori lay on her side in the darkness facing away from the door. She longed for sleep, ached for the sweet forgetfulness it would bring, but instead she lay awake, her senses, indeed every fibre of her body alert, tense.

When she heard the click of her door latch she

nearly cried aloud. The door swung open on silent hinges, then closed behind her midnight visitor. Though she couldn't have said how she knew, she was certain it was Grey. She held her breath as he approached the bed, his footsteps muffled by the thick pile of the carpet.

What could he be doing here? she wondered, her heart pounding furiously, her senses whirling. What did it mean? What should she do?

There was a swish of brocade as he discarded his robe. Then the bed gave beneath his weight and he was lying beside her, his body on its side, curled about hers. His hand fell onto her hip and he drew her back so that she half-reclined against him. "Grey?" she whispered wonderingly.

"You're trembling," he said softly. "Are you frightened? You shouldn't be. You know I won't hurt you." He brushed her cheek with something soft as velvet. "I've brought you the rose."

Taking it from his hand, Tori put it to her nose and the sweet fragrance of the blood-red blossom was so heady it made her senses reel. Was Grey really lying beside her, or was it all a dream, she wondered as his hand found the softness of her thigh beneath the folds of her nightdress. It savored the silken skin, explored the gentle curves, before slipping up over her hip and the narrow hollow of her waist where it lingered for a moment, caressing, teasing, before sliding up to cup the rose-tipped firmness of her breast.

Tori shivered, stunned into silence by the sensations, the emotions, he was arousing in her. She buried a groan in the depths of her down pillow as his mouth moved against the tender nape of her neck.

His hand retreated, retracing its way to her waist then descending to caress the hollow of her navel, the

41

smooth curve of her belly. Tori held her breath as it paused there for a moment—an eternity—before moving lower still.

Their sighs mingled as he touched her, caressed her, in ways she'd never dared dream of. A feeling began to build inside her, growing, rushing her toward something unknown and yet so desired. She hurtled toward it, beyond all reason, welcoming it as it engulfed her. She cried out, past caring if she were heard, and Grey held her, kissed her, touched her as she arched back against him, shuddering helplessly.

Her body had not yet ceased its quivering when the door opened. Her heart had not yet stopped its frantic pounding when Amanda entered the room, lantern held before her, and found her betrothed locked in an erotic embrace with her fifteen-year-old cousin. The sighs of Tori's ecstasy had not yet faded from her ears when they were replaced by the sound of Amanda's furious screams.

"Tori?"

Gasping, Tori looked up to find Christophe, elegant in evening dress, framed in the doorway.

"Yes?" she breathed, disoriented at being so suddenly jerked back to the present.

"Are you all right, *chérie*? You are so pale."

"I'm fine, Christophe. Fine."

He held out a hand to her. "Then come along. Our guest will be arriving at any moment."

Our guest. Steeling herself, Tori took up the painted silk fan that lay on her dressing table and went to slip a trembling hand into the crook of her husband's arm. Their guest—Grey Verreaux—the man she had hated, and loved, for seven long years.

42

4

Nothing in Grey's imaginings had prepared him for the moment when Christophe Duclaux's butler showed him into the first of the two adjoining parlors off the elegant, scarlet-carpeted entrance hall.

Though the overall impression of the twin rooms, separated by an ornately plastered archway, was one of formal elegance, he saw nothing clearly save the woman perched nervously on the edge of an emerald damask sofa.

He'd remembered her as a beautiful, delicate child. He saw her now as the magnificent fulfillment of beauty's early promise.

"Monsieur Verreaux," a low, French-accented voice said.

For the first time, Grey turned his attention to the third occupant of the room.

"Monsieur Duclaux," he replied, taking the

hand Christophe extended to him. His silvery gaze slipped quickly over Tori's husband. He was handsome, Grey allowed, in that dark Continental way that many Creole men were handsome. Older, of course, nearly thirty years his wife's senior, and the once jet-black hair was liberally sprinkled with gray. He was not so tall as Grey and his eyes were fathomless onyx far different from Grey's changeable silver which could take on the azure of a summer sky, the gray of a storm-tossed sea, or the dangerous glint of fine Toledo steel.

Christophe was saying, "I was surprised to discover, only today in fact, that you and my wife are acquainted. Indeed, she tells me the two of you were nearly related by marriage."

At last Tori lifted her eyes to Grey's face. In that single glance he saw that she had told her husband nothing of the pain—or pleasure—of the episode that had torn asunder his betrothal to her cousin.

"Yes, we were nearly cousins," Grey confirmed. "I was betrothed, briefly, to Madame Duclaux's cousin, Miss Amanda Hunter. How are you, Tori?"

Grey leaned toward her and she held out a hand to him. It lay for a moment—soft, white, trembling, dwarfed in his palm—before he lifted it to his lips. His finger against her wrist detected the fitful fluttering of her pulse and he wondered if her husband had heard the soft, sharp intake of her breath as his lips brushed her fingers and felt the icy hardness of the diamond wedding band that branded her as Christophe Duclaux's property.

"You haven't changed," she breathed, gently but firmly withdrawing her hand from his.

Grey's eyes met hers and he wondered precisely how she'd meant that.

"You have," he replied, his eyes glinting with

44

amusement. "You've grown up." Straightening, he smiled benignly at Christophe whose returning glance was filled with watchful curiosity. "The last time I saw your lovely wife, monsieur, she was a mere child of fifteen. Beautiful, to be sure, but not nearly as exquisite as she is today. Marriage to you must agree with her."

Christophe's answering smile was lifeless. There was a tension in the air he could not account for. Tori was plainly ill-at-ease—affected, he felt sure, by Grey Verreaux's mere presence. He did not like it—not at all. He longed to ask the arrogant Monsieur Verreaux to leave but dismissed the notion as foolishness. Still, it was business that brought the man to his home and there seemed no reason to prolong the social amenities any longer than strictly necessary.

"*Ma chère*," he said to Tori, "will you see if dinner will be served soon?" Turning to Grey, he explained smoothly, "At the risk of seeming rude, monsieur, I am anxious to discuss our business."

"As you please," Grey agreed, unable to tear his eyes away from the rustling sway of Tori's flounced skirt as she glided from the room.

In the hall outside the parlor, Tori paused. The cool poise she'd exhibited in the parlor shattered about her like crystal. She closed her eyes, trying in vain to will away the fit of trembling that had seized her the moment she made her escape from the parlor and from the heated weight of Grey's appraising stare.

How in the name of all that's holy, she wondered despairingly, am I going to make it through dinner if I can't even get past the introductions without losing hold of myself?

She glanced toward the darkened doorway of the sitting room on the other side of the hall. A drink, that was what she needed. One small, quick, calming sip and then she'd see about dinner.

The small family sitting room opposite the ornate twin parlors was shadowy, lit only by the golden lamplight that spilled through the open hall door. The clink of crystal on crystal was followed by the splash of whatever was in the first decanter she happened to grasp in the darkness.

Lifting the glass, she swallowed the dark, Jamaican rum. A cry died, strangled, as her throat closed against the onslaught of the burning liquor.

Tori closed her eyes and leaned against a table. Good Christ! Who would have believed that the mere act of meeting Grey again would have reduced her to this?

"Madame?"

Tori whirled. Like a child caught in some shameful act, her first impulse was to hide the glass amidst the whispering folds of her scarlet satin skirts.

"What is it, Lulu?" she demanded, her tone icy.

The girl, newly hired, began to fidget. "I thought . . . that is . . . I . . ."

Tori spared her further stutterings. "Never mind. Go tell Cook we want dinner as soon as possible."

Relief was plain on the girl's face as she scurried out of the room.

Alone once more, Tori drained her glass and set it aside. Found by a maidservant sneaking a tumbler of rum in the dark! It would be funny if it weren't all too likely to find its way into the swirling sewer of society gossip that abounded with tales of New Orleans matrons who kept spirits hidden but never far out of reach. One would think, considering the war that was raging ever nearer, that people would have better things to worry about. But gossip, it seemed, survived whatever the circumstances.

She should go back. They must be wondering what had become of her. A frown creased her brow. Would they be able to smell the rum? She hoped not. Christophe wouldn't begin to understand why the reappearance of Grey in her life would have sent his wife, who normally couldn't abide the taste of liquor, scurrying for a drink. And Grey—well, Grey would be too amused to bear. He was so arrogant, so filled with himself, so—so—

A shadow fell over her as the light from the doorway was blocked. Thinking it was the inquisitive Lulu returning, Tori swung about, scowling.

Grey stood there, his tall, broad-shouldered frame nearly filling the doorway.

—so handsome, the thought finished in Tori's mind.

"I thought you were the maid," she said distractedly, then, nervously, as he moved into the room, "Where's Christophe?"

"He went to see if there was a problem in the kitchen."

"Oh." She wondered what he would think when they told him she'd never gotten there. "I sent Lulu."

"I see." Those maddening silvery eyes took in the displaced decanter and the glass that teetered on the edge of the table. "While you . . ." He mimed raising a glass to his lips and tossing back a drink.

"Don't be vulgar," she snapped, turning her back amidst the swirl and swish of her rippling skirts.

Grey chuckled, a low, intimate sound that made Tori shiver with remembrance. "My sweet, I don't care if you're the biggest lush—"

"How dare you!"

The ice-blue fire in her eyes took not the slightest

edge off his amusement.

"Tori, Tori, I said I didn't care."

"I'll have you know I never drink!"

"Until tonight?" A mocking smile played at the corners of his mouth and his eyes sparkled with roguish enjoyment. "Whatever could have prompted this sudden change?"

Tori's creamy complexion grew mottled with exasperated anger. No razor-sharp retort sprang to her lips. Her tongue was infuriatingly tied. Clenching her fists, she strode to the door.

"We shouldn't be here," she decreed imperiously. "Christophe must be wondering . . ."

Grey whipped an arm about her waist as she would have passed him. "I've no doubt Christophe is wondering about a great many things, my love."

"Don't call me that!" she hissed. "Let me go!"

"I let you go once before. It was a foolish mistake."

He felt her tremble in the circle of his arm, smelled the slightly musky fragrance of her perfume, felt himself reacting to her nearness, her beauty. "Are you faithful to Christophe?"

Tori shivered, realizing the implications of his question. "Yes," she breathed. It was the truth.

"Do you love him?"

"Yes," she repeated, wishing that were true, too.

His arm fell away. "Then you're quite right. We shouldn't be here."

Tori hesitated, feeling oddly bereft, as though she'd lost something when he'd released his hold on her. She glanced up at him and found his eyes on her face, on the soft quivering of her curving pink lips. She knew beyond all doubt that another moment there in the dark would find them in each other's arms and that, given their circumstances, given the loyalty and allegiance she owed Christophe, and given the pain this man had inflicted on her in the past, was madness.

Grey made no move to stop her as she slipped past him and hurried up the hall toward the dining room. Waiting a moment in the silent darkness of the little parlor, he gave himself a moment to cool the heated blood that surged inside him—and gave Tori time enough to reach the dining room, and her husband, alone.

As she entered the dining room through one door, Tori found Christophe just entering through another, which gave onto the balcony that encircled the courtyard.

"Here you are, Tori," he said softly, more than a hint of stern disapproval in his tone. "I thought perhaps you and our guest had stepped out onto the balcony."

"No . . . we, that is . . ." She let the sentence trail off into nothingness, hoping he would not pursue the matter.

Grey's timely arrival spared her. "Madame was showing me the lovely painting of her that hangs in the small parlor," he explained smoothly. "Quite beautiful."

"It was a gift," Christophe replied, his black eyes betraying the fact that he believed not a single word of Grey's facile lie. "Commissioned by my wife as an anniversary present."

"You are fortunate, monsieur, to have so thoughtful a wife—and one so beautiful."

Onyx eyes locked with silver over Tori's head. The tension in the room ebbed and flowed; the hostility was undeniably mutual.

"Indeed," Christophe agreed. "A treasure

49

worth keeping—at all costs.''

Tori saw the icy calm of Grey's expression, the arrogant, confident set of the finely chiseled mouth, the dispassionate chill in his eyes, and could not help wondering if this face was the last thing his opponents saw just before he killed them in one of the numerous duels Christophe had told her Grey was notorious for.

Lifting the bell, she rang it too loudly, signalling her servants to serve the dinner she had gone to such lengths to order from her protesting Creole cook. As they took their places, she wished passionately that the meal was over and the time had come when she could retreat to the silken security of her room upstairs. At least there she could try to forget that merciless fate had swept Grey Verreaux back into her life to wreak havoc on the placid, passionless existence she'd led for the past seven years.

When the time came for her to retire, Tori bade Grey a brief farewell and fled. She undressed in silence, aided by her maid who, although puzzled by her mistress's mood, knew better than to venture more than the briefest of comments.

"You may go, Louise," Tori said when the girl lingered awaiting instructions.

As the door closed behind her, Tori lay back against her pillows. Though she wouldn't have thought it possible, she fell asleep as if the events of the evening had drained her physically as well as emotionally.

Several hours went by, hours of slumber haunted by dreams of Grey, by visions of duels, of Christophe lying dead in some meadow pierced through the heart by Grey's bullet.

She awoke, trembling, awash with guilt at the

thought of Christophe's death and wondering, while not really wanting to know, what she would do in such circumstances.

She gasped, coming fully awake, as her door opened. She held her breath, knowing it was foolish but half expecting to see Grey entering her chamber, coming to her beneath her husband's very roof.

Christophe appeared instead. His blue-black hair and rich, aged ivory complexion was set off to perfection by the deep royal blue of his dressing gown.

"Did I wake you?" he asked, crossing with silent steps to her bedside.

She shook her head, one hand reaching automatically to toss back a twining lock of her champagne-colored hair.

"I had a dream," she murmured.

"About Grey Verreaux?"

The haunted look in her eyes gave him all the answer he needed.

"Has he gone?" she asked, her betraying glance veiled by the long sweep of her lowered lashes.

"He has."

A sudden, aching constriction gripped Tori's heart. Gone! She bit back a desire to ask when he would return, saying instead: "Are you still going to do business with him?"

"Would you rather I didn't?"

Tori heard the unspoken question masked by the innocuous inquiry. She shrugged. "It's up to you. You know I've never had anything to do with your business."

Their eyes met then and Christophe was consumed with the need to possess her, to remind himself that she belonged to him, that whatever—whatever!—hold it was Grey Verreaux had over her, he could not—would not—ever have the right to touch her as her husband touched her.

Later, while Christophe slept, Tori gazed up at the lambrequins of tasseled crimson moiré that dressed the half-testor of her ornately carved bed. She lifted her husband's hand from where it lay on the smooth white skin of her belly and tucked it next to him. Her sigh was wrenched from the deepest wells of her despair. What was wrong with her? she asked herself, as she always did after those rare occasions when Christophe came to her bed. It was not him—it could not be, for he had enjoyed an enviable reputation as a lover in the days of his bachelorhood. Even now when they attended some social function, she would notice the eyes of more than one fine Creole beauty lingering on him hungrily, yearningly. Why, then, could he not arouse her, his own wife? Why could his passion not inflame hers and drive the hateful memories from her treacherous mind? Why, when she lay in his arms, did she see another man's face? Why, when he had had done with loving her, did she long for another man's touch?

Grey! Damn him to hell! In those few brief moments—in a single embrace—he had ruined her. He had stolen the key to her senses leaving her a helpless prisoner of the passion she bore for him.

She had hoped throughout these seven long, passionless years, that it would end. That she would someday cease to long for him and find the contentment she craved in her marriage. But now . . . Now Grey was back, back to reawaken all that need, that yearning, that she'd tried so hard to suppress.

Where was he now? she wondered. Lying in some other woman's embrace? Locked in another woman's arms, loving her, giving her all the pleasure his treachery had forever denied to Tori?

"I hate him," she whispered fiercely. "I hate him!"

But it was a lie and she knew it, to her shame. Beside her Christophe shifted in the bed. She held her breath, hoping he would not awaken. When he didn't, she sighed and returned to the tormenting images that plagued her.

Had she but known, Grey lay at that moment, not in the passionate embrace of some beautiful paramour, but alone in the big mahogany bed that dominated the master chamber of his Garden District mansion. He tossed beneath the sheets, his dark brow creased, trying without success to banish the pictures that taunted him—pictures of Tori and Christophe together—pictures of Christophe taking what was his by the right of matrimony.

A fierce emotion took hold of Grey then, an emotion with which he was unfamiliar, an emotion as sour as any he'd ever known. Grey scowled into the darkness. It was jealousy. He'd never known it before and now, having tasted it to the fullest, he decided it was not to his liking. But there was little he could do about it. Having found Tori again, having seen her and touched her, he knew he had to have her and damn the consequences!

5

"Tell me everything!" Clairesse urged, settling the folds of her violet silk skirt around her.

"Everything?" Tori hedged, wishing suddenly that she hadn't decided to come here, to the café run by Etienne Candé, husband of Clairesse, her closest friend. "What do you mean?"

"Victoria!" Clairesse cast an exasperated glance around the exquisite parlor of the apartment she and her husband shared above the café. "You know precisely what I mean. Grey Verreaux! Everyone knows Christophe invited him to dinner a few nights ago. I can't tell you how amazed we all were."

"It was business, Clairesse. Christophe wished to speak with Monsieur Verreaux . . ."

"Monsieur Verreaux." Clairesse's smile was feline. "Come now, Tori. Everyone says you've known him for years."

" 'Everyone' seems to be quite an expert on the goings-on in my household. If one of my servants told . . .''

"Now, don't get pettish, *chérie*. I don't know where the information came from. Likely one of Grey's servants overheard something. It doesn't matter. It's only that he is everyone's favorite topic of conversation. Any new information about him is like manna from Heaven."

"Why are they so interested?" Tori wanted to know. "For that matter, why are you?"

"Darling! Come now. It stands to reason. The man is gorgeous. He's rich, well-connected, and several shades less than respectable. His liaisons with married women are practically New Orleans legend! And he's fought far too many duels with cuckolded husbands and emerged from every one with nary a scratch to show for his troubles. But no one seems to know much about his life before his shipping concerns brought him to New Orleans. That's why the rumors about your having known him in Virginia have aroused such curiosity."

Tori sipped the strong coffee, wrinkling her nose when she found that Clairesse had laced it heavily with brandy. She set the cup aside.

"Well, I am sorry to disappoint anyone, but I really don't want to reminisce for the sake of providing more fodder for the gossip mill. Grey and I knew each other long ago. Our families were neighbors. After he left Virginia, I had no idea what had become of him. In fact, I kept so little track of him that I didn't even know he was in New Orleans until a few days ago."

"It's not surprising. I wonder that you know anyone at all! Christophe keeps you under such wraps—the sisters at the Ursuline Convent probably know as much as you." Clairesse touched Tori's sleeve. "I don't mean that as a criticism, *chérie*, but he does treat you almost like a schoolchild."

Tori sighed, turning her attention to one of the spring-green moiré d'antique bows trimming her bodice. It was the truth, she supposed. Cross as it made her, she couldn't really be angry at Clairesse for saying what so many others thought. Compared to other women she knew, she was treated less like a wife than like a child who needed constant supervision and protection. But privately she had to admit that after seven years, she had come to depend on Christophe for her sense of security. His presence was the one constant in her life. If nothing else, she could always depend on Christophe to keep the cruelties of a harsh world from trespassing into the serene, uncomplicated existence she'd led since her marriage. Not even to herself could she admit the extent of the turmoil into which his imminent departure plunged her. Nor could she bring herself to recognize the source of the turmoil—the fact that Christophe, her protector, her security, would soon be far away across the Caribbean, while she was left behind, alone, in New Orleans with Grey Verreaux.

It wasn't until Clairesse touched her arm that she realized she'd fallen into a reverie.

"You haven't heard a word I've said!" Clairesse accused her crossly. "Your mind is in the clouds today, Tori!"

"I'm sorry," Tori apologized dutifully, but she wasn't. In fact, she would far rather have been at home, tucked away in her elegant boudoir, safe in the little haven Christophe had created for her. "What were you saying?"

"About Marie Bellechasse. You do know Marie, don't you? Everyone—everyone!—knows Marie."

Tori vaguely recollected having seen the lady at some dinner or other shortly after her marriage. A hazy picture formed in her mind of an exquisite woman in a white silk gown who preened and primped before a bevy of admirers while her far older husband seemed torn between pride and chagrin.

"Yes," she agreed, "I know Marie Bellechasse."

"On the very day Grey came to dinner with you and Christophe, he fought a duel with Lucien Bellechasse."

Tori felt a sick quivering in her stomach. "Grey is Madame Bellechasse's lover?"

"Was, *chérie*, was. Marie has refuted him since he insulted her by refusing to kill her husband."

"She wanted her husband dead?"

"Oh, not really, I suppose." Clairesse waved a perfumed hand. "But Grey could at least have wounded him. Lucien is not so brave that he would have demanded a duel to the death. And I suspect Marie forced him to challenge Grey in the first place." Clairesse's giggle dripped malice. "I imagine she'd like people to believe she has some small bit of honor left to defend. Which, of course, she hasn't. But when Grey refused even to use live ammunition in his pistol—! It was as much as saying that Marie wasn't worth taking the duel seriously."

While it was hard for Tori to imagine being angry because one's lover refused to kill one's husband—indeed, it was impossible for her to imagine being so blatantly unfaithful to one's husband as to provoke a duel in the first place—she had to admit that in her secret heart there was a certain envy of Marie Bellechasse. She wasn't jealous, she reasoned, because she knew that with a single word of assent she, too, could join the apparently swollen ranks of Grey Verreaux's paramours.

But that word would never be spoken, she knew. It would lie unuttered forever inside her. Regardless of how she felt about Christophe, regardless of the fact that theirs had not been a love match and had been, in fact, more a futile attempt at a union of fire and ice, he was her husband and she would not— could not—break the sacred vows she had made to him on their wedding day seven years before. Furthermore, she had no desire to become merely one of the many women who passed in and out of Grey's life—and his bed. To know she was sharing him with other women, to feel that the words he was whispering, the touches, caresses, had all been used on someone else the night before and would all be used with someone else the next night would be beyond bearing for her.

Finally, she could not truly say that she had any great desire to have Grey reenter her life now. Her life with Christophe might well be as narrow, as unexciting and circumscribed as Clairesse was so fond of telling her, but it was that very sameness that she found somehow comforting. To know that there was unlikely to be pain, heartache, or sorrow waiting for her around the corner reassured her. If there was equally unlikely to be any great pleasure or wondrous joy, it seemed a reasonable price to pay. With Grey there would never be that sense of serenity. The morrow could just as easily bring agony as ecstasy, tears as laughter. The prospect of passion, the promise of discovery, almost frightened her now after the life she'd led since her marriage.

"Of course," Clairesse was saying—did the woman never run short of scandal? Tori wondered— "the break will be far the worse for Marie than for Grey. Grey still has Monique."

"Monique?" Some perverse side of Tori

59

couldn't resist asking the question.

"Grey's mistress."

"But I thought Madame Bellechasse . . ."

Clairesse's musical laughter rasped on Tori's nerves. "Marie! But no, *chérie*, you misunderstood. Marie is—was, I keep forgetting—merely one of Grey's many *affaires de coeur*. Monique is his mistress."

"This Monique," Tori murmured, all the while wondering what hitherto unknown emotion drove her to continue this pointless self-punishment, "Is she married? A widow, perhaps?"

"She is a quadroon. Very beautiful, as the wretches so often are. Fiery. With a temper to match."

Tori stifled a miserable sigh. She felt a little faint, even ill when faced with the sheer numbers of Grey's '*affaires de coeur*', as Clairesse chose to call them. Resolutely, Tori forced back the envy, the jealousy, and the tormenting images that filled her mind—images of Grey in the arms of one of his many pretty cocottes.

Gathering her skirts, she rose and signaled Clairesse's servant to bring her forest-green taffeta mantle and velvet-trimmed bonnet.

"Tori!" Clairesse protested, "you're not leaving!"

"I must," Tori lied, drawing the mantle, with its passementerie trimming, closer over her shoulders. "Christophe will be wondering what has become of me."

"Christophe!" Clairesse sighed, rolling her eyes.

Tori gave her a warning glance. "Please, Clairesse. Not another word against Christophe. I know you don't approve of our quiet life, but I am satisfied with it."

"Really, *chérie*, I can't remember your ever having been quite so defensive of him before. Is this something new?"

"Of course not," Tori assured her, but her voice was singularly lacking in conviction. "A wife should defend her husband."

"So virtuous! You make me feel like a bad wife. But then, perhaps Etienne likes me that way."

Clairesse's laughter was flat and unsure. She'd never seen Tori this way before and the change piqued her curiosity. She wondered if it had anything to do with Grey's visit to the Duclaux household and decided that it must. Any other reason would be just too boring!

The two women kissed each other's cheeks and Tori left wondering at herself for her sudden defensiveness toward her husband.

Was it really loyalty that prompted her or something else? Guilt? She thrust that thought from her mind. She had no reason to feel guilty. After all, she was not like Marie Bellechasse. She was not going to betray her husband by becoming a member of Grey Verreaux's seraglio. Her conscience was clear. Wasn't it?

Climbing into the carriage that would take her home, Tori tried not to examine her motives too closely. She didn't really want to think about Christophe or Grey or the feeling that might be lurking in her heart of hearts for either man. The day of reckoning would come—that much seemed inevitable. But just now she couldn't bear the thought of such a conflict shattering her calm, if unexciting, existence.

6

"No! I said I won't do it and I meant it!"

Elizabeth Phipps stamped her tiny foot for good measure, but the gesture was lost beneath the voluminous folds of her pink-sprigged, white piqué skirts and the swaying crinoline that supported them. She glared up at her husband. "You should be ashamed of yourself for even suggesting such a thing!"

Valentine Phipps shot Grey an 'I-told-you-so' glance. He had agreed, albeit reluctantly, to ask Elizabeth to befriend Tori after Christophe had departed aboard *Nightshade*. Grey's reasoning, Val knew, was that if Tori became a frequent visitor to the Phipps home, it would provide Grey with a convenient, discreet place to see her. After all, wouldn't it seem natural for Elizabeth's newest friend and Val's oldest to be invited to dine at the same time? Val had warned Grey that Elizabeth would not think too highly of the plan, but Grey had insisted he try.

"And you!" Elizabeth went on, waggling a finger in Grey's direction. "You should be doubly ashamed of yourself! It isn't bad enough that you involve your friend and try to involve his wife in your schemes—you're trying to corrupt an innocent woman!"

"Corrupt, my dear?" Grey asked, trying hard to conceal the amusement he knew would only fuel Elizabeth's temper. "I assure you, I've no intention—"

"No intention! No intention!" The petite brunette jammed her little fists into the gathers of piqué at her waist. "And pray, why then did you want me to turn my house into a place of assignation for you and this lady? Can you look me in the eye, Greyson Verreaux, and deny that it is your intention to make this lady the latest of your . . . your . . ."

"Paramours?" Val suggested, smirking at the sight of Grey being routed by his tiny dynamo of a wife.

"Stay out of this!" Grey snapped. "Don't give her any ideas." Sighing, collecting his thoughts, he suddenly smiled charmingly at the usually docile Elizabeth. "My dear," he said softly, entreatingly, "I assure you I've no intention of debasing Madame Duclaux in any way. I've the utmost respect for her and the greatest care for her reputation. It is not my desire to involve her in scandal nor to do harm to her marriage."

Sinking into the yielding comfort of the cream and gold striped silk cushions of the sofa, Elizabeth heaved a heartrending sigh and gazed mournfully up at her husband's best friend.

"But don't you see, Grey? That is precisely what

you will do. What if she falls in love with you? What then?''

"I should be delighted," he replied honestly, if not wisely.

"And when her husband returns from Jamaica? Would you expect her to continue her liaison with you beneath his very nose?''

"That would be her decision.''

"You would leave it to her to decide whether or not to destroy a union that has lasted seven years? Whether or not to disgrace herself and her husband? Whether or not she can live with the slurs and rancor of society once she had branded herself an adulteress?''

"Oh, come, Elizabeth!" Val interjected. "Half the women in New Orleans are adulteresses, if you want to be so prudish about it.''

"I agree, they are." His wife nodded. "And I think it is shameful. And you do, too, Val, even if you try to pretend you don't for your friend's sake. Can you deny that you disapprove of Grey's cuckolding half the husbands in New Orleans?''

"Hardly half!" Grey protested indignantly.

"Grey may do as he pleases," Val decreed, embarrassed to be so harangued in front of his friend. He shoved his hands into his pockets and cast Grey an almost sheepish look. "Really, though, Grey, I don't think much of this notion of yours of seducing Victoria Duclaux. It was different with Marie Bellechasse and Elise Renvielle and the others. They'd had lovers. Their husbands were too complaisant or at least too hen-pecked to protest. But in this instance . . . There's never been a whisper about Tori Duclaux.''

"No," Grey agreed. "She admitted to me that she's been faithful to Duclaux since their marriage.''

"Admitted!" Elizabeth cried. "You act as though it was some shameful secret. She should be proud of herself."

"Dammit, Elizabeth, I didn't mean it that way. It's only that I want—"

"Grey," she interrupted gently, cajolingly, "think for a moment not about what you want, but about what is best for this lady."

"And what if I think I am what is best for her?" he challenged her.

"You may well be," Elizabeth admitted, surprising both men. "But at this point, you may be a luxury she cannot afford."

It was a point Grey could not easily refute. He knew full well that Tori was not a woman who could deceive her husband. Should she decide to forsake her marriage vows and come to him, the break with Christophe Duclaux would be permanent and complete. And that, he surprised himself by realizing, was precisely what he wanted. If he could take her away from Duclaux, free her from the silken prison of her marriage, he himself would make a life for her. He would marry her.

The thought came as a revelation to him. To think that he, confirmed bachelor that he was, scornful of the all-encompassing bonds of matrimony as he had been since his abortive betrothal to Amanda Hunter, would seriously consider—no, desire!—giving up his freedom to marry any woman and particularly the wife of another man! What was wrong with him? Was he mad? No, there seemed only one logical conclusion . . .

"I love her, Elizabeth," he said simply.

Elizabeth and Val's eyes met over Grey's bowed head. Her glance was delighted, Val's astonished.

Elizabeth's beautiful, dusky eyes clouded with concern.

"She belongs to another," she told him gently. "Would she want to leave her husband?"

He shook his head. "I don't know. I don't believe she loves Duclaux, though she says she does. But I think she merely feels safe with him. As though his home were some sort of sanctuary for her, a wall protecting her from pain."

"Pain? What do you mean?"

"Heartache," he told his friend's wife. "Her heart was broken once. A man she loved treated her cruelly." He shrugged. "Perhaps she believes that, because she does not love Duclaux, she is in no danger of being hurt by him."

"But why should she fear you? What would make her think you would hurt her?"

Grey glanced toward Val, wondering if his friend had told his wife what had passed between Tori and himself in Virginia. Val shook his head; he had not.

Grey hesitated but then, deciding that having come this far he might as well be totally honest, he plunged on.

"Because I was the one who hurt her years ago."

Elizabeth stared, speechless. She looked from Grey to her husband and back again, but nothing in either man's face suggested that Grey's startling statement was anything less than the truth.

"I don't know what to say," she managed at last.

"Don't say anything," Grey told her, rising. "I apologize for involving you, my dear. It was a piece of errant foolishness and I do regret it."

Elizabeth rose as he turned toward the door.

"Wait. Why don't you stay to dinner? Perhaps we could talk . . ."

"There's nothing to talk about. But I thank you for the thought."

Bending, he kissed Elizabeth's cheeks. Then, with a nod for Val, he left, leaving Elizabeth to link her arm through her husband's and rest her cheek against his shoulder.

"I might have known," she sighed ruefully, a wan smile curving her lips.

"Known what?" Val demanded, as the sound of Grey's carriage wheels faded into the gathering twilight.

"I might have known that when the day finally dawned that Grey Verreaux found himself in love, it would be with a woman he couldn't have."

"I wouldn't be too certain," Val cautioned.

"Valentine! You don't think he would try to destroy . . ."

Val's shake of the head silenced her. "Perhaps he wouldn't set out to destroy her marriage, sweet, but you must remember that whatever Grey Verreaux does, he does with a passion, and if he decides that Tori Duclaux is the woman he wants, hellfire itself won't keep him away from her."

That very thought was on Tori's mind as the date of Christophe's departure drew near. She knew how determined Grey could be if he wanted something badly. Now, it seemed, he had decided he wanted her.

With Christophe nearby, she felt secure. He was so protective of her, there seemed no way that Grey could get close enough to do any harm to her fragile resolve. But with Christophe far away and her alone . . .

"Christophe?" she said meekly, hovering uncertainly in the doorway of her husband's study.

He looked up from the sheaf of papers scattered
over his desktop. "Come in, *ma chère*. What is it?"

Hands clasped in her lap to still their trembling,
Tori sank into a tufted leather chair opposite him.

"Why must you go to Jamaica?" she asked.

He sighed. He wished he could confide in her the
importance—and the danger—of the mission upon
which he was to embark, but secrecy was essential to
its success and the less Tori knew about it, the safer
she was likely to be in his absence.

"Victoria," he said at last, "we've gone through
this . . ."

"But there must be someone else you can send.
Surely you have competent people in your
employ—people you can trust to perform this task."

Her arguments would have been valid, had he
really been traveling to Jamaica on plantation
business. He understood and sympathized with her
confusion, but he had to maintain his charade.

"There are several reasons why I must go," he
explained lamely. "Not the least of these is that I
would not ask anyone else to risk their freedom, if
not their very lives running that damned Union
blockade."

Tori felt helpless, confused. Something inside
told her he was lying, but she knew it would avail her
nothing to argue. After several moments' silence, she
asked:

"Then can't I come with you?"

Christophe laughed, but the smile faded from
his lips as he realized that she was completely serious.
He leaned back in his chair.

"I cannot believe that you mean that," he
murmured. "Victoria, do you think, if I will not

allow any of the men who work for me to risk themselves, that I would allow you to go?'' He paused. ''Tell me, what is behind this sudden desire to accompany me?''

Rising, she turned her back to him. Guilt overwhelmed her even as she told herself sternly that she had done nothing to feel guilty for.

''Couldn't it merely be that I love you, Christophe, and that I am worried at your sailing off, running the Union blockade? You could be captured, imprisoned, even killed!''

She heard him rise from his desk and stiffened as he came to her.

''Can't you believe,'' she went on, ''that I merely want to be with you to share your danger?''

Taking her gently by the shoulders, he turned her toward him. His black eyes were probing as they scanned her face, watching the play of emotions there.

''It could be,'' he allowed. ''I wish it were that simple. But I don't think it is.''

Tori paled as the blood drained from her face. ''What do you mean?'' she asked, managing no more than a trembling whisper.

''There's no point in carrying on this charade any longer, Victoria. You've changed and I can chart the day, almost the moment, the changes began.'' He hesitated and Tori held her breath. ''It is Grey Verreaux, is it not, *chérie*?''

''No!'' Tori cried, whirling away from him. ''It has nothing to do with him! I haven't seen him since the night you brought him here! I haven't, Christophe, I swear it!''

''I know you haven't,'' he assured her, his tone and expression not unlike one he would use to soothe a skittish animal or frightened child. ''I didn't say you had. But I saw the way you reacted to Verreaux when he came to dinner. I felt the tension between you—it was as much on his part as on yours.''

Tori trembled but Christophe took her by the hand and led her to the window seat. He drew her down onto the garnet velvet cushions and took her hands in his as much to hold her there as to comfort her.

"Victoria, don't you think it is time you told me what happened seven years ago between you and Greyson Verreaux?"

Tori tried to pull away but Christophe held her fast. "Nothing happened," she lied. "Grey was betrothed—"

"To your cousin, Amanda. I know. But the betrothal was broken. Why, Victoria? What was your part in it?"

She tore herself away from him. "None! I had no part in it!"

"I don't believe you. Tell me the truth."

"There was nothing! Nothing! Why do you torment me this way?"

"Very well," he acquiesced coolly, returning to his desk. "Keep your secrets if you must. But I leave for Jamaica in one week and while I am gone, I expect you to resolve whatever feeling you have for Grey Verreaux. You are my wife, Tori—mine! And what is mine, I do not share with any man. Do you understand me?"

Tori nodded. She understood that while Christophe would not care to have his name dragged through the scandal mills of New Orleans, neither would he tolerate being the next *mari* to have the horns of a cuckold placed on his head by Grey Verreaux. The dreams she had had of the two men meeting under the dueling oaks—of one lying dead in the mists of the morning—were all too likely to come true if she didn't manage to exorcise Grey from her mind—and her heart.

But how, she wondered as she wandered dejectedly from her husband's study, how in the name of all that was holy was she to do that?

7

To Tori, the silence of the darkened house was ominous. Rising from her dressing table, she wandered about the shadowy bedchamber touching items Christophe had left behind: a shirt hanging over a Coromandel screen, left for the laundress; a book lying open on the table near the winged chair before the fireplace; a pair of slippers peeping out from beneath the edge of the bed. She could not have imagined how much she would miss Christophe. The house seemed so empty without him. She felt lost and a little afraid, like a child in the forest listening for the footfalls of the stalking wolf.

But the wolf she feared was no four-legged creature of the night, no fanged chimera out of a child's nightmare. He had a name, a voice, a face that haunted her dreams.

"Christophe," she whispered aloud, as though

invoking an angel to protect her from the demon lover who peered out at her with silvery eyes from within her own desires.

But Christophe was gone. His strength, the safety of his presence, had been stripped from her with his departure. She'd pleaded with him to allow her to come to the ship and say good-bye, but he had refused, saying it was a needless risk. Grey had agreed, but she could hardly have expected him to do otherwise.

Taking up a book, she climbed into her big, empty bed. It was useless trying to sleep. There were too many disturbing thoughts clouding her mind. She—

From the courtyard below came the sound of hooves and the grinding of carriage wheels on the cobbles. Fear clutched Tori's heart with icy fingers as she threw back the coverlet. In a mad swirl of linen and lace, she ran to the window and drew back the draperies. In the courtyard, touched by the silvery glow of the crescent moon, stood Grey's carriage. It swayed on its springs as Grey alighted. Dressed in black, he was a shadow moving with feline grace across the courtyard to the door where a lantern burned low.

"Christophe," Tori murmured. There had been trouble, she knew it! The *Nightshade* had been captured—she could not bring herself to consider the possibility that it might have been sunk—and her husband was a prisoner.

Not bothering to pull on a negligée, she left her room and swept down the corridor to the stairs. As she descended, she heard the butler explaining that "Madame has retired."

"Then wake her up," Grey ordered, striding past the disapproving old man.

"Monsieur, I cannot—"

"It's all right, Felix," Tori told him, flushing at the look on the butler's face when he saw the state in which his mistress had come downstairs. "I'll see Monsieur Verreaux in the library."

The butler's dark eyes darted from Tori to Grey and back. His reproachful gaze never left his mistress's face though he could not but have noticed the thin linen gown that betrayed her scandalous lack of corseting and the artful disarray of her hair as it tumbled in a gleaming golden shower down her back nearly to her hips.

"As you wish, madame," he said tightly. Closing the door, he disappeared into the depths of the house leaving Tori and Grey alone.

Descending to the bottom of the staircase, Tori led Grey into the library. Lighting a lamp on one of the leather-topped tables, she turned to Grey, her blue eyes alight with concern.

"It's Christophe, isn't it?" she asked tremulously. "The *Nightshade* has been captured?"

"Not that I know of," Grey said softly.

Tori paled. "It hasn't . . . it hasn't been sunk?"

"Good God, no! My crew is highly experienced, Tori. My first officer will get them through if anyone can."

"But you haven't heard . . ."

Grey laid his hat on the mantelpiece and smiled blithely. "I haven't heard a damned word. These things take time. In a few days, we'll likely get hold of a Union report of ships running the blockade and there will, no doubt, be a mention of the *Nightshade*. Until then, the less we hear, the better." He smiled in the face of her confusion. "I do assure you, we'd hear of it if the ship were captured or sunk."

Bewildered, Tori stood before him, her azure

eyes fixed on his starkly handsome face. If there was no news . . . If he had nothing to tell her . . . Then why . . ?

A shiver ran down her spine as she realized that his eyes had left hers and were slowly perusing the outline of her body beneath the sheer linen of her nightdress.

"Grey . .," she breathed, willing away the tantalizing warmth that had started inside her.

His gaze slowly, so slowly, returned to her face. A sardonic smile quirked one corner of her mouth. One black brow arched quizzically. "Yes?"

"If there's nothing else, I think you should go."

"Do you?" he asked, obviously amused by her discomfiture.

Folding her arms across her bosom, she turned, pretending to straighten a stack of books left lying on the table.

"Yes," she said, her voice quivering ever so slightly despite her best efforts to keep it steady. "I think you should because it doesn't look good for your carriage to be seen outside so late when Christophe is away."

"The carriage is in the courtyard," he disagreed. "It's dark, the streets are deserted, and very few people know Christophe is away."

"The carriage . . ." she objected.

"Tori, I came to tell you that if there is anything you need while you're here alone—"

"That's very kind of you," she interrupted, sidling toward the door as she heard him rise from his chair. "But I don't think . . ."

She cried out as his hands spanned her waist and turned her toward him. For a moment she could do nothing; his closeness, his touch, the steely fire in his

eyes mesmerized her. His hands stayed at her waist,
the tips of his fingers and thumbs nearly touching.
But he was close, so close that the tips of her breasts
nearly brushed the soft cloth of his coat. So close that
she could feel the heat of his body. Though he didn't
move, she knew he meant to kiss her, caress her,
make love to her if he could break through her
defenses.

She shook her head and the gilded cascade of her
hair glimmered in the lamplight. "No," she
whispered, fearful, pleading. "Don't."

"I must," he answered simply.

Her small hands pried his larger ones from
about her waist and she backed away. Silently,
gracefully, like some sleek black jungle cat, Grey
followed.

"Please," she breathed, one fragile hand outstretched as if to ward him off. "You mustn't." A
moan that was half terror and half despair welled in
her throat as her back struck the corner of the
mantel. "Grey."

"Tell me that Christophe satisfies all your
needs, all your desires," Grey challenged.

"He does," she vowed.

"Tell me that you've never thought of me during
these past seven years."

"I haven't!"

"Tell me that you don't want me—here, now,
the way I want you."

His shadow loomed over her as she trembled and
pressed herself back against the marble caryatids that
supported the mantel.

"I don't want you!" she wailed, tears welling
into her eyes.

He smiled, his eyes glittering. "Liar."

He reached for her and she skittered away, her linen gown whirling about her shaking legs.

"Leave me alone," she begged. "Why do you torment me this way? Wasn't it enough that you destroyed my life once? Must you try to do it again?"

"Is that what you think I want to do?" he asked, his passion fading to an icy calm. "Destroy you? You're wrong, Tori."

"Am I?" Sitting on a velvet chaise beneath the windows, Tori wrapped her arms about herself trying to ward off the chill that seemed to have taken hold of her. "Am I wrong? You came back into my life . . ."

"At your husband's request," he reminded her.

"Regardless of how it happened, you've come back. You see that I have a new life. I have a husband who loves me and whom I love."

Grey ran a hand through his hair. "Love! Who are you trying to fool, Tori? Me? Or yourself? Christophe doesn't love you."

"He does!"

"He owns you! You're a possession! He married you because he wanted a beautiful young wife to bolster his aging ego."

"How can you be so cruel!"

"It's the truth! As for your loving him . . . What you love is not having to grow up! Not having to become a woman! He lets you stay the same spoiled little girl you were when you lived in your father's house!"

"Spoiled little girl, am I!" Rising, Tori glared at him, too angry for tears. "You think I should grow up! Become a woman! Well, you're wrong! I am a woman! And Christophe does love me! Perhaps he did marry me for my youth—why should he have married me? For the same reason you were going to marry Amanda? Because you liked the way she behaved in your bed!''

"Leave Amanda out of this. That's over and done.''

"It's not over! It will never be over! What you did to me—''

"That was a mistake!'' he argued, remembering the tumult that had erupted at Barton's Landing after Amanda had discovered him in Tori's bed. "And I offered to marry you. You refused!''

Tori remembered being summoned to her father's study to be told that Grey had asked for her hand. "You didn't want to marry me!'' she accused. "You only offered to because you'd compromised me. Honor demanded that you offer for me.''

"That's right,'' he agreed. "Honor demanded it. And that's precisely what Gussie was thinking of when she stole the rose from Amanda's table and put it on yours. It would have worked if you had accepted my proposal.''

"But I couldn't—not knowing that you offered only out of a sense of duty.'' She waved a wearily dismissing hand. "You're right. It's over and done with. But you nearly destroyed me then—I won't let you do it again!''

"I told you, I'm not trying—''

"Aren't you? Isn't that why you came here tonight?''

"Tori—''

"Get out! I hate you! I never want to see you again!''

"Hate me?'' Grey's eyes swept over her. "You don't believe that any more than I do, Tori. And you will see me again.'' He picked up his hat and started toward the door.

"When Christophe comes back," she flung after him, "he'll challenge you! He'll kill you!"

"He's welcome to challenge me," Grey told her coolly, framed in the doorway, not caring that Felix stood frowning in the hall outside. "But I assure you the only possible outcome would make you New Orleans's loveliest widow. Good-evening, Madame Duclaux."

He disappeared and Tori hurried across the room and watched the butler bolt the door after him.

"You are never to admit that man again, do you hear me?" she demanded.

"As you wish," the butler agreed, bowing. "Will you retire now, madame?"

"In a few moments," she assured him. "I won't need you any more tonight, Felix. Go to bed."

"The lamp, madame," he objected, nodding toward the glow from the library.

"I'll blow it out before I retire," she assured him. "Good-night."

With another bow, the butler left her alone, small and trembling, in the library doorway. Tori turned back into the room intending to sit in the welcoming silence until she regained her composure. But scenes of the past few moments haunted her. She couldn't get Grey's face, his voice, out of her mind. The spicy, musky aroma of his cologne lingered in the air. Everything he had said, all the taunts, the jibes, were true. She knew it and, what was worse, he knew it. If he had touched her again . . . if he had held her, kissed her, she couldn't have resisted him. For the truth, the awful shameful truth, was that she had wanted him. Beneath her fear, beneath the terror his desire had evoked in her, had been an answering desire that shook her to her very soul. In those moments she had known a hunger, an aching, ravening need like nothing she had ever known with Christophe. And it was that realization more than her fear, more than the shame of betraying her husband, that had fueled her panic.

She had intended to sit only a moment in the library—allow herself a little time to gather herself—but in the end, she cried herself to sleep on the velvet chaise and spent the night trembling, pursued through her dreams by a love that was never meant to be.

8

The days following Christophe's departure passed
with monotonous regularity for Tori. They melded
into one another, becoming weeks. Though Grey did
not, as she feared, appear on her doorstep
demanding that which she could not give him, he
nonetheless seemed to haunt her days. He appeared
out of a crowd when she went to shop, when she
visited her modiste, when she stepped out of the
carriage in front of the Candés' cafe. He haunted her
nights as well. Her dreams seemed to center on him
with maddening, and increasing, regularity.

In the hope that not seeing him during the day
would exorcise him from her thoughts and from her
dreams, Tori began venturing outside the safety of
her own walls less and less until, nearly a month after
Christophe's departure, she had become a virtual
recluse.

It was then that Grey arrived. He found the wrought iron gates closed across the entrance to the Duclaux courtyard. A groom, summoned to the locked portal, hurried to the house only to return a few minutes later with the message that Madame Duclaux was not receiving visitors. Grey had left, unaware that Tori watched him from the safety of the shuttered loggia, and unaware also that, only moments after he left another carriage bearing Clairesse Candé would arrive and be granted *entrée*.

"Sit down," Tori invited her friend absently, her thoughts still upon the devastatingly handsome man to whom she'd just refused admittance to her home. "Let me send to the kitchen for something."

"Nothing for me," Clairesse replied, patting the cushion of the sofa beside her. "Sit down and tell me why you've immured yourself inside these walls. Heavens! I half expected to find you collapsed across your bed wasting away from consumption or something of the like."

"I'm fine," Tori assured her, perching on the edge of the sofa. "I simply haven't been going out."

"Well, I'm here to change that. Etienne and I want you to come with us to the Opera House tonight."

"Oh, Clairesse, I really couldn't. I . . ."

"Tori!" Clairesse tried her best to look stern. "There is no reason that you can't, since you have assured me there is nothing wrong with your health. Just because Christophe is away . . ." Her sternness gave way to curiosity. "When is Christophe coming back, anyway?"

Tori's delicate fingers twined nervously in the folds of her mauve silk gown. "I don't know, really. I should have thought he'd have returned long since."

"Well, you mustn't worry. Communication is difficult. It does you absolutely no good to sit here and brood about it. A night out is what you need. I'm sure Christophe would agree if he were here." She waggled an admonishing finger as Tori would have disagreed. "Tut, tut, my girl, no arguments. Come along, we'll go up and choose something absolutely ravishing for you to wear."

Night had fallen by the time the Candé carriage drew up before the imposing Bourbon Street entrance of the French Opera House. Etienne Candé—short, stout, with an air of bonhomie that belied his notoriously fiery temperament—stepped down first, then lifted his wife and Tori to the ground. He was proud of the admiring looks that followed them as they moved through the crowd toward the doors. Even now, after nearly ten years of marriage, he could hardly believe that the lovely, elusive Clairesse de Lisser, who had led the young men of her native Baton Rouge such a merry dance, had consented to marry him, a simple man with neither illustrious lineage nor impressive fortune. On his other arm lay the perfumed hand of Madame Christophe Duclaux, a lady of renowned beauty and great fortune and one about whom, since her husband chose to take her out in society but rarely, there was much curiosity. Puffed with pride, Etienne led the two ladies into the Opera House and up to one of the boxes overlooking the stage with its classically beautiful Corinthian columns.

Relieved to be away from the throngs, Tori settled her lace-frothed, rose-silk skirts around her. The air of anticipation had begun to affect her and she leaned forward, eager for the music to begin, unaware of the pair of steely gray eyes that watched her from the box opposite.

"Grey?" Receiving no reply, Val glanced toward his friend and found him staring intently, oblivious to his surroundings. "Who in blazes has caught your eye this time?"

"It's Tori," Grey said simply, rising from his seat as Elizabeth joined them, having retired for a few moments to one of the rooms set aside for the ladies.

"Tori?" Elizabeth repeated, taking her seat between the two men. "Victoria Duclaux?"

"Hmmm. There, just across the way."

Lifting her mother-of-pearl opera glasses, Elizabeth studied the woman who had so captured Grey's elusive heart and mind of late.

"How beautiful she is," the woman said, her tone completely devoid of envy or jealousy. Secure in her husband's love, she was free from any need to view other women as competition.

"She's exquisite," Grey agreed.

Taking the glass from his wife, Val studied Tori from the spray of rose-colored flowers pinned to her mass of golden curls, their diamond centers sparkling, to the billowing swell of her skirts before they disappeared behind the railing of the box in which she sat.

"I find it hard to believe you let that angel slip from your grasp," he told his friend, reluctantly relinquishing the glass to his wife.

"It was errant foolishness on my part," Grey agreed. "And my youthful pride when she refused my offer. But it isn't over yet."

"Are you going to speak to her?"

Grey scowled. "I tried—this morning. She refused to let me into the house."

"Perhaps she thought you wished to seduce

her," Elizabeth suggested slyly.

"Elizabeth!" Val was plainly shocked.

A smile quivered at the corners of Grey's mouth, then vanished. "She very likely thought exactly that. And who knows? Had the opportunity presented itself . . ."

"You're a wicked man, Greyson Verreaux," Elizabeth hissed as the curtain rose and a hush fell over the audience.

"Far from it," he disagreed good-naturedly. "I merely seized my opportunities the moment they present themselves."

The teasing good humor faded from Grey's face as Val touched his arm and drew his attention to a man seated in the box next to the Candés'. He was leaning over the railing staring at Tori, who seemed unaware of his perusal.

"Do you know who that is?" Val asked grimly.

Grey squinted through Elizabeth's opera glass. "Damn!" he muttered. "Randall Ramsey. He must know she's Duclaux's wife."

"He must also know that Duclaux has left New Orleans—and why."

"It may be that he doesn't know enough of the details," Grey suggested thoughtfully. "I'm convinced he would have followed him if he did. But if he knows who Tori is, he may think he can get the information out of her."

"She doesn't know anything," Val reminded him.

"But does Ramsey know that?"

Throughout their conversation, the object of their perusal felt uncomfortable, as though she were being watched, scrutinized like a specimen in a laboratory. Tori tried to ignore the feeling, realizing that she was no doubt the object of more than one curious stare, but it persisted and grew stronger until she found it impossible to concentrate on the music that ebbed and flowed from the columned stage before her.

Though scarcely turning her head, she cast serreptitious glances about her. There was no one who seemed to be paying her undue attention, yet the feeling remained and, if anything, grew stronger.

"What's wrong, Tori?" Clairesse asked, seeing the frown creasing her friend's brow.

"I don't know. I have the oddest feeling that someone is star—Oh, my God!"

"What is it?"

From opposite sides of the dimly lighted theater, Tori and Grey's gazes met and locked. Electric attraction crackled between them. The blood drained from Tori's face leaving her skin starkly white above the deep rose silk of her gown.

"Tori?" Clairesse touched her hand. It trembled. The painted fan she held between her fingers slid to the floor. "Tori!"

"I want to go home, Clairesse," she breathed, tearing her eyes away from the box opposite them. "I'll send back the carriage."

"You'll do nothing of the kind. You can't be out driving through the streets alone at night. What would Christophe say?"

"I won't be alone," Tori reminded her. "The coachman will be there."

"Tori, don't—"

"I'm sorry, Clairesse. I must!"

Rising, she swept out of the box, leaving Clairesse to stare after her, too surprised to collect herself and follow.

In the corridor outside, Tori paused, one hand pressed to her pounding heart. She started violently when a man appeared, having just left the box next to the Candés'.

"Madame Duclaux?" he said, his tones harsh in her ears. He was definitely not a Southerner.

"Yes?" She gazed up at him distracted. Though she was too upset to take careful note of him, the overall impression she got was one of polish and elegance. He was a gentleman, yet there was an air of slyness about him—a hint of danger that might have frightened her had she not been so bemused. "I'm sorry, sir, have we met?"

"We have not. My name is Devin—" The pause was miniscule—"Devin Sinclair. I have been trying to get in touch with your husband. There is a business matter . . ."

Desperate to get away, Tori interrupted him with a wave of her hand. "I'm sorry, sir. My husband is not in New Orleans at present."

"I see. In Baton Rouge, perhaps, or Natchez . . . ?"

"He is out of the country!" she snapped, wondering why this man persisted. "He has gone to Jamaica and I do not know when he will return. I—"

"Tori?" Clairesse appeared outside the Candés' box. She was surprised to see Tori in conversation with a man not in the least familiar to her. As she approached, the man mumbled his thanks and a hurried 'good-evening' and disappeared along the corridor.

She took Tori's arm. "Who was that man?"

"I don't know." Tori shook her head. "He wanted to know about Christophe. I'm leaving now. You don't have to come with me."

Clairesse kept up with her as she moved on. They were nearly to the corner when Grey appeared, blocking their way.

Tori heard the soft intake of Clairesse's breath as she saw him there, tall, starkly handsome in black-and-white evening dress. It was clear from his stance that he did not intend to let them pass.

"Grey," Tori breathed, her voice tremulous, her fingers tightening dangerously on the fragile ivory sticks and guards of her fan.

"Tori," he said softly. His silver eyes scanned the corridor behind her. When he'd seen her leave her box, he had also seen Ramsey leaving his. But the man seemed to have vanished. His gaze shifted lightly to Clairesse. "Madame . . ?"

"Candé," Tori supplied. "Clairesse Candé. Have you met Monsieur Verreaux, Clairesse?"

"Madame Candé." Taking Clairesse's hand, he raised it to his lips. His eyes met hers and Clairesse sighed, a little shiver coursing through her. "I regret, madame," he said, his fingertips imprisoning Clairesse's fingers, "that I must be rude and ask to speak to Madame Duclaux alone."

"No!" Tori cried.

Grey ignored her. "If you will excuse us for a few moments, madame."

"Clairesse! Don't go!" Tori begged.

"I assure you, madame," Grey went on, "that what I must say to Tori will take but a moment and then I will relinquish her into your care once more." His eyes shifted to Tori's pale face. "Unharmed."

Though Tori clutched at Clairesse's arm, her friend was already moving away. "I'll be back in a little while, Tori," she said, as she disappeared around the corner.

Tori started after her but Grey's hand clamped about her arm, pulling her back.

"I'll scream," she threatened.

"You're a fool if you do," he hissed. "Calm

yourself, Tori. I've no intention of seducing you here in the hall. Good Christ! what do you think I am? Some rutting satyr?" He chuckled in spite of himself at the defiant look on her face. "Yes, I can see that that is precisely what you think. Well, no matter. I have a legitimate reason for wanting to speak to you. Listen to me. There was a man, seated in the box next to yours just now. He was tall, dressed in blue with a blue brocade waistcoat."

"Mr. Sinclair?" she interrupted.

"Sinclair?"

"Devin Sinclair."

"He spoke to you?"

Tori shrugged, not understanding the look of dark concern on Grey's face. "He was coming out of his box just as I was coming out of mine. He said he had been trying to get in touch with Christophe."

"Did he say why?"

"Business."

"What did you tell him?"

"I told him that Christophe had gone to Jamaica and—"

Tori eyed him curiously. "It's the truth, isn't it?"

"Yes, it's the truth. Tori, that man was not Devin Sinclair. His name is Ramsey—Randall Ramsey. He is an agent of the North."

Tori almost laughed—would have laughed if Grey hadn't looked so deadly serious. "A spy? Are you trying to tell me that he was a Union spy?"

"That's exactly what he is."

"But why would he be interested in Christophe?"

Sighing, Grey drew Tori to the side of the deserted corridor. "Tori, Christophe did not go to Jamaica to see to his sugar plantation. He went there

91

to meet a man from France. If their discussions are satisfactory, he will go on to Paris."

"To Paris!" She was stunned. "But why? Why wasn't I told?"

"His business is secret. With him he is carrying papers from the Confederate government. I can't tell you more except that his mission is one which the Union would dearly like to see fail. They would do anything to prevent him from reaching Paris. Randall Ramsey, I'm certain, has orders to stop Christophe in any way he can by whatever means necessary."

"And I told him . . ." Tori's face was starkly white as the blood drained from it. "I told him Christophe had gone to Jamaica . . ."

She looked so small, so fragile, so frightened that Grey longed to hold her, to try to find some words to comfort her. In the end, he had to settle for catching her as she slid to the carpeted floor in a flurry of rose silk and white lace.

9

Tori awoke slowly, sluggishly, blinking in the dimly lighted room where the mid-morning sun glowed behind draperies of green and white striped silk. She felt confused and disoriented; nothing of her surroundings was familiar.

The door to the left of the bed opened and a pretty, chestnut-haired woman appeared.

"I thought I heard you moving about," she said brightly. Seeing the bewilderment in Tori's eyes, Elizabeth smiled gently.

"Good morning, Madame Duclaux. I am Elizabeth Phipps."

Tori lifted a hand to her head. "Where . . . how . . ."

"Grey Verreaux brought you here last evening. You fainted at the Opera House."

"Grey . . . oh, yes, I . . . I'm sorry, I don't

know why . . .''

"Tori?'' The door was opening once more and Grey appeared. Freshly shaven, he had obviously gone home at some point during the night and changed out of the formal attire he'd worn to the Opera House.

Elizabeth moved toward the door. Laying a hand on his chest, she halted him as he would have entered the room.

"She's very disoriented, Grey. I don't want you to upset her unnecessarily."

"I'm not going to upset her, Elizabeth," he promised, lifting her hand to his lips. "And I thank you for letting me bring her here and for putting her to bed. But I really must speak to her now."

"You'd better not distress her. If I come back and find her agitated . . .''

Grey's silver eyes twinkled. "It's no wonder to me that poor Val is so henpecked, married to a little shrew like you."

Elizabeth drew herself up until the top of her head nearly reached Grey's shoulder. "Who are you calling a shrew! I'll have you know that Valentine is the head of this household as he should be!"

"And he has your permission to say so, hasn't he?" Laughing, Grey steered his friend's pretty wife from the room. He closed the door before she could voice any further objections, and turned toward the bed. Tori, wrapped in one of Elizabeth's delicate, unbearably feminine nightdresses, watched him approach with wide, haunted eyes.

"I fainted last night," she said softly. "Mrs. Phipps told me so."

"You did," Grey confirmed. "Elizabeth Phipps' husband, Valentine, is my closest friend. We were together at the Opera House last night. When you fainted, they offered to take you in for the night." He saw her glance down at herself. "Elizabeth and one of the maids undressed you. It was all quite proper, I assure you."

"I'm sure it was." She gave him a little, wan smile. "I had the strangest dream last night, Grey. I dreamed that Christophe had gone away and someone wanted to kill him and I . . ." Her voice trailed off and she caught her bottom lip between her little pearly teeth to stifle a sob. Haltingly, she raised tear-filled eyes to Grey's face. "It wasn't a dream, was it?"

Grey shook his head. "No, sweeting, it wasn't a dream."

"That man wants to kill him. I told him where Christophe is."

Grey tried to steel his heart against the tears that spilled down her petal-soft cheeks. "Ramsey wants to stop him, Tori. It may not be necessary to kill him. He . . ." He let the thought die. There seemed little he could do to comfort her. For the truth was that Ramsey would likely be all too ready to kill Christophe. Grey felt like a hypocrite. He had not been sorry to see Christophe depart for Jamaica. He had often wished that Duclaux would simply disappear from the face of the earth leaving him alone with Tori. But now . . . no, this wasn't the way it happened in his fantasies. He'd always thought that once Christophe had gone there would be no obstacles standing between Tori and himself. He'd pictured them hurrying into one another's arms, unable to wait for that first embrace, that first kiss.

He looked again at Tori, who lay huddled amidst the tousled sheets, a thick feather pillow clasped in her arms, weeping softly.

They had kept her in ignorance of Duclaux's mission for her own protection. Now that decision had put Christophe in mortal danger. If something did happen to Duclaux, could he overcome Tori's feelings of guilt and claim her?

"Tori . . ." Lifting her gently, he sat on the edge of the bed and held her, comforting her as he might have soothed a child. She clung to him, her tears spotting the soft cloth of his jacket.

"I want to go home, Grey," she sighed, sniffling. "Please, take me home."

"He'll do nothing of the sort," Elizabeth decreed, sweeping into the room. "Valentine and I will take you home. With Grey's reputation, I'll not have you returning home with him, after being out all night. You'd be ruined by the gossips of New Orleans."

"You're very kind," Tori whispered, wiping her cheeks with the backs of her hands.

"Come along now. Psyche will bring in some warm water for you to wash and then she'll help you dress. Grey, I believe Valentine wants to speak with you downstairs."

Rising from the bed, Grey moved toward the door, pausing only long enough to tweak one of Elizabeth's long brown curls and murmur "meddler" under his breath. With a last glance at Tori, whose obvious and painful distress tore at his heart, Grey left the room.

He found Val waiting for him in the parlor at the foot of the stairs.

"You wished to speak to me?" he asked, helping himself to a sampling of Val's best brandy.

"Not really," Val admitted, lounging in a wing chair, one booted foot resting on the opposite knee. "Elizabeth wants me to speak to you. She's afraid

96

your feelings for Tori Duclaux might lead you to some foolishness.''

"She's afraid I'll take advantage of Tori's state, is that it?"

"I think so."

"I'm not as great a villain as your wife seems to think, Val."

"It's not that," Valentine assured him. "It's just that she has a great deal of compassion—"

"Not for me!"

"No, for Tori. This business of Duclaux's being stalked by Ramsey . . ."

"She feels guilty for having told Ramsey where Christophe had gone," Grey acknowledged. "But it's not her fault. He decreed that she be told nothing. Perhaps if he had confided in her she'd have known better than to speak of his voyage to strangers. It's his fault for always treating her like a foolish little girl instead of an intelligent woman."

"But she blames herself. If Ramsey kills Duclaux . . ."

Grey scowled. "She'll be devastated."

"And you don't like that?"

"Like it? I have visions of her burying herself in guilt—becoming a martyr to Christophe's memory."

"Do you think she would?"

Shaking his head, Grey rose and paced across the rich, jewel-toned Oriental carpet. "Elizabeth's volunteered you to accompany her in taking Tori home. See what impression you get, will you?"

"Of course, but what if my conclusions are the same?"

Grey sighed. "I don't know. I simply don't know."

In the glow of the tear-drop chandelier that hung

over Monique Bouladoux's mahogany dining table, Grey stared moodily into the ruby-red goblet of wine before him. Piqued by his absence the night before and by his moodiness over dinner, Monique could restrain herself no longer.

"Would you prefer I leave you alone to your brooding?" she demanded.

"Don't start," Grey warned.

"Is that all you can say? You were supposed to come to me last night after the opera. I waited until two."

Grey's eyes glittered a warning. "You should have realized I wasn't coming long before that."

"Where were you?"

"Monique, you should know better than to ask me questions like that."

"Should I?" Rising, the exquisite quadroon flounced across the room. "Haven't I the right to know why you left me here alone last night? Have I nothing to say after you break your promises and—"

"I've never made you any promises. And I don't intend to start now. If you are no longer satisfied with our arrangement . . ." He shrugged.

"There's another woman, isn't there?" she said, suddenly sure as she'd never been before that some other woman had captured the heart, the emotions, that had eluded her grasp for so long. "Who is she?"

"What I do when I am not here is none of your business."

Leaving the table, Grey strode toward the bedroom, where his coat of black superfine lay across Monique's rosewood bed.

"Grey . . ." She tried to stop him as he returned to the parlor but he brushed roughly past her, shrugging into his coat. "Don't leave me."

98

"The only reason I came here, Monique, was to tell you I may be leaving New Orleans for some time."

"No!" His mistress trembled at the thought. "Leaving! Don't! Grey, please! What will happen to me? What will I do? I'll be helpless."

"Don't be ridiculous!" he scoffed, positioning his high silk hat atop his head. "You took care of yourself well enough before I met you and no doubt you'll take care of yourself after I leave. In any case, I'm not saying you'll be turned out into the street. You'll still have the house. I'll provide for you. It's not as if I intend to be gone forever." He silenced her protests with a stern glare. "Take it or leave it, *chérie*."

Having no other choice, Monique inclined her head demurely, accepting his decree. But the moment he'd left her door, before he'd even had time to drive away, she was sending her maid to order her carriage and hurrying to the bedroom for a cloak. Grey had another woman, of that she was sure and that, of course, was his privilege. But she'd be damned if she'd give up the fight without first learning who the little lorette might be!

In half an hour, Grey stood in Tori's library watching with a sinking heart as she dabbed at her reddened eyes with a lace-edged handkerchief.

"If you want," he was offering, almost unable to believe that the words were falling from his own lips, "I will go to Jamaica and see that Christophe is warned. My ship is fast—I'm sure I could beat Ramsey there."

"Even if this man Ramsey left as soon as I'd betrayed my husband?" she asked haltingly.

"Tori. You didn't 'betray' anyone. Christophe

99

confided nothing in you. How could you have known?"

"Still, it is my fault," she whispered. She gazed up at him, a defiant light glowing in her cerulean eyes. "I want to go with you."

Grey shook his head. "It's too dangerous, Tori. Running the blockade is not child's play, after all. Those are real bullets and real cannon that the Union navy fires at us, you know."

"I don't care. Grey, I have to see that Christophe is safe. Don't you understand? I have to know I didn't sign his death warrant by speaking to that man."

"I can tell you that, Tori. I can see to it.",

"I must speak to him myself, Grey." She read refusal in Grey's very stance. Getting out of her chair, she went to him and laid her hand on his arm. "Please, Grey, I must," she said softly, persuasively.

"No. It's too dangerous." Moving away from her, Grey took up his hat and started for the door. "I've offered to go to Jamaica and see to your husband's safety, madame. That is the best I can do. As it is, I'll be risking my life and the lives of my crew. I won't be responsible for your life as well."

He strode out of the room decisively but Tori, taking up her rippling skirts, hurried after him. She caught up with him on the loggia where the shutters had been thrown open to the cool, scented breezes of evening and the flowers growing in pots along the railing swayed in the shadows cast by the lanterns burning along the balcony's edge.

"Grey, wait," she pleaded, reaching out to take his arm. "Please."

Stopping, he turned to look down at her, catching his breath at the sheer beauty of the fragile, upturned face and her cascading hair gilded by the lantern-light.

"Tori," he said, his voice scarcely more than a whisper borne on the evening breeze. "Don't ask this of me."

"I must. Don't you see? Can't you understand that this is tearing me apart with fear and guilt? I have to go to him, Grey. I have to see with my own eyes that he is safe, that my carelessness hasn't cost him his life. Please, please! If you go, the waiting and the wondering will drive me mad."

"And what if he is dead?" Grey demanded tightly.

"I can't bear to think of it," she whispered.

"Would you be able to listen to reason and realize that he understood the dangers of what he was doing when he accepted the mission? That is the truth, you know. Ramsey was on his trail long ago, Tori. Eventually, he would have discovered Christophe's destination without your help."

She trembled and Grey's hands rose and cupped her face. He wanted her, needed her so badly that the pain of his yearning had become a raw, gnawing ache that gave him no peace. "Tori . . ." he breathed, a catch in his voice.

"Take me to Jamaica," she pleaded. "I must go there, Grey. I must do what I can."

Grey's hands slipped from her cheeks to her shoulders and he turned her back toward the doors. With one arm riding lightly on her narrow waist, he led her back into the house and shut the door behind them.

From her carriage in the shadows on the opposite side of the street, Monique had watched them through the iron gates, seething with fury. The bastard! He'd left her to go to his blonde slut!

Rapping on the ceiling of the coach, she hissed up at her coachman:

"Do you know who lives in this house?"

"Duclaux. Christophe Duclaux and his wife," the man answered.

"Duclaux," Monique muttered. She had heard the name. A wealthy, ancient Creole family steeped in honor and pride, with strong ties to France. Well, she would learn more about this bitch Duclaux—she would learn enough to destroy whatever tenuous hold she'd gained over Grey. She'd be damned if she were going to lose the best protector she'd ever had to some hoity-toity snippet!

"Take me home!" she snarled, and settled back into the tufted leather squabs of her carriage already planning her next step.

10

Tapping her leather-shod toe in anticipation, Tori willed the carriage to go faster as it carried her toward Grey's Garden District home.

In the days following Grey's offer to follow Christophe and Randall Ramsey to Jamaica, she had begged, pleaded, wept, stormed, cajoled, and tried to bribe Grey to allow her to accompany him to Jamaica. Thus far he'd refused her best efforts—efforts that would have won her any concession from her husband during the long years of their marriage.

But now, Grey's ship had returned—without Christophe—and he planned to slip away from New Orleans at the earliest opportunity. Desperately, Tori had decided to try to convince him one more time and had promised herself that this time she would not fail.

She could not help admiring the fine, pillared façade of Grey's house as her carriage passed between the ornate wrought-iron gates that flanked the drive.

"This might have been my home," she mused, before chiding herself for such a fanciful—and dangerous—thought.

The carriage rocked to a halt before the house, and Tori steeled herself before stepping down and marching resolutely toward the front door.

An elderly man answered her knock.

"Madame?" he said coolly, as if the arrival of strange women on Grey's doorstep was an everyday occurrence.

"*Bonsoir*. I am Madame Christophe Duclaux. I wish to see Monsieur Verreaux."

"I am sorry, madame," he said, "but Monsieur Verreaux is out for the evening."

"Out?" Tori's face fell. "But I must see him! Please, monsieur, it is a matter of the utmost urgency."

The earnest gaze from those beautiful blue eyes tugged at the aged Merriweather's heart. Standing back, he allowed her inside and led her into a decidedly masculine room where the heavily carved rosewood furniture was watched over by a massive bronze and crystal chandelier. On a marble-topped table in the middle of the room lay a pair of Grey's white kid gloves. From beneath them Tori noticed the ivory and lace fan she'd carried to the opera the night she'd fainted. He'd kept it. She wondered why.

Before she had time to ponder the matter, her attention was captured by Merriweather clearing his throat.

He handed her a tiny, exquisite glass half-filled with brandy. Evidently, she reflected as she sipped it, she had seemed in need of a restorative.

"Thank you," she murmured. "Now, as you were saying, er—"

"Merriweather, madame," he supplied. "As I was saying, Monsieur has gone out. He is engaged to dine, then to go on to the opera."

"I see," Tori breathed, her disappointment apparent.

"Shall I tell him you called?"

Tori gave the butler a small smile, a daring plan already forming in her mind. "If you would be so kind."

Rising, she took her leave and ordered her coachman to take her home, where she lost no time in summoning her maid to her chambers.

With Louise's help, Tori dressed in a gown of cream silk with an elaborate overdress of illusion and lace. Her champagne curls cascaded over one shoulder from a diamond comb. A necklace of sapphires and diamonds banded her throat and long pendant earrings of the same stones swung from her ears.

Carefully, almost reverently, Louise laid a white silk mantle over her shoulders.

"Will Madame and Monsieur Candé be arriving shortly?" the maid asked.

"No, I'm going alone tonight, Louise."

"I see, madame," Louise said tightly, trying without much success to conceal her disapproval as her mistress swept out of the room and down to the courtyard where her carriage had been ordered to wait for her.

Butterflies fluttered in Tori's stomach as her carriage drew up before the Opera House. She remembered it all too clearly from the night she'd come with Clairesse and Etienne Candé, but when she told the usher who it was she had come to see, he escorted her to an entirely different part of the Opera House than she had visited before.

"If you will wait a moment, Madame Duclaux," the man asked.

"But of course," Tori agreed. She sounded serene, she looked calm and cool, but inside she was a mass of trembling nerves.

In a moment, the man had returned. "If you will follow me?"

Steeling herself, Tori painted a sweet smile across her face and followed the usher into an ante-chamber off Grey's private box. A table swathed in white lace was laden with delicacies arranged about an ice bucket in which two bottles of champagne reposed. Silver and crystal glittered in candlelight and a liveried servant stood expectantly, waiting for someone to serve.

Tori smiled her thanks to the usher as he bowed himself out of the room. When she turned back, she found herself the object of Grey's admiring scrutiny.

"When the usher told me you were here," he said, crossing the room to her, "I thought for a moment he had misunderstood. I couldn't imagine your braving scandal by coming here alone."

"If the cause is important enough, scandal is a small price to pay," she replied.

"And what is your cause, pray?" he asked, opening a bottle of champagne and pouring her a glass.

"I'm sure you have guessed," she said. "I have come to beg you one last time to take me with you."

Grey turned exasperated eyes heavenward. "Tori, I've told you. A blockade-runner is no place for a lady."

"Why not?" She set her champagne aside un-

106

touched. "I know you, Grey. You wouldn't leave New Orleans if you didn't have every intention of escaping the blockade safely. And even in the event we are captured, the Yankees are not so barbarous that they would harm a respectable woman."

"And if we're sunk?" he countered.

"I'm willing to take that risk."

"I'm not." He waved aside her further objections. "Blockade or not, Tori, I don't like the notion of a lone woman aboard a ship."

"Surely your vessel is not crewed by the sort of men who would—"

"Of course not, but—"

"If you trust your crew, Monsieur Verreaux," she purred with a feline smile, "whom is it you don't trust?"

A muscle quivered in Grey's chiseled jaw and he could not resist asking:

"Are you really so eager to be reunited with your husband, Tori?"

"I must see him, Grey," she replied, a breathless catch in her voice that stirred the ever-smoldering fires of his jealousy and hardened his heart to the beauty of her entreating eyes.

"I see," he murmured coolly. "Well, then, Madame Duclaux, perhaps we should dispense with our arguments and get down to business."

"Business?" Tori was confused by his sudden change of demeanor. "What do you mean?"

"Listen to me," he said. "Whenever I sail out of New Orleans, I am risking a great deal. I must, I am sure you will agree, ask a high price for my services."

Stung by his coldness, Tori lifted her chin. Her mantle slipped from her shoulders. In the flickering light of the candles burning in the chandelier, the diamonds and sapphires at her throat, ears, and hair glittered savagely. The bare flesh of her shoulders gleamed and the light shone on her gilded curls.

"Very well," she acquiesced, her tone as icy as his, "what is your price, Monsieur Verreaux? I will give you whatever you ask. Money, jewels, property . . ."

His eyes seemed to shimmer behind the glistening veils of his thick black lashes. One sun-burnished hand rose and brushed her cheek, her chin, her throat, her shoulder.

"You're so beautiful, Tori," he murmured, his voice darkly seductive, the voice she'd remembered from that night at Barton's Landing so long ago. A smile touched his lips. "What if you are my price?"

Tori's heart thumped in her chest. She had never imagined . . . !

Her hand swept up, but before she could strike his hand away, he caught her wrist.

"I see." His smile never wavered. "I thought you would give me anything I asked. But obviously, you did not mean what you said."

"Grey . . ." She was trembling. "Please, I—"

"Do you agree or do you not?" he demanded.

"I . . . but . . . please . . ."

"One night, Tori, one night in my bed. Would you pay the price to ensure your husband's safety?"

Trembling, Tori bowed her head. She had to go to Jamaica. She had to see for herself that she had done Christophe no harm by what she had told Randall Ramsey. She could search out another blockade runner, it was true, but time was of the essence and Grey Verreaux was the best.

"Tori?" he prompted.

"Yes!" she cried, tears sliding down her pearly cheeks. "Yes, damn you! I will pay your price!" She covered her face with her hands. "I hate you! Sweet

Jesus, how I hate you!''

There was a long, heavy silence before Grey said:

"Take heart, Tori, I would not force you if it is truly so repugnant to you.''

Tori looked up at him through her tears. "You would not—''

He averted his face, as much to hide the emotion her reaction evoked in him as to give her time to compose herself.

"No, I would not. But truly, I do not like the notion of taking a lone woman on a blockade runner. I wish you would reconsider . . .''

In Grey's private box, Monique chafed at the delay. What was keeping Grey so long? He was leaving her soon, she knew, and no amount of begging or arguing seemed to sway him. She had hoped for one last opportunity to persuade him tonight—but now his attention had been diverted by the arrival of his perfect little Madame Duclaux.

So he would sail off and leave her. Oh, she would have the house and enough money to keep her, but with the war escalating it was only a matter of time before the Yankees arrived. And where would she be then? A woman alone, without protection. A quadroon at the mercy of fate.

She puffed her cheeks in exasperation. Moreover, New Orleans seemed filled with strangers as people poured into the city, taking refuge with friends and relatives fleeing from the war that already raged in many parts of the South.

"What else can go wrong?" she asked herself wearily. "What else can happen to—''

She gasped as her eyes met a pair trained on her from a box nearly opposite Grey's. Monique's heart seemed to stand still. Her senses whirled, and she was suddenly a young girl again, weeping, frightened, alone in a cruel world and at the mercy of a vicious, vengeful woman—the woman who stared at her now with eyes filled with hatred.

It was the eyes she recognized, for the fragile form was otherwise unfamiliar to her. The woman's hair was snowy white, her face lined but still lovely. Her hand, bent with arthritis, rested on the knob of an ornate, gold-tipped ebony cane. She seemed frail beneath her jet-sprinkled black crepe. A black lace widow's cap perched atop her piled hair. She was like a mannequin, a phantom, a shadow out of some tale by Dickens. Only the eyes—the piercing, searching black eyes—were alive, and they drilled into Monique with unrelenting persistence.

Trembling, Monique rose from her chair and fled from the box.

The anteroom door swung open and the gorgeous, flame-haired woman in violent purple silk swished into the room.

Tori and Grey stared as Monique's precipitous arrival shattered the tense silence that had fallen in the room.

Monique's silk-lashed, violet eyes swept over Tori, taking in her angelic beauty and the rich shimmer of her jewels against the glory of her gorgeous gown. She could only thank God that this one was married, for she sensed that Grey's attraction to the beautiful Madame Duclaux was not merely another of his careless amours. Had Tori Duclaux been available, Monique thought, she might well have proved a serious threat to Monique's security as Grey Verreaux's mistress.

"I beg your pardon," she murmured, trying

without much success to regain her lost composure. "I didn't mean to intrude."

"Didn't you?" Grey asked, his tone dripping skepticism. "But since you are here—Madame Duclaux, permit me to introduce Mademoiselle Monique Bouladoux. Monique, Madame Victoria Duclaux. I have business to discuss with Madame Duclaux, Monique."

"How do you do, Mademoiselle," Tori murmured.

"Madame," Monique replied. Against her will, she had to admit that the petite Madame Duclaux was incredibly beautiful, as exquisite in her own way as Monique herself. She was so small, so delicate—like a French doll with her pink and gold and blue coloring. From the corner of her eye, Monique saw Grey glance once, then again, at Tori. She could not help feeling a flicker of resentment toward the lovely Madame Duclaux.

"Was there something you wanted, Monique?" Grey asked, his impatience apparent.

"Perhaps I should leave," Tori suggested. "I should like to speak with you later, Gr—" She caught herself. "Monsieur Verreaux."

"Don't go!" His distress was apparent and Monique ground her teeth in frustration. Regaining control, Grey smiled benignly. "Please, don't leave. I'm sure Monique will enlighten us as to the reason for her sudden appearance."

Tori toyed with the ruffled edge of her mantle. She felt uncomfortable there while Grey and his mistress looked daggers at each other.

"I wish to go home. I am not feeling at all well. But first I have to ask you—" Monique lowered her lashes demurely. "No, I have to beg you—don't leave me in New Orleans when you go, Grey. Don't leave me alone and unprotected.'' Casting a glance at Tori, she saw her already pale cheeks whiten still further. "You promised to take care of me, Grey. Don't abandon me now to my enemies!"

Tori clenched her hands in the folds of her skirt. The thought of Grey being Monique's protector, her lover, made her want to cry, or be sick, or both.

"Your enemies?" Grey asked skeptically. "And what enemies have you, pray?"

In her mind's eye, Monique saw again those eyes, those glittering, hate-filled eyes, boring into her, having lost none of their malice with the passing of years.

"You don't know, Grey, I've never told you."

"If it's someone not worth mentioning, how can it be someone to fear?"

"Grey! There are things in my past . . ."

"Your past is not my concern, Monique," he told her sternly. "And I am growing tired of these gambits to try and persuade me to take you . . ."

Rising, Tori smiled sweetly and moved to stand at Monique's side.

"Now, Grey, you must heed Mademoiselle Bouladoux's fears." She noted, with satisfaction, the stunned surprise on his darkly handsome face. "You have promised to protect her. How ungallant it would be to simply steam away leaving her alone. New Orleans can be cruel to a woman alone."

"What would you suggest I do, Madame Duclaux?" he asked tightly, fury seething inside him.

"Why, I suggest you take her with you." Her eyes never left his face but she registered Monique's shocked look. "In a way, this solves all our problems."

"It does?" Grey asked.

"It does?" Monique echoed.

"But yes!" She led Monique to a seat and sat down beside her. "You see, Mademoiselle. My husband is in Jamaica and it is imperative that I join him. But Monsieur Verreaux has objections to a woman traveling alone on a blockade-runner. If you were to come along, I would hardly be a lone woman and he could hardly object." She turned wide, innocent eyes to Grey's flushed countenance. "Isn't that so, Monsieur?"

Grey couldn't believe his ears. Could she really be so cold to him, so uncaring, as to be totally unconcerned that his mistress would be accompanying them aboard the *Nightshade*? Did she really care so little for him? Had he been mistaken all along?

His pride, his manly self-respect, was stung to the quick. His eyes glinted silver as he smiled grimly.

"Of course, you are quite correct, madame. My objections would be foolish should Monique agree to accompany us. Monique? I will take you home at once. Madame Duclaux? I suppose you are already—"

"Packed," she supplied sweetly. "As a matter of fact, Monsieur Verreaux, I am."

"Well, then, shall we consider the matter settled?"

"I should say so. And now—" She drew her mantle over her shoulders. "—I must be going." Holding out a hand, she took Monique's into her own. "Mademoiselle Bouladoux. So nice to meet you. Until tomorrow."

"*Oui*, madame," Monique murmured, still reeling from the swiftness of her change of circumstances. "Until tomorrow."

In a swirl of white, Tori left, not daring to glance at Grey, whose icy glare she felt boring into her back as she swept from the room.

That she managed to hold back her tears until she reached the sanctuary of her own home, she viewed as a monumental achievement. But the real test would come on the morrow when she began a journey aboard a ship with the man she loved—and his lover.

11

The *Nightshade*, a side-wheel steamer of six hundred tons, tugged impatiently at her mooring lines like a thoroughbred prancing at the starting gate. Aboard, Tori was shown to the small cabin that would be hers for the days and nights it would take them to reach Montego Bay. To her surprise, it was empty save for her own trunks that stood in the middle of the floor waiting for her to unpack them.

"Is this cabin my own?" she asked Grey, who had welcomed her aboard.

"Your own?" he asked. "What do you mean?"

"I thought perhaps I would have to share it."

"With Monique?" Tori nodded and a smile quirked the corner of Grey's mouth. "No, my cabin is larger so I've had Monique put in there." He noted, with some salving of his bruised pride, the blush that pinkened Tori's cheeks. "You don't mind, do you?'' he inquired smoothly.

"Mind?'' she repeated, averting her face so that the brim of her bonnet hid her expression. "Whatever can you mean?''

"You're not, perhaps, just a bit . . . jealous?''

"Jealous!'' She lifted her chin haughtily. "Don't be ridiculous. I've no reason to be jealous.''

Grey scowled, stung once more by her indifference. "This ship was not built to carry passengers,'' he informed her coolly. "She was built to carry cargo. Since I cannot, in good conscience, collect any other form of payment for this trip, I've taken on cargo to deliver in Jamaica. It takes up every inch of space available. I didn't think you would care to share a cabin with Monique nor she with you. And don't forget—it was your idea to bring her in the first place.''

Picking her way around the trunks, Tori drew off her gloves and tossed them onto the bunk. "I'm sure it's nothing to me where Mademoiselle Bouladoux stays, Grey. How much longer are we going to bob here before we get under way?''

Clicking his heels, Grey snapped a sharp, mocking salute. "We'll be on our way shortly, madame. Make yourself comfortable.''

Turning away, he left the cabin and strode up the passageway whistling. There was something in her tone, something in the stiffness of her carriage, that told him she was nowhere near as indifferent to the sleeping arrangements aboard his ship as she wanted him to think. His spirits lifted, he went to give the orders to sail.

The trip downriver from New Orleans was less eventful than Tori had imagined. Grey knew his business and, as even he had to admit, the Union

Navy did not have the stranglehold on New Orleans that it already enjoyed at Charleston and other eastern Confederate ports.

Once in open water, Grey ordered the *Nightshade* to set course for Montego Bay at its full speed. Even so, he told Tori, the trip would take five days.

By the third day the novelty of life aboard ship had worn off and Tori chafed to reach Jamaica. It was not that her accommodations were lacking in any comfort—her cabin was small, but it was fully furnished and she had it completely to herself. Nor was it the food. If she told the truth—and she would rather have died than admit as much to Grey—it was the thought of his sharing his cabin with his mistress that made Tori pettish and sour.

During the nights, the long, silent nights when the iron plates that sheathed the wooden hull creaked and groaned, she lay in her bunk tormented by images of Grey and the beautiful Monique locked together in a passionate embrace, sharing the kind of love Tori could only dream of. The damnable pictures kept her awake until exhaustion overcame her, and even then she dreamed of them only to awake and start the whole vicious cycle over again.

In the daytime she climbed to the deck of the sleek, white-painted steamer and strolled in the sunshine twirling the parasol she carried to protect her skin from the punishing rays of the hot Caribbean sun. It was then, during her morning and afternoon strolls, that she noticed the most bewildering aspect of the journey. Monique, who was often to be found above decks enjoying the air and the sun, seemed to regard her with a malicious resentment that Tori could not explain. Every time their paths crossed, every time their eyes met, the beautiful quadroon fixed her with a heated glare filled with such anger that Tori had to turn away. She was thankful that Grey was nearly always nearby for she had heard of Monique's fiery temper and wondered if she might not be planning some violence against her.

But that was ridiculous, wasn't it? After all, it was Monique who was sharing Grey's cabin—and no doubt Grey's bed as well, since she was his acknowledged mistress. Why on earth should she be filled with such resentment toward a woman whose marriage vows put her out of Grey's reach? Why, when it was Tori who had made it possible for Monique to accompany her lover, should the woman dislike her so? It seemed to Tori beyond all understanding.

For Monique, however, the reason was all too apparent. Having gained—through Tori's good graces, she grudgingly admitted—Grey's permission to flee New Orleans aboard *Nightshade*, she had boarded the ship feeling giddily triumphant. However much Grey might lust after the lovely Madame Duclaux, it was she, Monique, who was sharing his cabin.

And then she learned the truth. It had come as a shock to her when, upon preparing for bed on that first night out of New Orleans, she discovered that Grey had had a second bunk fitted into his cabin. He did not, nor apparently had he ever, intended to share a bed with her aboard his ship. She knew that, to a man, Grey's crew assumed their captain enjoyed the favors of his beautiful mistress nightly—she hoped desperately that Madame Duclaux believed it as well—but she and Grey knew the truth. At night they lay in separate beds as chaste and innocent as if they were siblings rather than lovers. What was more, on the few occasions when she had gathered her courage and approached Grey, he had rebuffed her in no uncertain terms. He seemed to have lost his appetite for his beauteous Monique, and she thought she knew the reason.

From across the deck, she fixed Tori with a resentful stare. That little hussy had become a threat to her comfortable existence. She had blighted Grey's desire for her and, in doing so, threatened to destroy the elegant life Monique had built for herself.

There she sits, Monique thought to herself spitefully, pure as a lily. A little holy madonna secure in her title of 'madame' but in truth little more than a common adulteress. It was what she was—what she had to be—for one night Monique had heard Grey leaving the cabin they shared. She had heard his footsteps echoing down the passageway in the direction of Tori's cabin. He was her lover now, Victoria Duclaux's. What hypocrites they are! Tori seemed so concerned with her husband's welfare. Why couldn't they simply conduct themselves with some modicum of discretion in New Orleans? This entire journey made no sense to Monique unless—she studied Tori wondering—unless they had some ulterior motive. But what could it be? Time would tell and Monique intended to keep a close eye on them both.

On the last night out, the night before they would drop anchor in Montego Bay, Grey could bear it no longer. If Tori was tormented by images of him and his mistress, and Monique was struggling in the clutches of the green-eyed monster, Grey was wracked with the frustration of sharing a cabin with a beautiful woman he had ceased to desire, while the door of the woman he hungered for was locked against him.

Night after night he left his cabin and paced the passageway, stopping again and again outside Tori's door, raising his fist to knock only to let it fall, knowing she would only send him away more confused and dissatisfied than ever. He had held himself aloof from her for the greater part of the voyage. He doubted they had exchanged more than a dozen words and those little more than impersonal remarks on the weather or the accommodations. But now—one night out of port—he could bear it no longer. He had to see her, speak to her, touch her. It had ceased to be a desire for him—it was a necessity.

Leaving his cabin, he strode purposefully down the passageway. Without pausing to consider the consequences, he rapped at the door and was surprised by Tori's immediate response.

"Grey? Come in."

Entering, he found her seated beneath one of the gimbals in which an oil lamp moved gently with the rise and fall of the ship. An open book lay in her lap.

Grey drew a breath. His heart ached. All his senses screamed with the need of her. Wrapped in a delicate gown of pink lawn foaming with fragile, creamy lace, she seemed as soft, as alluring as an angel with her magnificent hair spilling over her shoulders and curling at the piquant swell of her bosom.

He tore his gaze from her, shielding himself from the sight of her with the thick screen of his black lashes.

"What is it, Grey?" Tori asked. Her heart ached. His distant manner of the past days seemed a rejection to her—as if by having his mistress so near, so accessible, he had no need of Tori. And yet as he stood before her, so strong, so breathtakingly handsome, she felt emotions and needs stirring inside her that had not come to life in seven long years—emotions that he himself had awakened, if only briefly and incompletely, on a night that seemed forever ago.

He longed to go to her, to gather her into his arms, to carry her to the bunk that stood so invitingly nearby. His lips, his arms, his body ached to feel her against him. He wanted to still her protests with kisses and caresses; yet, in the end, he merely said:

"We should reach Montego Bay by midday tomorrow."

Tori lowered her gaze to mask her disappointment. "And Stockton Hall?"

"If we take all your trunks, it may be early evening before we reach your husband's plantation."

"Perhaps we could take only the necessities."

Was she really so eager to be reunited with her husband? Grey wondered. Half of him could not bear the thought of seeing her once more at Christophe's side—the other half longed to purge his soul of her and put an end to the raw aching that plagued his nights and days.

"If you wish," he acquiesced calmly. "The rest could be sent after us."

"Grey," she said carefully, not knowing what his reaction might be. "Would you be terribly angry if Mademoiselle Bouladoux did not accompany us to Stockton Hall? Perhaps she could come later if your stay proves a lengthy one, but—"

"Christophe would object to my mistress setting foot in his house?" Grey asked archly.

Tori bit her lip. Was he really so loath to be parted from her, even for a day or two? "Christophe insists that propriety be observed at all times."

"As you wish," he agreed, his tone chilly. He hesitated before asking, "Are you looking forward to seeing your husband again?"

Ever mindful that Grey's mistress was just down the passage, very likely lying awake in his bunk waiting for him to come and love her, Tori forced her eyes to meet his and coerced a small, innocent smile to her lips.

"But of course I am eager to see him again, Grey. After all, he is my husband and we have been apart for too many weeks. I long for him."

Grey felt as if a needle-sharp stiletto had pierced his heart and been turned slowly, excruciatingly. To think of the nights that he had lain awake in his bunk needing her, hungering for her, his body afire with desire for her—and she was here, all prim and proper, tucked into her chaste bed yearning for Christophe Duclaux! It was more than he could bear.

Turning, he strode to the door. "Well, Madame Duclaux," he said, his voice icy with disdain, "tomorrow you will be reunited with your fine Creole husband. No doubt he will be pleased to put an end to your longing!"

Tori stared as he wrenched open the door, flung himself out of the cabin, and slammed the door behind him. How dare he speak to her that way! What did he expect her to do? Throw herself on her knees and make a passionate declaration of her desire for him after he had spent the past four nights lying with his mistress a few doors away? Did he think she had no pride? No self-respect? Should she declare herself and allow him to reject her in favor of his quadroon whore's charms? If that's what he thought, she told herself, he must be mad!

Laying her book aside, Tori extinguished the lamp and climbed into her bunk. Sometimes she thought she was the one who was mad—torn between her desire for Grey and her loyalty to Christophe. It seemed as if she would be torn apart as her heart, her mind, her senses were tugged this way and that. What was the answer? There seemed no way the situation could resolve itself without someone—and perhaps all of them—getting hurt.

And what if, upon arriving in Jamaica, they found Randall Ramsey had beaten them there and harmed or even killed Christophe? How would she cope with the guilt of having been the instrument—however unwitting—of her husband's misfortune?

She heard the door of Grey's cabin open and close. The soft, alluring laughter of a woman reached her—Monique's. Was Grey even now kissing her, caressing her, loving her?

She was consumed by a wave of self-doubt. For all her beauty she felt inadequate—less a woman than the commonest tavern maid 'round whom the patrons flocked with lustful gleams in rum-blurred eyes. The only men close to her were the one she loved and another on whom she depended. The former she knew to be closeted even then with another woman. And the latter? If Ramsey had not harmed him, how was Christophe passing the time in Jamaica? Had he found some comely and willing woman to give him the satisfaction his wife could not?

Tori squeezed her eyes shut against the tears that forced their way out to dampen her lashes and trickle down her porcelain cheeks. She wished she could unlock the fires inside her that would warm the hearts of the men in her life but it seemed an impossibility. And for all that she had willed Grey's ship to speed toward her destination, she now wished the ocean would open up and swallow her whole and save her the pain, the uncertainty that she was sure were all that awaited her in the murky future.

12

Most of Stockton Hall's four hundred acres had been planted to sugar cane since its founding over seventy years before. Begun at the turn of the century by Nathaniel Stockton, it had passed to his son and grandson before being sold by trustees acting on behalf of Charles Stockton's widow to Christophe Duclaux. He had purchased it with an eye toward forsaking the United States eventually to live in the tropical paradise of Jamaica.

Tori and Grey approached the massive iron gates that flanked the long, climbing drive leading to the Great House. The green of the sweeping canefields was matched in beauty only by the azure of the cloudless sky above and the endless cerulean sea upon which Tori had gazed so often during their ride from Montego Bay.

"Why didn't Christophe change the name?"

125

Grey asked as they passed through the gates and started toward the huge, rambling mansion that stood like a fortress at the end of the drive.

"He said it wouldn't have done any good. It has always been known as Stockton Hall and it always will be."

"Is it famous hereabouts?" he asked doubtfully. Though the sweep of the cane was undeniably impressive, the place had an air of decadence and decay that was not at all to his liking.

"Say rather, infamous," she told him. "Notorious. The previous owner, Charles Stockton, married a young, beautiful widow, Melanie Frazier, who had arrived in Kingston not long before from England. Apparently, she had left England under a cloud of suspicion. It was said that her first husband, a wealthy man far older than she, had died under circumstances that caused suspicion that she may have murdered him. The investigations turned up some unsavory tales about her life before her marriage. At any rate, she seems to have felt it necessary to take whatever she could pack from among her husband's treasures and embark for Jamaica and a new life.

"Once here, so the story goes, she portrayed herself as a wealthy widow—which, of course, she was, even if her widowhood was her own doing. Her beauty captivated Charles Stockton, who was then the most eligible bachelor in Jamaica.

"Soon after their marriage, however, he discovered that her fiery beauty hid a heart of ice. What was more, she held the slaves of Stockhall Hall in thrall through fear. One of the house slaves, an old woman, was apparently a Haitian well versed in the rites and powers of voodoo."

"And the husband?" Grey interrupted.

"He objected, of course. He realized that he had

126

married a monster, but by then there was little he could do. He was found, so they say, at the foot of the stairs with his neck broken—this, despite his having injured himself in a fall from a horse but a day or two before and being incapable of climbing the stairs in the first place.''

"His wife murdered him?"

Tori gazed ahead at the stone mansion that had sheltered so much horror. "So everyone suspected. But nothing could be proven. He had taken a beautiful slave girl as his mistress and Melanie was thought to be insanely jealous. That may have been the truth, for the girl was found dead in her cabin in the slave quarters. There were no marks on the body, so it was presumed she was poisoned. Then again, it was said that a voodoo charm was discovered near the body. Perhaps she believed in her mistress' powers so strongly that the mere sight of the charm brought on her death.''

"What became of the wicked Mrs. Stockton?" Grey wanted to know.

"Ah, well, therein lies the mystery. For a few years she continued to live here. Local legends abound with tales of her cruelties. Finally, the locals had enough. A band of her slaves decided to mutiny. They armed themselves and broke into the house one night when she was supposedly locked in her chambers performing her voodoo magic. All sorts of terrifying sounds came from her chambers, and the mutineers waited until the sounds died, thinking to catch her unawares. But when they broke into the rooms, they had been torn apart. There were signs of a terrible struggle, but there was no sign of Melanie Stockton. She had disappeared.''

Grey turned a skeptical stare on her. "Disappeared?"

"It's true," she assured him. "There was only one set of doors to the rooms and they had been locked from within. All of her belongings—her clothes, her jewels, everything—were accounted for. But the mistress herself was gone. Not a trace of her was ever found." She gazed doubtfully toward the mansion and Grey saw a shiver of foreboding run through her. "The locals say she was so wicked that the Devil rose up out of Hell and took her away with him."

"What do you suppose happened to her?" Grey asked.

Tori shook her head. "I can't imagine. The estate was heavily in debt—Melanie Stockton had expensive tastes—and after her disappearance the creditors took over its management. For nearly twenty-five years the mansion lay empty. At last Melanie was declared dead and the creditors sold the estate to Christophe. It was his intention to leave New Orleans and live here."

"But you do not want that?"

"The stories frightened me," she admitted softly.

"He shouldn't have told them to you."

"It wouldn't have mattered. I would have learned them from the locals. Ah, well, I suppose it is simply foolishness on my part. All that is past; Melanie Stockton is no more and Stockton Hall is as peaceful a house as any, I'm sure."

"And you're a little girl whistling in the dark," Grey told her, smiling.

Tori shot him a withering glare, but before she could counter it with a wry remark, they arrived before the sweeping stone staircase that rose to the grand, columned entrance of Stockton Hall.

"No one seems to be about," Tori said

nervously as she and Grey climbed the stairs.

"It does seem deserted," Grey agreed. With the sweep of a hand, he signaled the men who'd ridden with them to hold off in their unloading of the bags. "And yet there are workers in the cane fields, so the place isn't abandoned. Let us not jump to any conclusions, shall we?"

At the head of the stairs Tori hesitated. Then, reminding herself that she was, after all, mistress of this estate, she pushed open one of the great paneled doors and preceded Grey into the cool, dark, marble-floored foyer of Stockton Hall.

Like the exterior of dull grey stone, the interior of the mansion had an air of melancholy decay, as though the life of the once-magnificent house had gone bad somehow, been soured by the tragedy and misery that had been played out within its walls.

Ahead, framed in a columned archway, a broad staircase rose to a wide landing lit by a grimy window that had nevertheless retained much of its former elegance and beauty. Flanking the landing were two smaller staircases that rose out of sight toward the second floor.

From the foyer, they could see little of the rooms that opened off the larger chambers at the foot of the stairs. But high up on one wall a pediment with a coat-of-arms cartouche had obviously once surmounted a painting that was no longer there.

"Perhaps it was a portrait of the notorious Mrs. Stockton," Grey suggested.

Tori shivered. "I don't think you should joke about it," she chided. Grey might think it foolish, but Christophe had recounted the dark tales to her in far greater detail than she had used in telling them to Grey. Now, standing inside the house, she saw some of the places where the horrors had reputedly been committed. In her mind's eye, she could almost see the terrors Christophe had described to her.

"Tori, don't be a child. Likely the legends are just that, legends. Melanie Stockton, if indeed there ever was such a person, was probably a harmless woman maligned by jealous gossip."

"There certainly was such a person, sir, I assure you," a masculine voice said from the shadows at the side of the archway. "And the legends about her are, unfortunately, all too true."

Grey stepped a little to the side, placing himself in front of Tori as the man stepped out of the shadows. His clothing, though he was in shirtsleeves, seemed presentable. The man himself, tall and slender with sandy hair, would have seemed respectable enough, benign even, were it not for the pistol that dangled from his right hand.

"Is that necessary?" Grey asked, his body tensed and ready to spring into action should the man show signs of becoming violent.

The man glanced at the pistol. "I don't know. Perhaps I would if you were to tell me who you are and what your business is at Stockton Hall."

"My name is Greyson Verreaux. The lady with me is Madame Christophe Duclaux. I have brought her from New Orleans."

Astonishment replaced the suspicion on the man's face. "Madame Duclaux? I had no idea. That is, Monsieur Duclaux did not tell us to expect his wife."

"Who are you?" Grey demanded.

The man shifted the pistol from hand to hand as though suddenly embarrassed by its presence. "My name is Jared Whitney. I am the overseer of Stockton Hall. Please, let me show you into the salon and send for something cool to drink. You must be parched after your ride from Montego Bay.''

Bristling with questions, Tori and Grey followed him into a small parlor whose walls were painted a once pristine white. The tarnished gilding of the once elaborate cornices gleamed dully in the afternoon sun shining behind faded gold draperies.

After dispatching a serving girl to the kitchen for lemonade, Jared Whitney settled into a threadbare armchair and regarded Grey and Tori, who sat at opposite ends of a scarred Empire sofa, with obvious curiosity.

"Once more, let me apologize for the nature of my welcome," he said, casting a glance toward the pistol he had laid aside on a table. "Monsieur Duclaux said there might be people looking for him—dangerous people. He said nothing about his wife's arriving."

"My husband is safe, Mr. Whitney? He is well?"

Jared Whitney lifted his shoulders slightly. "I presume so, madame. He was when last I saw him."

"When last you saw him?" Tori frowned. "Pardon me, Mr. Whitney, but you speak of my husband in the past tense—almost as if he were no longer here."

"He isn't," Whitney assured her, pausing long enough for the young servant girl to serve the lemonade that would sit untouched before them. When she had gone, he turned his gaze back to Tori. "Monsieur Duclaux took ship two weeks ago for France."

13

"It's out of the question!" Grey stormed, his broad back toward Tori as he stood at the window of the parlor looking out over the long, steep drive toward the sea in the distance.

"But, Grey—" Tori began.

"No!" He swung toward her. "Tori, think what you are asking! I didn't want to bring you to Jamaica! Now you ask me to take you to France!"

"You have family there. You could visit them."

He ground his teeth, exasperated by her relentlessly feminine logic. "There is a war on," he reminded her with exaggerated patience. "My place is at home, not paying social calls on relatives I've never met!"

"War! War! War! The war is not going to be won or lost on the issue of your participation." She fixed him with an accusing glare. "You're only

133

running the blockade to make yourself rich—or is it richer?''

"Richer! Is that why you think my ship's made two trips to this god-forsaken rock?'' With a savage sweep of his hand, he dismissed every inch of the lush green paradise that surrounded them.

"Christophe's trip was in the service of the Confederacy,'' she reminded him coolly.

"And what of this voyage?'' he challenged. "It damned well hasn't been a pleasure cruise!'' Tori opened her mouth to protest but he went on, ignoring her. "And now—now!—you expect me to spend months chasing your husband across the goddamned ocean! Well, I won't do it! You wanted to be certain he was safe, that Ramsey hadn't gotten to him. Well, now you know. He left Jamaica bound for France alive.''

"But what if Ramsey followed him to France?'' Tori asked.

"That is not my concern. Good Christ, Tori! Christophe is a grown man! He undertook this mission of his own free will and with full knowledge that the Yankees might send agents to try to stop him. He will be on his guard.''

"But, Grey! I only want to see that . . .''

"No! If Christophe had wanted you to come with him, he would have taken you. He did not. And I will not. And that's an end to it!''

Tori turned wide, haunted eyes to Grey's face and the tears she'd tried so hard to hold back spilled in crystalline rivulets down her soft, pale cheeks.

Coming to her, Grey enfolded her in his arms. Her cheek rested on the soft lawn of his shirt and the hard wall of his chest. He held her tightly as she wept and clung to him, warmed and comforted by his nearness, grateful for his strength.

His face buried in the scented silk of her hair, Grey tried to control the hunger her nearness evoked in him. Now was not the time for passion, but his rampant senses knew only that she was there, in his arms, as he'd longed for her to be since that first night when she'd come back into his life. She was like a child now—a frightened, bewildered little girl who needed to be held and soothed. It was comfort she needed most, not passion. That, he hoped, would come later when her concern over Christophe had lessened. If only his raging senses could accept the logic of it as easily as his mind did!

"You should lie down," he told her, his lips moving gently against the shining crown of her head. "Did you get much sleep last night?"

"Almost none," she admitted.

"Come on, we'll find a servant and have them show you to the master suite."

His hand at the small of her back, Grey guided her out of the parlor. In a chamber nearby, they found the young serving girl busily dusting a stack of books on a table against the wall.

"Persephone, isn't it?" Grey asked.

The girl's big dark eyes darted from Grey to Tori and back. "Yassuh?" she said shyly.

"Were you here when Monsieur Duclaux was here?"

"De new massah? Yassuh, I was. But he be gone now."

"Yes, I know. This lady—" he indicated Tori— "this lady is his wife. Madame Duclaux. She is tired and would like to lie down. Will you show us to the master's suite?"

"Ain't nobody use de massa's rooms, suh. Dey been nailed shut since . . ." She hesitated.

"Since Melanie Stockton disappeared?" Tori

suggested.

"Yas, missis," the girl whispered, one hand going to a little leather bag that hung by a thong about her neck.

"Well, then, suppose you show me to whatever rooms my husband used during his stay."

Nodding, the girl started from the room. With Grey and Tori following, she mounted the stairs to the landing then turned to the staircase on the left and climbed to the second floor.

"De massa's rooms," she whispered as they reached the second floor corridor.

Tori and Grey peered down the length of the corridor. At the far end, hidden in the shadows, stood a pair of massive double doors. Rough planks had been laid across them and big, rusted spikes held them in place. Beneath the dust and cobwebs of a decade's neglect, it was possible to see that the once-gleaming surfaces of the doors were scarred with jagged gouges around the battered brass latches.

"What happened to them?" Tori asked.

Persephone fingered her charm. "When de missis disappeared, de men chopped open de doors. But nobody be dere."

"What do you suppose happened to her?" Grey asked, curious.

The girl's eyes widened to saucer size. "De Debil come to git her. Or de Obeahman come."

"Obeahman?" Tori repeated, her voice loud in the echoing corridor.

"Shhh!" Persephone hushed. Then, as though suddenly aware she had just shushed her mistress, she turned a worried face toward Tori. "Is not good to say some tings out loud, missis."

Tori and Grey exchanged a glance. "I see," Tori said seriously, humoring the girl. "Then perhaps it would be best if you showed me to my rooms."

Only too pleased to comply, Persephone led them up the corridor toward the end opposite the old master suite.

The room into which they were shown had rich cream walls and draperies of bright yellow silk. An old fashioned tester bed dominated the room. It was clean and inviting, restful even, once Persephone had drawn the draperies against the relentless glow of the Jamaican sun.

Tori sank gratefully onto the edge of the bed. With a smile, she dismissed the flighty Persephone.

"Lie down now, and rest," Grey advised. "A good night's sleep wll do you the world of good. In the morning, we'll head back to New Orleans."

"No, we won't," Tori disagreed.

Grey groaned as he lowered himself into a chair near the foot of the bed. "I'm not going to argue with you about this, Victoria."

"Good. I had hoped you wouldn't."

"I'm leaving for New Orleans in the morning."

Her blue eyes shone with a determined light as she returned his steady stare. "If you do, you go without me."

"I won't leave you here alone."

"I'm not asking you to. I'm asking—"

"The impossible!" Pushing himself to his feet, he began pacing the room like a restless jungle cat. "Tori, it's madness for you to pursue Christophe to France."

"Then I'm mad," she agreed serenely. "It is something I am driven to do, Grey."

"And what if he simply tells you to go home and await his return as a good wife should?"

Tori lifted her chin and took a deep breath to help control her emotions. "Then I shall have to accept that and go home, shan't I?''

"Tori . . .''

"It's no good, Grey," she sighed. "You can't change my mind. If you won't take me to France, I'll simply have to find someone who will.''

"Do you think I'd let you go sailing off across the ocean by yourself?'' he demanded.

She arched a brow and the ghost of a smile appeared at the corner of her mouth. "Do you think you could stop me?'' she asked slyly.

Grey chuckled. It was the first sign in a long time that the mischievous Tori he'd known so long ago lived on inside the cool, distant woman she'd become.

"Probably not," he admitted. "If you were determined.''

"I am.''

"We'll discuss it.''

Tori bit back a smile. For him to even agree to discuss the matter was a minor victory. "I think that we . . ." she began.

He fixed her with a stern look. "But not now. Now I want you to lie down and rest. Since it appears that we're going to be here at least for the night, I am going to send to the *Nightshade* for our things. And you, my stubborn little she-cat, are going to obey me, if only this once, and take a nap.''

Pleased with his concern, Tori obediently lay back atop the fringed and embroidered coverlet. Taking a silky shawl from the chaise at the foot of the bed, Grey tucked it around her. His eyes were gentle, wistful even, as he brushed back a wisp of hair that clung to her temple.

"Sleep now, won't you?'' he asked tenderly.

"I'll try,'' she promised.

His eyes glittered with mischief. "And no lying

awake up here planning your strategy, do you hear me?"

"Yassah, massa," she drawled, imitating Persephone.

Laughing, Grey left the room and Tori, sure of her eventual success in persuading Grey to take her to France, drifted into a soft, dreamless sleep from which she didn't awaken until the glaring Caribbean sun was lowering toward the western horizon.

Tori stretched, lifting one hand to her mouth as she yawned. Despite her ever-present chagrin over Christophe, she felt sheltered and cared for here, and it was all due, she knew, to Grey. He did care about her, she was certain. He was concerned for her well-being. Perhaps, she allowed herself to dare hope, he even loved her.

Pushing back the shawl she had wrapped herself in, she swung her legs over the side of the bed. The ivory taffeta of her gown was hopelessly creased—why, she wondered, hadn't she had the presence of mind to take it off before lying down? She hoped Persephone had some experience in caring for a lady's gowns but doubted there was much chance of it. After all, Stockton Hall had not had a mistress in residence in nearly twenty-five years and Persephone was little more than a child.

Yawning again, she reached up to toss back the long, loose locks of her golden hair. The gesture was stayed in mid-air as the doorlatch was jiggled from without.

Tori held her breath. Was it . . ? But no, she chided herself, rising from the bed's edge and striding toward the door. She was allowing the dark legends of Stockton Hall to fire her imagination.

Resolutely seizing the door handle, she pulled

the door open only to have Persephone nearly fall at her feet.

The girl gave a startled little scream before she realized that it was Tori who stood there.

"Missis!" she cried. "You scare de life out of me!"

"I'm sorry." Tori held back a smile at the girl's skittishness. Apparently she was not the only one with an overactive imagination.

"I come to see where de trunks go." With a jerk of her thumb over her shoulder, she indicated Tori's baggage piled in the hall to avoid waking Tori.

"Well, you may as well have them brought in, since it seems we're going to be here at least a short while."

Persephone nodded, but her dark eyes roved over Tori's disheveled gown. "You should not sleep in dat dress."

"I know," Tori agreed. "But I was so dreadfully tired. Have Monsieur Verreaux's belongings arrived?"

"Marse Grey's clothes be in his room, missis. But I doan know where to put his . . . his . . ."

"Yes? His?"

"His woman, missis. She stay in de house too?"

"His wo . . ." Tori caught her breath. She had forgotten about Monique! When Grey said he would send for their 'things,' she had not thought he might include his mistress. What choice did she have but to extend the hospitality of the house to Monique since she herself was in large part responsible for the woman's being there? She could hardly demand that Monique be left aboard the *Nightshade*.

"Yes," she said at last. "The lady should be given a room close to the monsieur's."

"Ah. She be his—"

"Indeed," Tori cut her off. "See to it, Persephone, then come back and help me change."

The girl disappeared up the corridor and Tori closed the door behind her and leaned on it. All the pleasant musings of a few moments ago crashed around her like shattered crystal. Of course Grey would want Monique with him. She was, after all, his mistress. But how, in Heaven's name, could he be so callous as to bring her into Tori's home—house her beneath Tori's roof—make love to her—?

Steeling herself, Tori pushed this last, unwelcome thought out of her mind. That was that, she told herself sternly. No more delusions. Who was she deceiving but herself? These schoolgirl fantasies only made it harder to accept the inevitable. Henceforth, she must master her treacherous emotions and deal with Grey strictly as business demanded. Her heart—her foolish, credulous heart—must never, never be allowed to lure her into the sweet temptation of succumbing to Grey's persuasion. What he wanted—if indeed he wanted anything more than a brief *affaire de coeur*—she couldn't imagine. But she was determined that from that moment on, there would be nothing between them but business and he would never—never!—know the depths of her feelings for him. He would never know just how close she had come to losing herself in the love that had burned in her secret heart for him since she was fifteen.

14

Tori awoke to find Persephone peering anxiously around the half-opened door.

"Come in," she said, pushing herself up in the center of the big bed. Reaching up with one hand, she smoothed back her tousled curls. The morning sunshine was already fading behind the drawn draperies.

"Is it late?"

"Near eleben, missis," the girl told her. "I was gittin' worried 'bout you."

"I suppose I was overtired from the long voyage," Tori mumbled.

It was a lame excuse at best, particularly since she had had a long and restful nap the previous afternoon. But she couldn't admit the truth to Persephone. It wouldn't do at all to have the girl accidentally tell Grey that Tori had slept half the morning away because she had lain awake most of the night tossing and turning, knowing in her heart that he was there, but a few doors away, doubtless in the arms of his mistress.

Noticing that Persephone was about to draw the draperies, Tori stopped her and dispatched her to order a bath and breakfast for her 'missis.'

A little over an hour later, Tori sat amidst the billowing skirt of a rose-sprigged muslin dress. A matching parasol and brown leghorn straw hat with rose-colored plumes and rose silk ribbons lay waiting while Persephone, with a skill Tori would not have suspected the girl possessed, dressed her hair artfully, confining the rippling tresses into a chignon which was in turn confined in a fine net.

"Did Grey rise early this morning?" she asked, forcing an air of casual interest which she hoped concealed her far greater concern.

"Marse Grey were up with the sun, missis. He go to Montego Bay. Someting 'bout a boat."

"Ah." Tori's heart quavered somewhere between hope and despair. Grey's going to see about his 'boat' could mean that he was considering going on to France, that he was having the *Nightshade* made ready for a return trip to New Orleans, that he was seeing to the delivery of the cargo he'd brought from America, or it just might mean nothing at all. There was, after all, little for him to do at Stockton Hall, since it did not belong to him and its affairs seemed to lie securely in the capable hands of Jared Whitney. It was only natural that he would wish to spend his time aboard *Nightshade* where he was the indisputable master.

Tori leaned toward the mirror, displaying a somewhat curious interest in a small, scarcely noticeable beauty mark just to the right of her mouth. She sighed, asking with feigned indifference:

"Did he say when he would be back?"

Persephone fingered the soft silk of the parasol wondering why it was that fine white ladies took such pride in keeping their skins so pasty. True, it was not healthy to spend too long beneath the scalding Jamaican sun, but a little color wouldn't hurt any one of them.

"No, missis," she answered absently.

Rising, Tori tied on her hat and took the parasol from Persephone. "I see. Well, perhaps I'll go exploring outside. Is there anything of interest nearby?"

Persephone shrugged. "Dere use to be a garden behin' de house. No one's touched it for years but dere was a pretty waterfall dere 'mongst de weeds."

"Perhaps I'll see if I can unearth it after all this time." Tori turned toward the door, pausing in the doorway as though just struck with an afterthought. She turned back toward the maid who was already tidying the bedchamber. "And Mademoiselle Bouladoux? Is she still abed?"

"Oh, no, missis. De mam'zelle got up near tree hour ago. She ask for Marse Grey, den she ask for a horse and ride out."

"I see. Thank you, Persephone."

Forcing a smile, Tori swept from the room and down the stairs, seeking the privacy of the overgrown garden in which to vent her frustrations.

A flagged terrace behind the house, its stones cracked and uneven from having been pushed out of place by weeds and trees, led down to a path scarcely visible to the naked eye. The pathstones had been reclaimed by the wild tangle of flowers and ferns where parrots and parakeets chattered and swirled amidst the branches of giant silk cotton and rain trees. Tori picked her way carefully through the undergrowth.

The once beautiful garden now all but concealed its former centerpiece, a small, rippling stream that had been painstakingly trained to run through the lush greenery. A dam, certainly man-made but seeming completely natural, had been constructed so that the sparkling water tumbled over carefully placed rocks and danced among the overhanging foliage, spotting the bright green leaves with droplets that glistened in the sunshine like diamonds.

With a whispering puff of muslin and lace, Tori sank to her knees beside the little man-made falls. Furling her parasol, she laid it aside and dipped her hand in the water. The chill of it, in such marked contrast with the heat of the day, sent a shiver of sheer delight coursing through her.

She let the water trickle through her fingers, caught a leaf as it floated by, and watched another as it fell, end over end, in the glittering falls. She was enchanted—so much so that she did not hear the footsteps of the man in white linen who approached equally unaware of her presence.

As he shoved aside the wild foliage that blocked his path, he suddenly noticed the gleaming white and pink of Tori's gown as it spilled over the flagstones she knelt on.

"Ah!" He drew himself up, pulling off his bowler. "*Scusatemi*, Signora!" he said, his voice heavily accented. "I beg your pardon."

Tori started violently. The man who stood above her was not as tall as Grey but he was as dark, perhaps even more swarthy, with coal-black hair that sprang into tight little curls as he pulled off his hat. A black moustache quivered between his full month and his aquiline nose. A deep cleft divided his strong, prominent chin.

146

Rising, Tori curled her fingers about the handle of her parasol. It was a frilly, fragile accessory at best, but it would be enough, she hoped, to defend herself should such drastic action become necessary.

"Sir?" she asked, looking almost directly into his startlingly blue eyes. He was a scant few inches taller than she—had her slippers of Moroccan leather had high heels, they would have been of a height.

"I am sorry, signora," he said in his halting English. "I was told the house was empty. I came to visit because I had heard of the . . ."

"The legends?" Tori suggested. "They seem to be a favorite subject for discussion hereabouts."

"Yes. My host and hostess recounted them to me at length. But ah! I am forgetting. Permit me to introduce myself. I am Count Niccolò da l'Armi." He made her a little, charmingly formal bow. "And you, signora. You are . . . ?"

"I am Madame Duclaux. Victoria Duclaux."

The man's amazing blue eyes lit up in recognition. "Duclaux! You are, perhaps, a relative of Christophe Duclaux, the owner of this estate?"

"You know my husband, monsieur?"

"We have met. He was, on one occasion during his recent stay in Jamaica, a dinner guest at the home of my host, Signor Chesney. Do you know him?"

Tori shook her head. "I'm afraid not. I arrived only yesterday, you see. This is my first time in Jamaica." She eyed the dapper, handsome man curiously. "You are Italian, are you not, Signor—pardon me—Count da l'Armi?"

"I am," he confirmed.

"Forgive me, but it seems a bit curious to find an Italian count in Jamaica."

"I suppose it does," he agreed good-naturedly.

"I came to visit acquaintances and also because my doctor said the warmth would do me good."

"You are ill?"

He smiled brilliantly as though charmed by her instant concern. "No more. I am cured—well, as cured as one can be." He patted his chest. "I suffer from a . . . pulmone . . . how do you say it . . . lung! An ailment of the lungs."

"I'm so sorry. But you are better now?"

"Much. And I thought, on this my first day out of bed, I could come visit this house of legend. As I said, I did not think anyone was here. It is an unexpected delight to find such a lovely lady as yourself in residence."

"Oh, not in residence," Tori corrected. "I intend to follow my husband to France on the first available ship."

"Indeed?" The Count seemed disturbed by her announcement. "Your husband never mentioned that you would be joining him."

Tori was puzzled by his agitation. "Why, no." She felt some vague uneasiness but could not fathom the reason for it. "You see, Christophe has been traveling for some weeks, so I was unable to let him know of my intentions. Nonetheless, I am determined to rejoin him."

"Alas, Signora, I fear that will prove difficult. There are no ships bound directly for France now. I know, because I myself wish to book passage on one. I am attached to the Italian Embassy in Paris and must return at the earliest opportunity."

Tori's mind raced. She recognized an opportunity when she saw one.

Smiling flirtatiously, she toyed with the ruffles of her parasol. "Tell me, Count, are you truly interested in the legends that surround Stockton

Hall?''

"Indeed I am," he assured her. "They are *affascinante*. Fascinating."

Gliding toward him, Tori slipped an arm through his and smiled up from beneath the brim of her hat.

"Then you must allow me to show you the house. What sort of hostess would I be if I let you go home with your curiosity unsatisfied?"

The Count, ever enchanted by a pretty, flirtatious woman, lifted her hand to his lips and kissed it lingeringly as they started toward the house.

15

Together Tori and Niccolò toured the Great House exploring rooms Tori herself had not yet seen, rooms that looked as if they had not seen the light of day since the morning Melanie Stockton had been discovered missing.

"How beautiful it all must have been," Niccolò said, running a finger among the tinkling prisms of a candelabra, one of a pair that stood on either side of a magnificent piano whose ivory keys were darkened with age and whose once-gleaming mahogany case was smeared with thick, gritty dust.

Nodding, Tori paused in an archway where a pair of purple velvet portieres hung limply, their once-luxurious nap overlaid with a fine network of cobwebs. Two rooms, each immense, both hung with enormous crystal chandeliers, were divided by the archway. There was little in the way of furniture in either room save for the piano, a tall, gilded harp, and assorted tables, chairs, and ornaments.

"I suppose these rooms were meant to be used for balls," she mused. "It must have been magnificent."

She smiled at the Count. "Can you imagine it, sir? The ladies in their glittering jewels, the gentlemen in evening dress, the musicians, the liveried servants . . ." She stopped, blushing at her own enthusiasm.

"No, no, please continue," the Count urged her. "You make it come alive."

Tori shook her head. "I don't know what's wrong with me. I'm not normally so fanciful. It's this house. There's something about it that stirs the imagination."

Niccolò looked around the room. "The stories, I suppose. Do you know, I was told there were bloodstains on the floor of Signora Stockton's room. Is that the truth?"

Tori shivered, remembering Christophe's telling her that Melanie Stockton had once had a slave who displeased her slain in her presence—had his throat slit before her very eyes in her own bedchamber.

"I don't know if it's true," she replied. "Quite honestly, those rooms are boarded up. I've never been inside."

"Never?" The Count gave her a teasing look. "And are you not in the least curious? If not, you are a rare woman, Victoria." He looked suddenly distressed. "Ah, you must forgive me. I had not meant to be so bold."

"Not at all," she assured him. "You may call me Victoria."

"You are gracious. And you must call me Niccolò. It would make me very happy."

Tori flushed. He really was overbold, but there

was something so charming about him that she could not take offense. And the admiring light in his astonishing blue eyes soothed her pride, which had taken a beating in the past few weeks.

"Very well," she acquiesced shyly. "Niccolò."

Seizing her hand, he kissed it loudly. "Now, why do we not go and explore Melanie Stockton's rooms, eh?"

Feeling like a child off on a new adventure, Tori followed Niccolò up the staircase. At the head of the stairs, she pointed toward the barred doors in the shadows at the end of the hall.

"No one has been inside for years," Tori told him as he examined the planks crudely nailed across the beautifully paneled and carved doors.

Surprising her with his strength, Niccolò pried the boards loose. The heavy bronze hinges groaned as he pushed one of the double doors open. The room within was dark and heavy draperies covered the windows. The priceless carpets were thick with dust; ancient cobwebs hung like tattered lace curtains from every doorway, every piece of furniture, every lamp chimney. It was like a scene from a fairy-tale—the sleeping palace no one had disturbed for a hundred years.

"Shall we?" Niccolò asked, obviously eager to explore the fantastic chambers.

Tori hesitated. There was something eerie about the rooms. An atmosphere of death and decay that sent shivers down her spine. And yet she could not help being intrigued by the thought of entering Melanie Stockton's inner sanctum.

Together she and Niccolò toured the boudoir, blowing the dust off discolored miniatures of nameless men and women. As they peered into discolored mirrors with tarnished backs of ornately chased silver, marveling at the variety and value of the objects that had simply been left to decay after Melanie's disappearance, it was obvious that the best of Stockton Hall's, furnishings had been brought here, to the mistress's chambers.

Niccolò opened doors until he found the bedchamber, and they entered slowly, fascinated.

"What do you suppose . . . oh, Lord!" Tori cried.

Niccolò looked up from his perusal of a Boulle cabinet to find Tori staring in horrified fascination at an ugly brown stain that marred the jewel-toned beauty of the oriental carpet.

"Blood, I think," the Count said dispassionately. "So the stories were true."

He nudged the stain with his toe, but Tori laid a hand on his sleeve.

"Don't . . . oh, please don't," she begged, feeling queasy.

The Count took her arm and steered her away. "Come, Victoria, I should not have asked you to come here. It was cruel of me."

"No," she assured him. "I'm fine. It's only the thought of having someone . . . of wantonly ordering the death . . ."

"I understand. Come, we will go back to the boudoir."

Willingly, Tori followed him back to the sitting room. He dusted off an ornate Regency armchair and lowered her into it before returning to his perusal of the room.

He stopped before the fireplace of white Carrara marble. As Tori watched, Niccolò toyed with the carved decorations of the ornate mantel.

"What is it you expect . . ." she began. Then, to her astonishment, there was a loud click as he pressed the breast of an amply-endowed nymph. A panel at the side of the fireplace opened, revealing an empty space and a narrow staircase just behind it.

Rising, Tori went to the fireplace. "How amazing!" she marveled. "I suppose someone like Melanie Stockton would have need of secret panels and hidden tunnels." She peered inside. "I wonder if that was how she disappeared all those years ago?"

"I do not doubt it," Niccolò replied. "Such hidden passages are not uncommon in my own country. Well," he said cheerfully. "Now that my curiosity is satisfied, I can go home with no qualms."

"Niccolò," she said as they left the suite, leaving the planks for a servant to replace. "Is it truly so important that you get back to France?"

"It is," he assured her, taking her elbow as they started down the sweeping staircase. "Most important."

"Perhaps—and mind you, I say perhaps—I can help you."

At the foot of the stairs, he turned to her eagerly. "Can you?" he asked. "You know of a ship?"

"I really cannot say more, Niccolò, until I make same inquiries. It may not be possible at all and, if it is, it may be very expensive."

He waved a dismissing hand. "That is of no moment." He seized her hand in his. "If you can help me, Victoria, I would be grateful. Forever grateful."

Gently, she disengaged her hands from his grasp. "As I said, I cannot make any promises until I know more. But why don't you come to dinner tonight? Perhaps by then I will be able to tell you something more."

Agreeing, Niccolò took his leave and Tori, summoning Persephone to help her, put her plan into motion.

"Be dat man comin' to dinner, missis?" the girl
asked as she dressed Tori's hair into a mass of golden
curls at the side of her head and fastened a spray of
silk flowers to the other side.

"That man?" Tori paused as she fastened an
emerald bracelet about her wrist. "Count da l'Armi,
you mean? He's coming, yes. He and Monsieur
Duclaux met while Christophe was staying alone
here. They were dinner guests one evening at the
home of the Count's host and hostess here in
Montego Bay. It is only polite that he be invited."

"De massa doan go nowheres to dinner wile he
be heah, missis."

"You must be mistaken, Persephone. The
Count said he met Christophe over dinner at the
Chesneys'."

In the mirror, Tori saw the girl shake her head.
"Ain't nobody 'round heah wid a name like dat,
missis."

Tori rose from her dressing table and shook out
the skirts of her emerald silk gown. It was cut low
and left her shoulders and a great deal of her bosom
bare, providing a beautiful showcase for the emerald
necklace that had been in Christophe's family for
generations.

"You must be mistaken, Persephone," she said
again. "The Count clearly said his host's name was
Chesney. Perhaps they are new to the area and you
are not familiar with them."

Persephone shrugged. She was sure of her facts,
but it didn't matter to her either way and she knew
better than to argue with her mistress.

"Has Monsieur Verreaux returned?" Tori
asked.

"Marse Grey? Yass'm. He come in near a half hour ago."

"Do you know where he is?"

"His room, I tink."

Leaving her chambers, Tori swept down the corridor to Grey's door. Saying a silent prayer that Monique would not be there with him, she rapped on the panel.

Grey, in shirtsleeves with the open throat of his shirt displaying the dark furring of his chest, whistled softly as he saw her there.

"Are we celebrating?" he asked, his silvery eyes alight with admiration and desire. "What is the occasion?"

"Does there have to be an occasion?" she hedged, casting him a flirtatious sideways glance from beneath lowered lashes. "Would you mind so much dressing for dinner?"

He stepped back to admit her into the room. "I'm not sure what Merriweather packed in the line of evening dress," he told her. "But I shall do my best."

Perched on the edge of a chair, Tori took a deep breath and plunged into the matter that had brought her there.

"Grey, what exactly is your objection to going to France?"

He sighed. "Not again. I told you, Tori, it would be an expensive and foolish venture. For me to sail with you to France simply because—"

"What if it was not just for me?" she interrupted.

"What do you mean?"

"What if there was a passenger? A wealthy passenger, willing to pay handsomely to be taken to France?"

"He'd have to be willing to make it worth my while. And I mean well worth my while."

Pleased, Tori rose. "Good. That's all I wanted to know. Dinner is at eight."

Grey's eyes followed her as she flounced out of the room. She was up to something, the scheming little minx. He had the distinctly unpleasant feeling that he had walked right into her trap. But there seemed no way he could have avoided it since he didn't know what her trap was!

16

When he came downstairs sometime later, Grey found Tori in the dining room. He paused in the doorway, startled by the changes she'd wrought there.

Like the rest of the house, the room had been kept barely clean enough for habitation. But after the Count da l'Armi's visit earlier that day, Tori had enlisted Persephone and a few of the female slaves out of the cane fields and gone to work in the dark and dingy room.

The results spoke for themselves. The long narrow room fairly glittered in the glow of the twin bronze and etched-glass chandeliers. The long mahogany table gleamed beneath a cloth of delicate lace that Persephone had produced from Heaven only knew where. Fine china shone, reflecting the glistening silver of the tableware and candelabra.

The windows had been freshly washed, and the
sky-blue Scalamandré draperies had been taken
down and carried outside, where the thick
accumulation of dust had been shaken out of them.
Against one wall a huge French mirror, whose heavy,
gilded frame touched the elaborately corniced
ceiling, reflected the room with startling clarity.

It was in the mirror that Tori noticed Grey for
the first time. She smiled at his reflection and it
smiled back. For an instant, they were unguarded,
frank in their mutual admiration, each aware of the
powerful attraction that constantly threatened to pull
them together—and tear them apart.

With a feeling of wistful resignation, Tori came
back to herself. "Did you tell Monique to dress for
dinner?" she asked.

Grey toured the sparkling chamber slowly, his
hands clasped behind his back. In his black-and-
white evening dress, he was surely the most
devastatingly handsome man Tori had ever seen.

"I haven't seen Monique," he replied,
straightening his watch-chain after catching sight of
himself in the mirror.

"If she intends to eat with us, she'd better dress.
I won't hold dinner for her. If she's not ready in
time, she'll simply have to eat in her room."

Grey turned to her with a puzzled look on his
face. "Why are you making such a fuss over dinner?
Last night we ate in the parlor. You didn't seem to
mind."

"I've invited a guest for dinner tonight, and I
want things to be proper. He's a gentleman.
European. Do you want him to think we're
savages?"

"Who is this man?" Grey demanded, his voice
tightening, and his eyes as darkly gray as a storm-

tossed sea.

"His name is Niccolò da l'Armi—Count da l'Armi. He is attached to the Italian Embassy in Paris."

"Da l'Armi!" Grey seemed startled.

"Do you know him?"

"Oh, I think I heard his name mentioned by someone in Montego Bay." He took on an air of indifference that seemed somehow false. "Did he say what he is doing in Jamaica?"

Tori noted the edginess in his voice and smothered a small, pleased smirk. How delicious it was that he was so quick to anger over the least hint of another man in her life.

"He came for his health and to visit friends."

"How did you meet him?"

Tori shrugged her bare shoulders and busied herself arranging a bouquet of flowers which Persephone had gathered from the remnants of the garden.

"I was walking outside this afternoon and he simply appeared. He had no idea that anyone was here. Apparently, he'd heard the legends of the house and met Christophe during his stay here. Christophe invited him to visit the house. He has been ill and today was his first opportunity to do so."

"And are you taking him on a tour after dinner?"

Tori glanced at him from the corner of her eye and noticed the heightened color of his face. "Oh, no," she purred. "We had our tour this afternoon. We broke into Melanie Stockton's rooms. It was quite exciting. Niccolò found a secret passage. Can you imagine that?"

"Niccolò?" Grey repeated grimly. "It sounds as if the two of you are fast friends."

"Well, he is a charming man. And he asked me to call him Niccolò. It would have been rude of me to refuse."

"And I suppose you told him to call you Victoria?"

She shrugged. "Of course. Really, Grey, how stern you look. He is a delightful man. Truly he is. You'll see when you meet him."

"I'm looking forward to it," he growled.

"Now, Grey, I hope you'll be cordial, because—"

She broke off at the sound of the front door opening and closing. Monique, in a riding habit, appeared in the hall outside the dining room door.

"Monique," Tori said coolly. "We are having a guest for dinner tonight. If you intend to join us, I suggest you hurry and dress. I cannot insult the gentleman by asking him to wait for you to get ready."

Monique's violet eyes flickered over Tori, then skimmed over Grey. She shook her head and her wind-loosened hair shimmered, catching the flames of the candles in sparkling highlights.

"I'd prefer to eat in my room tonight, if you don't mind," she replied with hauteur.

"As you wish," Tori acquiesced, almost grateful to Grey's mistress. She had no great desire to try to explain Monique's presence to Niccolò.

Turning back to Grey as Monique's footsteps echoed in the cavernous stairwell, Tori said:

"I hope you won't be pettish just because Monique declines our company."

"I'm never pettish," he said pettishly. "I'm going out onto the terrace for a cigar. Call me when the Count arrives."

"I will," Tori promised, and when Grey had left

the room, she giggled. There was nothing in the world that soothed her battered pride like the sight of Grey in a fit of jealous pique. Even if the Count da l'Armi were not such a charmer, he would be worth cultivating if only for his effect on Grey!

Out on the terrace, Grey stared unseeing into the dusky twilight. The wild beauty of the tangled gardens went unnoticed and the cigar he'd gone out to smoke remained unlighted as he rolled it back and forth between his thumb and forefinger.

Da l'Armi. He'd been warned of the wily Italian's presence in Jamaica. Here for his health, indeed! Christophe's contact on the island—a sugar planter and partner in a prosperous shipping business named Edward Lytton—had told Grey only that afternoon that da l'Armi had appeared on the island only a few days after Christophe's arrival. He'd met with Randall Ramsey, who'd arrived only days before Grey and Tori. Ramsey had disappeared —whether he'd returned to New Orleans or gone on to France, no one seemed to know—but da l'Armi had remained in Montego Bay. Lytton suspected Ramsey had warned da l'Armi that Grey and Madame Duclaux were on their way and da l'Armi had remained in Jamaica to see what, if anything, they did when they arrived.

Grey scowled. Da l'Armi's presence would seem to indicate that word of the Confederate plan to enlist French aid had already reached unsympathetic ears in Paris. But if da l'Armi had been sent to stop Christophe, why had he remained behind while Christophe went on to France? Did Christophe know what da l'Armi was? Did he know he had enemies in the French capital working to see that his plan failed?

It was a pointless question, since the answer was simply unavailable to him. The real question was

what he should do about it. And how many of the
details should be given to Tori.

The fewer the better, the cautious side of his
nature counseled. If she knew who and what da
l'Armi was, her behavior might warn the Italian that
he'd been exposed as more than merely a casual
visitor to the island.

Grey pursed his lips, pondering the matter.
Lytton had told him that da l'Armi had enquired
about ships bound for France and had seemed more
than a little annoyed that none were expected for
some time. Now Tori, who had been pestering him to
take her to France, had suddenly arranged a dinner
party to introduce him to da l'Armi. And she'd been
asking him earlier about taking a passenger. It was
obvious that she'd decided to bribe him to take her to
Europe with a wealthy passenger for profit's sake.
What should he do? It seemed obvious. Da l'Armi,
though doubtless not the leader in the conspiracy to
see the Confederate plan fail, was one of its agents. It
would be much easier to keep track of his movements
if he were on board the *Nightshade*. He would
take da l'Armi to France, he decided, and Tori as
well.

The sound of a carriage approaching the front
of the house captured Grey's attention then. He put
away the unsmoked cigar and turned toward the
French doors of the dining room, preparing himself
for his part in the evening's charade.

Persephone, who had been persuaded out of her
colorful skirt and loose cotton blouse for the
occasion, swept into the room dressed in one of
Tori's plainest cotton gowns.

"Missis?" she said, drawing Tori out of her
pleasant musings. "De Count be heah."

"Thank you, Persephone. Why don't you go

and see how dinner is progressing."

As the girl disappeared in the direction of the kitchen, Niccolò da l'Armi appeared, looking suave and sophisticated in black with a white brocade waistcoat and white cravat. A thick gold watch chain glittered across the front of his waistcoat and a ruby glowed from the little finger of his right hand.

Taking Tori's hand, he bowed over it, his blue eyes heavy lidded and seductive.

"How beautiful you are, Signora," he murmured, his lips moving gently against the back of her hand. "I thought you lovely this afternoon, but now I see that you are truly exquisite. You would put the ladies of the Court of France to shame."

"Surely you flatter, Niccolò," Tori scolded. "The Empress Eugénie is reputed to be outrageously beautiful and your own countrywoman, the Countess Castiglione, has been called the most beautiful woman of the century."

"Only by the uninformed—those who have not beheld you, *cara*," he breathed.

"I'm sure the lady's husband would feel much the same way," Grey said from the doorway. His voice was low and dark, edged with contempt.

Niccolò turned toward him smiling, entirely unabashed, not even relinquishing his hold on Tori's hand.

"Without doubt, Signor, and he would be correct."

Withdrawing her hand from the Count's grasp, Tori glanced from the Count to Grey, inordinately pleased with the angry flash of silver in Grey's eyes. He really was jealous, she told herself, delighted. How wonderful!

"Niccolò," she said warmly, her voice soft and alluring. "I should like to introduce Mr. Greyson

Verreaux, master of the *Nightshade*, which brought both my husband and then me to Jamaica. Grey is an old friend of the family. Grey, this gentleman is Niccolò da l'Armi—the Count da l'Armi—of whom I spoke earlier.''

"Signor Verreaux." Niccolò's eyes glistened. "You are master of the ship . . ." He looked at Tori, his eyes wide with delight. "This is what you were speaking of earlier!"

"Yes, but I have scarcely broached the subject with Grey. I'll leave you gentlemen to discuss it after dinner. Now, shall we sit down?"

The three of them sat down to a meal of roast suckling pig, baked sweet potatoes, fried plantain, callalu, oysters, and stewed guavas and coconut cream—not, perhaps, as elegant a repast as Tori might have ordered at home, but one which, for all the haste employed in its planning and preparation, everyone seemed to enjoy.

"As you may have suspected," Tori told Grey as dinner was drawing to a close, "Niccolò greatly desires to return to France. In fact, it is imperative that he do so."

"May I ask why?" Grey said, his silver eyes fixing Niccolò with a long, cool stare.

The Count patted his lips with a napkin. "Alas, Signor, I cannot disclose that information. I am, as you may know, attached to the Italian embassy. My reasons are reasons of state and therefore not mine to reveal."

"In any case," Tori continued, "Niccolò intends to book passage on the first ship bound for France that puts into Jamaica. I told him I might be able to help. And you told me you might consider sailing to France if the trip was worth your while."

"I may," Grey agreed. "But I must warn you,

Count, that passage aboard the *Nightshade* is not inexpensive. I am a blockade runner by trade, and there is a great deal of money to be made just now at my trade. For me to tie up my ship carrying passengers to France . . .''

"I understand," the Count assured him. "And I would be prepared to compensate you handsomely for any losses you estimate you would incur during the voyage to France."

Grey pursed his lips, feigning reluctance. Although he had already decided to take da l'Armi to France and there to try to discover what steps had been taken to sabotage Christophe Duclaux's mission to the French Court, it would not do for him to appear too eager. He must let da l'Armi think that his willingness to sail to France was motivated purely out of greed. He said:

"It is something we would have to discuss. I'm not at all certain you realize precisely how profitable a business mine is. I would suggest we discuss the matter before you make such rash statements."

"Very well, then let us discuss it. I am most anxious to be on my way, Signor Verreaux."

Grey tossed his napkin aside, a sardonic smile curving his lips. "It is a boring subject for ladies, Count. Why don't we retire to the parlor while Madame Duclaux refreshes herself?"

Niccolò rose and, after complimenting Tori lavishly on her table and hospitality, left the room. Behind him, Grey exchanged a calculating glance with Tori.

"This was clever of you, *ma chère*," he told her, determined to keep her as much in the dark as he could concerning all the plots and counterplots developing around them. Christophe was obviously in danger because of his mission to aid the

Confederacy. Steps had apparently been taken to stop him, and it was impossible to say precisely how far their enemies were willing to go to do that. It seemed to Grey that it might be easier for them all if Tori, like da l'Armi, believed that greed was Grey's only motivation. "Your friend da l'Armi is going to have to pay and pay dearly if he expects me to transport him to France."

Tori rose, her face a mask of cool indifference. "Ask any fee you desire, Grey. If it is too high, Niccolò will simply turn you down."

"I don't think so. He wants it too badly. And there may not be another ship for weeks, even months. I think the prospect of such a long, boring wait would deter him from refusing my price too quickly."

"Not necessarily," she countered.

As he was leaving the room, she caught his arm and he turned back to her. "I want to go to France, Grey. If you won't take me, I too will wait for the next ship. Niccolò and I will simply have to keep each other company."

Silver flame flared in Grey's eyes. He took a step toward her, then another—but then Niccolò appeared in the doorway and whatever harsh words he had intended for her were left unsaid as Grey accompanied the Count from the room.

Smiling smugly, Tori went to order wine for the gentlemen, serenely sure that Grey and the Count would come to some agreement that would permit her to get what she wanted—passage to France aboard *Nightshade*.

"You asked him for how much!" Tori cried later, after Niccolò had left. "That's obscene! That's not a fee, Grey, that's extortion!"

Grey shrugged one elegant shoulder. "He's willing to pay it. In fact, he seemed pleased. I expect I could have asked him for much more."

"Well, I only hope you don't intend to ask me for a similar fee."

His eyes sparkled with deviltry as his gaze slid slowly over her. "The fee I'd ask from you, *chérie*, would help you as much as it would help me."

Tori turned her back, her cheeks flaming. "Don't be disgusting!"

"Disgusting?" He came up behind her. "Is that what you think it would be between us? You should know better. I think you do. Or have you developed a taste for Italian counts?"

Whirling around, Tori slapped him hard across the face. "Don't speak to me that way again! Damn you! Must everything come down to—"

"Yes!" he snarled, savagely cutting off her diatribe. "In the end, that's exactly what it must come to between you and me. I want you, Tori, so much it's eating the heart out of me. And if you'd admit it—if for one moment you'd let yourself be a woman instead of a damned piece of ice—you'd admit that you want me just as much!"

"Never! I won't be one of your conquests—one of those pathetic women who run after you panting for your favors! Go up to Monique, if that's what you want. That's what you keep her for, isn't it?"

Grey's eyes were hard, boring into the very soul of her. "At least she's a woman," he snarled cruelly. "Look at you. You flaunt your beauty under men's noses, flirt with them, tease them, but when they desire you, you spurn them, treat them like rutting animals not fit to touch your hem."

"I'm a married woman," she flung at him.

"And I've no doubt you treated Christophe the

same way. That's why he's kept a mistress from the day you were married!''

Tori gasped, feeling as if he'd struck her, as though he'd plunged a searing dagger into her heart. She fell back, trembling hand to her throat, as he strode from the room, oblivious to her pain and too angry to care for her tears.

17

"Don't bother with that," Tori told Persephone as the girl began putting away her discarded clothing and jewels. "Leave it until the morning."

The girl eyed the magnificent emerald silk gown carelessly thrown to the floor. By morning it would be a mass of wrinkles. "But missis—"

"Just leave it!" Tori hissed. She was immediately contrite, for none of this was Persephone's fault. The girl had done her best and had succeeded surprisingly well for being so young and inexperienced at being either a housekeeper or a lady's maid. But right now Tori couldn't bear to have anyone near her. Right now she needed quiet and solitude and a good, long cry.

Still, the hint of gentle reproach in the girl's liquid brown eyes sent a pang of guilt through her.

"Persephone," she called softly as the girl

opened the door to leave.

"Night, missis," Persephone replied over her shoulder. "Tings be better in de mornin'."

The door closed behind her with a click, and Tori was left alone. A moment passed, then another. Then the tears she'd barely been able to hold back misted her eyes and trickled down her cheeks.

Not bothering to blow out the candle, she threw herself across the high bed and let the tears, the pain, the longings flow out of her. Was it true? she wondered. Were those angry, hurtful words Grey had spoken true? Was she less than a woman? Had Christophe kept a mistress because she couldn't be the woman he wanted—the woman he needed?

"I can't help what I am," she sobbed into the soft feather pillows whose cases were blotted with the marks of her tears. "I've spent too many years hiding my feelings, my desires, to suddenly turn into a woman like Monique or Joséphine Morande. How can they expect me to change the habit of so much time so quickly? How can Grey expect me to give him my heart again when he's already broken it once?"

She heard footsteps approaching her door, heard the click of the latch, saw the flicker of the candle flame as the air currents in the room changed.

"What is it, Persephone?" she managed, only a sniffle betraying her anguish.

There was no answer, yet she knew she was no longer alone in the room. Without looking, she realized who her midnight visitor was.

"Grey . . ," she whispered.

The bed gave as he sat down on the edge. His hand closed over her shoulder and he turned her over.

"Go away," she whispered, averting her face to hide the evidence of her sorrow.

"You've been crying," he said gently, almost wonderingly. She was so careful with her emotions most of the time that this evidence of tears touched him.

"No, I haven't," she insisted, but the proof was there and they both knew it.

"Liar," he taunted in a tone that was more like a caress.

She rolled away from him once more. "Go away! I hate you!"

"Another lie," he murmured, fondling the rich, fine silk of her hair as it lay across the silken counter-pane. Unable to resist, he lifted a thick strand of it to his lips, then pressed his mouth to the soft, fragrant skin of her temple. She lay on her side facing away from him, and the gentle rise of her hip beneath the fine linen of her gown was more than he could resist.

She stiffened as he caressed her. "Don't touch me!" she hissed. "I don't like it!"

"Another lie," he said quietly, a hint of amusement in his voice. He pulled her over onto her back so that she rested in his arms. "You love it and you know it!"

"I don't!" she insisted. "I don't want you!"

"Your mind may not," he told her, his voice a dark velvet caress, "but *you* want me here . . ." He kissed her lips. ". . . and here . . ." Her breast, where the tight coral tip jutted against the sheer white linen. ". . . and here . . ." The soft curve of her belly. ". . . and here . . ."

"No!" Tori writhed away as his head moved lower. "You can't!"

"I can," he disagreed. "And I intend to."

She huddled near the tall, carved headboard of the ancient bed. "Grey, please . . ," she whispered, her thoughts, her emotions, awhirl as he edged

173

closer.

On the other side of the bedroom door, Monique pressed one ear to the panel. She had heard Grey moving about in his room long after he should have been asleep and hoped it meant he was going to come to her. When she'd heard his door opening and closing, she had held her breath, wanting him, hoping against hope that his too-long absence from her bed was at an end. But his footsteps had passed her door and faded off into the distance.

Tiptoeing to her door, she had peeked out and had seen him pause before Tori's door, waiting, as if gathering his courage, then disappearing into her bedchamber.

Leaving her room, Monique had followed him, her silken wrapper whispering over the deep pile of the hall carpet. At Tori's door she listened, needing to know Grey's feelings, yet afraid of what she might overhear.

"Grey, please, I can't," Tori pleaded, as his arms pulled her tighter, drawing her back down into the bed beside him. Her mind reeled as he touched her, kissed her, showed her in a hundred ways how much he needed her and wanted her.

"You can, Tori, if only you'll let yourself."

"No, no," she wept, tears of fear and frustration glistening in her eyes and bedewing her lashes. "I can't, Grey. Christophe . . ."

"Forget Christophe!" he snarled savagely, pulling her closer. "Let him go. You don't need him."

"Grey . . ," she moaned, torn between guilt and desire.

"I love you, Tori. I know I hurt you before, but I didn't know . . . didn't realize . . . Don't punish me forever for a moment's foolishness."

174

Monique's heart contracted painfully as she listened to Grey's voice so low, so caressing, so filled with yearning. What she would have given to have heard him murmur those words to her! She wished—how she wished—that she had not come here, followed him, eavesdropped. But she had had to know. And now she was certain.

Footsteps on the stairs warned her of Persephone's approach. Lifting the rustling skirt of her wrapper, she fled back to her room before the servant girl could mount the stairs and see her there.

In Tori's bedroom, Tori lay consumed with desire, helpless as she had never been, beneath the caresses of Grey's hands and lips. His fingers had found her, caressed her, his tongue thrust lazily between her lips mimicking the movements of his fingers, tearing asunder the last vestiges of her resistance.

She moaned softly, a sound that was half desire, half despair. She could not resist him any longer. She was burning, aching with the need of him. He had won their battle of wills. All that was left was for him to claim his reward.

"Missis?" Persephone rapped at the panels, her knuckles like gunshots in the stillness of the room.

Tori cried out, writhing away from Grey, pulling her half discarded nightdress over her nakedness, while Grey muttered an oath that would have put his crewmen to the blush.

"Tell her to go away!" he hissed.

"I can't," Tori whispered, her voice trembling even as her body shuddered. "You have to go!"

His tone was savage, furious; his eyes glittered with the remnants of his passion. "Send her away!"

Near the other end of the corridor, Monique

paced the floor like a great, restless cat. Schemes and desires and loathing whirled through her mind.

It was obvious that Grey no longer needed her now that Victoria Duclaux had come back into his life. As much as it hurt her, as sharp as the pains were that cut into her pride at the thought, she knew the time had come for her to move on.

But Providence was kind sometimes. She had gone riding that afternoon. She had intended to look for the obeahman Persephone had spoken of. In her desperation, she had thought to ask for one of the potions for which the voodoo queens of New Orleans were so famed. No doubt they existed here in Jamaica as well, although careful questioning of Persephone had told her that the practice of voodoo was far more prevalant on Haiti than on Jamaica. Still, it existed and she had hoped beyond hope that she would be able to buy something that could bring back Grey's desire and thus salvage the luxuries that being Grey Verreaux's mistress had afforded her.

She knew she could not go back to New Orleans alone, without the protection of a powerful man. It was not the war—oh, no, there were worse things in life than war, more fearful dangers. In her mind's eye she saw again those hate-filled eyes that had confronted her at the Opera in New Orleans on the night Tori had come to beg Grey to take her to Montego Bay. Those eyes belonged to a phantasm from out of the murky past. They belonged to Dorothée Arnault—the woman who had murdered Monique's father and destroyed her mother as surely as if she had strangled her with her own two hands. She had vowed to destroy Monique as well—for Monique's father had been Dorothée Arnault's husband and Monique's mother his mulatto mistress.

176

Yes, Dorothée Arnault had vowed to destroy her husband's quadroon daughter and, if she could judge anything by the black hatred burning in the woman's eyes, the determination had not dimmed with the passing of the years.

A trembling hand to her throat, Monique made a silent vow never to return to New Orleans and instead turned her thoughts toward the future—and to the chance of happiness which Fate had given her that morning.

As she rode along the roads winding down from Stockton Hall toward Montego Bay, she had become lost. Confused, she had followed the lane to another Great House. Dismounting, she'd been ushered into an entrance hall of such beauty that she'd caught her breath. Here, she told herself, was the splendor that Stockton Hall had once possessed. Here, with the sunshine streaming through the beveled panes of classical fanlights beneath the plastered rosettes and century-old crystal fixtures, was the beauty and elegance that even the fine mansions of the American South could not surpass.

"I lost my way," she had told the grand, intimidating housekeeper who had come to ask her business. "Could you tell me where I am?"

"Dis be Woodbridge," she told her. "De massa been't heah jist now."

"I'm not here to see your master," Monique told her. "I need directions to Montego Bay."

The hall was flooded with light as the front door opened and closed again. Monique turned and found herself the object of admiring scrutiny from a pair of bright blue eyes.

"Dis lady be loss, massa," the woman told him.

"Lost?" The man gave his hat and gloves to the

woman, who disappeared as silently as she'd come. His eyes skimmed over Monique, whose ivory and flame coloring was complemented by her habit of heather blue trimmed with gold. "How fortunate . . . for me." The sunlight streaming through the fanlight touched his golden hair, setting it afire. "Permit me to introduce myself," he said. "I am Edward Lytton. Welcome to Woodbridge. And you are?"

"Monique Bouladoux."

"French?"

"American. I come from New Orleans."

"Ah, New Orleans. And so, Madame Bouladoux, I would be pleased to direct you to Montego Bay."

"It is Mademoiselle, sir," she corrected him, feeling suddenly as if she were drowning in those deep blue eyes.

One golden brow arched. "Mademoiselle? In that case, may I invite you to lunch?"

They had eaten together on the terrace of Woodbridge and Monique had felt an attraction, an excitement, she had not known since she had first met Grey. Edward Lytton had made no attempt to seduce her, had not exceeded propriety in any way save, perhaps, in the outrageousness of his compliments. He had, in fact, treated her as if she were the grandest lady ever to grace the halls of Woodbridge.

She could stay here in Jamaica, she knew. Doubtless Tori Duclaux would be so pleased to see her out of the way that she would grant her the hospitality of Stockton Hall. Eventually, she hoped, she would become Edward Lytton's mistress. More than that, she could not aspire to, for it was inevitable that he would one day discover that she was a quadroon and even in Jamaica, gentlemen did not marry women of color.

But whatever the outcome of her flirtation with Edward Lytton, she knew there was no future with Grey and she could not return to New Orleans alone.

Monique sank onto the tufted bench of her dressing table, her fiery spirit momentarily subdued. Yes, her future lay in Jamaica. Only time would tell what she could make of it.

18

"Are you certain you wouldn't like to come along, Persephone?" Tori asked as she sat on the edge of the bed while the girl swiftly and efficiently packed her trunks. "Aren't you at all curious about how life is lived in faraway places?"

"No, missis," Persephone replied honestly. "I be happy heah. I tink I rather stay at home and leave de adventurin' to other people."

Tori laughed. "I hope we won't have too many adventures. I, for one, would settle for a nice, quiet uneventful voyage."

"Dat man be goin' wid you?" she asked quietly, never lifting her wide brown eyes from her work.

"That man? You mean Count da l'Armi?" Persephone nodded. "You don't care for him at all, do you?"

"No, missis," the girl replied solemnly. "I

don't."

"But why?"

"He argue wid de massa. Dey have bad words."

"I thought you said my husband never met the Count," Tori replied.

"No, missis. I say de massa doan go nowheres to dinner. De Count, he come here one day."

Tori shook her head. The Count had told her he'd never been to Stockton Hall before the day he'd met her. But Persephone seemed so certain—adamant, even.

"What did they say?" Tori asked at last, her curiosity getting the better of her.

Persephone did not pretend that she hadn't been eavesdropping. "De Count, he say de massa have papers he want. De massa, he say he doan. De Count say he lie—dat he best fergit 'bout goin' anywheres. De massa say he be goin' to see Napoleen and de Count best stay out of it."

"Napoleen?" Tori repeated. "You mean Napoleon?"

Persephone shrugged. "I 'spose so."

"How could Niccolò possibly know that Christophe was traveling to see Napoleon?"

"I doan know, missis. But de Count say de massa best go home to 'merica and fergit 'bout France. He say dat if de massa try and go dere, he die."

"Die!" Tori paled. "Are you telling me that the Count actually threatened Christophe's life?"

"Dat what he say, missis."

Tori leaned back against the carved bedpost. It was incredible. Why should Niccolò be concerned with Christophe's business with Napoleon III of France? What difference could it make to an Italian diplomatic attaché on leave for his health . . . ?

"Missis?" Persephone's voice broke into her bewildered musings.

Tori looked up. "Yes?" Persephone gave a jerk of her head in the direction of the door, where Monique stood framed in the doorway.

"May I speak with you for a moment?" the flame-haired quadroon asked.

"Of course." With a sweep of her hand, Tori invited her into the room. "Persephone, you may leave us."

Monique sat in a chair near the hearth. When they were alone, she said:

"I've come to tell you that I've decided not to go to France."

Tori was stunned. That Monique would decline the chance to accompany Grey to Europe was beyond her imaginings.

"I see," she managed, not bothering to hide her surprise. "It may be months before you will be able to secure passage back to New Orleans. With the war . . ."

Monique shook her head, her long, elegant fingers twining themselves in the ruffles that trimmed the wide sash of her bright blue gown. "I won't be going back. The situation there . . ." She shuddered delicately, remembering with startling clarity the hate-filled gaze of her nemesis, Dorothée Arnault.

As Monique had known she would, Tori assumed she was referring to the war. "You wish to stay in Jamaica?"

Monique lowered her beautiful, almond-shaped violet eyes. "I'd like to stay here, at Stockton Hall."

"I see." Tori was astonished, but could think of no valid objection. The house would only stand empty after their departure. "Very well. But what about Grey?"

Monique fastened her gaze on a point somewhere above Tori's head. "My arrangement with Grey was, in a sense, a business arrangement. I cared for him and I believe he cared for me. He provided protection and I provided"—her cheeks colored faintly—"companionship. I had a beautiful home, beautiful clothes, a comfortable life and a handsome, exciting lover." She noticed the flush that rose in Tori's cheeks, but went on: "But my usefulness to Grey is at an end. It is you he loves now."

"But there is nothing between us," Tori told her honestly. "We are not lovers."

Monique's great violet eyes came to rest on Tori, and in them Tori saw that she had accepted the death of her affair with Grey as if it was inevitable.

"An affair of the heart," Monique told her, "can sometimes run deeper than an affair of the flesh."

"I suppose that is true," Tori agreed. "But whatever it is, so long as my husband lives, there can never be anything between Grey and me. Even an affair of the heart is a betrayal."

The two women gazed at each other, feeling a strange kinship—they were both imprisoned by the dictates of society, one by the sacred vows of marriage, the other by the barriers of blood. Several minutes ticked by before Tori broke the silence to say:

"I wish you happiness, Monique. I hope you find someone to take Grey's place in your life."

A pretty, dusty rose flush pinkened Monique's ivory cheeks. "I think I may have," she confided, with charming girlishness."

"Monique!" Tori was surprised and intrigued. "Who is he?"

"He is a planter. He is very handsome and his

home is beautiful. I met him when I became lost while out riding.''

"And that is where you have been going these mornings when you rise so early and ride out?"

Monique nodded. "He cares for me, I think. I believe he does."

"And he is the reason you wish to remain at Stockton Hall?" She smiled as Monique nodded. "That's wonderful! I hope the two of you—"

"He does not know," Monique interrupted.

"Does not—?" The breath seemed to leave Tori's lungs in a rush. "He doesn't know you are a quadroon?"

Monique shook her head. "I don't know how to tell him. They view things differently here than in New Orleans." Forcing a smile that quavered visibly at the corners, she stood. "Well, I won't worry about it now. I wish you a safe voyage."

Tori stood and the two women embraced, unlikely allies in the struggles against the unfairness of life—and love.

"You are welcome to Stockton Hall for as long as you need it," she told Monique. "I will tell Jared Whitney myself. And Persephone, since she doesn't wish to come to France either, will be most helpful to you. I wish you happiness with your gentleman."

"Persephone," Tori said thoughtfully when the girl returned to the room to finish her mistress's packing. "What would be the chance of a gentleman—a planter—marrying a woman with one quarter Negro blood?"

"None," Persephone answered succinctly.

"No matter if he loved her and she him?"

Persephone shook her head. "If de woman has color, she has color. One drop be all it take."

"What if she doesn't tell him?"

"When he finds out de truth, he kill her. It happen sometime."

Tori sighed, depressed by the futility and unfairness of it all. Her case, suddenly, seemed far brighter, for her circumstances could change. But for Monique, things would never change. Her blood was her blood, her ancestors were her ancestors. And nothing that had gone before could ever be undone at this late date.

The two women did not see each other again, for the *Nightshade* steamed away from Montego Bay at first light the next morning. Monique watched it go as she rode back from her morning ride to Woodbridge. She was restless and worried. Edward had not been at home, and his housekeeper, Emerald, had not known when he would return. There seemed little to do but return to Stockton Hall and hope for some word from him.

Word arrived, in the form of Edward Lytton himself, late that night. He appeared unexpectedly at the front door and was ushered into Monique's presence by Persephone, whom she had promoted from lady's maid to housekeeper of Stockton Hall. A young girl, Selma, was brought in from the fields for Persephone to train as a house-maid and lady's maid for Monique.

"Mam'zelle," Persephone announced, feeling as grand as the rustling petticoat that Tori had given her to wear under her hand-me-down cotton gown. "Marse Lytton be heah."

"Edward?" Her heart pounding, Monique hurried to the entrance hall, where she found Edward, his blue and gold masculine beauty out of place in the gloom of the mansion, waiting, his hat in his hand.

"Mister Lytton," she said softly, unable to address him more familiarly beneath the prying eyes of the maid-turned-housekeeper. She cast a glance toward Persephone. "Bring something for Mr. Lytton to drink, Persephone. What would you prefer?"

Edward shook his head. "It doesn't matter. Actually . . ." He seemed ill-at-ease. "It is Monsieur Verreaux and Madame Duclaux I have come to see."

Monique's spirits sank. "I see."

"No, I don't think you do. You see, I am part owner of a ship called the *Peregrine*. I was called this morning to meet with the other owners, only to learn the ship has been lost. It is thought her boilers exploded."

Monique was nonplussed. "I don't understand what this has to do with . . ."

Edward's gaze fell. "It was aboard the *Peregrine* that Madame Duclaux's husband was sailing to France."

"Christophe!" Monique caught her breath. "Were there any survivors?"

Edward shook his head. "It is thought not. A few bodies were found. One was thought to be Christophe Duclaux but it was impossible to be certain. I really must speak with Madame Duclaux."

"She is not here."

"Where has she gone? When will she return?"

Taking Edward's arm, Monique led him into the parlor. After settling him into a comfortable chair, she brought him a drink.

"She won't be returning," she told him, sinking into the chair opposite his. "She left Jamaica this morning aboard Grey Verreaux's ship. They are bound for France even as we speak."

"Oh, lord," Edward groaned. "There is no way

I can send word to her. All I can do is write to her and send the letter on the next ship bound for France. But even so, I don't know where she'll be. How can I let her know her husband is dead?''

Monique shook her head. She thought of Tori's words to her the night before when she had said:

"So long as my husband lives, there can never be anything between Grey and me."

Well, her husband was dead. She was free to love and be loved, but she didn't know it. And what was worse, there didn't seem to be any way of telling her.

Monique's attention was brought back to Edward, whose handsome face was set in an expression of grim resignation.

"It had to have been the boilers," he was saying. "Nothing else would have caused an explosion tht would have destroyed the ship—blown it to smithereens. But there wasn't anything wrong with the boilers when she left port. I know there wasn't. They'd just been repaired and inspected. It had to have been sabotage, but I don't understand how—"

"Sabotage!" Monique eyed him curiously. "Have you enemies who wish to destroy your shipping company, Edward?"

Edward gazed into her eyes. Evidently, Grey had not confided either the nature of Christophe's mission, nor his own involvement in it to Monique. Therefore, it was not for him to reveal that he had been their contact in Jamaica.

He shrugged. "There are always unscrupulous men who would try to gain an unfair advantage by such practices. Occasionally one meets such men, whom one knows instinctively cannot be trusted."

"Such as Niccolò da l'Armi," Monique murmured, frowning.

Edward started. "Da l'Armi?" he asked carefully. "What do you know of him?"

"Nothing, really. He was here a few times. But there is something about him I do not trust."

Edward relaxed a bit. "You're right. I intend to keep an eye on that one."

Monique smiled faintly. "You'll have a difficult time doing that, Edward. He sailed this morning with Grey and Tori, bound for France."

"Sailed . . ." Edward caught his breath. He knew, from his conversations with Grey, that Grey was aware that da l'Armi was working against Christophe's mission, that he was connected with Randall Ramsey in his efforts to stop Christophe. What could Grey have been thinking of to take da l'Armi with him?

He sat back, resigned. Presumably, Grey had his reasons, incomprehensible as they seemed to Edward. Edward could only hope Grey realized how dangerous da l'Armi was—for he suspected it had been da l'Armi who had masterminded the destruction of the *Peregrine!*

19

In her little cabin aboard *Nightshade*—the same one she had occupied on the trip from New Orleans to Jamaica—Tori sat brushing her hair. There were so many unanswered questions, so many mysteries whirling through her mind. Everything seemed hopelessly muddled.

Footsteps passed her door. She heard the precise, pleasant sound of Niccolò humming some gay tune. The tale Persephone had told her came to her mind. Arguments. Death threats. What did it all mean? How was Niccolò involved? What had the Italian Embassy to do with a treaty between the French Empire and the American Confederacy? Had Niccolò truly threatened Christophe or was that the product of Persephone's imagination? Still, the girl seemed remarkably level-headed and sensible. Certainly she would have had to be during the time she shared that great, sinister house with only Jared Whitney and the shadows of its violent past.

The only person who could have provided her with the answers she needed was Niccolò and he, she already knew, would deny everything. Hadn't he claimed never to have visited Stockton Hall before the day they'd met? He was a most unusual man, particularly in Jamaica. It seemed unlikely that Persephone would have been mistaken about having seen him there before.

Perhaps she should speak to Grey about it; heaven knew she longed to talk to someone. But he disliked Niccolò. For that matter, he was hardly fond of Christophe. Doubtless he would simply counsel her to forget the whole thing, return to New Orleans, and be his mistress.

His mistress. Therein lay her other problem. Lord! she thought irritably, for a woman who led such a placid, orderly existence for seven years, I'm certainly paying for it now!

Grey. She loved him. Hadn't she admitted as much to Monique? And he loved her. She didn't need the beautiful quadroon to tell her that. But she didn't trust him not to hurt her. And she didn't trust herself not to betray Christophe in Grey's arms. The answer to that dilemma seemed to lie with Niccolò. Regardless of her doubts as to his character—those, at least, she could keep to herself until they reached Paris and she had a chance to talk to Christophe—she knew that Grey was inordinately jealous of every moment, every bit of flattery, every smile that passed between her and the charming Italian Count. For the time being, the easiest way to keep Grey at arm's length seemed to be to keep him in a perpetual fit of jealousy.

She smiled at her own reflection in the mirror as she pinned up her long curls and confined them in a net to keep them safe from the brisk sea wind. It wasn't going to be easy. She would have to appear receptive to the Count's advances without letting him think she was willing to move from flattery to intimacy. Considering Niccolò's hot-blooded temperament, the task wouldn't be a simple one.

Over her gown, she pulled on a mantle of purple taffeta and a close-fitting leghorn bonnet with ribbons to match. The night air was damp and cool, but the sky was clear and the first glittering stars heralded the canopy that would soon stretch from horizon to horizon over the endless sea.

"Victoria?"

Turning, Tori found Niccolò striding toward her as she would have climbed the stairs to the deck.

"Good evening, Niccolò," she said with a smile that masked her suspicions.

"May I join you for a walk or are you walking with our illustrious captain tonight?"

Tori's smile was teasing. Though her motives for encouraging Niccolò's attentions were purely selfish and had nothing to do with any real attraction on her part, she could not deny that it was pleasant to have two such handsome and dashing men looking daggers at each other over her.

"I'm sure Grey has a great deal to keep him busy on this first night out of port," she told the Count as they climbed the stairs and emerged on the deck of the paddle-steamer.

The deck stretched before them, pale, almost ethereal in the gathering twilight. Like many other blockade runners, the ship was painted entirely white so that, on a dark night, skimming along the surface of a night-black sea, she might be mistaken for clouds. Her two smoke-stacks and two tall masts were silhouetted against the sky and the latter, their

sails furled as they would remain unless trouble arose
with the engines that drove the paddle-wheels,
seemed ominously skeletal. The eerie sound of their
riggings creaking and groaning in the wind was un-
nerving.

Niccolò offered Tori his arm and she slipped a
hand into it.

"I hope," he said as they strolled toward the
prow, "that you will come to Paris and remain there
for some time. There is much to see and much to
do."

"That," Tori replied primly, "will depend upon
my husband. If Christophe wishes to remain there,
then of course we will do so."

"Of course, your husband." Niccolò gazed out
over the sea. "I look forward to renewing our
acquaintance."

This was her chance and she knew it. Taking a
deep breath, Tori forced herself to sound casual as
she said:

"The oddest thing happened, Niccolò. My maid
at Stockton Hall—Persephone, you remember—told
me that you had been there during my husband's
stay. In fact, she said that harsh words had passed
between you."

"What?" To his credit, Niccolò seemed
genuinely mystified. "She must have been
mistaken."

"It hardly seems likely. I can't imagine who on
Jamaica you could be mistaken for."

"Do you doubt my word, Signora?" he said, his
tone changing from lazy amusement to distant
coolness.

"I did not say that. I only said that it was odd.
Don't you think it is?"

"Very odd. Indeed, most peculiar." Niccolò

seemed deep in thought. "Did your maid say what this imaginary disagreement was about?"

"She said it was something about some papers or other." She glanced up at him curiously. His eyes narrowed and the lines around his mouth deepened as his full lips tightened.

Tori studied the planking of the deck as if abashed.

"I did not mean to make you angry with me, Niccolò."

"Angry?" He relaxed almost imperceptibly; he was obviously still on his guard. "I am not angry, *cara*. But I do not like people who overhear something and put their own interpretations on it. Your maid very likely heard your husband having words with his overseer or some tradesman. Perhaps she did not approve of my coming to visit you, and she sought to cause a breach in our friendship."

While Tori did not for a moment believe that to be the case, it seemed wise to let the matter drop. She had no evidence, nothing she could point to as proof, and it seemed unwise to antagonize Niccolò without it.

"Perhaps you're right," she agreed at length. "It may have been that Persephone did not approve of your visits. I think she is very fond of Christophe."

Only too willing to let the subject die, Niccolò turned to Tori, his eyes warm and soft with admiration.

"Let us forget Jamaica and prying servants, *cara*, and think of ourselves. When we are here this way, I find myself longing for this voyage never to end."

Tori simpered prettily as he lifted her hand to his lips. For all that she had been cloistered during her marriage to Christophe, she had not forgotten the skills of coquetry she had learned as a young, flirtatious belle in Virginia.

"Niccolò," she murmured, when he had lingered too long over her gloved fingers, "do not forget that I am a married woman."

"Whose husband is far away," he reminded her.

"But married, nonetheless. I take my vows seriously. I am determined to be faithful to my husband—wherever he may be."

"Admirable," he murmured. "But how deeply has this determination of yours been tested?"

A flush stained Tori's cheeks as she remembered the scene of the night before in her bedroom at Stockton Hall. Her determination had been tested to its very foundations—and been found wanting, at least where Grey was concerned.

She sighed, turning her pinkened cheeks out toward the gathering darkness of the night sky. "It has been tested to its limits, I assure you."

"And it held firm?"

"I am still a faithful wife, Niccolò," she said softly, hedging on the truth the tiniest bit.

"*Brava*, Victoria," he said, a slight mocking air to his words. "But I wonder if your resolution will be as strong with another man."

"Do you mean to test it?" she asked, slightly breathless that he should be so bold in stating his intentions.

"I do. Before this voyage is at an end."

"I must warn you, sir," she countered, her tone growing cooler, more distant, "that Grey Verreaux is, as I believe I've already said, an old friend of my family. I doubt that he would take a kind view of your attempting to seduce me."

"I can deal with Signor Verreaux," he said

confidently. "I have dealt with jealous men before."

"Jealous?" She was plainly surprised and Niccolò laughed.

"But of course, *cara*. One has only to look at him when he looks at you to see that he is enamoured of you. I would expect him to take a dim view of my attempts to steal your heart. But his anger would not, as you seem to think, stem from any familial protectiveness on his part. It would, I think, spring from the far more understandable fact that he wants you himself."

They turned and started back, and Tori saw Grey's tall figure silhouetted against the white wheelhouse. Hands braced against the railing, he made no pretense that he was doing anything other than watching them.

Tori shivered. She was playing a hazardous game and it seemed that, without her knowing, without any warning, the stakes had just been raised.

20

The brilliant morning sunshine was muted behind drawn draperies and the artificial twilight in the parlor at Stockton Hall seemed somehow ominous as Persephone recounted her tale to Monique.

Monique's flame-hued brows drew downward in puzzlement as the servant girl finished her tale.

"Have you thought what you are saying?" Monique demanded. "You think that this Italian, this Count da l'Armi, somehow murdered Christophe Duclaux?"

"I doan know," Persephone admitted. "Dere is no proof. But de Count, he say if de massa go to France, he die. And now . . ." Her spread hands said more than words ever could.

Rising, Monique paced across the room. Her crimson riding habit skimmed over the brilliant carpet that had been a gift from Edward Lytton not long after Tori and Grey's departure.

"But how is it possible?" Monique wanted to know. "Christophe was at sea. The Count was here. How could he have been responsible?"

Again Persephone shrugged. "I doan know, mam'zelle. I only know what I tole you."

"Well, none of it matters now. The *Nightshade* is at sea. There is no way for us to get a warning to Grey."

"A warning?" A familiar voice asked from the doorway. "A warning to whom? And for what?"

Casting discretion to the wind, Monique rushed into Edward's arms. Gently, he held her, delighted that she should be so pleased to see him. But presently he felt her trembling and knew there was more to her unorthodox greeting than mere affection.

"Monique?" He held her at arm's length and saw the worry in her beautiful eyes. "Here now, what's happened? You must tell me."

"Oh, Edward." Leaving his arms, she went to the window and stood gazing out toward the endless expanse of blue sea in the distance. "It may be nothing. Then again, it may be murder."

"Murder?" Edward's blue eyes shifted to Persephone and back to Monique. "What is this all about?"

Sighing, Monique sank onto the cushions of the window seat. "It's about Christophe Duclaux and the sinking of the *Peregrine*. Persephone thinks it may not have been an accident."

Edward's head shot up and he turned to the maid. Did she have evidence to support his own suspicions?

"What do you mean?"

With Persephone substantiating the story,

Monique recounted what information they had been able to piece together. When they'd finished, Edward paused in the rhythmic, nervous pacing he'd begun halfway through their story.

"I was afraid da l'Armi was involved," he said, shaking his head.

"But that is what I do not understand," Monique put in. "We can speculate as much as we like, but the fact remains that the *Peregrine* was at sea when she exploded and Niccolò da l'Armi was here. How could he have caused the explosion?"

Edward frowned. "It would not be impossible. If the gauges that show the boiler pressure were tampered with, then the pressure would build and build. Eventually, they simply could not stand the strain." He groaned, rubbing his brow. "He likely paid one of the workmen to sabotage the gauges while working on the boilers. It would have been all too easy."

"But if that were true," Monique objected, "if the Count was responsible for the explosion, why would he be so impatient to go to France himself?"

To keep Grey and Tori from asking too many questions and rousing suspicion, Edward thought. He said only, "We may never know."

Monique toyed with her riding crop. "I wish there was some way to get word to Grey and Tori. The man could prove dangerous to them!"

"Not while they're at sea." Edward shook his head as he took Monique's hand and led her out to where their horses waited for them at the bottom of Stockton Hall's grand front entrance.

Taking Monique's foot into his hand, he lifted her into the saddle. "Don't forget, my dear, that he is aboard the *Nightshade*, too. He would hardly bring about its destruction when he himself would go with it to the bottom.'' Lifting a finger, he silenced her as she was about to speak.

"Now, enough about Italian counts and their plots. I will try to learn what I can about Niccolò da l'Armi and I will send word to France as soon as possible concerning the *Peregrine* and Monsieur Duclaux and our suspicions. In the meantime, let us enjoy this glorious day, shall we?"

As they cantered off down the long, sloping drive, Monique let herself, for a moment, forget the barrier, the secret, that she feared would tear their budding love asunder. She still had not told Edward the truth about herself. She feared it would drive him from her, ending this marvelous interlude when this handsome, cultured gentleman treated her as a woman worth the wooing and not merely as a beautiful woman to be hired and dismissed like a glorified chamber maid. She was heartily tired of being little more than a servant who, because of her desirability, was employed in the bedchamber rather than the scullery. She wanted more than admiration, more than desire—she wanted love. She had thought for so long that it was merely a foolish dream, but now she had found it. She was determined to know it in all its splendor before the issue of her blood—and she believed it would inevitably arise—tore them apart.

Aboard the *Nightshade*, tensions seemed to grow with the passing of each day. For Grey, Tori's nearness was a torment. He ached for her, craved her; his thoughts constantly strayed to her. His passions frayed his nerves, and his temper was often held in check by the slenderest of threads. And the fuel that fed the fire and the breeze that fanned the flames were embodied in the dapper, dashing form of

Count Niccolò da l'Armi.

While Grey was busy with the affairs of his ship, Niccolò was busy courting Tori. It seemed that whenever Grey saw Tori, the Count was at her side. Whenever he met her in the passage or saw her emerge onto the deck Niccolò was beside her. When Niccolò spoke to her, Grey's anger flared; when she laughed at some witty quip, Grey's jealousy reared its head; when Niccolò touched her, Grey's fury knew no bounds.

And so it was almost a relief when Tori awoke one morning with a vicious cold and took to her bed to wait out its course.

Determined to be kind, Grey visited her when he could, taking pains to amuse her and cheering her as best he could. That Niccolò visited her as well, he had no doubt, although generally by the time he left the wheelhouse and made his way to Tori's cabin to bid her good-night, the Italian had already retired to his own cabin.

After only a few days, Grey began to enjoy the close warmth of the little cabin, where a fire was kept burning in the stove in an attempt to keep the chill, damp sea air at bay. He looked forward to sitting in the armchair at the foot of the bed and talking to Tori until she could no longer keep her eyes open. And even then, he would often sit, watching her sleep, loving her and railing against the fate that kept them apart. He cursed himself for every kind of a fool for having so callously thrown away her love those long years before when she had given her heart to him with the naive, trusting innocence of a schoolgirl.

Smiling, pleased to at last be done with the day's work and free to visit Tori, Grey paused outside her door. Tonight, despite the late hour, there were sounds coming from within the cabin, voices speaking in hushed tones.

"Da l'Armi!" Grey muttered to himself. Why in hell hadn't that blasted man gone to bed and left Tori alone!

His knuckles whitened as he seized the latch and swung the cabin door open. His normally ruddy, sunbaked face flushed with the hot blood of his fury when he found Niccolò seated on the edge of Tori's bunk holding her gently in his arms.

"Take your goddamned hands off her!" Grey snarled. "What in hell do you think you're doing!"

He crossed the small floor in scant strides. His hands closed brutally about Niccolò's arm and he jerked him away from Tori nearly yanking her out of bed in the process.

Taken unawares, Niccolò made no move to defend himself. His breath left him in a sickening 'whoosh' as he fell against the opposite wall, his head narrowly missing a lantern that burned low in its wall-mounted gimbal.

Grey towered over him, his eyes ablaze with murderous rage. "I don't know how things are done in Italy, da l'Armi," he snarled. "But in America, we don't take kindly to men laying their hands on other men's women! Now you can either get out of here and keep to your cabin for the rest of this voyage, or we can go up on deck and settle this now."

Pulling himself to his feet, Niccolò straightened his clothes with an air of injured dignity. His eyes were twin orbs of blue ice as they skimmed contemptuously over Grey.

"There is nothing to settle, Signor," he told Grey coldly. "Though if there were, you need not wonder if I would rise to the challenge. Rest assured I have fought more than one duel and I will doubtless

fight many more. I remind you as well that Tori is
not my 'woman' as you say, but neither is she yours,
however much you may desire that she were. But I
will not argue that point with you now. If you would
care to curb your temper and look at her, you will see
that she is in no condition to be seduced by either of
us!''

Dragging his eyes away from the Count, Grey
looked to where Tori lay, huddled miserably under
the blankets, trembling so violently that her
movements were visible even under the thick quilts
Grey had piled on her.

"Tori!" Grey's anger faded into concern. As he
moved toward the bunk, he didn't even notice
Niccolò slipping out of the cabin to return to his own
quarters and nurse his shredded dignity.

Tori's eyes opened to slits. From beneath the
quilts, she reached a shaking hand toward him.

"Oh, Grey," she whispered. "I'm cold—so
terribly, awfully cold."

Grey frowned. It was stifling in the room. The
fire blazed in the little stove—he didn't dare try to
build it up any more. And with the pile of quilts on
top of the bunk and the heated bricks that had been
wrapped in flannel and tucked at her feet, she should
have been roasting. But it was plain to see that she
was freezing. Grey didn't know whether to be happy
or sad. On the one hand, she was miserable; on the
other, at least the fever that had plagued her the past
few days had broken. Strands of hair stuck to her
forehead and little beads of perspiration stood out on
her forehead and upper lip.

"Grey?" she asked plaintively, pleading with
him to help her.

He ran a hand through his hair. There was little
he could do. The ship had no doctor in residence.

Oh, the cook could stir up possets and stitch cuts but that was the limit of his medical skills. Grey himself, blessed with good health, knew little about illnesses and their treatments. But he knew that he had to do what he could to make her comfortable.

Working swiftly and silently, he warmed water on the stove and rummaged through Tori's things until he found a fresh nightdress. Over her protests, he pulled off the heavy quilts that she clung to for warmth.

"What are you doing to me?" she demanded, almost weeping.

"Just be quiet," he ordered.

As if she were a doll, he stripped off the dampened gown that clung to her body. With the basin of warmed water and a cloth, he bathed her face and neck and then the rest of her, working methodically. But if he managed to concentrate his mind on his task, the rest of his body was concerned only with the beauty of her as she lay there, helpless, trusting as a child. He was almost grateful when he pulled the fresh gown over her head and shoved the innumerable pearl buttons through their holes, fastening it up to her chin and down her waist. He pulled the blankets up to her chin, then went out, ostensibly to empty the basin of water, but in fact to take a turn on deck in the chilling night air that enveloped the ship.

By the time he returned, Tori was asleep. Her lashes lay like delicate wings across her cheeks and her forehead was dry. Her face had lost the flushed, fevered look it had worn for days past. Grey breathed a sigh of relief as he lowered himself into the chair at the foot of the bed. He didn't want to think about her beauty or about the rage that had erupted inside him at the sight of her in Niccolò da l'Armi's arms. Least of all did he want to consider the fact that sooner or later she would return to her husband and be lost to him. At that moment, in that hot, cramped cabin, all he wanted to do was watch her and love her.

21

Tori awoke with the dawn, feeling more alive than she had in days. Though the headache and sore throat that had plagued her would doubtless be with her for several days, the awful fever, racking cough, and suffocating congestion of the lungs seemed to be nearly gone.

Peering over the mound of blankets she saw Grey, sound asleep, slouched in the chair, his feet on the foot of her bed. From his disheveled appearance and the dark shadowing of beard on his chin, it was obvious that he had been there all night.

A wave of tenderness engulfed her. How dear he was! How sweet he could be. His concern touched her heart in a way his obvious desire never could. It meant so much more to her to know that he cared for her than to know that he wished to make love to her. It was infinitely harder to find a man who loved one than to find a lover.

She loved him so much it hurt her. The knowledge that she could never be his—and he could never be hers—gnawed at her day and night. Fate had been kind to tear them apart so many years before, as if knowing that their love was never meant to be. Why, then, had it been so cruel as to throw them back together now, when there was no hope?

Hot tears stung her eyes and she turned onto her side and let them trickle down her cheeks to the pillow. She didn't realize that Grey had awakened until he rose from his chair and came to the side of the bunk.

"Tori?" he said softly.

"Yes?" she replied, not daring to look up at him.

He sat on the edge of the bunk. Taking her gently by the shoulders, he turned her onto her back. Her cheeks were flushed with the effort of holding back the sobs that ached in her throat. For a moment, Grey thought her fever had returned.

He lay a hand on her forehead. "How are you feeling this morning?"

"Better," she told him. "Much better, truly."

"Your fever broke last night. While da l'Armi was here. Do you remember?"

She frowned, shaking her head. "All I remember is the cold. I was so very cold."

His smile was sheepish. "I'm afraid I leapt to the wrong conclusion when I walked in and found the Count holding you."

"Grey!" Her eyes twinkled, pleased by his jealousy. "What did you do to him?"

"Nothing. Well, at least I didn't hit him. But I'm afraid I challenged him to a duel."

"A duel!" Knowing Grey's reputation, Tori felt

a very real sense of alarm.

He eased her back onto the pillows as she struggled to sit up.

"Calm down, Tori. It wasn't a real challenge—more of a threat of a challenge. In any case, the Count did not accept. Although he threatened to."

"The two of you are like two stags prancing and bellowing."

"Rivals for the same doe?" he suggested mischievously.

"That will be enough," she chided with mock severity. She stretched luxuriously beneath the covers. "It's odd," she mused aloud. "Considering that my fever broke during the night, I feel amazingly fresh. It's almost as if I'd had a ba—"

A horrified suspicion crept into her mind and over her face. She looked up at Grey who beamed down on her with angelic innocence.

"Grey, you didn't . . ."

"You were freezing, Tori. And your gown was soaked. I could hardly have left you like that. You'd have awoken this morning with pneumonia."

A crimson flush stole into her cheeks. "You should never have . . ."

"Who, then?" he demanded. "The Count? The first officer, perhaps? Don't forget, you are the only woman aboard. It's not as if I can snap my fingers and summon a maid." The devilish light faded from his eyes; his expression lost all hint of levity. "You're a beautiful woman, Tori. Even I never dreamed how beautiful."

She rolled onto her side, facing away from him. "Grey, please don't," she begged.

She did not mind the thought of his having seen her, touched her, as much as she minded the thought of his having desired what he had seen and touched.

The thought of what he did made her curse the fever that had called for such drastic measures. For it seemed, somehow, that the knowledge of his desire fueled hers. She wanted him the more for his wanting her.

And yet, the loathsome voice of reason taunted her, such emotions were wrong. They should be cut out of her heart and mind and cast aside like the malignant cankers they were. But as with any deep cut, there was pain, such pain that it seemed the cure was worse than the disease.

Grey saw her shudder, saw the teardrops that glistened like sparkling dew on her golden lashes.

"Tori," he said softly, with such tenderness that she felt as if her heart would shatter. "Why are you crying? I told you you are beautiful. Why should that make you weep?"

Tori steeled herself, hardened her battered heart, fought down the urgings of her traitorous senses. She had to put some distance between them before it was too late and foolishness overcame them.

"Christophe," she lied, "Christophe used to say the same thing to me. Your saying it reminded me of him and how very much I miss him."

Grey stiffened. Tori could almost feel the pain her seemingly callous words evoked in him. The air seemed suddenly charged with tension, chilled with the icy coldness of his hard stare.

"Well, it won't be long before we are in France," he told her stiffly, biting out each word with taut precision. "Then you will be reunited with your precious Christophe. Until then, I'll not trouble you further."

Tori bit her lip, holding the tears at bay until Grey had stormed from the cabin and slammed the door behind him.

Then, and only then, did the storm of her anguish break over her, and she lay beneath the heaped quilts weeping until it seemed she had no more tears left to shed.

In Jamaica, the morning sunshine appeared with its usual, unrelenting regularity. In her moiré-draped bed at Stockton Hall, Monique stretched beneath the light silken sheets that, like the ornately carved rosewood bedroom suite that now decorated her room, had been a gift from Edward Lytton.

Smiling, Monique kicked back the sheet and climbed out of bed. She felt wonderful, like a princess in some children's fairy story who had been awakened to a beautiful life by a handsome prince.

Her flowing nightdress swirled about her as she waltzed across the room in the arms of an imaginary lover. In her mind, she danced in a grand ballroom wearing a Parisian gown. All around her were faces—admiring men, jealous, envious women. And she was the belle of the ball. And it was a proper ball, in a proper ballroom, not some hole-in-the-wall affair for quadroons attended by gentlemen as a lark and shunned by their high-nosed, respectable wives who could look the other way and pretend the pretty, painted creatures into whose beds their husbands crept did not exist.

Once it would have been merely a dream—a fantasy in which she was a fool to indulge. But now her dream was about to become reality. And her fairy godmother was one Edward Lytton.

Only yesterday, while they had been dining bathed in candlelight at Woodbridge, Edward had mentioned the upcoming ball at Faircrest, the home of Pierce and Mary Wynter. It was to celebrate the visit of Pierce Wynter's sister, Iris, Lady Devizes, from England.

Monique's heart had leapt. Visions of grandeur such as she had never known swam in her head. But then reality had come crashing down, shattering her lovely illusions.

"Perhaps I shouldn't," she had murmured, gently withdrawing her hand from his.

Edward's instant concern had been touching. "But why?" he asked. She could not answer immediately and he went on, coaxing: "You must. I've already accepted for us both."

"But, Edward . . ." she began.

In the privacy of her bedroom, Monique recalled with a smile and a lighthearted, delicious sensation of being truly loved, that he had overridden every one of her wan objections with a single-mindedness that bordered on the dictatorial. In the end, she could do nothing but bow to his wishes.

And so, incredible as it seemed, she would attend the grand ball at Faircrest as a welcome guest on the arm of Edward Lytton.

Monique wound her arms about the tall, fluted post of the canopy bed. She was happy—almost too happy, it seemed, for it all to be true.

The doorlatch clicked as a hand pushed it down; the hinges creaked as the door opened.

"Good morning, Perseph—" Looking up, Monique found not the maid come to see if she was still asleep, but a small, veiled figure in black that glided into the room with soundless steps like some phantom of the night.

Before the woman in widow's weeds threw back her veil, Monique knew by some unerring instinct who her unwelcome visitor was.

"How did you get in here?" she demanded.

Dorthée Arnault lifted the black lace from her

head. Her face was still beautiful; the years had silvered her hair but the fine, porcelain flesh of her face seemed curiously, almost diabolically, untouched. As always it was the eyes, the burning hate-filled depths of those fathomless black eyes that struck a frightening chord of remembrance in Monique's heart.

"Does it matter how I came to be here?" the woman demanded.

Monique was struck by the deep, precise sound of the woman's voice. For all that Dorothée Arnault had once destroyed Monique's world—almost her life itself—nary a word had ever passed between them.

"My servants . . ." she objected.

"Your servants!" Madame Arnault sneered. "As if you were the mistress of this house! Your kind are all the same. You ape your betters trying to take more than your due."

"What do you want here?" Monique asked, fighting to keep her voice steady. To show fear to his woman, she knew instinctively, was to give her the upper hand.

"I want you to know that I will not allow you to ruin a gentleman the way that slut, your mother, did."

Monique drew herself up. "My mother did not ruin Vincent Arnault! It was you—you who killed him! But you made it seem that it was my mother's fault." Her violet eyes flashed, and in their depths was a glimmer of remembered pain. "You killed him and you killed her, too—just as surely as if you had run a dagger through her heart."

"She deserved to die! Half-breed bitch breeding more just like her! I will not allow you to perpetuate your vile kind at the expense of a gentleman like Edward Lytton."

Monique summoned all the bravado inside her,

but it was not enough to conceal the fear this woman inspired in her.

"What can you do about it?" she challenged the woman, some part of her knowing the game was lost but refusing to give up until the bitter end.

"I can expose you. You haven't told him, have you?" Dorothée Arnault's malicious chuckle grated in Monique's ears. "No, I can see you haven't. But you will. You must. For if you don't, I will. You believe that, don't you?"

"Yes," Monique admitted freely. "I believe that." Her eyes narrowed, and her lip curled with distaste. "You're so filled with hate—it's devoured any shred of humanity you ever had."

"Hate! Bah! What do you know of hate! What do you know of humanity? You're nothing but the mongrel product of the union between a gentleman and a half-blooded bitch who used her body to—"

"Stop it!" Monique shrieked. "I won't listen to you! Get out! God, how I hate you!"

"Do you? And do you think I care for the hatred of a creature like you? All I want is for you to leave Edward Lytton alone. The place for you is not among decent people, but in the fields or the scullery—not in the bed of a gentleman."

Monique turned her back to hide the emotions she could no longer conceal by will alone. But she could not shut out the hateful sound of Dorothée Arnault's taunting voice:

"Remember what I have told you. Get out of Edward Lytton's life or he—and all of Montego Bay—will learn what you really are!"

Monique clenched her fists to still the trembling of her hands. "I'll fight you!" she vowed. "I won't cower, and I won't run. I won't let you destroy me the way—"

She swung about, determined to face her fear and her enemy. "I won't . . ." Her threat trailed off into nothingness. She was alone. As stealthily as she had come, Dorothée Arnault had departed.

Flame hair streaming down her back, her silken nightdress billowing behind her, Monique ran to the door and swung it wide. The morning sunlight streaming through the huge window on the landing cast the giant silhouette of a woman against the staircase wall. Monique ran to the head of the stairs but found only Persephone mounting the treads.

"Where did she go?"

"Go?" the girl asked. "Who, missis?"

"Madame Arnault! A woman in black. She just left my room. You must have seen her on the stairs!"

Persephone peered back down the stairs. "Nobody be heah, missis."

"But she was here!" Monique insisted, an edge of hysteria tingeing her words. "She was in my room only a moment ago!"

From the look on Persephone's face, Monique could see that the girl knew nothing about Madame Arnault's visit. Yet they should have passed on the stairs or in the hall below. How could she have come and gone without being seen? A shiver passed through Monique's body, and she wrapped her arms protectively about herself. Dorothée Arnault had always loomed in her mind as the epitome of evil—the bugbear that had haunted Monique's childhood. Would she now become the phantasm that would haunt her womanhood as well?

22

In the wan glow of the lamps that burned on either side of her dressing table, Monique gazed at her reflection in the ormolu-framed mirror. Her finely boned, ivory-complexioned face stared back at her through haunted eyes. She was beautiful, exquisitely so, but in the classic manner of the quadroon. There was little to be found in her of her father, Vincent Arnault, but much of her mother, the magnificent Ninon.

Ninon, like many women of color in New Orleans, had been the mistress—the *placée*—of Vincent Arnault. For years he had kept her in fine style with a beautiful cottage all her own. To all outward appearances, Vincent's legal wife—the hateful Dorothée—had looked the other way, pretending not to know where her husband was when he went out in the early evening and didn't return until very late, sometimes not at all. But it was obvious that the woman had harbored such loathing, such hatred, for the beautiful Ninon and her daughter, that it seethed inside her like lava in the dome of a volcano.

It erupted just two months before Monique's eleventh birthday. Vincent Arnault had arrived at Ninon's little cottage complaining of pains. He had died in agony a few hours later in Ninon's bed.

Dorothée Arnault had used all her resources to prevent an investigation into her husband's death, and Ninon and Monique were sure they knew the reason. Unable to bear the humiliation, the morification, Dorothée had poisoned her husband, knowing he would expire in the arms of his mulatto mistress. But nothing could be proven. Still, the venom that spewed from Dorothée following her husband's elaborate funeral left New Orleans in no doubt that she had wreaked her final vengeance on the gorgeous *placée* and her lovely violet-eyed daughter.

Society was divided in its opinion of her actions. Surprisingly, many fine New Orleans ladies looked on her with distaste. She had been Vincent's legal wife and her sons were his heirs. She should have been content to leave him his other life amidst the sheltering shadows of the world of *plaçage* and the *placées*. By her actions she had effectively had her revenge on both her husband and his mistress, but she had also violated the rules of Polite Society by lifting its concealing skirts and exposing its soiled linen to the world.

For Monique and her mother, the sordid death of Vincent Arnault spelled utter ruin. Though Dorothée Arnault left New Orleans shortly after her husband's funeral, the damage had been done.

Penniless, too notorious for any other gentleman to consider making her his *placée*, Ninon had barely kept herself and her child from starvation.

Monique had not only lost the kind, gentle man who had been her beloved Papa, she had had to watch her mother, torn by grief and worry, grow old before her time and lose all will to live. Her health had broken down swiftly and, when Monique was barely fourteen, Ninon had died, leaving her child to make her own way in the world.

Leaving her dressing table, Monique went to her trunk and drew out the hinged leather case she took everywhere with her. Inside, carefully cradled in velvet, lay a delicately colored miniature painted on ivory. In the other half of the case, a lock of shining black hair lay sealed under a domed crystal.

"Maman," Monique whispered. "She is back. Madame Dorothée is back. What shall I do? I thought when she left New Orleans that she was gone forever, but she came back and now she is here, in Jamaica. Will she follow me forever? Will she never give me peace, Maman? Will she never be satisfied until she destroys me the way she destroyed you—the way she destroyed Papa?"

The answers were there, in her own heart, and it took all Monique's courage to face and accept them. She would have to end her romance with Edward.

There! she thought. She allowed the thoughts that had been festering inside her to emerge in all their hateful ugliness. It would be better, she told herself resolutely, trying desperately to steel herself against the aching sorrow in her breast, to break it off herself rather than to allow Dorothée Arnault to destroy any more of the people Monique loved.

Taking a deep breath, Monique pressed a kiss to

the miniature and replaced it in her trunk. With the grace and dignity of a queen, she rose and prepared to face an ordeal that pained her to the depths of her very soul.

Tori cried out as the coach in which she and Grey were riding hit a hole in the road and lurched violently.

"It would behoove the French to put springs on these contraptions," she complained, scowling out the streaked window at the lush green countryside of the Loire Valley.

Grey said nothing. His silver eyes were riveted to the opposite window, and it was as if he were under the spell of the land of his ancestors.

Tori felt almost jealous. Reaching out, she gently touched his sleeve. "Grey?"

"Hmmm?" He glanced at her, a soft smile at the corners of his mouth.

"Why did you lie to Niccolò?"

"Did I lie to Niccolò?" he asked with admirably feigned innocence.

"When we docked, you told him we couldn't accompany him to Paris. But that is where we're going."

"If I told him that, Tori," he said, the tiny smile fading and his tone taking on a hint of impatience, "it was because I had no desire to spend any more time with the man." One jet-hued brow arched and his eyes glinted darkly. "Did you?"

"I didn't say that. But you told him we were going to spend the night at your cousin's château. That was a rather clumsy lie, wasn't it?"

"Not at all. In fact, I've sent a messenger ahead to warn my cousin of our arrival. I expect we'll be more comfortable there tonight than your friend the

Count will be in some roadside inn.'' He turned his attention back to the window. It was another lie, but Grey felt no remorse. They were, in fact, on their way to meet Christophe Duclaux's next contact, but for Tori's own good it was better for her to believe they were merely passing the night with Grey's relatives. He hoped his messenger arrived safely and his contact was willing to go along with the charade of being his French cousin.

They lapsed into silence again as the miles passed. Then Tori broke the silence to ask:

"Grey, why do you suppose no one knew anything about Christophe's ship when we docked?''

With a sigh, he turned his head toward her once again. "They may have had to change their course, and so alter their destination. There are hundreds of ports where they might have put in if an emergency arose. I'm sure it's nothing to worry about.''

"Christophe could be in Paris by now, couldn't he?'' she persisted. "I wonder what Niccolò will do when he gets there.'' Her blonde brows drew together. "I hope Christophe doesn't get involved with him. The Count is an unscrupulous man, I'm sure, and he—''

"Tori!'' Grey interrupted impatiently. "Christophe is a grown man. He can deal with Niccolò da l'Armi by himself. He dealt with him in Jamaica, didn't he?''

"But if I were there,'' she argued, "I could—''

"Victoria! Will you stop this fussing! Christophe can manage without you. After all, he came to France without you, remember?''

Tori lifted her chin, haughty as a princess. "He would have taken me along if I had been in Jamaica with him.''

"But you weren't in Jamaica, were you?'' Grey

said grimly, some perverse part of him enjoying her pique.

"You're a despicable man, Grey Verreaux!" she snapped. "You can't bear to think that I might love Christophe and he might love me! I know it pleased you no end when he left me all alone in New Orleans."

"Did you ever stop to think that he may not have wanted you under foot?" Grey asked archly.

"Oh! You are the most loathsome, maddening, wicked, cruel . . ." She struggled to think of more adjectives.

"Vile, nefarious, villainous, corrupt, obdurate, ne'er-do-well . . ." he went on, thoroughly enjoying himself.

"Why do you taunt me this way?" she demanded, pouting prettily. "Why don't you find someone else to irritate?"

"Why, Tori, my love." He lifted her hand to his lips. "There's no one in this world I'd rather irritate than you."

"Am I supposed to be honored?"

He shrugged. "I've known women who would have been."

Tori laughed, scornfully rolling her eyes. "And conceited into the bargain!"

"Why is it," he asked ruefully, "that one cannot tell the simple truth without being branded an egotist?"

"Oh, Lord! Grey, I do believe you've been away from the adoring women of New Orleans too long. Pray tell, how do you imagine your many women are managing without you?"

"Poorly, no doubt," he answered quickly, teasingly. "I suppose they'll simply have to make do with the Union Army—although I expect it will be a hardship for them.''

"If I thought you were serious, I'd be sick," Tori said, then patted his hand with mocking sympathy. "Well, never mind. Here we are in an entirely new country. It's just lying in wait for you. Think of all these poor, deprived Frenchwomen who have yet to discover the wonders of Greyson Jérôme Dieudonné Verreaux." She giggled as he winced at her use of his entire name. "Tell me honestly, Grey, is Dieudonné really one of your names?"

"Indeed," he assured her. "Jérôme de Verreaux was a great-uncle of mine who was very close to my father and Dieudonné Rousseve was an ancestor of my mother."

"But Dieudonné? God's gift?"

He waggled a comical brow at her. "Prophetic, don't you think? And apt!"

She groaned. "Now I know I'm going to be sick!"

Grey's rumbling laughter filled the coach. With eyes that twinkled with amusement and admiration, he pressed his lips to the backs of Tori's gloved fingers.

Rapping on the roof of the coach, Grey instructed the man to pull into the courtyard of the next inn they passed and ask directions to the Château de Saint-Rémy. When the coachman returned, he told them it was not far—a few miles more on the main road then three more on the lane that led to the Château.

"You'd best tidy your hair and tie on your bonnet," Grey told her as the coach turned off the main road and into a narrow, tree-shaded lane. "You want to look your best when you meet the Duchess."

"Duchesse?" Tori asked, opening her travel case, which was fitted with toilet articles in the finest of ivory and gold. "The Duchesse of what?"

"The Duchesse de Saint-Rémy. Who do you think lives at the Château de Saint-Rémy?"

"What has she to do with you?" A sudden suspicion dawned on Tori. "Your cousin! Your cousin is the Duchesse de Saint-Rémy! But I thought . . ."

"You thought it was just another batch of Verreauxs, didn't you?" Grey chuckled and decided to embroider the tale further. "Didn't you listen to all the gossip back home in Virginia? My cousins came out of the Revolution and all the ensuing changes of government here in France quite well. They retained all their property, their titles, most of their money . . ."

"But a duchesse! Grey!"

"She married the Duc, Hubert des Bouffleurs, very young. My mother wrote me that the Duc died nearly a year ago and the Duchesse came here from Paris to wait out her year of mourning." Lies, all lies, he thought, but for Tori's own good. He hoped the Duchesse went along. "That must be the château." He nodded out the window.

The Château de Saint-Rémy rose up out of the mists like an enchanted castle in a child's fairy tale. It seemed to be all towers and turrets and crenellated battlements; tall spires disappeared into the wafting fog and the water of the little river that flowed around the château lapped at its white stone walls.

Tori gasped as a stag with a magnificent rack bounded across the lane just in front of the horses.

"How beautiful it all is!" she sighed. "Oh, Grey, how could you never have come here before?"

He shrugged, feeling himself being drawn ever deeper into a web of lies of his own making. "I was always happy in America. Can you picture me as the lord of such a manor as this?"

Tori laughed. "No doubt the girls of the nearby villages would be glad the days of droit du seigneur are past!"

"Well, I always said a good custom is worth reviving." He leered, sending Tori into a fit of giggling. "You know, the Duchesse was considerably younger than the Duc. I wonder if she is as beautiful as I've heard."

"She is your cousin, Grey!" Tori reminded him sharply.

"Distant cousin," he pointed out. "It may be my familial duty to comfort the grieving widow."

"May be?" She felt the unpleasant pricklings of jealousy.

He smiled slyly. "I'll let you know after I see the Duchesse."

"Hah! If she's that young and beautiful, she'd no doubt put you in an early grave! You're not as young as you used to be, Grey."

"I'm no doddering old man, either!" he objected, just the smallest hint of hurt in his tone. "I'm just reaching my prime, I'll have you know."

"Your prime! Your prime passed by about five years ago, I'd say."

"And what makes you an expert?"

"You don't have to be an expert to see when time has taken its toll," she taunted. She glanced pointedly toward his hair. "I see a few gray hairs up there, sirrah."

"I don't care if I'm sprinkled with them," he retorted. "I assure you all my parts are in perfect

227

working order." He shot her an arch glance. "As I'd be more than happy to demonstrate any time you'd like."

Flushing, Tori busied herself packing away her toilet case as the coach passed over the arched stone bridge and into the château courtyard.

"I wouldn't want to tire you," she told him coolly. "After all, you might need your strength—for comforting the Duchesse."

Together they climbed down out of the coach and approached the iron-banded door. It swung open at their knock and a handsome young footman in cerulean blue and gold livery appeared.

"*Oui*, Monsieur? Madame?" he asked.

"I am . . ," Grey began. Seeing the man's confusion, he switched to the French he had learned as a child. "*Je suis* Greyson Verreaux."

In short order they were ushered into an entry hall, up a short corridor, and into a gallery that stretched off into the distance. Floored in black and white marble, its long walls were pierced with arched windows before which stood gilded sofas. Lifesize gilded nymphs held torches aloft and massive chandeliers dripping crystals hung down the center of the vaulted ceiling.

Tori unconsciously stepped nearer to Grey. She was beginning to feel intimidated.

Please, please! she begged Heaven above. Don't let the Duchesse be as young or as beautiful as Grey says—

"Good afternoon," a deep, heavily-accented voice said. "Welcome to Saint-Rémy."

One glance dashed all Tori's hopes. From the far end of the gallery a woman appeared and glided toward them. She was dressed entirely in black, but her bodice sparkled with the exquisite jet embroidery that also banded each of the seven deep flounces on her skirt. Against the stark black mourning, her skin seemed as pale and ethereal as moonlight. Her hair, which at first seemed grey beneath the vaporous veil that floated behind her as she moved, proved to be an extraordinary silver blonde such as Tori had never seen before. Upon closer inspection, the Duchesse proved to have eyes of clearest turquoise, a perfect retroussé nose, and full, pouting lips that in themselves seemed capable of driving any man to distraction. Worse still, her tightly fitted bodice was molded to a deep, high bosom and a waist so small it seemed Grey could span it with his hands. Tori, always accustomed to being celebrated for her angelic beauty, felt for the first time in her life, plain and lacking in femininity. Her dusty clothes and travel-worn fatigue only compounded the feeling.

"You must be my cousin, Monsieur Verreaux, from America."

"I am," Grey replied in faultless French, relieved that the Duchesse was going along with his scheme. "I was enchanted by the château, madame. But it pales in comparison to its mistress."

The Duchesse's low, musical laughter surrounded them, seeming almost to caress them. "How kind you are to flatter a poor, grieving widow." The incredible turquoise eyes skimmed quickly over Tori. "And you, madame?" she began.

"This is Madame Duclaux," Grey informed her.

"You are also a widow, madame?" the Duchesse inquired sweetly.

"No," Tori replied, chagrined that her French was not as smooth as Grey's. "Monsieur Verreaux is taking me to Paris to join my husband."

"How sweet of him." She smiled intimately at

Grey. "Perhaps, after you have delivered Madame
Duclaux to her husband, you will come back and visit
your poor *cousine* for a while, no? I have been very,
very lonely these past ten months."

Grey grinned and Tori could almost feel the heat
emanating from him. The satyr! The lecher!

"I'm very tired, madame, and dusty," she said,
her tone bordering on insolence. "If I could be
shown to my room . . ."

"But of course." The Duchesse snapped her
fingers and a footman appeared, seemingly out of
nowhere. "Take Madame Duclaux to the tapestry
room, François."

"Thank you," Tori said shortly. "I believe I'll
rest and leave you two to"—she cast a pointed glance
at Grey—"get acquainted."

The footman led the way and a fuming Tori
followed. She'd been lonely! Tori sneered to herself.
Lonely, indeed! This was the second footman she'd
seen thus far, and both had been extraordinarily
handsome young men. And the livery the Duchesse
put them in! Tori's eyes skimmed the back of the
young man from head to foot. Why, those satin
breeches were so tight he couldn't get goosebumps
without everyone knowing about it! The Duchesse de
Saint-Rémy—it was a high-sounding title, to be sure,
but all it masked was another little trollop who
couldn't wait to get her hands on Grey.

She was still scowling when the footman opened
the door and ushered her into her chamber. If he
expected an answering smile or any other reward, he
was disappointed. All she wanted to do was shut
herself in, away from Grey and his pretty little
cousine, and wait for the morning to come so they
could leave!

23

Whatever she felt for the Duchesse, Tori could not fault her hospitality. The rooms to which she had been shown were beautiful in a way no other chambers she'd ever seen were beautiful. The walls were covered from floor to ceiling with rich, undoubtedly ancient, tapestries. Worked in brilliant colors, they seemed not to have faded with the passing of the years. The lords and ladies and mythical beasts that cavorted across them were as bright and vivid as they must have been the day they were finished. The furniture that decorated the bed-chamber and adjoining sitting room was all heavy and dark, almost medieval in appearance. It made Tori think of Renaissance princes like Lorenzo the Magnificent and the Borgias. Even the Duchesse, Tori reflected, seating herself in an X-shaped Savonarola chair, somehow reminded her of a miniature she had once seen of Lucrezia Borgia!

At the tug of a bell-rope another footman appeared—Tori wondered if there were no women at all in the Duchesse's employ. She found she had but to express a whim and it was gratified. She was sent a maid to unpack her belongings, and a tub was filled for her bath and scented with precious oils.

She was reclining on a century-old chaise tasselled in gold, reading a novel someone had left in a massive carved oak cabinet in the sitting room, when a tap on the door interrupted her.

"Come in," she called.

The door opened and yet another of the Duchesse's footmen appeared. This one was blond as an angel with long-lashed eyes the color of the Jamaican sea.

"Madame Duclaux?" he said in nearly accentless English. "I am Armand. Madame la Duchesse has sent me to ask if you will come to dinner downstairs or dine in your rooms."

"In my rooms, I think," she told him. He bowed, smiling, then turned to leave. "Armand," she called, halting him as he reached the door. "May I ask you a question?"

"But of course, madame. Madame la Duchesse has told me I am to serve you in any way you wish during your stay at the Château de Saint-Rémy."

"Any way?" Tori asked.

The beautiful young man took the question in his stride. "Any way, madame."

"Is that usual?" she asked, amazed.

He seemed surprised that she needed to ask. "It would be rude if a guest's wishes were not fulfilled, madame."

Good Lord! Tori thought. In New Orleans hospitality meant a good meal, a comfortable bed, and pleasant, convivial company. Hospitality in France took on a whole new meaning!

She realized that the footman was waiting expectantly. Flushing, she wondered if he thought she meant to ask him to make love to her. Pulling her dressing gown closer about herself, she rushed on:

"I only wondered if Monsieur Verreaux's rooms are nearby."

"Oh, no, madame. Madame la Duchesse has given Monsieur Verreaux the suite that belonged to Monsieur le Duc."

"And where is that?"

"On the other side of the château."

"I see." Well! The Duchesse certainly didn't waste any time in separating them! The Duc's suite, indeed! Grey just might get his wish to be lord of a great manor. She returned her gaze to the footman. "And where is the Duchesse's suite?"

His reply, when it came, was no surprise. "The Duchesse's rooms adjoin the Duc's, madame."

"I see. Thank you, Armand. You may go."

With a graceful bow, the footman left and Tori tried to get back to her book. She had struggled through three pages without comprehending so much as a paragraph when another rap, this one more forceful, sounded on her door.

"Come in?"

The door opened and Armand appeared, followed by two other footmen bearing covered silver dishes which they swiftly arranged into a perfect setting on a table near the window.

"Your dinner, madame," Armand told her.

"Thank you. I'll ring when I've finished."

Armand bowed his way out of the room, but Tori could not find the interest in eating it would have taken to get up and go to the table.

Yet another knock sounded on the door. Tori smiled. Armand not only had the face of an angel, he was persistent!

"Come in, Armand," she called, laughing.

The door opened and Grey appeared. "Who in the hell is Armand?" he demanded, his silvery eyes darting suspiciously around the room.

Laying aside her book, Tori rose from the chaise. "Armand," she told him, casting a flirtatious look over her shoulder, "is part of your little *cousine*'s notion of hospitality." She smiled a mysterious, feline smile and his eyes narrowed. "Armand," she said again, enjoying his agitation, "is one of the Duchesse's footmen. An absolutely beautiful young man who has told me he is here to serve me in any way." She glanced at him from beneath lowered lashes. "Any way!" she stressed.

"You're not serious!"

"Am I not? Come, come, Grey. I'm sure the Duchesse would have assigned some pretty ltitle maidservant to you if it were not that she wants you for herself." She made a face at his pleased smirk. "Where is your little *cousine*, by the way?"

"After dinner she retired to her rooms. She says it's time for her milk bath."

"Milk bath?" Tori repeated, poking disinterestedly among the dishes on the table. "She actually bathes in milk?"

A smile twitched at the corners of Grey's mouth. "Apparently it is the great beauty secret of the women of her family. She told me that her great-great-great-grandmother, in the reign of Louis XIV, had the tub emptied after her bath and the milk given to the poor."

"That's disgusting!" she groaned.

Grey came to her and stood gazing out the

window. "There must be something to it," he told her thoughtfully. "Gabrielle is certainly beautiful."

"Gabrielle?" Tori repeated, not at all liking the way he said the Duchesse's name. "The two of you must have had quite a conversation over dinner."

"You could have come down," he reminded her. "You chose to remain in your rooms."

"Which, you'll notice, are rather a long way from your rooms—and the Duchesse's."

"I am in the Duc's rooms," he told her.

"I know. Armand told me. And the Duc's rooms adjoin the Duchesse's rooms. Convenient."

"The Duchesse gave me the rooms, Tori. I didn't ask for them."

Tori swung away from the window. "Are you going to sleep with her, Grey?"

He tried hard to conceal how much her concern pleased him. "Would it matter to you if I did?" he asked.

"Why should it?" She forced herself to sound cool and disinterested.

"I don't know. You asked the question so I assume you must be concerned."

"Well, I'm not. I assure you it means nothing to me where you sleep—or with whom."

Grey stared into her eyes trying to gauge how much she really meant of what she was saying. His confidence was ever so slightly shaken when he saw that she apparently meant every word of it.

"Then perhaps I should leave," he said softly.

Tori refused to meet his gaze. "Perhaps you should," she agreed coolly.

Turning, he strode out of the room. Behind him, as the door closed, Tori's cool indifference gave way to a weary resignation. Grey cared nothing for her. A woman was a woman as far as she was concerned. It wasn't that he desired her, it was only that he had been without a woman for too long. Now that he had seen the Duchesse—so beautiful, so willing—he was only too happy to have Tori exiled to some remote part of the château while he played the lord of the manor.

Ah, well, it was only for a short time. Once he took her to Paris and they found Christophe . . .

She bit her lip. Aggravating as he was, maddening as he could be, she could not bear the thought of their time together coming to an end. It wasn't that she didn't want to be reunited with Christophe, she assured her guilty conscience, it was just that . . . that . . . Grey made her feel so desirable, so much a woman. With Christophe she had always felt like a pampered child.

And she loved him. Those old emotions had been buried, banked like glowing embers waiting to be stirred into life. And she had thought . . . had wished . . . had dreamed . . . that he felt the same.

"You fool," she scolded herself, casting aside her dressing gown and climbing into the massive tester bed, whose gold-fringed, purple velvet draperies made her feel as if she had entered some mystical cave. "You stupid, stupid fool! How could you have fallen into this trap again? Didn't you learn anything? Did you think he would moon after you like a lovesick fool when you couldn't give him anything? Especially when there are so many beautiful women so willing to give him what you refuse him."

Lying in the darkness, she heard footsteps in the adjoining room. Thinking it was Armand returning for her dinner dishes, she climbed out of the bed and went to the sitting room door.

"You can leave those—" she began, swinging the door open.

Grey looked at her from where he stood in front of the massive fireplace. Nothing was said; there seemed no words to express their emotions.

Lifting her skirt, Tori ran to him and Grey gathered her into his arms. She didn't care, suddenly, about the future. She knew there was none with Grey; she belonged to Christophe and would until one of them was dead. But for now, for tonight, he was there with her, and she was determined to love him while she had the chance.

"Tori, Tori, I need you. Say you won't send me away tonight," he murmured, his lips in her hair, on her forehead, her cheek.

"I won't . . ." She trembled. "I want . . ."

"Tell me," he urged.

"I . . ."

The rapping at the door tore them apart. Tori blushed crimson and fled to the bedroom just as the sitting room door opened and the Duchesse appeared.

"Here you are, you wicked man," Gabrielle scolded him. "I thought you were coming to see me. I wanted to tell you about the time Hubert . . ." Her seductive smile wilted as Tori reappeared, buttoned primly in her wrapper. "Ah, Madame Duclaux. I hope you enjoyed your dinner. When Armand said you had asked to eat in your rooms, I was afraid you were ill."

"I'm quite well," Tori told her, wondering spitefully if the Duchesse was disappointed to hear it.

If so, she concealed it well. "I am delighted to hear it," she said. She and Grey exchanged a glance that made Tori uneasy. It was as if they possessed a

237

secret that Tori knew nothing about. The Duchesse went on, "I have a wonderful notion. There is to be a house party in two days' time at the Château de Lurneaux. The Marquis de Lurneaux is a very dear friend of mine." Seeing the amused expression on Tori's face, she hastened to add: "And the Marquise, his wife, as well. Perhaps we could all go. I do so long to see some of my Paris friends. It will be months before I can enter society again, but surely no one could object to my paying a little visit to a neighbor."

"It sounds fascinating," Grey said casually. He was fully aware of Tori's outrage, but there was little he could do. He could hardly tell her that Christophe had never made contact with the Duchesse and that Gabrielle had told him they might be able to glean more information at the Marquis's house party. He was determined to keep Tori from becoming a part of this dangerous scheme. If it took lies and subterfuge to keep her safe, then so be it!

"It is urgent that we reach Paris, Grey!" Tori reminded him sharply.

"Surely a few days will not matter," Grey argued.

"Grey!" Tori could not believe her ears. Why was he doing this?

"How devoted you must be to your husband, madame," the Duchesse purred. "I wonder what he would think if he knew you were alone in your room with another man."

Tori bristled and Grey took the Duchesse's arm. "I think this matter can better be discussed in the morning, Gabrielle. Now, why don't you and I go and let Madame Duclaux rest?"

The Duchesse was only too pleased to agree. Grey's little *amie* was stubborn, she was thinking.

Perhaps it would be best if she took matters into her own hands to insure the success of their plan. There was no need to consult Grey, who was obviously besotted with the girl.

Returning to her bedchamber, Tori cast aside her dressing gown and was about to climb into her bed when there came yet another knock at the door. When she opened it, Armand was standing there, a steaming mug of chocolate on a silver salver in his hands.

"Madame la Duchesse sends this, madame, with her apologies."

Taking the mug, Tori thanked him and, reluctantly, the Duchesse. She extinguished the lights and climbed into bed, determined this time to get to sleep before there were any other interruptions.

The chocolate was warm and thick as she sipped it. Perhaps the Duchesse really was sorry. Perhaps it was only that she was lonely and Grey was handsome . . . Perhaps . . .

Suddenly Tori was tired, so very tired, that nothing mattered except sleep. Setting the mug aside, she was asleep by the time it slipped from its precarious perch on the edge of the bedside table and fell on its side on the thick carpet.

24

It was the pain that woke Tori just after the streaked dawn had broken over the Château de Saint-Rémy. She moaned, drawing her knees up beneath the silken counterpane.

"Madame?" Armand appeared at the door that joined the sitting room to the bedchamber. "Are you unwell? I thought I heard—"

"Armand!" Tori gasped. "Find Monsieur Verreaux! Please! Tell him to come!"

"*Oui*, madame. At once—" Armand's eyes went to the floor beside the bed. The chocolate mug lay there, dark droplets still adhering to the rim. Beside it, sprawled on the jewel-toned pile of the carpet, lay a mouse, undeniably dead.

"Please, Armand," Tori begged, too anguished to wonder what it was that so fascinated him. "Please, bring Grey!"

Quickly, Armand scooped up the mug and the
mouse and hurried out of the chamber.

It seemed an eternity before Grey arrived. Tori
lay huddled beneath the coverlet, frightened, in pain,
not knowing what was wrong. She squeezed her eyes
tight shut and clenched her teeth as another pain
contracted her stomach.

"Tori?" Grey knelt on the edge of the bed. Over
her moaned protests, he eased her onto her back. His
hand was warm on her clammy forehead. "Tori, can
you hear me?"

"Oh, Grey! It hurts! It hurts so much!"

"Where? In your head or only in your
stomach?"

"Only my stomach. But . . . oooooh!"

Grey ran a hand through his hair. "Have you
ever felt this way before?"

"No! Help me, Grey!"

"Tori, I don't know . . . Perhaps it was something you had for dinner. What did you eat?"

"I didn't eat dinner! All I had was a mug of
chocolate that the—the Duchesse!" Her arms
wrapped protectively about herself, and she shot an
accusing glare at Grey. "It was the Duchesse! After I
told her we couldn't stay, she put something in the
chocolate to make me sick!"

"Tori." Grey's tone was blatantly skeptical.

"It had to be, Grey! She wanted us to stay!"

"Tori . . ."

"Its all her fault! That . . . that . . ."

"Stop it, Tori! You're deluding yourself! Now,
calm down. It's probably the water here or some
feminine complaint."

"It's not a feminine complaint, damn you!" she
snarled. "Oh! Damn you to hell, Grey Verreaux!

242

Will you just once try to think with your brain and not with your—"

"Victoria!" The Duchesse swept into the room. Seeing Tori curled up in agony on the bed, she clucked sympathetically. "Oh, *pauvre petite.* Armand told me you were ill. Do you feel any better now?"

Tori, groaning, did not answer, so Grey did.

"She's no better, Gabrielle. Is there anything you can do for her?"

"She's done enough," Tori gasped.

Ignoring Tori, the Duchesse said, "I have sent to the village for my physician, Dr. Poussaint. He should be here soon."

"That's not necessary," Tori told her.

Gabrielle's smile was kindly, almost fond. "Nonsense, *chérie.* We cannot be too careful with your health, can we? It is better for *un médecin* to look at you, don't you agree, Grey?"

"I do, Tori," Grey told her.

"I'm sure you do," she hissed.

A tap at the door was followed by the appearance of Jean-Baptiste, Gabrielle's current favorite among her handsome young footmen.

"*Pardon, madame. Le médecin est arrivé.*"

"*Merci,* Jean-Baptiste. Please show him in."

The footman bowed and disappeared, to return a few moments later followed by a tall, handsome man of middle years whose thick, dark hair was tinged attractively at the temples with silver.

"Madame la Duchesse," he said, bowing formally to Gabrielle.

"Good morning, Doctor," Gabrielle said. "I am sorry to awaken you so early but this lady, Madame Duclaux, has taken ill. She assures me it is nothing, but she is in pain.''

"Pain is never nothing," the doctor said seriously. His dark eyes went to Tori, who lay curled on the bed. "Madame will permit an examination?"

Tori eyed the doctor suspiciously. The nearest village was some miles away. He seemed to have arrived awfully quickly. It was almost as if he'd been summoned beforehand—almost as if Gabrielle had sent for him knowing Tori was going to have need of him this morning. But of course, it was impossible for her to voice her suspicions to Grey—he would never believe anything against the Duchesse.

"Madame?" the doctor prompted.

"Tori," Grey said softly, forbidding her to refuse.

"Oh, very well," she snapped. "If you must!"

Gabrielle ushered Grey out of the room and Tori reluctantly submitted to Doctor Poussaint's poking and prodding and embarrassing questions.

"Are you certain, madame," he asked, "that you are not *enciente*?"

"*Encie*—?" Tori repeated, wishing she had complied with Christophe's wishes and learned to speak French properly. "Oh!" Realization dawned on her, and a crimson flush pinkened her cheeks. "No! I am not with child."

"Are you certain, madame?" he persisted.

"Yes, monsieur, I am absolutely certain."

"Well, then, I must presume the cause lies in something you have eaten."

"I haven't eaten anything since midday yesterday, Doctor. I did, however, drink a mug of hot chocolate last night just before I retired."

"Aha! Perhaps there was something amiss with the chocolate."

"That is what I thought, monsieur. The

Duchesse herself sent the chocolate and—"

"Oh! If Madame la Duchesse sent the chocolate, it must have been perfectly fine."

Tori rolled her eyes. Sainte Gabrielle could do no wrong! Did the woman have everyone under her spell? It seemed she had—at least all the men!

"What is your diagnosis, monsieur?" Tori asked impatiently.

"I must assume it is a complaint of the stomach, madame, since none of your other organs seem to be involved."

"And the cause, Doctor, since you insist it was not the Duchesse's chocolate?"

"I cannot know, madame," he replied, a touch of irritation in his voice. "For I cannot know what it is you have eaten in the past day or two. There are complaints that incubate within the system for days. The humors, you know . . ."

"Humors," Tori repeated disgustedly. My God! They could find the Duchesse in the act of plunging a knife into someone's back and find a way to excuse it! "I see. And what do you prescribe?"

"Bed-rest, I think. And a bland diet. But bed-rest is essential. For at least two days."

"Two days!"

"At least, madame. I will give to Madame la Duchesse instructions as to your diet. You must follow it *exactement*."

"But doctor!" Tori protested over the pains that were already easing. "I must get to Paris. Monsieur Verreaux and I were supposed to leave this morning."

"*Non, non, non*," the doctor protested. "That would be impossible. Two days, at least, in bed and then nothing strenuous for a few days afterward."

"But, doctor, I simply cannot . . ."

"Listen to me, madame, I am the expert. Now, I will go and tell the Duchesse my findings. Meanwhile, I will leave a sedative for you. If the pain persists, you should take it. It will put you to sleep until the pain eases."

"Whatever you say," Tori sighed, resigned, sensing that arguments would gain her nothing.

The doctor left and it was not long before Grey appeared.

"Doctor Poussaint said it is merely an irritation of the stomach, Tori," he told her, sitting on the edge of her bed.

"Doctor Poussaint is a quack," she told him sweetly.

"Tori—"

"Don't 'Tori' me, Grey!" she snapped. "The Duchesse could poison more people than Lucrezia Borgia, and the good doctor would say they all died of inflammation of the tonsils!"

"This is doing you no good, Tori. This is only aggravating your condi—"

"I don't have a condition! I'm telling you that all that is wrong with me is that the Duchesse wanted us—no, you!—to stay here."

He sighed. "I'm going to have some of Doctor Poussaint's sedative mixed for you."

"I don't want it! I won't take it!"

But he gave the order and it was brought to her by Armand on a platter. Though Tori raged and stormed, she finally swallowed the strangely sweet mixture and fell into a deep, sound sleep.

It was early evening by the time she awakened. The sun was lowering behind the thick, verdant forests that surrounded the château, setting the rich, green leaves aglow.

Tori groaned. The sedative had certainly made her sleep and the pain in her stomach was but an unpleasant memory, but her head ached abominably. There was nothing seriously wrong with her, she was certain, and the cure was all too clear—climbing into a coach and driving away from the château and the Duchesse and her toadying minions. If only she could get Grey's attention away from that woman long enough to show him the sense of their leaving. But that, given the amount of time they spent closeted together, seemed impossible.

The creaking of the door hinges seemed like the crack of thunder in the silent room. Tori looked up to find Grey peering around the half-open door.

"Come in," she said.

"I looked in on you earlier, but you were sound asleep," he told her, pulling a chair up to the bedside. "Do you feel any better?"

"The pains are gone," she told him. "But the sedative gave me the very devil of a headache."

"At least the pains are gone. I expect you'll be up and around within a day or two."

"I shall be perfectly all right in the morning," she assured him. "And I see no reason why we can't leave for Paris then."

"No."

"What did you say?"

"I said no. And I don't want any arguments. In fact, I have told Gabrielle that as long as we can't go to Paris, we will accompany her to the house party at the Marquis de Lurneaux's château."

"You told her what!" Tori screeched, pushing herself up against the pillows.

Grey despised the ruse he had to practice on her, but he was firmly convinced that it was for her own protection. Christophe had not reached the Duchesse, and Grey had to talk to the Marquis to try and discover if Christophe was known to have reached France at all. He was beginning to suspect that Randall Ramsey and his anti-Confederate associates in Europe had done their work all too efficiently. If so, there was all the more reason for secrecy. Their own lives might be in danger if Ramsey learned of their presence in France. Added to which, he could not tell her of his fears for Christophe's life until he had more evidence one way or the other.

"Now, Tori," he soothed, we can't go anywhere for a few days and by then it will be time for the party. Aren't you curious about—?"

"What I'm curious about is what my husband is doing in Paris!"

"Tori, Tori, settle down."

"Settle down! For God's sake, Grey, sleep with the woman and be done with it so we can leave this place!"

"That was uncalled for, Tori."

"But true! Now go away and leave me alone. My head aches."

Without another word, Grey rose and strode out of the room. Lying back against her pillows, Tori smiled. She had struck a nerve, she knew. That might be a small, petty victory, but it was a victory nonetheless.

She sighed. Well, it certainly looked as if they were going to be here for a few days and then become the guests of the Marquis de Lurneaux, whoever he was! There didn't seem to be much she could do about it, so she might as well make the most of it.

Propping herself comfortably against the pillows, she prepared herself to play the part of the pampered, petted invalid to the hilt.

25

The silence that reigned in the dining room at Stockton Hall was almost palpable. Edward Lytton's attempts at conversation failed to elicit any but the scantiest of responses from Monique. At last, unable to maintain the pretense of a normal evening, he suggested they go for a drive, hoping the cool, scented breezes of the Caribbean night would help relax Monique enough to make her confide in him.

Edward drew the carriage to a halt near the edge of a bluff overlooking the endless sea. The night sky was thick with clouds, but now and then the moon would appear, shining its silvery path along the black, sensuously undulating surface of the ocean.

Climbing down from the carriage, Edward reached up and drew Monique down beside him. Hand in hand, they walked to the very brink of the bluff, taking refuge in the swaying shade of a tall palm tree.

Pulling her into his arms, Edward kissed her, his lips at first gentle, then savage and demanding. Monique shivered in his arms. The moment was bittersweet, filled with the thrill of love and the sorrow of imminent parting.

Feeling the hesitation in her lips, the reluctance in her body, the way she held herself, refusing to hold him near as he longed to hold her, Edward sighed and loosed her from his apparently unwelcome embrace.

"Tell me," he begged, confused, almost frightened by the distance that had begun as a crack and seemed rapidly to be widening into a chasm between them. "Tell me what I've done, what has happened to drive you away from me."

"Nothing," Monique whispered. "You've done nothing. Except . . ."

Catching her breath, she turned away, fighting to retain what fragile control she maintained on her emotions.

"Except?" Edward prompted, desperate to know.

"Except to make me fall in love with you," she whispered.

More bewildered than ever, Edward stared out at the ocean. He couldn't begin to understand why she was drawing away from him. Because she loved him? That was hardly a reason to end any relationship, was it? People prayed for love, longed for it, died for it, but now they had found it together, she seemed despondent.

"I don't understand," he told her honestly. "I love you, Monique. You tell me you have fallen in love with me also, yet I sense that I'm losing you. Tell me why."

"I . . . it is only that . . . it is because . . ."

Monique closed her eyes, despairing of ever finding the words to tell him her secret. If she didn't, she felt sure, Dorothée Arnault would, out of spite and hatred. It wasn't fair to Edward to keep her secret only to have him enlightened one day by a bitter, evil old woman who wanted only to have her petty vengeance on her dead husband's love child. On the other hand, was it fair to Edward, a white man, a member of the landed gentry, to continue their romance—a romance that would be anathema to his family, his friends, perhaps even to Edward himself? They had never discussed such matters. For Edward, the slaves who labored in the fields of Woodbridge were a matter for his overseer. He himself saw few of them, saving those who kept his house. And even they seemed to regard him as a being set apart. How he truly felt about them, she didn't know. If he regarded them as people—and she knew that many landowners did not—he never said so.

How would he feel about her—a quadroon—a woman whose ancestors had labored in the fields of great Southern plantations? That there was no future for her as mistress of Woodbridge she had accepted from the outset. But would he even be willing to keep her as his mistress? Would he keep her near him in silken concubinage, as so many of her sisters had been kept? If that was what he offered, she would accept it. She could bear any indignity if it meant being near him. What she couldn't bear—and what she feared the most—was losing him. The thought of watching the tenderness in his eyes turning to repulsion sickened her, terrified her. At that moment, as never before in her life, she would have sold her soul to be one of the high-nosed, pampered

Sandra DuBay

daughters of some lily-white English planter.

"Because?" Edward prompted.

"Because I am not what I seem to be," she managed at last, her voice scarcely audible over the whispering of the wind in the trees and the pounding of the waves on the beach not so far below them.

"What do you mean?" he pressed. "Please, Monique, this is driving me mad. You must tell me. There is nothing—nothing!—you could tell me that would be worse than this suspense, this worry. You're putting me through a hell I can't bear any longer!"

"Please, Edward, I'm trying. It's only that it's very hard for me. . . . I am frightened."

"Of what?"

"Of your hating me!" The words were a wail of sheer anguish erupting from her breast.

"Hating you?" He was astonished, utterly stupefied. "How could I ever hate you? I love you! And I thought you loved me."

"I do. No matter what, you must believe that always. Always!" She shook her head mournfully. "But I shouldn't. You shouldn't. I must tell you . . ."

Edward sighed. "Is that all there is to this? Are you hiding some shameful secret?" He looked out toward the ocean and so missed the look of utter horror that flickered across her beautiful face. "Some lover in your past? Is that it?"

He was not taking her seriously, Monique realized. How could she make him understand? How could she tell him? Should she simply blurt out the truth and let him make of it what he liked? That would be cruel. But this—this was torture for them both. And to what end? If she left Edward and Jamaica, who was to say Dorothée Arnault would

254

not pursue her, haunt her, dog her footsteps, not satisfied until the daughter of her hated one-time rival had been ruined.

A sudden determination welled in her. She did not doubt for a moment that Dorothée Arnault would expose her secret in the end. She was too filled with malice to let such a golden opportunity pass by. Monique's love affair with Edward Lytton was doomed, she was convinced, but that was no reason not to savor the precious last moments like the last sweet drops of vintage wine. Later, after Madame Arnault had done her wicked work, Monique would have these gilded days to look back on—these magical nights to remember when she loved and was loved as an equal.

A flash that lit the sky took them by surprise. The rumble that followed was a warning neither could ignore.

"Come on, we'd better go back to Stockton Hall before this storm breaks. I've had enough to contend with without pneumonia."

"Edward," Monique murmured as he helped her back into the carriage, "take me to Woodbridge."

He glanced at her in surprise. "Woodbridge? But why?"

"I want to be with you, Edward. I want you to keep me with you tonight. Will you do that? Do you love me enough to do that?"

They kissed and even as the first chilling drops of rain splashed against the shining black carriage, Edward turned the horses in the direction of Woodbridge.

Monique leaned against him, savoring his strength, his warmth, his love. Tonight they would lie in the great master's chamber of Woodbridge together—one. For tonight—and for as many nights as she had left, a melancholy voice whispered from the depths of her heart—she would be mistress of Edward's heart, the object of his love. For him—for now—she would be the perfect lover, and no vicious, loathsome old woman would stand between them and use her hatred like a razor-sharp sword to cleave them in two.

26

The only nice thing Tori could say about taking the trip to the Château de Lurneaux was that the Duchesse's coach was far more comfortable than the one Grey had hired to bring them to the Château de Saint-Rémy. For the rest, she had not yet forgiven Gabrielle for what she would always believe—Grey's skepticism notwithstanding—had been an underhanded ruse to keep them there long enough to go to the Marquis de Lurneaux's house party.

"How long will this party last?" Tori asked the Duchesse, who was busily perusing her coiffure in a mirror held by her maid.

"Now, now, *chérie*," the Duchesse said soothingly, waving the mirror away with an imperious sweep of her hand. "We have not even arrived. Do not speak yet of leaving."

Tori cast an angry glare toward Grey, but he

only smiled benignly, in the manner of a kindly uncle bestowing a well-meant, if unappreciated, gift upon a favorite child.

"Relax, Tori," he said brightly. "Enjoy yourself. Give yourself a chance to recover. Paris—and Christophe—will wait for you."

Tori said nothing, knowing that arguments were useless. She would go to the Marquis's house party, since it seemed she had no choice in the matter, but if, when the party had ended, Grey showed no inclination to leave the board—and no doubt the bed—she thought jealously—of the Duchesse de Saint-Rémy, she would find her own way to Paris.

"There it is!" the Duchesse exclaimed as they emerged from the thick cover of a lush forest, "the Château de Lurneaux."

Tori peered out the window. Looming up in front of them was a fortress, the gray stone walls rising like cliffs. There was nothing here of the kind of fairy-tale castle that had so enchanted her on her first glimpse of the Château de Saint-Rémy. The Château de Lurneaux had been built for defense in the dark, feudal days of centuries before. Oh, the grounds were beautiful. After the Revolution, during which the radicals of the nearby village laid seige to the château but failed to force the Marquis into submission, the lord of the château had called in master landscapers who turned the park surrounding the château into a wonderland of temples and meadows, grottoes and bowers.

The carriage rolled beneath the deadly spikes of the raised portcullis and into an ivy-walled courtyard. Unlike the exterior of the château, where only tall, narrow slits pierced the massive walls, the courtyard was lined with leaded mullioned windows, some with intricate stained glass renderings of coatsof-arms of the Marquises de Lurneaux and their wives over the generations.

Several coaches and carriages stood in the courtyard, which swarmed with footmen in orange-and-black livery. The guests, the cream of Paris society, had already disappeared into the château where refreshments and entertainments awaited them.

As they reached the door it opened as if by magic. A footman—not sufficiently attractive to find employment at the Château de Saint-Rémy, Tori reflected—made them a low, courtly bow.

"Madame la Duchesse," he said.

"My guests, Madame Victoria Duclaux and Monsieur Greyson Verreaux," she informed him grandly.

With another bow, the footman led them into the great hall where the Marquis and his guests were assembled, then departed to see that their rooms were ready for them.

With the air of a queen, Gabrielle swept through the great room. From everywhere came greetings, coos of sympathy, sly invitations, compliments—some, it seemed to Tori, couched in terms that rendered the saccarine words almost insulting.

Drawn along in Gabrielle's wake, Tori found herself inundated with introductions to Comtes, Comtesses, Marquis, Marquises, Ducs, Duchesses, even a Prince or two. It seemed strange that, in a country which had been torn apart less than a century before by Revolution, a nation that had sent its king and the most famous queen in all its history—Marie Antoinette—to the guillotine, the aristocracy had reinstated itself with remarkable success. It was hard to imagine that all this blue-blooded decadence was ruled over by Bonaparte, Napoleon III, nephew of the general who had led France out from under the ruling fist of the Bourbon dynasty.

Her head nearly whirling with the flood of new sights and sounds, new faces and names, it was a moment before Tori realized that she had become separated from Gabrielle and Grey in the press of people. She looked around, but there was little she could see. The room seemed packed to the walls with people and their bodies blocked her view.

"Madame?" a velvety voice said from beside her. "Is something wrong?"

Turning, Tori found herself looking into a pair of eyes the color of mahogany. Glossy brown hair brushed into silken waves gave way to long side whiskers and a neatly trimmed moustache above a pair of full, sensual lips.

"I seem to have misplaced my companions," she confessed, feeling foolish.

"Ah, well, never mind. They will, no doubt, come looking for you. In any case, we will all be here for two days. Sooner or later you will come across them. In the meantime, permit me to introduce myself—I am Marc-François, Chevalier d'Archambeault."

"I am Victoria Duclaux."

"And was the tall, dark gentleman with you Monsieur Duclaux?"

"No. He is Monsieur Verreaux. He is taking me to Paris to join my husband." She sighed. "At least he is supposed to take me to Paris. We do not seem to be making much progress toward that city."

Taking two glasses of champagne from a passing footman, the chevalier led Tori to a brocade-cushioned bench near the wall.

"As it happens, madame, I myself am soon

returning to Paris. If your friend does not seem amenable to departing, I should be delighted for your company on the journey.''

"That is very kind of you, sir . . .''

"Now . . .'' He held up a cautioning finger. "Marc-François.''

She smiled, nodding her agreement. "Marc-François.''

And I may call you . . ?''

"Victoria,'' she supplied.

"*Enchanté*, Victoria.''

Taking her gloved fingers into his hand, he lifted them to his lips. His dark eyes caressed her face as his lips caressed her fingers. It was Tori's first experience with the charm of a practiced courtier and she could not help being enthralled by him.

Over Marc-François's bowed head, she saw Grey through a parting in the crowd. Standing apart from the rest of the throng, his silvery eyes skimmed the assembly as if searching for someone. Then, at the same moment that she saw him, he saw her. His eyes narrowed dangerously.

Abandoning his champagne glass to a footman, he started toward them, his eyes never leaving her, as if afraid that to glance away would be to lose her.

"Tori,'' he said, standing over them like an angry guardian confronting his strayed ward. "I wondered where you'd run off to.''

"Run off?'' Tori said. "I assure you, Monsieur Verreaux, I did not run off. We were separated in the crowd and Marc-François was kind enough—''

Grey's eyes shifted to Tori's companion. "Marc-François? I was not aware that you had acquaintances in France, Victoria.''

Tori's eyes glinted. Smiling sweetly at the Chevalier d'Archambeault, she said: "Marc-

François, would you excuse us for a moment?"

"But of course, Victoria. Will I see you again later? I am told there is to be an exhibition in the north meadow in an hour. May I escort you?"

"I should like that," she agreed, cheeks pinkened prettily.

The chevalier bowed. Taking Tori's hand, he brought it to his lips once again. "Until then."

As his handsome form disappeared into the crowd, Grey took her arm and steered her into an anteroom off the Great Hall.

"What is the meaning of this?" he demanded.

"I don't know what you're talking about. I was left by myself while you went off with the Duchesse. Marc-François kept me company and—"

"Did he try to arrange an assignation?"

"Grey! What are you saying? The Chevalier d'Archambeault behaved like a perfect gentleman."

"Grow up, Tori. The object of these house parties is to allow husbands and wives the opportunity for discreet adultery."

"Well, you need not disparage a gentleman simply because some people abuse—"

"Grey?" From behind him, a silken voice caressed his name. "Here you are, you wicked thing. No sooner are we introduced than you disappear from sight. Are you hiding from me?"

Grey swung around and Tori saw the owner of the voice. She was petite, slightly built, with a doll-like face surmounted by a mass of golden curls. Her long lashes fluttered as she gazed up at Grey with unabashed invitation.

"Mademoiselle Sayce," he said. "Certainly I was not hiding. I was merely speaking to Madame Duclaux."

"Madame . . ." The woman's pale blue eyes

shifted to Tori. The smile faded from her eyes while she carefully maintained the sweet curving of her lips.

"Mademoiselle," Tori said, her eyes demanding an explanation of Grey.

None was immediately forthcoming and then it was too late, for the tall, commanding figure of their host was suddenly nearby.

"Carlotta, *chérie*," he was saying, his hand caressing her neck with shocking familiarity. "Would you like to go to the stables and choose your"—his eyes twinkled roguishly—"mount? Or do you trust me to choose for you?"

"I trust you completely, *mon coeur*," she cooed.

Tori glanced up at Grey, wondering what he would think of the woman's being so sweet to him one moment and so seductive to the Marquis the next. To her surprise, he seemed to care not at all.

"*Bon*." Lifting her hand, the Marquis gently nipped her fingers. "In half an hour, then."

With a curtsy to the Marquis, she left them and disappeared through the doorway and up the stairs.

"Are you looking forward to the exhibition, monsieur?" the Marquis asked Grey.

"It promises to be fascinating," Grey replied.

"And you, Madame Duclaux?"

"I had not heard, Monsieur le Marquis. What sort of exhibition is this to be?"

The Marquis gazed at her for a long moment, his dark eyes, set in the seamed face of a jaded sensualist, searching for something he seemed not to believe might actually be there. At last he said, more to Grey than to her:

"Perhaps Madame would find our little entertainment not to her liking. It might be better for her to take the opportunity to rest in her rooms."

With a bow to Grey and a kiss for Tori's hands, the debonair Marquis left them.

"What was that all about?" she demanded. "Who is Carlotta Sayce and what is this exhibition?"

"Carlotta Sayce is a courtesan, Tori. A 'grand horizontal' as they are called."

"A whore?" Tori breathed. "The Marquis welcomes her into his house?"

"The grand horizontals are not mere whores, Tori, they are a group apart. They cater only to the rich, the nobility. Many become wealthy women in their own right."

"And what is this exhibition I am not supposed to attend?"

"The Marquis has come across several antique prints depicting an Indian Rajah and his concubine making love on horseback. This afternoon, Carlotta Sayce and the Comte de Bertin will attempt to duplicate the prints."

"They will make love? On a horse? In front of everyone?"

Grey smiled at her obvious shock. "I think the Marquis was correct, Tori. It would be better if you stayed in your room."

"Perhaps," she agreed. Another thought occurred to her. "Grey? We are leaving for Paris as soon as this party is over, aren't we? Promise me."

"Unless the weather is bad," he hedged, wanting more time to talk to the Marquis—to learn his opinion about the mysterious disappearance of Christophe Duclaux.

"The weather!" Her eyes narrowed with anger. "I warn you, Grey—the Chevalier d'Archambeault has offered to take me to Paris. If you do not take me, I will go with him!"

Before Grey could object, a footman passed through the room announcing that the Marquis invited them all out to the north meadow. As the room began to empty, Tori asked a footman to show her to her room.

By the time she reached her chamber, she wanted nothing more than to lie down. But a footman appeared before she had even closed the door. On a silver salver, he held a note.

Tori took it and thanked him. Closing the door, she opened the letter and read:

> 'It is urgent that I see you privately. I have information concerning the whereabouts of your husband. Please come, alone, to Cupid's Grotto.
>
> Niccolò da l'Armi'

Niccolò! He was here! And he had information about Christophe! She had to go.

Slipping the note into her pocket, she left her room and asked a servant for directions to Cupid's Grotto.

Once out of the château, she followed a flagstone path into the picturesquely tangled gardens to the south of the castle. From the opposite side of the massive château, she heard the faint sound of applause and wondered what complicated maneuver the Comte and Carlotta had accomplished.

She was deep in the forest and beginning to wonder if she had been mistaken in her wanderings, when she saw Niccolò standing in the shadows of a man-made grotto whose walls were decorated with cherubs and hearts.

"Niccolò!" she cried, taking the hand he

offered and stepping carefully over the rough stone steps. "Tell me quickly! Where is Christophe! How is he!"

The Count said nothing but only gazed at her, his expression a curious mixture of affection and regret. He was still gazing at her when the blow fell from behind and darkness enveloped her.

27

Tori awoke and immediately wished she hadn't. Her head ached with such ferocity that she could not move, could barely think, could not bear to open her eyes for fear some movement in the room would set her senses to reeling.

"Signora?" A timid voice sounded like thunder in Tori's aching head. "Signora?"

Tori ventured a one-eyed glance. Even with the white, cut-velvet draperies drawn at the window, the brilliant scarlet of the walls hurt her eyes. "Where am I?" she demanded.

"*Mi scusi*, Signora," the maid said, turning to leave.

"Wait!" Tori called, the sound of her own voice agonizing in her ears. "Come back. Please tell me—"

But the maid had gone and Tori lay back against

the pillows, exhausted by the effort. She flung one
arm across her aching head, wishing that something,
anything, would put her out of her misery.

The door creaked as it opened. Footsteps, like
the thudding of a giant fist, crossed the floor. Tori
groaned, expecting to hear the incomprehensible
Italian of the maid once more. Instead, an all-too-
familiar voice said softly:

"*Buon giorno*, Victoria."

Niccolò! Through the aching pain in her head,
Tori was aware of a blossoming of hatred inside her.
He had tricked her! Lied to her! Lured her into the
dangerous isolation of the grotto only to steal her
away to this place—whatever and wherever it was.

"Victoria?" Niccolò repeated. "I know you are
awake. Isabella, the maid, said you were."

"Go away, Niccolò," she hissed through gritted
teeth. "Leave me alone. Can't you see that I am ill?"

"Ah, poor sweet. Your head is aching, I
imagine. Damn that Luca! I told him to be careful."

"Where am I, Niccolò? What is this place? Your
home?"

"Oh, no. This is the home of a very important
man. We are not far outside Paris."

"Paris!" She struggled to sit up but fell back
with a groan. "Why did you have to hurt me this
way, Niccolò?" she breathed.

"It was regrettable, *cara*," he said, a genuine
note of remorse in his deep, accented voice.

"Then why?" she persisted.

"There was no other way to get you away from
your watchdog—Grey Verreaux."

"You lied to me, Niccolò! You said in your note
that you had information about Christophe!"

"I have," he replied simply.

"Then tell me! Tell me now!"

"I will tell you," he promised. "When the time is right. And only if you cooperate with us."

"Cooperate in what way? And who is 'us'?"

"Later, *cara*, later. In time all will be revealed. First, I will send Isabella back to you. She will help you bathe and dress and she will bring a powder for your headache."

"But I want to talk about—"

"After you are dressed, we will talk."

Isabella returned. A stout, no-nonsense woman of middle years, she spoke no English—which, Tori suspected, was why she had been chosen to serve her—but went about the business of bathing and dressing Tori in a steady, dogged way that brooked no interference.

The gown into which Tori was buttoned was of deep wine silk elaborately flounced and embroidered with gold thread. It was far more ornate than any gown Tori would have chosen for herself, and the color was not one she could ever remember having worn. But it shone with a dark iridescence and, to her surprise, it seemed to flatter her fairness. Isabella, despite her stoic silence, proved a capable maid—talented, even—particularly when it came to dressing Tori's hair in the intricate cascade of curls so much the fashion.

Isabelle left, leaving Tori standing alone in the center of the beautiful crimson room. In a few moments, however, she had returned, a glass of cloudy water in her hand.

Handing it to Tori, she mimicked a person drinking. Tori looked from the glass to the maid with suspicion. She remembered all too clearly the mug of chocolate at the Château de Saint-Rémy and the bogus note that had lured her into the grotto and Niccolò's clutches.

"You can drink it, Victoria," Niccolò said from the doorway. "There is nothing in it but a headache powder. I'll drink some first, if you insist."

Resigned, Tori took the glass. Even if there was something in the water to render her unconscious, at least she would have respite from the pounding in her head.

Niccolò beamed as she emptied the glass and handed it back to the maid. He complimented her on her toilette, thanked Isabella, pressing a gold coin in her hand, and led Tori from the room.

Together they walked down the long, darkly paneled corridor. It was flooded with the sunlight that shone through a tall window at the far end. The beveled panes of the window sparkled like diamonds, and Tori squinted in their brilliance.

"This way," Niccolò directed as they reached the head of a winding mahogany staircase.

Lifting her skirts, Tori followed him down the stairs and across a parquet-floored foyer. They passed through a room walled in azure, trimmed with gold, and furnished in the ornate, delicate style of Louis XV.

"Where are we going?" Tori demanded. "Whose house is this?"

But Niccolò did not answer—they had reached their destination.

"Come in," a voice called in answer to Niccolò's knock.

Entering the room, Tori saw a large man in black seated in an ornately carved Flemish armchair of solid oak. His eyes were scarcely visible, shadowed as they were by thick heavy brows and round, reddened cheeks. His hair was nearly grey, although streaks of black showed that he had once been as dark as Niccolò.

With one fleshy hand, he motioned them forward. His dark eyes skimmed over Tori appraisingly. Thick lips curved into a smile revealing startlingly white, perfectly even teeth.

"Well, Count, she is indeed as lovely as you told me. I will admit that I was skeptical." He shifted his eyes to Tori. "Madame Duclaux. I am Gianfrancesco Quaratesi. Please, sit down. Make yourself comfortable."

"Why was I brought here against my will, Signor Quaratesi?" she demanded. "You realize that there will be a search for me. Inquiries will be made."

"It is to be hoped that a scandal can be avoided. All that is desired of you, Signora, is information and, perhaps, your help in a small matter."

Tori took the chair Niccolò held out for her and regarded her host curiously. "You may ask me anything, Signor. But I warn you that I know nothing that could possibly be of use to you."

"We shall see," Quaratesi replied.

"Niccolò said you have news of Christophe—of my husband."

"'I have had word of him, *è vero*," the man admitted. "But first, I must ask you several questions."

Exasperated, Tori leaned back in her chair. "Ask whatever you like."

Quaratesi smiled and Tori felt as if she were eye-to-eye with a cobra. "Tell me, Signora, why did your husband depart from New Orleans for France?"

Tori recalled what little Grey had told her of Christophe's mysterious 'mission' to Paris. These men must be in league with Washington somehow. They must be working against the Confederacy— against Christophe.

271

"He did not leave for France, monsieur, he left for Jamaica where we own a sugar plantation."

"Nevertheless, he continued to France, did he not?"

There was little point in lying—it was obvious they knew Christophe's destination.

"He did," she admitted. "What Creole does not long to see Paris? It is a part of their collective ancestry."

Quaratesi's stare was calculating. Tori could feel his skepticism and knew he believed not a word of her facile lie.

"And Monsieur Verreaux, madame? What is his part in all this?"

"He was hired by my husband to take him to Jamaica, monsieur. And he was hired to bring me to join my husband here, in France."

"Come now, madame. A successful blockade-runner such as Greyson Verreaux does not abandon his lucrative trade to turn passenger carrier."

"My husband made it well worth his while, monsieur. And so, I might add, did the Count da l'Armi who paid an exorbitant amount to be brought to France."

"And if, as you say, you are here to join your husband, why are you dallying at the Château de Saint-Rémy and the Château de Lurneaux?"

Tori lifted one slim shoulder. Her unease was growing, for it was obvious that they knew far more what was going on than she did. She felt as if she were walking a tightrope over a deep, black pit fraught with unknown terrors.

"The Duchesse de Saint-Rémy is a cousin of Monsieur Verreaux and he suggested we break our journey there. I became ill while at the château, and the visit to the Marquis de Lurneaux's château was a part of my convalescence."

The glance exchanged between Quaratesi and Niccolò did not go unnoticed by Tori, who tried, but failed, to decipher their looks.

"Either you are the most innocent, or the most foolish woman I have ever met, madame," Quaratesi said at last. "I prefer to believe it is one or the other because if you are simply lying, you are doing a very poor job of it."

Lifting her chin, Tori rose and glared down at him imperiously. "If you are finished insulting me, Monsieur Quaratesi, I would appreciate being allowed to leave this place and continue on my way to—"

"Not just yet, Signora," Quaratesi said. He held up a hand as if to stay the bitter disappointment that clouded her face. "But soon . . . soon."

"But I have told you what I know! I have answered your questions! If you have my husband, you must take me to him. Please!"

"Patience, Signora. Enjoy the hospitality of my home for a short while. I promise you that you will be with your husband soon enough."

There was something in his voice, something in the feral gleam of his black eyes, that sent shivers down Tori's spine—something that told her that his promise was not one to be thankful for.

Quaratesi dismissed them with a wave of one meaty hand, and Niccolò ushered her out. As they passed along a loggia that opened onto a small, exquisite garden, Tori noticed a man moving among the blossoms, a cheroot hanging loosely between his fingers.

"Randall Ramsey!" she breathed, recognizing him from the Opera in New Orleans and remembering what Grey had told her about the Union spy to whom she had inadvertently revealed Christophe's movements.

"What was that, *cara*?" Niccolò asked. His dark eyes darted to the man in the garden, then back to her pale face. "Do you know that gentleman?" he asked.

Tori could hear the tension in his tone and knew that this was yet another treacherous step in her dangerous path. "Oh, no," she assured him. "He did look familiar, but I suppose it is only that he reminds me of someone Christophe knew in New Orleans." She cast Niccolò a dazzling smile. "Is he Italian?"

"I don't believe so." Niccolò said no more, but it seemed to Tori that his dark eyes searched her face with more than their usual intensity. What was more disquieting was the glimmer of pity—almost of remorse—that she thought she saw in their fathomless onyx depths.

28

Having managed to elude Gabrielle following the
exhibition in the meadow, Grey mounted the worn
stone steps to the top of the southwestern tower of
the Château de Lurneaux. Petit, the Marquis's
steward, had directed him to Tori's room and he
wondered if she had calmed down since their little
talk downstairs.

Arriving at her door, he rapped at the rough,
iron-banded planks. Footsteps sounded on the flagstone floor then the door swung open.

"Tor—" Grey began.

"Monsieur?" One of the Marquis's maid-
servants stood there eyeing him curiously.

"Where is Madame Duclaux?" Grey demanded,
looking over the maid's head into the obviously
empty room.

"I do not know, monsieur. I was sent by

Monsieur Petit to tidy this room.''

Casting another bewildered glance into the deserted chamber, Grey retraced his steps and searched out the steward once more.

''Pardon me,'' he said, feeling ever so slightly foolish, ''would you direct me to the chamber of the Chevalier d' Archambeault?''

''His chamber is located on the second floor of the northwest tower, monsieur. Any footman in that tower can direct you.''

''*Merci*, monsieur.''

Grey turned to leave. Behind him, a footman stepped up and whispered into the dapper, whippet-thin Petit's ear.

''*Pardonnez-moi*, Monsieur Verreaux?''

Grey looked back at him. ''Yes?''

''I am reminded, monsieur, that the Chevalier d'Archambeault is no longer in his room.''

''He has moved to another?''

''He has left the château. Apparently, he was called back to duty in Paris unexpectedly.''

''I see.'' A sudden anxiety gripped Grey. ''Would you know if Madame Duclaux left with him?''

''I am sorry, monsieur, I did not see either the lady or the gentleman leave the château, although they did, apparently, depart at approximately the same time.''

Dumbfounded, Grey could only shake his head and walk away. Left! She had left! He remembered her threats downstairs, remembered that she had told him the handsome young Chevalier d'Archambeault had offered to take her to Paris with him. Had he come to her room while the rest of the assembly was off watching the Comte and Carlotta disport themselves on horseback? Had he told her he'd been called back to his duties at the court in Paris and convinced her to accompany him rather than waiting to see if Grey really ment to take her himself? And where was she now? Had the Chevalier also convinced her to partake of his hospitality once they had reached Paris?

His first reaction of stunned amazement passed, giving way to a hot anger that had its beginnings in jealousy and disappointment. That she was alone, somewhere between the château and Paris, with a handsome young officer who was obviously attracted to her and to whom it seemed she was attracted . . .

"Damn her!" he hissed beneath his breath. "Why the hell couldn't she wait! Doesn't she understand the danger? Can't she . . ." But a niggling voice in his mind reminded him that he had sought to protect her from danger and worry by telling her almost nothing of her husband's mission to Paris or his apparent disappearance. How could she know that there could be others out there—desperate, ruthless men—who might think it wise to eliminate not only Monsieur Duclaux but also his wife, thereby reducing the risk of her asking too many inconvenient questions?

"Monsieur Verreaux?"

Grey looked up and found the Marquis de Lurneaux standing beside him. "Monsieur?"

"Disturbing news, monsieur. May we retire to the privacy of your chamber?"

Together the two men went to Grey's room. As he swung the door wide, Grey found that his chamber was already occupied.

"Good evening, Grey."

Sprawled on the bed, naked as she had been in the meadow hours before, was Carlotta Sayce.

Smiling, Grey stepped aside and allowed the

Marquis into the room. Carlotta's smile never wavered.

"Ah, *mon cher,*" she cooed at the Marquis, "will you not come and join us?"

"I am sorry, monsieur," the Marquis apologized. "I did not realize you had an assignation."

"I did not," Grey assured him. He smiled charmingly at Carlotta. "Mademoiselle, I am honored by your attention, but the Marquis and I have important matters to discuss."

For once, the pale, beautiful courtesan was at a loss. "You mean," she murmured, "that you wish me to leave?"

"That is what I mean," he confirmed.

"Please, monsieur," the Marquis asked, "do not inconvenience yourself on my account. I can return—"

Although he did not wish to examine his feelings too closely, Grey found himself devoid of desire for the admittedly lovely woman. She was not—damn her eyes!—Tori, and it was only Tori who filled his days and nights with longing.

"It is no inconvenience, Marquis," Grey replied. "If you will excuse us, mademoiselle."

Unaccustomed to rejection, Carlotta pulled a rustling silk robe about herself and flounced out of the room. Left alone, Grey and the Marquis laughed, then, sobering, sat down to discuss the Marquis's 'disturbing news.'

In Paris, at the Hôtel Quaratesi, Tori stood in the shadowy library of the townhouse gazing out through the mullioned windows toward the Seine at the end of the gardens. She had come to the library to try and find something to take her mind off

Christophe and the possible reasons for her imprisonment here, but she knew it was useless. Somehow Niccolò and Quaratesi and who knew who else were involved with Randall Ramsey. And Randall Ramsey, so Grey had said, had been sent from Washington to try to stop Christophe from reaching Paris and the French emperor.

Sinking onto the cushions of the window-seat, she laid her head in her hands. It was all so fantastic. One day she was the demure, sheltered wife of a simple Creole gentleman, the next she was the prisoner of spies and secret agents determined to alter the politics of nations. And to think Clairesse Candé had taken her to task because of the uneventful life she led! It would have been laughable had it not been that she knew the men involved were ruthless, cold-blooded, and capable of violence to insure the success of their schemes.

And they had Christophe. Where was he? What were they doing to him? What had they done? Could they have . . . ?

But no! Resolutely, she rose and left the library. She would not allow her mind to wander in such morbid directions. She would find Christophe, and together they would return to New Orleans. The war would seem positively tame after this! And she would love him, and take care of him, and be a good wife. And she would never be unfaithful—why did Grey's image dance in her mind at the thought of being unfaithful to Christophe?—and she would—

"Oh!" Isabella, the maid who had dressed her, started as Tori swung open the door to her room.

"It is only I," Tori told her. "I came up to—" She stopped, astonished, when she noticed what it was the maid was doing. "Those are my things! That is my trunk from the Château de Lurneaux!"

279

Isabella gazed at her uncomprehendingly. "*Mi scusi*, signora. *Non capisco.*"

"No, no. I know you don't understand English. I'm sorry. It is only that . . ."

"*Mi scusi*, signora?"

Frustrated, Tori shook her head. "Never mind, Isabella. Go on with what you were doing."

"*Mi scusi?*"

With a wave of her hand, Tori indicated the trunk, and Isabella went back to her unpacking, leaving Tori to ponder yet another mystery.

Below, in the salon to which Niccolò had conducted her to meet Signor Quaratesi, the Count faced his host and Randall Ramsey. His swarthy face was mottled with anger.

"You cannot do this!" Niccolò hissed, his clenched fists resting on the polished surface of the mahogany table.

"It is regrettable," Ramsey admitted, his handsome, sharply planed face showing not the slightest hint of remorse. "But I do believe it is necessary."

"No!" Niccolò argued. "Her husband is dead! The papers are at the bottom of the sea with him. It is Verreaux who is the danger to us, not Victoria!"

"Agreed," Ramsey said, bored with arguing. "It is Verreaux who is asking all the questions. But how do we know if he has told Madame Duclaux anything? Perhaps her husband told her before he left—"

"She knows nothing!"

"She will suspect something when Verreaux dies. She will hardly think the two deaths a coincidence, will she?" He waved a weary hand. "Why did you simply not kill them both in Jamaica, or at least at the Château de Lurneaux?''

"There were too many others around," Niccolò defended himself lamely. "I thought to lure Verreaux here where—"

"Luca told me you left no clues as to your destination. How was Verreaux to find you?" Quaratesi's black eyes bore mercilessly into Niccolò. "No, you hoped to keep the little Duclaux for yourself. You have a *tendresse* for her. That is a dangerous weakness for a man in your position, my friend."

"Verreaux will come to Paris looking for her," Niccolò insisted. "When he does, he will be killed. All I want is to be allowed to take Victoria home with me to Ital—"

"It is not enough," Ramsey interrupted. "They must all be killed. Your Madame Duclaux, even if she does not know the details of the Confederate offer, knows enough to get me hanged should I be captured in Confederate territory. And I am sorry, Count, but I do not intend to hang for the sake of your romantic tendencies." He looked at Quaratesi. "I must return to Washington. But first I must have your assurances that this matter will be dealt with to our satisfaction."

Quaratesi nodded his assurance, and Ramsey took his leave with no word of farewell for Niccolò. As the door closed behind the American, Niccolò sank into a chair opposite his countryman.

"Once Verreaux is dead," he persisted, "we will be perfectly safe. If we send false documents purporting to be a refusal from the Emperor of the offer, they will believe there is no help available from the French and they will abandon their plans. There will be no need for Victoria—"

Quaratesi shook his head. "I am sorry, my

friend, but there is too much at stake. She has nothing to lose if we are betrayed. Her husband is already dead. Her cooperation—even simply her silence—will gain her nothing. If she were to reach the Emperor's ear, nothing—not even the influence of the Emperor's mistress, our countrywoman the Countess Castiglione—will save either of us.''

''But if she can be convinced not to betray us?'' Niccolò persisted. ''If a way can be found to make her wish to protect us?''

Gianfrancesco Quaratesi sighed, leaning back in his great chair. ''My dear Count—my friend—again and again I warn you against involving your heart in your work. You desire this beautiful little American.'' He smiled as Niccolò averted his eyes guiltily. ''No, I see you don't deny it. Alas, there is nothing I can do. Enjoy her now, my friend, for she will not protect us once she discovers she is a widow instead of a wife. And because she will not be loyal to us''—he shrugged—''she must die.''

''I will not kill her,'' Niccolò vowed grimly. ''Mine will not be the hand that does it.''

Quaratesi held up a broad, beringed hand. ''I would not ask so much of you, my friend. It will be done quickly and as painlessly as possible. But when the time comes, you must allow it. Search your heart—you know it is necessary.''

Leaving the room, Niccolò wandered through the grand chambers and corridors of the hôtel, his thoughts racing, turning over scheme after scheme to keep Tori safe. He could tell her that Christophe was dead and hope that, in her grief, she would turn to him and agree to keep their secret, but he feared that instead she would simply refuse to help them and loathe him as the instrument of her husband's death.

But there had to be a way! If she felt any loyalty

282

to him—if there was some tie that bound them to
each other, that would prompt her to want to protect
him from Imperial retribution—but what? How?
What could he do?

Without realizing it, he had mounted the stairs
and gone to Tori's door. It opened and Isabella
appeared.

"Isabella, is the Signora inside?" he asked in the
maid's native Italian.

"She is," the maid affirmed. "She is confused.
She does not understand something."

Niccolò nodded, dismissing the woman. There
are a great many things she does not understand, he
reflected as he knocked on Tori's door. And for the
present, she is better off not knowing.

"Come in," Tori called from within the room.

Niccolò entered. Tori sat in a chair near the
window, her hands folded in her lap.

"Good evening, Victoria," he said. "Isabella
said you seemed confused by something."

"I came in and found her unpacking my trunk
from the Château de Lurneaux. How did it get
here?"

Sighing, Tori rose and went to the window.
Unlike the library window, her bedchamber windows
overlooked the interior, enclosed courtyard around
which tall stone walls rose. She could see nothing of
the beautiful city that surrounded her.

"Niccolò," she said quietly, her back to him. "I
don't understand why I was brought here and why
I'm being kept here. I have told Signor Quaratesi that
I can tell him nothing. I don't understand why I
should be forced to comply with his schemes when
they do not involve me." She swung toward him and
regarded him with wide, pleading eyes. "Take me
away from here, Niccolò. Take me to Christophe."

He spread his hands helplessly. "I cannot. If I could, you know I would."

"Oh, Niccolò!" With an anguished cry, she swept across the room and into his arms. "I'm frightened! I don't know what is happening!"

Niccolò's heart, which he'd thought too jaded by the numerous, shallow *affaires de coeur* he had enjoyed with the women of Italy and France to feel anything beyond a passing desire, turned over in his breast.

His determination to keep Tori from harm redoubled. If only there were a way to convince her to protect the conspirators with her silence and to keep her from learning of his part in her husband's death! On the other hand, she had to be told of her widowhood. Only then, he believed, would she feel herself free to love again. Only then could he hope to marry her. As the Contessa da l'Armi, living with him in Italy, she would be safe. But how could he tell her? How could he keep her from branding him a murderer?

Questions. They were all he had. But if he lacked answers, he lacked nothing in the way of determination. Standing there in the cool, dark chamber with Tori trembling in his tight and loving embrace, Niccolò da l'Armi vowed to find a way!

29

Lying in the darkness of his room at the Château de
Lurneaux, Grey gazed up toward the ancient canopy
lost in the night shadows. His thoughts were
muddled, his mind a turmoil, despite his best efforts
to think carefully and rationally and plan his next
step with an eye toward his own safety—and Tori's.

Tori. His brow furled at the thought of her. He
was sure there was more to her disappearance than
there had at first appeared. He was certain she had
not merely thrown in her lot with d'Archambeault.
Or was that merely his pride—his love—indulging in
wishful thinking? If only he could fathom the depth
of her feelings for him. If only—

He sighed. Until now, her loyalty to Christophe
had kept them apart, had kept her from revealing the
secrets of her tightly-reined heart. But now that
Christophe was dead . . .

Dead. The notion still seemed unbelievable. He wondered if Tori could know, but dismissed that idea. The intelligence had only just reached France, and Tori did not have access to the sources that Grey did in his capacity of blockade runner for the Confederacy.

Tori was a widow. She was free. They were free. But she was gone. How could he find her? And if he did, would she want to be his as he wanted her to be?

And there was Christophe's mission—failed now that the papers he'd carried were lost at sea. The Confederacy would have to send a new emissary. Precious time had been lost, and the desperately needed aid was not yet forthcoming. Frustrated by his own helplessness to aid the cause he loved, Grey doubled his fist and struck the mattress with it.

He wanted nothing more, at this point, than to find Tori, board the *Nightshade*, and return to America. He was sick to death of missions and intrigue and danger. Running the Union blockade, once so exciting and fraught with tension, seemed like child's play after the rigors of international politics.

He started as a knock sounded on the door. Tossing back the coverlet, he lit a candle and hoped against hope it might be Tori waiting on the other side of the iron-bound portal.

Swinging it open, he tried to hide his disappointment from the Duchesse, who stood there smiling up at him.

"Grey?" Her smile was dazzling, her beauty enchanting, but somehow she held little attraction for him. The promise of pleasure that once would have tantalized him had dimmed.

"Gabrielle," he said, bending dutifully over her hand. "You were looking for me?"

She glanced past him into the dimly lighted room. Though Grey had made no attempt to seduce her when they were staying in such close quarters at the Château de Saint-Rémy, she still had hopes.

"May I come in?"

Stepping back, he allowed her to pass. When she had entered the room, she turned to him, but he stood near the door, his hand still resting on the latch. She could see he had no intention of making their acquaintance any more intimate.

"I wanted to ask a favor of you, she said. "Would you mind terribly if we did not stay for the entire weekend? I know it is too late to leave tonight but perhaps in the morning—"

"I am leaving for Paris in the morning," he told her.

Gabrielle seemed taken aback by this sudden turn of events. "And Madame Duclaux?" she asked. "She will accompany you?"

"Tori has already left for Paris. She departed much earlier, apparently with the Chevalier d'Archambeault."

"But no, she didn't," Gabrielle disagreed.

"What do you mean?" Grey demanded. "How do you know?"

"Just after the exhibition in the meadow, I went to my room for a wrap. I met Marc-François d'Archambeault. He had just come from Tori Duclaux's room. Apparently, he had been called back to Paris and had gone to ask if she wished to accompany him. He said he had been told by the person packing her trunk that she had already departed and that her trunk was to be sent along as soon as it was packed."

"Are you certain about all this, Gabrielle?"

"Quite certain. Why?"

He shook his head absently. "Nothing. Gabrielle, listen to me. I must go to Paris. Now, immediately. I cannot take the time to return to Saint-Rémy. May I leave the rest of my and Tori's belongings there for the time being?"

"Of course you may. But please, wait until morning. It is already dark and the roads are not entirely safe. In the morning you can make a fresh start."

Grey could see the sense of her arguments, though his heart rebelled at the delay. In the morning he could set out for the capital without having to worry about being robbed or losing his way in the concealing darkness.

"In the morning," he agreed. "But by that, I do not mean five minutes before noon. That may be a courtier's notion of the morning, but I mean to be on the road to Paris before the sun is fully above the horizon."

Gabrielle nodded, understanding that he meant this to be good-bye. He would not seek her out in the morning, nor would he expect her to get in the way of his preparations for departure. She found herself wishing, as she left his room, that he was not so zealous in his concern for the now-widowed Madame Duclaux!

Paris! Beautiful Paris! The jewel of western Europe had never been more beautiful, more sophisticated, more gay than it was under Napoleon III and the exquisite Empress Eugénie. The city seemed to sparkle. Love and beauty and pleasure ruled supreme, but they were only a veneer masking the intrigue that seethed beneath the surface, endangering the fragile empire of the nephew of the great general, Napoleon.

Grey arrived in the city and was, like most who passed its gates for the first time, dazzled. But its tempting diversions could not sway him from his goal. Without even looking for lodgings for himself, he set about searching for the Chevalier d'Archambeault.

It was late afternoon by the time he found his rooms in the Avenue des Champs-Elysées.

"*Oui*?" Marc-François appeared at the door in his shirtsleeves.

"*Pardonnez-moi*," Grey told him. "I am Greyson Verreaux. I have come from the Château de Lurneaux. I must speak to you."

The chevalier waved him inside. The chambers, though cluttered, were furnished elegantly, though the young chevalier could not take credit for their luxury. The apartment had belonged to his parents and had been given to him only when he had entered the Emperor's service and needed to maintain a private residence in the capital where he could entertain his friends and amours.

Marc-François offered Grey a glass of wine, which he accepted with alacrity. The road from the Château de Lurneaux had been long and dusty, and he had stopped only once when his horse had thrown a shoe.

"How may I help you, monsieur?" the chevalier asked, sitting in an armchair opposite Grey.

"I am looking for Madame Duclaux. Victoria Duclaux. You met her at the château."

"I remember her. A beautiful woman. Were there not a war raging in America, I would consider visiting that nation—if only to see the women."

Grey permitted himself a small smile. "In any case, Madame Duclaux, it appears, has disappeared."

"Disa—" Concern chased the lazy good humor from the chevalier's face, and he sat forward in his chair. "But I thought someone had accompanied her to Paris."

"And I thought that someone was you until another person told me you had left alone."

"I was called back to Paris unexpectedly. I went to Madame Duclaux's room to ask if she cared to accompany me. A man was there—he was packing her belongings into a trunk. I asked him where Madame Duclaux was, and he said she had already left for Paris."

"Had you ever seen this man before?"

The chevalier shook his head. "Never. He was obviously not one of the Marquis's footmen. No, this man was big, rough. I assure you I would not like to meet him on the bank of the Seine on a dark, foggy night." He sipped his wine thoughtfully. "The man was dark, swarthy. With a beard. His voice was deep, gruff. He spoke with a thick accent."

"An accent?"

"Hmmm. Italian, I'd say."

"Ital—" Grey's face was suffused with the hot blood of fury. "Da l'Armi! That bastard!"

"Da l'Armi? You mean Count Niccolò da l'Armi? Cavour's agent?"

"Cavour?" Grey asked.

"Count Camillo Cavour. The chief minister of the King of Sardinia. He is a thoroughly distasteful man. Nothing is beneath him if it will accomplish his goals. His agents are for hire—at a stiff price—to anyone."

"And da l'Armi is one of his agents?"

Marc-François shrugged. "I don't really know. No one does. That is part of Cavour's genius. No one in Paris, or anywhere else in Europe, could connect any of his agents with him. He has a network of intermediaries so complicated it's like a spider's web, with Cavour sitting in the center spinning his plots and waiting for his victims to fall into his trap.'' He gazed at Grey, perplexed. "But what could da l'Armi have to do with Madame Duclaux?"

"They met in Jamaica," Grey told him. "In fact, he sailed with us to France." Setting aside his glass, he rose and held out his hand to the chevalier. "I thank you for your friendship, monsieur. I don't suppose you could tell me where to find da l'Armi?"

Marc-François shook his head. "I'm sorry. He is attached to the diplomatic corps but I don't believe he resides at the embassy. I could make discreet inquiries, if you like."

"I would be grateful."

Grey walked to the door, accompanied by the handsome chevalier. As he stepped out the door, Marc-François laid a restraining hand on his arm.

"You don't think da l'Armi would harm her, do you?"

Grey shrugged. "I don't know. I believe he harbors a certain tenderness for her, but whether that would protect her if she got in the way of his orders, I simply don't know."

Darkness had fallen early as black, threatening clouds gathered over the city. Not so far away from the chevalier's lodgings, a carriage drew to a halt near the Tuileries Gardens.

"Come, Victoria," Niccolò said, stepping down from the vehicle. "We will walk in the gardens."

There was a tension about him, an air of nervous impatience, that troubled her. "It is going to rain," she objected lamely. "Couldn't we come back another—"

Sandra DuBay

"No," he interrupted, too sharply. He softened his tone and forced a thin smile. "Let us go now."

Reluctantly, Tori laid her hand on Niccolò's arm and they started down the steps of the terrace toward the tree-ringed, shadow-filled lawns of the gardens. At the bottom of the step, Niccolò suddenly stopped.

"Ah, I have forgotten something in the carriage."

"We will go back," Tori said instantly.

"No, no. You and Bernard go on. I will catch up."

"But—"

"Please, *cara*, stop arguing," he asked, already turning away.

Tori cast a glance at the tall man who had accompanied them—Bernard, one of Quaratesi's men. Reluctantly, fear prickling her spine with warning fingers, she started into the gardens.

At a discreet distance, Bernard followed. In his hand rested the needle-sharp stiletto Quaratesi had ordered him to slip between Tori's ribs in the secluded darkness of the garden. When dawn broke over Paris, Victoria Duclaux would be no more. There would be merely another mystery, yet another victim of her own foolishness in walking alone in the shadowy gardens by night. No doubt, Quaratesi had reasoned confidently, the police would blame her death on brigands who roamed the night-shrouded streets preying on foolish innocents. And that would be the end of the investigation and the end of the threat Victoria Duclaux posed to their future safety.

292

30

Tori trembled as she walked along the shadowy allée between the tree-fringed lawns of the gardens. At first the night had seemed silent as the grave—she shuddered at the thought—but she could hear, as her ears grew acute, the sound of the Seine not so far away and the clatter of hooves and the rumble of carriage wheels on the Rue de Rivoli just beyond the Terrasse des Feuillants. Footsteps followed her but she dared not glance over her shoulder—the hulking silhouette that was Bernard was not far behind her.

The allée down which she had just walked was deserted. Even the dogged Bernard seemed to have abandoned her. The carriage that had brought them was barely visible in the darkness at the edge of the garden. It was empty.

Some ancient, primitive instinct warned her of the mortal danger in which she stood. Lifting her

Sandra DuBay

black velvet skirts, she turned to run. It was too late.

A long, looming shadow detached itself from
those of the swaying trees. It fell across her even as
she turned, even as her small, booted feet gained
purchase on the slippery path.

Casting a terrified glance back over her
shoulder, her eyes strained into the darkness. The
shadow was moving . . . approaching . . .

"Niccolò!" she wailed, pleading for him to help
her, pleading for him to save her from Bernard.

But Quaratesi's henchman came forward,
moving with astonishing swiftness on silent feet. In
the instant between the heart-stopping realization of
her danger and Tori's first sight of him, he was upon
her. The light of a moon half-concealed by clouds
glinted on the long, narrow, lethal blade of his
stiletto.

There could be no question of his intent.
Without thought, without reason, without wasting a
moment to beg for her life, she tried to angle toward
the concealing trees, but it was hopeless. The blade
flashed in Bernard's practiced hand. A white-hot
pain slashed through her upper arm.

And then, even as she'd thought her life was at
an end, there was a thud. With a soft moan, Bernard
fell to the thick grass at the edge of the Quinconce.

Tori found herself gazing at Niccolò over the
lifeless body of Quaratesi's assassin. Her eyes slipped
down to the corpse at her feet. The blade of a knife
protruded from his broad back.

"Victoria . . ." Niccolò whispered. He took a
step toward her.

Ignoring the pain in her arm, she whirled away.
Grabbing fistfuls of her black velvet skirts, she lifted
them away from her flying feet as she fled in the
direction of the Terrasse des Feuillants and the Rue

de Rivoli on the opposite side.

"Victoria!" Niccolò called as loudly as he
dared. "Wait! Come back! I mean you no harm!"

But Tori was beyond reason. In the breadth of
an instant she had been nearly killed and had
witnessed a murder. She would not, could not,
remain a moment longer with these people—these
maniacs.

Her arm ached. Her heart pounded. Her lungs
burned with the pumping of the damp, chilled night
air. She was nearly to the terrasse, only a few steps
separating her from safety, when Niccolò, swifter,
unhampered by skirts, petticoats and hoops, threw
an arm about her waist and yanked her off her feet.

The impact knocked them both to the ground.
They fell on the grass between two towering trees.

Tori struggled like a mad thing in Niccolò's
embrace. "Let me go!" she screamed. "Let me go,
you madman! You killer!"

"Victoria. Victoria!"

"You murdered him!"

"Of course I murdered him!" Niccolò hissed
impatiently. "He was sent to kill you! Quaratesi
ordered you killed! Bernard was his assassin."

"Quaratesi . . ." She lay still beneath him.
"But why? Why? You're lying to me!"

"Am I?" He touched her arm. Leaning over
her, he showed her his bloodied fingers. "He cut
you. He was trying to kill you. He had every
intention of carrying out his orders."

Lying on the grass, her pulse slowing, she gazed
up at Niccolò in bewilderment. "But I don't understand! What have I done? All I want is my husband.
Why does Quaratesi want to kill me?"

Niccolò sighed, gazing off into the darkness of
the garden. How could he tell her? How could he

explain?

"And Christophe?" Tori interrupted his musing to ask. "Where is he? What has Quaratesi done with him? When will I see him again, Niccolò?"

"So many questions," the Count sighed. "Your arm is in need of attention, *cara*. Come, let me take you somewhere where we can get a doctor for you."

"Niccolò, I want to know—"

"And you will, *cara*. But first, your arm is bleeding. We must take care of it." He pushed himself to his feet. "Come, I know a place—"

"Not back to Quaratesi's!"

"No, no." Taking her hands, he pulled her to her feet. "I know a place where we will be safe from Quaratesi until we can summon help for you."

They started back toward the carriage, Niccolò's arm about Tori and Tori leaning slightly on him as the pain of her injury began to seep through the numbness of her shocked senses.

Behind them, in the Rue de Rivoli, a carriage was passing. Inside a man sat heavily against the tufted leather squabs. He was melancholy, frustrated with his inability to find out where da l'Armi might be holding Tori, for he had no doubt she was being held against her will. He blamed himself for leaving her alone at the château. But he couldn't have foreseen that da l'Armi could have found her there. Could he?

Glancing out the window, he noticed the two figures walking in the tree-shadowed gardens. The man had his arm about the woman and she leaned on him. They looked like lovers, and Grey envied them. He sighed and looked away, turning his attention to his own worries and his fears of Tori's safety.

Niccolò helped Tori into the carriage, then climbed onto the coachman's box. With Bernard lying dead in the garden, it would be up to him to drive them to their destination—a house on the Île St. Louis.

Tori winced as Niccolò lifted her out of the carriage and down to the cobbled courtyard of he hôtel. As they reached the door, it swung open and an elderly woman smiled uncertainly as Niccolò led Tori inside.

"Send for a doctor, Margherita. This lady has been injured.

"*Si*, Signor."

"I will take her upstairs. Bring the doctor up when he arrives."

The Count helped Tori up the dark, winding stairs and down the lamplit corridor to a chamber full of delicate gilded furniture, most of which had been culled from the loot stolen from the homes of the aristocracy during the Revolution. Niccolò had prized it for its beauty and workmanship, and he had traced certain pieces and bought them from their current, if dispossessed, owners.

Tori sat on the edge of the bed while Niccolò moved around to its other side. Reaching around from behind her, he unfastened her pelerine and drew it off. She looked at her right arm. The black velvet of her gown was torn and the thick blood oozing from her wound stuck her sleeve to her flesh.

She felt his fingers at her back, slipping the faceted jet buttons from their holes, and twisted away. "Niccolò! Stop!"

"*Cara*, the doctor is going to have to treat you, and your sleeve is in the way. Come now. I will not harm you."

Sitting like a child, she allowed him to pull off her bodice. She stood as he unfastened her black skirt

and hoops. Then, in her camisole and a single
petticoat, she was tucked into the bed with all the
tenderness of a beloved nursemaid toward her
charge.

From another room, Niccolò fetched a basin of
warmed water and a soft cloth to bathe Tori's arm.

"Oh, Niccolò," she hissed. "It hurts!"

"It is deep, *cara*. The doctor may have to stitch
it."

"Stitch?" Tori looked down at the pad of gauze
the Count held on the wound.

"It may be necessary." He lifted the pad,
peeked beneath, then replaced it. "We must decide
what we will tell the doctor."

"What do you mean?"

"Victoria, we can hardly tell the doctor you
were wounded by a would-be assassin, can we?" He
frowned, thoughtfully. "Let me see. We could tell
him a glass was broken and you fell on it."

"Do you expect him to believe that?" Tori
asked.

"It doesn't really matter what he believes. He
will not question us."

There was a knock at the door and Margherita
appeared. "The *dottore* is here, signor," she
announced.

"Show him in," Niccolò told her.

Margherita disappeared and in her place
appeared a short, stout, white-haired man whose
dapper appearance gave no indication that he had
been at all ruffled by his precipitous summons to the
Hôtel d'Eygalières, the home Niccolò rented in Paris.

"Bonsoir, monsieur. Madame," he said,
removing his hat. "I am Doctor Ferrand. His dark
eyes went to Tori. "Madame is ill?"

"My wife dropped a glass of wine. She slipped

and fell. Her arm was cut on a shard of the glass."

"Ah. *Pauvre madame*." Removing his coat, the doctor asked that a basin of water be brought. Niccolò dispatched Margherita and it appeared quickly along with several towels.

Tori looked up at the doctor with wide eyes as he approached. He smiled down at her, kindly, reassuringly.

"Never mind, *belle madame*," he said softly. "I will endeavor not to hurt you."

He lifted the pad and scowled down at the ragged wound. "Ah, this is a wicked slash. Still, it could have been much worse."

"Will you have to stitch it?" she asked anxiously.

"I think, perhaps, I will. But you must not worry. I am very careful with lovely young ladies. You should have no more than a tiny white scar to show for your misadventure."

Tori's eyes met Niccolò's over the doctor's bowed head. Why had he lied? she wondered. Why had he told the doctor she was his wife? His reasons may have been honorable—perhaps he thought that the doctor would think less of her if he learned that she was not Niccolò's wife despite being there, mostly unclothed, in the middle of the night. But a nagging skepticism kept her from accepting this attractive explanation. He may also have—

A cry was wrenched from her as the doctor slid a needle threaded with silk into her flesh. Instantly, Niccolò was beside her, his arms about her, her head cradled—and her cries smothered—in the warm hollow of his shoulder.

Again and again the needle pierced her, and she felt the slick tickle of the thread as it slipped through her skin. She moaned, and the tears she could not hold back stained Niccolò's coat.

"A moment, *pauvre petite*," the doctor cooed, "and it will be over."

Tori trembled as he knotted and cut the thread. "Are you finished?" she whispered.

"All finished." He held her arm as he bandaged her wound. "You must change the bandage every day. You must keep the stitches dry. When the wound is well on the way to healing, you must call me to clip the stitches and pull out the silk."

"We will," Niccolò promised.

"*Bon*. Then all I can do now is prescribe sleep for tonight and rest for a few days."

Niccolò held the doctor's coat and walked with him to the door. "Thank you for your prompt arrival, doctor."

"Not at all. That is what I am here for."

Smiling, Niccolò paid the doctor handsomely for his services, then saw him out the door. Turning, he said to Margherita:

"Bring some laudanum up to madame. I fear she may have need of it to help her rest."

The housekeeper nodded and went to do her master's bidding. It seemed only moments before she was at the door of Tori's room.

"Thank you, Margherita," Niccolò told her, taking the glass from her tray. "That will be all for tonight."

"Niccolò?" Tori said as he brought the glass to her bedside. "Tell me about Christophe. You know where he is, don't you?"

"Drink this," he urged, holding out the glass to her.

"I don't want it. I want to know about—"

"And I will tell you," he interrupted. "But only after you are a good girl and drink this. Doctor

Ferrand left it for you. Do not tell me you are going to disobey his orders already.''

Taking the glass, she eyed it skeptically. "What is it?''

"A sedative," he hedged. "It will help you sleep.''

Obediently, she lifted the glass to her lips and drained it. Handing it back to him, she waited impatiently for the answers to her questions.

"Christophe," Niccolò said. "Victoria, are you certain this cannot wait until the—''

"No!" She shook her head, fighting the effects of the laudanum. "I've waited so long, come so far. You must tell me.''

"Very well." He sat beside her and tucked the quilts beneath her chin as if she were a very small child. He hesitated, gauging her condition. She was groggy, her eyelids dropped, and it was obviously a struggle for her to lift them. "Tori?" he said softly.

"Hmmm?" she murmured. "Christophe?''

Taking her hand, he stroked it. "Christophe is dead, *cara*. Quaratesi ordered him killed.''

Her eyelashes, lying on her pale, pearlescent cheeks, never fluttered. "I see," she murmured. "Thank you, Niccolò." Then she drifted off to sleep.

31

Tori woke with the feeling that she had just emerged from the depths of some warm, soothing ocean. Her head seemed filled with cotton, her mouth was dry, and her throat was parched. And her arm—her arm!—ached with a kind of burning, raw pain such as she'd never experienced.

"Victoria? Victoria, come, you must wake up."

"I am awake," she whispered. "Oh, Niccolò! My arm, it aches! The pain . . ."

"I will give you something for it in a little while. Now you must get up. You must wash and dress because we have to leave as soon as possible."

"Leave?" She squinted toward the window where the sun had not yet risen enough to show through the draperies.

"Hurry." He was already at the door. "Get up. Your water is there, on the wash stand."

"But, Niccolò . . ."

It was too late; he had already gone. Tori
climbed out of the bed gingerly, desperately trying to
avoid bumping her arm, and made her way to the
washstand. With her left hand she poured the warm
water into the basin, then washed herself, slowly,
clumsily, spilling far too much water onto the
polished floor at the edge of the rug.

She looked around as a tapping sounded at the
door. If it was Niccolò, she thought, glancing down
at her scanty attire, she'd better find a robe.

But the door opened and Margherita appeared.
In her arms she carried Tori's black bodice. The
sleeve still showed signs of the damage and staining
that had occurred the night before, but it had been
repaired to the best of Margherita's ability.

With Margherita's help, Tori dressed. But when
the housekeeper brought her pelerine, Tori looked at
her, perplexed.

"The Count says you are to come down the
stairs when you are dressed, signora. You are to be
ready to leave as soon as you can."

"Ready to leave?" Tori paused, her
befeathered, beribboned hat in her hand. "But
why?"

But like Niccolò, Margherita had not waited for
her to ask questions.

Curious, Tori left her room and followed the
corridor to the stairs. She descended cautiously, her
hand sliding along the bannister. She felt unsteady,
still groggy from the laudanum Niccolò had given
her the night before.

At the foot of the stairs, Niccolò paced back and
forth like a caged and restless animal. Glancing up,
he saw her on her way down, and hurried to meet
her.

"Come, Victoria, we must go."

"Help me with my hat, Niccolò. I cannot tie the ribbons."

"In the coach," he told her, propelling her toward the door with a firm hand in the middle of her back.

"But, why—?"

"Victoria, by now Quaratesi knows we are gone. He knows Bernard is dead. He will send people to look for us. We must leave. Now!"

A vague, disquieting memory flitted through Tori's befogged mind.

"Wait, I must tell you about the dream I had last night."

"Tell me in the coach," he persisted. "Margherita has packed a hamper of food for us. You can tell me over breakfast."

Brooking no more of her delays, Niccolò bustled her out the door and into a closed traveling coach that had been drawn up in the courtyard. They settled inside and Niccolò drew the curtains down over the windows.

With a rap on the coach wall, he signalled the coachman and they were on their way.

"Where are we going?" she demanded, as the coach rolled out between the gates.

"To the country, *cara,*" he replied absently. "My dear friend the Comte de Mérimée has a château. We will be safe there."

"Safe . . ." Tori reached under her pelerine and gently touched the bandages covering her wound. "That reminds me, Niccolò. I had the strangest dream last night. I dreamed that you told me Christophe was dead. You said Quaratesi had ordered him killed. Isn't that ridiculous? I suppose it was the shock of learning that Quaratesi had ordered

305

me killed. That must have been it, wasn't it, Niccolò?
Christophe will meet us in the country, won't he?
Won't he?''

Grey had just picked up his hat and strode
toward the door of his suite at the Hotel Bristol when
the sound of knocking surprised him.

"Oui?" he said, cautiously opening the door.

"Good morning, Monsieur Verreaux," Marc-
François d'Archambeault said. With him was a large
man of middle years wearing a bowler hat at a jaunty
angle and a brown-and-cream checked suit. "May we
come in?''

Grey stepped back to allow them to enter.
"What can I do for you gentlemen this morning?''

"This gentleman is Mr. James Twysden. He is
attached to the American Embassy in Paris. He has
been looking for you."

"For me?" Grey was on his guard. The
American Embassy—Washington's Embassy—was
all too likely to be looking for him for all the wrong
reasons. "But why?''

From the inner pocket of his coat, the attaché
produced a dispatch that had arrived some days
before.

"This was sent from Jamaica, Mr. Verreaux. It
was addressed either to you or to a"—he consulted
the paper—"or to a Madame Christophe Duclaux. It
comes from a Mr. Edward Lytton, Woodbridge,
Montego Bay, Jamaica.''

Grey remembered his meetings with Lytton, but
thought it wiser to reveal nothing. "The name does
not ring a bell, sir. Nor does Madame Duclaux know
such a person.''

"Is Madame Duclaux here at the hotel?''

Grey and Marc-François exchanged a glance.

"No," Grey replied. "She is not. The dispatch, Mr. Twysden?"

"Oh! Of course!"

He handed the packet to Grey who broke the seal and skimmed the contents. It was the sudden flush of his cheeks and the flash of fire in his eyes that alarmed Marc-François, prompting him to say:

"Good God, Verreaux! What can it be?"

"What it is, d'Archambeault, is proof that Tori is in the custody of a madman—and a murderer!"

"You can't mean to say—"

Grey silenced him, warning him with a glance to say no more. Instead, Grey turned to James Twysden.

"Can you tell me, Mr. Twysden, where I might find Count Niccolò da l'Armi? I am given to understand that he is attached to the Italian embassy."

"Count da l'Armi?" Mr. Twysden repeated. "Is this an official matter, Mr. Verreaux? Because if it is, I must refer you to my superior. I am, you will understand, merely an—"

"No, no," Grey assured him, sensing that the man would only enmesh him in a tangle of dangerous official red tape if he thought it was a matter of any importance. "It is a purely personal matter, Mr. Twysden. Madame Duclaux and I came from Jamaica to visit relatives. I have reason to believe that the Count might have some information concerning a long-lost ancestor of mine whose descendants I am trying to locate. That is all."

"Ah," the attaché looked immensely relieved. "I see. In that case, I don't suppose there would be any harm in my telling you that the Count da l'Armi is known to be renting a residence on the Île St. Louis. The Hôtel de la—no, that's not it. Let me see. The Hôtel dy—no, wait a moment . . ."

Grey glanced at Marc-François, who shrugged apologetically.

Providentially—for Grey could take scarcely another moment of the man's fumbling—James Twysden's round face lit with remembrance and relief.

"I have it! The Hôtel d'Eygalières! On the Île St. Louis."

Scarcely taking time to thank Marc-François or Mr. Twysden or bid them adieu, Grey set off for the Hôtel d'Eygalières. As he rode along, chafing with impatience whenever his carriage was forced to halt in traffic, he could not help remembering the dispatch.

> "The steamship, *Peregrine* (it had said), of which I am part owner, was destroyed some days out of Montego Bay. There were no survivors after an apparent explosion of the boilers. Sabotage is suspected. Although I cannot offer proof positive, my suspicions rest upon Count Niccolò da l'Armi as the agent provocateur in this incident. Allow me to extend my gravest sympathies to Madame Christophe Duclaux on the loss of her husband.
>
> Yours sincerely,"

It was signed, "Edward Lytton." Curiously, the packet contained not only Lytton's letter of explanation and regret, but another letter from Monique Bouladoux. Grey wondered how Monique had managed to make the acquaintance of Edward Lytton, for the letter had been inside a sealed packet from Lytton's plantation. He wondered, too, why the letter was addressed to Tori and not to him.

Women, he thought, bewildered—who could understand them? Tori and Monique had existed on terms ranging from barely civil to openly hostile from the moment they'd met in New Orleans. Now, instead of writing to him, Monique had written to Tori. He turned the letter over in his hands. He would not open it. He would give it to Tori when he found her. And he would find her. And when he did, he would kill Niccolò da l'Armi!

The carriage turned into the courtyard of the Hôtel d'Eygalières. Another carriage stood there, a black, closed, somehow ominous-looking vehicle. The reins were tethered to a post and no coachman manned the box.

Grey climbed out of his carriage. He strode to the door and lifted his hand to knock. But the door merely swung wide. From within the dark, ancient house, he heard a man moan, sounding more frightened than pained. Voices were raised in anger—and in fear.

"Tell me!" a gruff voice raged. "Tell me where they have gone!"

"Please, Signor Quaratesi," a woman wailed. "Do not harm my son! He knows nothing. He is only the gatekeeper."

"Then you tell me, Margherita."

"I cannot."

The voice, when it came again, was sly, silky, filled with menace:

"Tell me, Margherita. Or my friends here will use their own methods on your son."

"No!" The housekeeper's voice quavered. It was rich with fear for her son. "I beg of you, signor."

"Tell me! Or he will die!"

The young gatekeeper moaned—a desperate sound filled with mortal terror. His mother's broken weeping filled the air until a slap abruptly silenced it. Her voice, halting, despairing, went on:

"Mérimée. The Count has gone to the Château de Mérimée."

"Is the woman with him? The American?"

"*Si*, signor. She was wounded by the man, Bernard, in the Tuileries last night. The doctor stitched her arm after the Count brought her here."

"But her life is in no danger."

"No, signor."

The man snarled an epithet, and Grey did not dare wait to hear any more. Whoever this cruel man was, he wanted da l'Armi badly enough not to waste any time in leaving for this Château de Mérimée, wherever it was. He had to get there first.

Racing back out to his carriage, he ordered it to Marc-François's rooms on the Champs-Elysées. He would find Tori if he had to chase her all over France! But somehow, he would have to beat da l'Armi's enemies to him. They wanted da l'Armi and, from the sound of it, they wanted Tori as well. She had been wounded, the woman, Margherita, had said. It was a relief to know that her life was in no danger from her wound, but the fact that she had been harmed at all was something else da l'Armi would answer for!

He looked back at the house as the carriage drove out through the gateway. Three men emerged from the hôtel. One was large, his florid face twisted into a mask of fury. He was followed by two others, both big, rough-looking men. One of them climbed into the coach with the first while the third climbed onto the box and took up the reins. They looked like the kind who enjoyed killing and who took care not to leave witnesses to their dirty work. They could do as they liked with da l'Armi—although if Grey had his way, he would deprive them of the pleasure of their vengeance—but with Christophe Duclaux dead, Tori was his—his!—and he would rescue her from her captors and have his revenge on them for daring to put her in danger. They would pay and pay dearly. Of that simple fact, he was in no doubt.

But the task of locating this Château de Mérimée lay ahead. As the coach left the Île St. Louis and sped in the direction of the Champs-Elysées, Grey sent a silent prayer heavenward that Marc-François d'Archambeault, already the font of so much useful information, would be able to supply him with this essential piece of the puzzle.

32

Turned away from Marc-François's apartment by his concierge with directions to the chevalier's post at the Palais des Tuileries, Grey chafed at the delay that gave da l'Armi's pursuers more and more of an advantage over him.

The Tuileries Palace fronted on the Tuileries Gardens. Begun in the sixteenth century by Queen Catherine de Médici, it had grown over the centuries. It was a mix of the old and the new, the ancient and the modern, the tastes and fashions of three centuries of French monarchs.

Grey searched along the crowded corridors and galleries for Marc-François. At last, after several wrong turns and many questions, he was directed to an anteroom near the king's apartments.

"Are you on duty?" he asked, having surprised Marc-François.

The chevalier shrugged. "Supposedly. But I wouldn't be missed." His smile was charming, almost boyish. "My father secured this post for me, but I am not really necessary to the running of this palace."

"I need to speak with you. It is about Tori and da l'Armi."

Laying a finger to his lips, Marc-François led him to an even smaller anteroom and locked the door behind them.

"It is never wise to speak too freely in a public room," he told Grey. "Now, tell me what you've learned."

Grey recounted the events at the Hôtel d'Eygalières. When he'd finished, the chevalier whistled softly.

"Gianfrancesco Quaratesi. An unsavory man. I didn't know da l'Armi worked for him."

"Who is he?" Grey demanded.

"Quaratesi? Supposedly, he is merely an importer of Italian silks and wines. Reputedly, he is a ruthless agent for—can you guess?—Cavour. He makes Niccolò da l'Armi look like a choirboy."

"I've got to get to Tori before this Quaratesi does. He's tried to have her killed once. He's not likely to let her go once he's dealt with da l'Armi."

"There was a body found in the Tuileries gardens this morning. A man named Bernard Lippi, known to work for Quaratesi. He had a knife in his back and another in his hand. The stiletto in his hand was bloodied. It is likely that he was sent to kill Madame Duclaux but someone, probably da l'Armi, killed him before he could complete his task."

"Now I have to find her before Quaratesi can complete Lippi's work. This place, the Château de Mérimée, do you know of it?"

"I do. It belongs to the Comte de Mérimée. But I don't know him well, and I don't know where his château lies."

"How can we find out?"

Marc-François rose. "Come, I know of someone who may be able to help."

The chevalier led Grey to an apartment on the first floor of the palace. They were admitted by a pretty, flirtatious maid and ushered into the presence of the most beautiful woman Grey had ever seen.

"Madame la Comtesse," Marc-François said, bending reverently over the woman's hand. "Allow me to present Monsieur Greyson Verreaux, an American."

"Monsieur Verreaux," a throaty voice purred.

Grey stepped forward. Upon closer inspection, he could see the petulant pout that spoiled the lines of the mouth and the calculating hardness that glittered in the magnificent eyes. But these flaws aside, the woman possessed beauty of a magnitude Grey had never imagined possible.

"Madame la Comtesse Castiglione," Marc-François said as Grey kissed the Countess's outstretched hand.

Grey looked into her almond-shaped dark eyes. She was extraordinary, but even the most superficial contact revealed the fact that she saw her beauty as her due, not as a gift. She wore it as some kings wore their crowns—believing it bestowed upon her by divine right.

"How sweet of you to bring this handsome *americano* to meet me, Marco," she purred.

"You must excuse us for interrupting your morning toilette," the chevalier apologized. "Though what you could possibly need with a beauty regimen I cannot imagine."

"It is true," she agreed, with none of the blushing modesty with which most women would have greeted such a compliment. "But it is expected of great ladies."

"Then we will crave your indulgence for a moment only. Monsieur Verreaux has come from America to visit his ancestral holdings. One of these, so he was told, lies near the Château de Mérimée. I told him I did not know where the château was, but I knew a lady who might be able to help."

"Mérimée." The Countess's perfect nose wrinkled. "You remind me of Fabien, and I do not wish to be reminded of the Comte. But since it is only directions . . ."

Grey and Marc-François left the Countess's rooms with detailed directions to the château. There remained only to try and reach it before Quaratesi and his henchmen did.

"You will make better time riding than taking a carriage," the chevalier told him. "Come with me. I have several superb horses."

"You're too kind," Grey told him. "I don't know how I can repay—"

"There's no need. I, too, would hate to see the lovely lady harmed." He stopped to take Grey's arm, struck with a new notion. "Why don't I come with you? No"—he silenced Grey's protests—"I mean it. Quaratesi has at least two men with him and there's always da l'Armi to contend with. I insist."

Within the quarter hour, Grey and Marc-François were riding out of the city and on their way to the Château de Mérimée, some thirty miles southeast of Paris.

Even as Grey and Marc-François were starting out and Gianfrancesco Quaratesi and his

316

companions were rumbling over the roads in Niccolò
and Tori's wake, the coach carrying da l'Armi and
his distraught captive drew up before a small château
that was, in fact, little more than a rectangular
hunting lodge built of honey-colored stone. In the
late seventeenth century, one of the Comtes de
Mérimée had surmounted the center of the lodge with
a soaring dome. But it was the park surrounding the
château that was its saving grace. Long, flower-
bordered parterres stretched off toward the forest
and, when the Comte was in residence, fountains
played on each of the château's four sides.

But it was autumn and the flowers had long
since died. The château had lain unused for some
time and the fountains were empty and dry, clogged
with leaves. To Tori, shocked and desolated by the
realization that the nightmare she had related to
Niccolò was no mere bad dream, it seemed isolated
and forbidding, a prison.

The moment the coach stopped, she leapt out of
it, past the footman and across the lawns, her heavy
velvet skirt rippling behind her. Her bonnet, its
ribbons loosened in the coach, fell off and her hair,
tucked hastily into a net that morning by Margherita,
streamed out behind her as she ran.

Behind her, watching the lithe figure receding
into the distance, Niccolò stood beside the coach. He
did not bother to follow her—there was no need. She
could run until she dropped, and she would still be
thirty miles from Paris—thirty miles from help. He
watched, biding his time, until her steps faltered and
slowed, and she collapsed onto the leaf-strewn grass.
Then he walked to where she lay.

"Victoria," he said as he stood over her.
"Please, listen to me."

"Victoria." Leaning down, he stroked her hair.

Sandra DuBay

She writhed away, pushing herself to her feet.
"Don't touch me!" she hissed. "Do not
ever—ever!—touch me again."

He held out his hands to her, pleading, his dark
eyes filled with remorse and longing. "I love you,"
he said simply.

A bitter laugh died in Tori's throat. "How dare
you!" she breathed. "How dare you speak of love to
me! Did you murder my husband because you loved
me?"

"That was not my fault. Quaratesi ordered—"

"I don't give a damn about Quaratesi! You
killed him! It was you and that bastard, Ramsey!"

He stared at the ground, the picture of misery.
"Victoria, I cannot undo the past. When I . . . when
I carried out my orders . . . I did not know you. It
was not until after your husband had sailed that I met
you. You remember, *cara*, in the garden at Stockton
Hall. *Dio*! I thought you were the loveliest woman I
had ever seen. I think I would have done anything for
you in that moment."

"Including making me a widow?" She glared at
him, loathing him. "I am a widow, Niccolò. And
you—you are a murderer!"

"I am what necessity has made me, Victoria.
Nothing more. You know nothing of the
machinations of politics. You know nothing of the
workings and methods of governments."

"Governments! I am talking about the taking of
an innocent life, Niccolò! My husband's life! What
had Christophe done to threaten your precious
government?"

"He involved himself in a scheme to aid your
Confederacy—a scheme which certain parties would
do anything to stop. He condemned himself to death
from the moment he agreed to be the envoy to

318

Paris."

The stricken look on Tori's face moved him. He reached toward her, wanting to comfort her, but she recoiled.

"Victoria, please! I have changed. I—"

"Changed!" she spat. "Into what, pray? You are a monster, Niccolò! A monster!"

"I love you," he breathed.

"Love me?" Her eyes glittered with malice. "Is that the reason you kidnapped me from the Château de Lurneaux? And why you took me to that fiend, Quaratesi?"

"It was—"

"I know, orders," she supplied bitingly. "Is there nothing you won't do if you are told to?"

"It was not entirely because of Quaratesi's orders," Niccolò insisted.

"Then why? Why!"

"Because I wanted to get you away from Verreaux! He guarded you like a jealous husband! You reject my love—did you also reject his lust?"

"Damn you! Damn you to hell!" she hissed. "Leave Grey out of this! There is nothing you can say about him that will excuse you for what you have done!" She raised a hand to ward him off as he approached. "You say you took me from Lurneaux because you wanted me with you. Then why did you take me to Quaratesi?"

"Because I knew he would hunt you down with or without my help. He believed that your husband may have told you of the Confederate scheme to enlist help from France in their war against Lincoln's government. He thought that if you discovered that your husband had been killed to prevent him from completing his mission, you might have gone to the French authorities and exposed him. That is why he

319

ordered you killed, to protect himself.''

Tori's obvious skepticism pained him. ''I swear it is the truth. I thought that if Quaratesi saw that you knew nothing, he would leave you alone. I believed that if he saw you were innocent, he would let you go unharmed.''

''And when you discovered he had no intention of doing so, you put me in danger of my life! You let me walk into that garden knowing Bernard was following me with a knife! You let me go into the Tuileries Garden knowing I was never meant to come out of it!''

''Yes! And that was why I followed Bernard! I never meant to let him kill you.''

''He nearly did,'' she reminded him, her voice cold as the winds of deepest winter. ''He nearly succeeded.''

''But he did not succeed! I saved you as I had always intended to do!'' The ice in her blue eyes pierced him to the heart. ''Victoria,'' he moaned. ''Do not think of the past, I beg of you. Think of the future. Let us begin anew.''

''I cannot, Niccolò. The shadow of Christophe would forever stand between us.'' The anguish in his eyes was pathetic. Tori felt the smallest flicker of pity for him, but ruthlessly stamped it out. ''Do not hope, Niccolò, for there is no hope for us. For me you will always be my husband's murderer.''

''In time—''

''No! Time will change nothing. Take me back to Paris, Niccolò.''

''You don't want to—''

''What I want—all I want—is to go home. Home, to New Orleans. I don't care if there is a war there. I don't even care if the whole Yankee army is billeted in my home. I want to be there.''

His face twisted into a sour grimace. "And I suppose you want Grey Verreaux to take you there."

"It is Grey's home as well. We are Americans, Niccolò, and America is where we belong. I've had enough of France and its so-called beauty and culture and sophistication. It is nothing but a sewer in fancy dress." She bit her lip to hold back her tears. "I wish I had never set foot here!"

The tears of fatigue, of fear and pain and anger that she had managed to hold back until now, began to fall, blurring her vision, muddling her thoughts, clouding her overtaxed mind.

"Do you truly want to go home, Victoria?" Niccolò asked.

"I do," she assured him. "It is all I want."

"And there is no hope for us? You will never be able to love me?"

"Never," she insisted. "Never."

He nodded, accepting defeat gracefully. "Then come. Come with me into the château and rest for a little while. Let Madame Rodolphe, the wife of the caretaker, clean and bandage your arm."

"And then?" Tori persisted suspiciously.

"And then we will start back to Paris."

Knowing she could not stand outside all day with the chilly autumn wind whipping across the open lawns, Tori lifted her skirts and started toward the château. Niccolò, coming abreast of her, reached out to touch her arm, but she twisted away from him, quickening her step just enough to keep out of his reach.

As they climbed the shallow steps to the entrance, the ornate, twelve-foot door swung open as if on command.

Tori squinted as she entered the foyer. Although the day was cloudy and overcast, as dull and gloomy

321

as Tori's mood, it was bright compared to the dim, weak light that filtered down from the obscure heights of the dome and the small, nearly opaque round windows that had been set into its soaring curve.

"*Bonjour*, Monsieur le Comte," a woman said, appearing from the depths of the château and approaching across the wondrous marquetry sunburst floor. She eyed Tori uncertainly, unsure of how to address her.

Niccolò came to her aid. "Madame Rodolphe, this is Madame Duclaux. Will you show her to a room where she can rest for a time?"

"Of course, Monsieur le Comte. This way, if you please, madame."

Unable to ignore her fatigue any longer, Tori followed the woman up the grand staircase. At the top, she was led to a chamber not far from the landing. It was small, yet exquisitely furnished with priceless Empire pieces and draped in gold silk. The floor, a marvel by the same artisans who had fashioned the foyer floor, was protected by an ancient Oriental carpet Tori imagined must be more valuable than the other furnishings of the chamber combined.

Tori looked longingly at the gold-draped bed nestled into a niche in the floral-papered walls.

"I will help madame off with her gown?" Madame Rodolphe asked.

Though she wanted nothing more than to lie down, Tori saw the sense in discarding her gown—it was the only one she had and definitely the worse for wear—and the hoops that supported the billowing skirt. With Madame Rodolphe's help, she was partially undressed and tucked into the bed.

"You are hurt, madame?" the caretaker's wife

asked, seeing Tori's bandaged arm and the pinpricks of blood that dotted the white gauze covering it.

"A cut," Tori told her. "Perhaps you could change the bandages before the Count and I leave."

"Of course, madame."

"And—Madame Rodolphe?"

"Please, madame, my name is Olivie."

"Very well, Olivie. Would you bring me a pitcher of water?"

"You wish to wash, madame?"

"Not now. Before I leave I will, but now I am simply thirsty."

"As you wish, madame."

Olivie left and Tori laid back against the pillows. The room was filled with shadows, for the draperies had been drawn at the tall, leaded windows. The bed was so soft, so warm. The fine lawn sheets were perfumed with lavender. As she lay there, the strain of the past days overcame her and her eyelids fluttered shut as she slid into slumber.

Niccolò looked up as Olivie came down the stairs.

"Is she resting?" he asked.

Olivie smiled. "She is very likely asleep even now. The poor lady is exhausted, Monsieur le Comte."

"Yes." Niccolò sighed. "The past few days have been more than she can bear." He saw the curiosity in Olivie's eyes—the questions she did not dare ask.

"Poor lady!" the salt-and-pepper-haired woman cooed. "And so young to be a widow."

"Yes. Her husband—her late husband—was a dear friend of mine. I feel it is my duty to care for Victoria until she is well again."

"I noticed that she was injured. She asked me to

323

change her bandages later.''

"That would be kind of you. The doctor said the wound should be kept clean and bandaged.''

"She said it was a cut.''

Niccolò suppressed a smile. How concerned—how curious—the woman was. And how eager to be involved.

"It is. But I fear it was self-induced.''

"Self—'' Olivie was plainly shocked. "You cannot mean—''

Niccolò nodded mournfully. "I fear so. In her grief over her husband's death, the poor lady tried to end her life.''

"Mon Dieu!'' Madame Rodolphe crossed herself in the face of such a grievous sin.

"Will you help me, Madame Rodolphe? Will you help me get the lovely, deluded lady well again?''

"If I can,'' Olivie agreed instantly.

"I will need you. You see . . .'' He lowered his eyes as if greatly pained by what he had to say. ". . . you see, the lady blames me for her husband's death.''

"Oh! Surely not!''

He shook his head. "As God is my witness, dear Madame Rodolphe, I was nowhere near Christophe Duclaux when he died.''

"I am certain you were not, Monsieur le Comte. You must not feel badly. The poor, sweet lady is out of her mind with grief.''

"I wish I could believe that. I wish I could believe that one day she will hold me in the same esteem she once did. But now . . . now, it is as if she sees an assassin behind every tree.''

"We will help her, you and I, Monsieur le Comte. You will see.''

Niccolò nodded, smiling gratefully. "You make

me believe that. I think you will agree that it is best if she does not wander about the house. If you would be so kind, I should like you to lock her door and bring me the key."

"*Certainement*, Monsieur le Comte," Olivie agreed. "The lady asked that a pitcher of water be left in her room for her."

"Then do so. But, Olivie . . . ? Put the water in something she cannot break. We do not want broken glass in the room."

The woman's face was a mask of horrified pity as she remembered the bandaged cut on Tori's arm. "I understand, monsieur," she assured him.

"And Olivie?" Niccolò called as she would have turned away.

"Monsieur?"

From his pocket, Niccolò extracted a packet. "This is laudanum. Perhaps it might be wise to mix some of it in her water."

Olivie nodded as she took the packet. "I think you are correct, monsieur. I will do as you say."

Tori stirred as Olivie entered the room. Her eyelids fluttered, then opened, blinking to banish some of the heaviness that weighed them down.

"Your water, madame," she said, pouring a serving of the laudanum-laced water into a pewter mug chosen for its softly-rounded edges.

Tori propped herself up on her good arm and sipped the water, feeling its delicious chill sliding down her throat.

"Thank you," she said faintly, falling back onto her pillows.

"Monsieur le Comte said . . ." Olivie began.

Tori's head tossed restlessly on the pillow. "Don't speak to me of Niccolò," she ordered tersely.

"He killed my husband! Your 'Monsieur le Comte' is a murderer!"

Olivie moved away as Tori's eyes closed and she sank into a sleep that was half fatigue and half drug-induced.

The poor lady, Olivie thought, slipping the key from the lock. She left the room and, after closing the stout oak door, locked it securely from the outside. Poor sweet lady—to be so young, so beautiful, and so deluded. Ah, well, with the Comte's help and her own, she would be well again. All she needed was rest and quiet. A nice, long stay in the country and all would be right.

33

Grey leaned forward into the wind as he and Marc-François rode toward Mérimée. The horses belonged to the justly famous stables of the chevalier's father, the Comte de Rochebaron. But though the deceptively fragile-looking legs and tiny hooves of the finely bred Arabs flew over the dusty, rutted roads, Grey chafed to go faster. If the horses had sprouted wings like Pegasus and flown over the treetops, they still would have been too slow to suit him.

Ahead, at the side of the road, a coach stood—or rather leaned—for one wheel had shattered. Three men stood beside it—two scratching their heads in apparent bewilderment and the third berating them viciously.

Grey reined in his horse and the chevalier followed suit. When Marc-François leaned close, he told him:

"That is the coach I saw at the Hôtel d'Eygalières. And those are the men who were threatening the woman and her son."

Marc-François squinted into the distance. "It is Quaratesi and two of his men. I will be honest with you, *mon vieux*, I have no desire to take on Quaratesi or any of his henchmen. Given my choice, I'd prefer to get to Mérimée, get Victoria out, and leave before this one can get there."

Much as Grey hungered for vengeance against anyone and everyone who had had anything to do with Tori's injuries and imprisonment, he could see the sense in not exposing her to any more danger. If this Quaratesi had ordered her death once, he would likely take advantage of any opportunity to kill her now.

He nodded his agreement, albeit reluctantly. "I agree with you. It will take some time for them to get that wheel repaired. We can make it to Mérimée before them."

"Let's cross this field behind the cover of those trees. I wouldn't like Quaratesi to see us. If he recognized me, he might wonder why I'm riding hell for leather toward Mérimée."

Taking to the fields, then, they passed Quaratesi and his men, hidden from them by the screen of trees and the bulk of the damaged coach.

In her room at the Château de Mérimée, Tori awoke.

Damn Niccolò! she thought. It had been the water! He'd put more of his damned laudanum in the water. She owed him a piece of her mind and she was determined to give it to him!

Sluggish and clumsy with the lingering effects of the drug, she shoved back the coverlet and slid her legs over the side of the bed. It was an effort to stand. Minutes passed before she could manage to make her slow, halting way to the door.

Her hand closed about the cool brass latch. She pressed it. Nothing happened. For a moment she did not comprehend the significance and then, when she did, her fury banished all lingering traces of the laudanum with which Niccolò had laced her water.

"Niccolò!" she shrieked. "God damn you to hell! You let me out of this room! Do you hear me!"

Silence was her only reply and she pounded at the solid oak panels with her doubled fists. Pain shot through her shoulder and down her arm from her wound. Gasping, she turned away from the door. The effort had exhausted her; the thick wood of the door had bruised her fists; the thought of being imprisoned here, with Niccolò, depressed her. Surely someone would come to her rescue. Perhaps Grey—

Her mouth twisted bitterly. Grey! Where was he now? Likely still at the Château de Lurneaux with the Duchesse. Or perhaps they had returned to the Château de Saint-Rémy. In all likelihood, she would never see him again. Just as she would never see Christophe again.

Christophe . . . His face swam in her mind's eye. Dear Christophe. She had never been his wife in the sense that Clairesse Candé was a wife to Etienne or, she imagined, as Elizabeth Phipps was a wife to Grey's friend Val. But she had been faithful and loyal to him and she had loved him, in her fashion, even if it were a gentle love, composed more of affection than passion.

"Forgive me, Christophe," she whispered to the empty room. "Perhaps you would have been happier with one of your fiery Creole beauties—perhaps you could have found the passion you sought with

Sandra DuBay

Joséphine Morande with a wife more suited to your
needs. But I did love you . . . in my way. I did.''

Weary, resigned to remaining at the château
until a means of escape presented itself, she crossed
the room and slumped into a chair near the pink
marble fireplace.

Help me, she prayed silently. Show me a way out
of this place.

The rattle of the key in the lock shattered the
cool silence of the room. Tori held her breath as the
door swung open, but it was Olivie Rodolphe and not
Niccolò who appeared.

"You're awake, I see," the woman said
brightly.

"Yes," Tori agreed bitingly. "No thanks to you
and your laudanum."

Olivie had the grace to flush and cast her eyes
down in embarrassment. "I am sorry about that,
madame, but you must be calm. The Comte only
wishes for your safety. He fears that you will try to
harm yourself again."

"Again?" Tori repeated, bewildered. She saw
Olivie's eyes dart to the bandage on her arm.
Realization dawned on her with awful clarity. "He
told you I did this to myself? But why? Why should
try to kill myself?"

"In your grief, madame. It is understandable.
When someone loses a person they love . . ."

"Christophe?" Tori rose, torn between disbelie
and outrage. "He told you I cut myself because o
my husband's death?"

"Yes," Olivie admitted. "He said—"

"And you believed him!"

"There seemed no reason not to."

Tori held out her arm toward the woman. Th
creamy linen that was wound about her upper arm

330

contrasted sharply with the delicate pink of her skin. "And why, pray, if I were trying to kill myself, would I cut myself here!"

"Reason does not always prevail when one is maddened by grief."

"Maddened by grief! I am not maddened by anything, Madame Rodolphe. Yes, I grieve for my husband. He was a good man. A kind and handsome man. But I did not try to kill myself—oh, no. A man tried to kill me. An evil man who worked for another evil man—the same fiend that Niccolò da l'Armi works for. They are a band of killers, Olivie. All of them. And Niccolò is one of them. It was he who killed my husband! My Christophe! I hate him! I wish he were dead!"

She stopped, seeing the wary, worried light in the woman's dark eyes. Sighing, she looked away. It's no good, she told herself wearily. Niccolò has done his work well. She believes me mad and everything I say only reinforces her belief. My only hope lies in appearing to recover from my 'dementia' and in gaining her confidence.

"I'm sorry," she whispered, looking fragile, wan, incredibly delicate. "I am not myself just now." She lifted a hand to her lips. It shook convincingly. "Please forgive my outburst."

Olivie's tender heart went out to her. She might be mad—certainly Olivie had never seen evidence to suggest that the charming Comte da l'Armi was capable of the kind of violence this pathetic creature attributed to him—but the fact remained that she was young and alone and had suddenly become a widow. Olivie, having herself lost a husband while still a young woman, sympathized with her. She herself had been fortunate; she had met and married Timothé Rodolphe after three long years of impoverished widowhood. She could only hope for as much for this pretty creature. The Comte da l'Armi obviously adored her, and what a ravishing comtesse she would make.

"The best thing for you just now, *chérie*, is rest. Quiet and rest, that's the thing. Come now, I've ordered a bath drawn for you in the next room and I've found something fresh for you to wear—an ensemble left behind by the Comte and Comtesse de Mérimée's daughter, Arabelle, when she and her parents left for Paris the last time. She is a small, slender girl, like you, and though the gown may be a trifle young for you, it is white and lilac which, after all, are also colors of mourning."

Tori nodded, demure and shy. "Thank you, Olivie, you are kindness itself."

But if Tori had hoped for an opportunity to escape when she was being taken to her bath, she was disappointed. Olivie merely locked the hall door then unlocked another which connected Tori's bedroom with a boudoir.

The tub, a stunning, gilded and enameled confection shaped like a sea-shell, was suspended well above the floor on tall, slender, golden scrolled pillars. Steam rose from its frothy surface and the scent of roses filled the air.

Tori paused by the bedsteps that had been set beside the precariously poised tub. She looked at Olivie who showed no sign of leaving.

"I'm sorry, Madame Rodolphe," she said, "but I am truly not used to bathing in another's presence."

Olivie's plump cheeks pinkened. "Nor am I used to being present at such a time, but Monsieur le Comte . . ."

"Don't tell me," Tori groaned. "Niccolo

ordered you to remain in the room so that I don't drown myself in my sorrow?''

The woman's averted eyes told her she was right. ''Very well, madame, but may I request that you turn you back? If you hear gurgles, then silence, you may feel free to summon aid.''

Looking every bit as embarrassing as she felt, Olivie took a chair near the window, her back carefully turned toward the golden tub. She heard Tori undress, then the creak of the steps and the splash of the water as she climbed into the tub.

The warmth of the water seeped into her very bones as she washed away the dust of the road and the fatigue that had seemed to shadow her footsteps like a faithful dog since she'd been taken from the Château de Lurneaux. She hadn't had a moment's relaxation, an instant when she'd been able to let down her guard. To her overtaut muscles and frayed nerves, the penetrating warmth of the sweetly-scented water was paradise.

Dipping her head into the water, she washed her hair before she realized she had no way of rinsing it.

''Olivie?'' she called. ''Could you call for another bucket of water to be brought for my hair?''

''There is another, just there,'' the woman replied. ''I'll get it for you.''

Leaving her chair, Olivie brought the spare pail and left it on the top tread of the bedsteps.

''Thank you,'' Tori said, as Olivie returned to her chair. Before she upended the pail over her head, however, she dipped her hand in it and sipped greedily at the water she caught in her cupped hands. It was warm, unappetizingly so, but at least she knew it contained none of the laudanum she so despised and of which Niccolò was so fond.

When she'd left the tub and toweled herself and

her hair dry, Olivie brought the clothing she'
borrowed from Arabelle.

The underthings, the pantalets, camisoles
corset, corset cover, and petticoats were delicat
things, streaming satin ribbons, frothed in lace a
delicate as a spider's web. The gown itself was high
necked and long-sleeved, a virginal confection with .
full, bell-shaped skirt sporting a wide flounce. O
white lawn, it was light as a summer cloud and a
sparkling white, with a row of pearl buttons dow
the front. A wide sash of lilac moiré wound about he
waist and tied in a big, stiff bow at the small of he
back; its two streamers flowed down to the ver
bottom of the flounced skirt.

Standing before Arabelle's mahogany-frame
cheval glass, Tori combed her long hair until i
gleamed golden and rippled down her back to th
bow of her waist. She looked up in wonderment a
Olivie took the comb from her.

"What are you . . ?" she began.

Olivie only smiled as she captured a broad
curling lock of Tori's hair from either side of he
head and tied them at the back with a ribbon tha
matched her sash.

"I look like a schoolgirl," Tori mused, turnin
slowly before the mirror.

"That you do," Olivie agreed. "And you wi
feel as young as one after you've rested. Your arm wi
heal—the wound is clean, not festered—and you
heart will heal with even less of a scar."

Tori bit back a scathing remark about he
wounded heart not healing until the canker that wa
Niccolò da l'Armi had been scraped out of it, but sh
thought better of it. She had to convince Olivie tha
she was beginning to accept her fate and that he
reason was returning. To do this, she must refrai

from ranting against Niccolò, who had obviously wheedled his way into Madame Rodolphe's gullible affections.

"I'm sure you are correct," she said demurely.

Olivie beamed with approval. "Well, then, shall we return to your room? I'm sorry I have to lock you back in there, but . . ."

"I know," Tori nodded. "Niccolò is concerned for my well-being."

"He is," Olivie agreed, delighted. "I'm sure it will not be much longer before you are free to go where you like."

"I hope you're right," Tori said as she preceded Olivie into the room. She clenched her teeth in frustration as the key was twisted in the lock, making her once more a prisoner. "Oh, Lord!" she said fervently. "I hope you're right!"

Sitting on the brocade-cushioned settee that had been built into the oriel window at the end of the long room, she glared out at the sun lowering toward the western horizon. Already it seemed balanced on the very tops of the trees in the forest that bordered the lawn at the westernmost end of the château. It would be evening soon, then night, then morning again, and she would still be here. And how many nights and mornings would follow, she wondered. How long could Niccolò imprison her here? How long before he understood that she could never love him? How long before Quaratesi found them and they were forced to flee further into the countryside?

The key rattled once more in the lock, and she pushed herself to her feet wondering if, perhaps, Olivie had gone to Niccolò to plead her case and ask that she be at least given the freedom of the château.

But it was not Olivie. Instead, Niccolò stepped

out from behind the concealing door.

His black eyes skimmed over Tori from the shining crown of her head to the tips of her slippers peeking out from beneath the flounce of her skirt.

"Victoria . . ." he breathed.

She turned her back to him. "Go away, Niccolò. Even a prisoner has a right not to be tormented."

"I do not mean to treat you like a prisoner—"

"You don't?" Her laughter was harsh and unpleasant. "What do you call it, then? I am locked in, drugged, treated like a madwoman." Her eyes glittered with loathing as she pointed an accusing finger at him. "You! You made me out to be some sort of suicidal lunatic! She believes—no doubt because it is what you told her—that you are trying to help me recover from the death of my husband! Why didn't you tell her the rest? That I would not be a widow had you not murdered my husband!"

"Victoria, please, listen to me. I must tell you that—"

"No! No, no, no! I will not listen to another of your lies, Niccolò! Not even one more! Just go! Keep me a prisoner in this place if you want, but for God's sake, give me some peace!"

"Victoria, you say this now because you are angry with me—"

"Angry?" She stared at him, incredulous. "Angry? You say that as though it were a trifle! If you had spoiled a new gown, I would be angry. If you had broken some precious object d'art, I would be angry. But you killed my husband, Niccolò! You murdered, in cold blood, the man to whom I was wedded as a child of fifteen! The man to whom I belonged! The man I thought would be my companion of a lifetime! That is no mere trifle, even you will agree!"

"Very well," he acquiesced sourly. "You hate me."

"Indeed I do. And I always shall."

"I do not believe you," he insisted stubbornly. "You were fond of me once—aboard the *Nightshade*. No, do not deny it. And you will be fond of me again. More than fond. You will."

"Never, Niccolò. Never! Whatever affection I felt for you has gone now." She shook her head. "No, I will never change. In my loathing for you, I will remain constant as the earth itself."

The last traces of humility faded from Niccolò's face to be replaced by stark, angry determination.

"You will change, *cara*. You will. When you are hungry enough!"

Whirling on his heel, he slammed out of the room and twisted the key savagely in the lock. To Tori, the sound of his footsteps ringing on the parquet floor of the corridor sounded like the hollow echoes of the gaoler in every child's nightmare.

"When you are hungry enough," he had said. Tori felt a shiver of horror coursing down her spine. Surely he couldn't mean to starve her into submission! Even Niccolò couldn't be that inhuman—could he?

With a feeling of dread, she realized that he could, indeed, be that cruel. He was determined to have what he wanted. It was not difficult to believe that he meant to do precisely what he threatened. After all, a man capable of killing another man—a man for whom he bore no ill-will—on orders from a third man, was capable of almost anything.

Leaving the window, she wandered about the room. She was restless, frightened, desperate to escape. She wondered if she could flee through one of the windows; it was true her room was on the second floor but perhaps, just perhaps, she could think of a way to let herself down by means of—

"And then what?" she asked her reflection in the dressing table mirror. "Where will you go? How will you get there? Can you ride one of the coach horses bareback? You don't even know where you are!"

The key rattled in the lock once more and Tori whirled toward the door. She steeled herself, fearing that Niccolò had come to torment her again. A sigh of relief escaped her as Olivie appeared.

"How are you?" the woman asked.

"Quite well," Tori replied, praying the woman hadn't heard her talking to herself. "What have you there?"

Olivie closed the door and locked it. Nearly concealed beneath a towel was a small basket with half a loaf of bread and a wedge of cheese.

"I am not supposed to bring you anything to eat," she told Tori. "Monsieur le Comte said he thought you should fast for a day or two to cleanse your system. He said it was a treatment used at Baden-Baden." She frowned thoughtfully. "Or was it Marienbad? Ah, well, in all events, I see no sense in starving oneself. I will bring you some water." She glanced guiltily at the carafe she'd brought the night before. "Without laudanum, I promise."

"Thank you, Olivie. Without you, I should truly go mad in this place."

The woman left and returned shortly with fresh water. Tori had no choice but to trust her and she drank greedily of the fresh, cold water. The bread and cheese were manna from heaven after a day's fast, and she had consumed them both before she knew it.

"I must take the basket back to the kitchen,"

Olivie told her, pleased with Tori's appetite.

"I thank you again," Tori told her. A disquieting thought occurred to her as the woman walked toward the door. "Olivie?"

She turned back toward Tori. "Madame?"

"Do not put yourself in any danger for me. I could not bear to cause you pain."

Olivie looked genuinely perplexed. "Danger? From whom?"

Smiling wanly, Tori shook her head. "Trouble, then. Do not get yourself into trouble for my sake."

"Don't worry about me. I will take care."

Left alone once more, Tori returned to the oriel window and sank onto the cushions. At least she was no longer ravenous. She felt sated—stuffed, actually. She had made an unashamed pig of herself. But then who knew how long it would be before Olivie managed to smuggle her another meal?

Sighing, she gazed out the window. The trees seemed but skeletal silhouettes in the glow of the setting sun and the—

She blinked, squinting toward the forest that bordered the lawn. Was her imagination getting away from her? Was she truly losing her mind as Niccolò wished Olivie to believe? Or had she seen two horsemen at the edge of the forest, visible only for a moment before they disappeared once more into the cover of the trees?

34

Monique Bouladoux stretched beneath the fine silk
sheets that swathed the brass-and-iron bed in Edward
Lytton's bedroom at Woodbridge. She had grown to
love this room. Behind the white shutters closed over
floor-to-ceiling windows, the Jamaican sky was overcast and threatening. It seemed somehow
appropriate, she mused, that the unusually gloomy
weather should so well match her feeling of dark
foreboding. Tonight was the night of the Wynters'
ball.

"Ah, you've decided to join the living," Edward
teased her as he entered the room and crossed the
gleaming mahogany floor to the bed.

He looked so devastatingly handsome in his
brown leather knee-high boots, tan trousers and
open-throated white shirt that Monique wondered
how she could ever have deserved the love of such a

man. She reached up and twined a lock of his sun-kissed blond hair about her finger. Smiling, he turned his head and kissed her wrist.

"I've brought you a gift," he told her, leaving the bed and crossing the room to a table near the door, where a leather-bound case lay.

"A gift?" Monique repeated. "But, Edward, there's no occasion. It's not my birthday. It's not Christmas."

"Does there have to be an occasion for me to give a gift to the woman I love?" he asked. "Must there be a reason for me to wish to give a beautiful woman beautiful things?"

Monique took the case from him with trembling fingers. She hesitated, gazing up into his eyes, torn between her love for him and the heartrending dread that Dorothée Arnault would carry out her threat and destroy their romance.

"Open it," he urged. "I want to see your eyes when you see what I've brought you."

"Open it!" he said sternly, though the dictatorial tone of his voice was softened by the roguish twinkle in his gold-lashed eyes.

Monique fumbled with the chased-gold latch. The leather was old and cracked. The decorative design on the latch and hinges was worn from many years and many feminine fingers.

When at last the latch gave and the lid lifted, Monique gasped in surprise and stunned admiration.

"Oh, Edward . . ." she breathed, dazzled.

There, on a bed of black velvet, lay a necklace of diamonds from which great ruby teardrops, like droplets of heart's blood, depended. Matching eardrops lay one on either side of the diamond clasp.

Monique gazed at it. "It's the most beautiful

thing I've ever seen," she managed, breathlessly.

"It belonged to my mother—it was my father's wedding gift to her. Before that it was his mother's, then my grandfather's mother's. It is the traditional engagement gift in my family and has been for more than a century."

"Engagement," she whispered. "But; Edward . . ."

"I want you to have it. All you must do is say you will marry me."

Closing her eyes, Monique let the leather case close. "Edward, you know I love you. But I cannot . . ."

Laying a finger across her lips, he silenced her protests. "Don't answer now," he told her. "I know this comes as a shock to you. Take some time. Think about it." He pushed the case back into her hands as she would have given it to him. "Keep this while you are making your decision. I want you to wear it to the Wynters' ball at Faircrest."

Dorothée Arnault's hate-filled face danced in her mind's eye. "It might be better if I did not go. I—"

"Not go? Nonsense! What's gotten into you today, Monique? You're positively dismal this morning."

"I'm sorry." She shook her head. "I don't know what's wrong with me today." A part of her wanted desperately to confide in him, but she couldn't. She wanted this day—which she was convinced would be her last with Edward—to be perfect. "Will you forgive me?"

The look on his face was so loving that Monique felt her heart turn over.

"This once," he teased. "Now, get up. We're

Sandra DuBay

going riding. Then I expect you to go home and start getting ready for tonight.'' He held the jewel case toward her. "Take these—and wear them!"

The ballroom at Faircrest opened onto the terrace from which the ocean, its endless black expanse streaked with silver moonlight, was visible in a vast, panoramic vista. The ballroom itself, a vision of white moiré, was lit by Waterford crystal chandeliers. The cornices were of intricately carved mahogany with tall archways over the door and windows. The cream of Jamaican planter society milled about in the glorious room, strolled on the terrace, and stood conversing with studied grace on the elegant staircase that wound upward in a lacy, oval spiral.

Monique, her flame-colored hair piled high, swept into the room feigning a confidence she was far from feeling. She knew she was beautiful. Her gown was of blood-red moiré d'antique, cut plainly with a billowing skirt, short puffed sleeves and off-shoulder décolletage.

As they were meant to be, Edward's jewels were the focus of her ensemble. The ruby teardrops fell over her shoulders and bosom and the pendant earrings swung from her lobes catching and reflecting the light like a shower of fire.

Among the women in the room, there were many who were old enough to remember Edward Lytton's elegant, much-mourned mother. Those jewels had been her favorites, and their appearance about the throat of this dusky beauty could mean only one thing. It was tantamount to a proclamation of intent. Edward intended to marry this woman.

"Lady Devizes," Monique murmured, smiling

344

into the eyes of the tall, graceful sister of their host, Pierce Wynter.

"How lovely you are, my dear," Iris, Lady Devizes, said, her tone utterly devoid of any emotion save genuine admiration. "You would create a sensation in London. I vow, the Prince of Wales would number himself among your most ardent admirers."

"You flatter me, my lady," Monique protested, charmed.

"Nonsense. I don't believe in flattery. And your jewels. Magnificent!"

"You've won over the guest of honor," Edward whispered as they moved on into the ballroom.

"She's charming," Monique replied. "I admit I was in awe of her. After all, she is an English lady. She is a friend of the Princes of Wales."

"And you are the most beautiful woman in the room. Now relax, and let's dance."

As the evening progressed, Monique found herself the center of masculine attention. The gentlemen vied with one another for her attentions. One after another, they partnered her on the dance floor. Even Edward seemed ever so slightly jealous when more than one attempted to entice her to take a romantic stroll with him on the moonlit terrace. The evening, for Monique, would have been perfect, but for one flaw in its genteel veneer.

As she and Edward circled the floor, a chill, like the cold fingers of doom, seemed to prickle its way up her spine. Her violet eyes darted about the room until they found the source of that chill.

Dorothée Arnault, swathed in black, a gauzy veil covering her face, sat in an immense, carved armchair. Though Monique could not see her face, she could feel that cold, hard, hate-filled stare.

When, after the third time, he repeated a question and Monique failed to respond, Edward led her off the dance floor and out onto the terrace.

"Monique, what is the matter?" he demanded. "I've been speaking to you and you haven't heard me. Your mind is a thousand miles away."

She shook her head, turning her face toward the bracing ocean breezes. "I'm sorry, Edward. I can't explain."

Bending, he kissed the curve of her shoulder. "Stay here, I'll get us both some champagne."

Before Monique could stop him, he had returned to the ballroom. She watched him cross the gleaming floor, saw, as if in a nightmare, the black-swathed phantasm rise from her throne and move with surprising nimbleness to intercept him.

"She's going to tell him!" Monique murmured, her voice quavering with terror. "Oh, dear Lord, she's going to tell him!"

Terrified, Monique fled along the terrace to the front of the Great House. Shaking, she ordered Edward's carriage.

"Stockton Hall," she told the driver as they started off down the drive. She lifted a hand to her throat as they drove away and felt the heavy gold and cold stones of Edward's necklace. She had to give them back to him. After Dorothée Arnault was done with Edward, he would want nothing to do with her.

"Driver?" she called, sliding the earrings from her lobes and releasing the necklace's diamond clasp. "I've changed my mind. Take me to Woodbridge."

Sitting back against the seat, the jewels lying in a glittering heap in her lap, she tried in vain to keep the hot, salty tears from flowing down her ivory cheeks.

"Wait for me," she told the driver as she alighted from the coach in front of Edward's beautiful home. "I will need you to take me to Stockton Hall in a moment."

She entered the house. Her first impulse was simply to drop the jewels onto the nearest table and depart. Every moment she spent there, in Edward's home, in the beautiful house she had dreamed might one day be hers, was sheer torture. But she couldn't just leave them—they were too precious, too valuable.

"Emerald?" she called, wondering if Edward's housekeeper mightn't have stayed up to see if her master needed anything when he returned from Faircrest. "Emerald?"

The house seemed deserted. And yet Monique knew it couldn't be. There had to be someone around.

Looking for someone in a position of responsibility to whom she could entrust Edward's family heirlooms, Monique went from chamber to chamber, exploring rooms she'd never seen before.

"Emerald?" She opened the door to a small rear sitting room after seeing a glimmer of light under the door. "Emerald, are you in here?"

The room, like the others, was deserted. Monique entered, thinking that the housekeeper might have fallen asleep in one of the winged chairs near the hearth. It was then, as she approached the fireplace, that she saw it.

A portrait, in an ornate gold frame, hung over the mantel—a portrait of a woman with fiery red hair and piercing black eyes. Dorothée Arnault.

The jewels slipped from Monique's hand to fall in a shimmering pile on the carpet beneath her feet. She stared at the portrait, recognizing her old

Sandra DuBay

enemy—recognizing the horror of her childhood, the chimera that had haunted her days and nights, the driving force behind the deaths of the two people she had loved more than anyone in the world.

Filled with a fury like nothing she had ever known, a blind, scarlet hatred that knew no rhyme or reason, Monique seized the fireplace poker and attacked the portrait. Hacking and slashing at the canvas, she wept with the release of wreaking her vengeance at last, if only on the image of Dorothée Arnault.

So engrossed was she in her fury that she did not hear the door open, nor even sense Edward's presence until he rushed forward to wrest the poker from her hands.

"What are you doing?" he demanded. "Monique? Monique!"

She struggled with him. "Give it back to me! Give it back! I have to kill her! I have to destroy her!"

"Stop it!" Casting the poker aside, he seized her shoulders. "Stop it! What's wrong with you?"

"Dorothée! Dorothée Arnault! I'm going to kill her."

"What are you talking about? Dorothée Arnault?"

"There! There! The portrait! Why is her portrait here at Woodbridge?"

"Monique, I don't know what you're talking about. The woman in that portrait is dead! She's been dead for twenty-five years!"

"No, she isn't! She was there, tonight, she—"

"Stop it! Now listen to me! I don't know what all this is about, but I assure you that woman was not at Faircrest tonight. That portrait came from Stockton Hall. That is Melanie Stockton, and she

348

isappeared twenty-five years ago.''

"Melanie . . . Stockton . . . ?'' Monique whispered.

"Yes. Melanie Stockton. She's gone, dead, isappeared.''

"Melanie . . .'' Suddenly, so much made sense, o many dark mysteries were suddenly bathed in ght. "Melanie . . .'' she whispered. Her eyes locked ith Edward's for a single, long moment, before she lid into a faint at his feet.

35

The sun sank behind the trees and Tori scanned the lawn's edge for some sign of the two horsemen she was certain she'd seen earlier. She had seen them. She had! Hadn't she?

She went to the windows and peered out, longing desperately for some reassurance that her rescue was at hand.

Meanwhile, concealed from the château by the forest, Grey and Marc-François tethered their horses to a tree and stood perusing the windows of the mansion.

"How are we going to find her?" Marc-François asked. "We cannot simply burst into the château. Da 'Armi may have men with him. Even if he does not, he may do Tori some harm before we can reach her."

"If we could get her out before confronting da 'Armi—if we could be certain she was safely away,

before da l'Armi knew we'd found her . . . '' Grey
mused. "We could—"

"Look there!" the chevalier interrupted,
clutching Grey's arm.

He pointed toward the château where the setting
sun glinted on leaded diamond panes as one of the
tall, second-floor windows was pushed wide.

Though from their vantage point they could see
little beyond a snow-white gown and long, rippling
blonde hair, there was no doubt in Grey's mind as to
who it was leaning out that window.

"It's Tori," he hissed. "Let's go!"

With a sigh of despair, Tori closed the window.
It was no use. She had obviously imagined the two
horsemen she'd hoped had come to free her. Escape
seemed impossible.

Sinking onto the cushions of the window seat,
she folded her hands in her lap and tried not to think
of the apparent hopelessness of her situation. To give
in to despair would be to abandon all hope of
eventual freedom and that she must never do.

Her head came up as she heard the sharp crack
of a stone hitting the windowpane. She listened,
wondering what it was she had heard. She sighed. It
was likely nothing. Perhaps some poor bird flying
into the windows. Or it could have been—

She heard it again. Not daring to hope, she went
back to the window she had looked out of earlier.
Even as she reached for the latch, she heard the crack
of another stone against the glass and felt the
vibrations of the stone striking the window.

Unfastening the latch, she swung the tall
window wide and leaned out. Looking down, she
found Grey and the Chevalier d'Archambeau
smiling up at her.

"Grey! Marc-François!" she breathed, nearly

weeping. "It *was* you I saw in the forest!"

"Are you alone?" Grey hissed up to her.

She nodded. "All alone. There's no one in the château but for myself, Niccolò, and a woman, Madame Rodolphe. She has a husband but he is not here now."

"Can you get out?" the chevalier asked.

She shook her head. "They've locked me in."

Grey's expression never changed. "You'll have to jump," he told her calmly.

Tori gazed down at him from her second story window. "Pardon me?" she asked, not believing she had heard him correctly.

"Jump," he repeated. "I want you out of there before I confront da l'Armi."

"But, Grey, I—"

"Do it, Tori, now. There's no other way. Marc-François and I will catch you."

"You and . . ." Tori looked down at their serene, confident faces. Jump, he said—as though it were as easy as skipping through a field of daffodils. He made it sound so simple, but she was the one who was supposed to step off a ledge and into space for a two-story drop.

"Come on, Victoria," he said impatiently. "We haven't got all night!"

Pulling a chair to the window, she climbed to the wide stone ledge. She squeezed her skirts through the window and stood poised on the sill.

"Grey, are you certain that . . ."

"Quaratesi is coming," he told her grimly.

Without another moment's hesitation, Tori stepped off the ledge. Her breath left her with a 'whoosh' as her body hit the two men on the ground. It seemed that one moment she was falling through the air, her skirts billowing out like one of the hot air balloons that were so fashionable on summer society outings, and the next she was lying sprawled on the ground, her skirts squirming as Grey and Marc-François fought their way out from beneath the yards of fabric and lace.

"Did you break anything you may need?" Grey asked, appearing from beneath Tori's lace-frothed petticoat.

"I don't think so," she assured him. "Where is Marc-François?"

He appeared from beneath her skirt with one of the lace flounces of her petticoat clenched in his teeth.

Tori giggled in spite of herself but Grey's lips tightened disapprovingly.

"If the two of you have quite finished," he said haughtily, "I'd like to get on with the business at hand."

The three of them stood and shook the grass from their clothes.

"Take Tori to the horses," Grey directed. "I'm going to finish matters with da l'Armi."

Tori clutched at his arm. "Grey, no, please! Let's just go! Please! Take me home. Forget Niccolò!"

"Don't you care that because of him, you got this?" He jabbed at her bandaged arm.

"Of course I care! I hate him for what he's done! But what difference can it make now?"

Ignoring her, Grey looked at Marc-François. "Take her to the horses," he repeated.

Over Tori's protests, Marc-François led her away from the château toward the forest where the horses tugged impatiently at their tethers. The last she saw of Grey was when he disappeared around the end of the château moving toward the great front door.

"What will he do, Marc-François?" Tori asked the chevalier after they'd reached the horses.

The handsome young chevalier shook his head. "I don't know, *chérie*, but I would not give a sou for da l'Armi's chances against Grey in a fair fight."

"A fair fight?" Tori scoffed, her brow furled with worry. "Niccolò da l'Armi doesn't know the meaning of that phrase."

They fell silent, the tension unbroken by either the rustling of the autumn leaves overhead or the restless shifting of the horses, their dainty, iron-shod hooves churning the soft soil.

"What can he be doing?" Tori wondered aloud. "It's as quiet as . . ." She couldn't bring herself to finish the phrase. "What's taking so long?" she substituted quickly.

Marc-François rubbed her back with a comforting hand. "Don't worry, *ma chère*, it will not be long now, I feel certain."

The evening sky was streaked with the shaded glow of a magnificent sunset, but Tori had eyes for none of its beauty. She crossed her arms and rubbed them with her hands. Though the evening was not cold, a chill seemed to have taken hold of her.

Marc-François stripped off his jacket and draped it about her shoulders. She looked up at him, her great cerulean eyes filled with such worry that his heart seemed to burst with tenderness for her. Encircling her with his arms, he drew her against him and cradled her head on his shoulder.

"Oh, Marc-François, Christophe is dead—my husband—did you know that?"

"Yes, *mon ange*, Grey told me."

"Grey?" She lifted her head from the chevalier's shoulder. "How did he know?"

"Word arrived from Jamaica. The man who wrote was part owner of the ship your husband sailed on. He said the ship exploded."

Tori nodded. "Niccolò did it. I don't know just how, but he—oh!"

Marc-François looked in the direction of her transfixed stare. Two men were walking across the lawn, followed by a woman. Niccolò, Grey, and Olivie.

"What are they going to do?" Tori whispered.

"From the looks of the pistols in their hands," the chevalier replied, "I'd say they were going to duel."

"No!" Tori struggled but the chevalier held her fast. "Let me go!"

"Hush! Anything you do now will only distract Grey. He would not duel with da l'Armi if he was not confident that he would win."

Knowing he was right did nothing to allay Tori's fears. She watched in horrified fascination as the two men stood back to back, pistols at the ready. On a signal from Olivie Rodolphe who was, Tori could see even at that distance, trembling violently, they began pacing off the steps that would culminate in the death of one of them.

Tori held the chevalier close, longing to hide her face in his shoulder but unable to tear her eyes away from the drama unfolding before her. As she watched, the distance between the two men widened. Time seemed to slow. As they turned toward each other and raised their weapons, an eternity seemed to pass before the guns belched fire and the sharp explosions of powder echoed across the wide, manicured lawns. Time stood still—the two men stood, frozen for an instant like one of the Empress Eugénie's tableaux vivants, and then . . . Tori's pent-up breath left her burning lungs in a whoosh as Niccolò slid quietly to the ground.

Tori's knees wobbled beneath her and Marc-François crossed himself and said a hurried prayer for the repose of the Count's troubled soul.

"Tori," he said softly, meaning to comfort her, but she was away, skirts held up from her flying feet, curls bouncing, the chevalier's jacket sliding from her shoulders to fall on the grass behind her.

"Grey!" she cried, ignoring Niccolò's body and the weeping Madame Rodolphe, who stood beside it. "Oh, Grey, I was so frightened!"

"Were you, my love?" he asked, gathering her into his arms. Slipping a finger under her chin, he tilted her face up toward his. "Do you want to know a secret?" She nodded. He grinned. "So was I!"

Then Marc-François was beside them with the horses. "Come along, we've already lingered longer than we ought."

"He's right," Grey agreed. "Up you go, sweetheart."

He lifted Tori into the saddle of his horse then swung up behind her. Over her head, he saw the coach-and-four that had just turned into the drive at the end of the park.

"Here comes Quaratesi," he told the chevalier. "No doubt he'll be disappointed to find his friend dispatched."

"Only because it will deny him the pleasure of doing it himself."

"He'd never lower himself," Grey disagreed. "He'd order one of his henchmen to do it for him."

357

Marc-François nodded. "At all events, they will soon be close enough to see us here. I suggest we depart. Quaratesi is not da l'Armi, after all. I doubt he would content himself to settle any dispute in the manner of gentlemen."

Grey agreed and Tori was only too happy to ride away from the Château de Mérimée and the remains of Niccolò da l'Armi.

Amid fond farewells and promises of future friendship, Tori and Grey and the Chevalier d'Archambeault parted company halfway between Mérimée and Paris. Grey hired two fresh horses for them at an inn and bribed a serving girl for her warm cloak to cover Tori's flimsy gown, and they were on their way again. For Marc-François, Paris was home for all its intrigues and sordid adventures. For Tori, Paris, and indeed all of France, was merely somewhere to leave. She did not care if she never saw its shores again. She wanted only to be home in New Orleans. A sudden, unwelcome thought occurred to her. She might not even have a home in New Orleans any longer. Ah well, she was safe now—safe with Grey. He would care for her and, if they could not return to New Orleans right away, at least they could be together.

They broke their journey at an inn just outside a picturesque village. The houses and shops nestled close to the winding lanes and the geese that waddled contentedly across the roads to the pond that shimmered in the moonlight seemed blithely unaware that they might be in any danger from passing travelers.

A fire crackled in the hearth of the chamber to which Tori and Grey had retired after dining in the parlor of the ivy-covered inn. Tori lay snuggled beneath three warm quilts propped up on fat feather pillows that felt like Heaven. She was reading Monique's letter, a smile curving her lips.

"I think it's wonderful," she told Grey. "She seems truly in love with this man, Edward Lytton. Don't you think it would be marvelous if he married her?"

"It's not likely to happen," Grey told her, not looking up from where he was polishing his boots by the fire.

"Grey," Tori pouted. "Don't be so pessimistic."

"It's true. She's a quadroon. No gentleman, let alone a great landowner, would marry a quadroon."

"Not even if he loved her?"

"Not even then."

Her mood spoiled, Tori cast the letter aside. "What will we do now?" she asked.

"I suppose," he replied, rising from his place by the fire, "we should go to the Château de Saint-Rémy and collect our things. Then I'll take you back. What do you think of returning to Jamaica for a while?"

She nodded. "I'd like that. Perhaps we can learn more of how the war is progressing at home."

His face utterly serious, he came to sit on her bedside. "What will you do now?"

"What do you mean?" she hedged, cheeks flushing.

"I think you know what I mean. You're a widow. There is no one standing between us. Not anymore."

Tori looked away. She could not deny that the fire that glowed in his eyes, the unabashed desire, stirred the banked embers of her own passion. But now was not the time. She could not take a lover—not even one she'd loved in her mind, in her heart, in her soul long before she'd ever laid eyes on Christophe Duclaux. No, her conscience—fickle, troublesome, animal that it was—demanded that she mourn her husband properly, as a wife should.

"Please, Grey, be patient with me. Christophe . . ."

"Christophe was dead before we even left Jamaica," Grey reminded her.

"I know. But it is as though it only just happened. I need a little time. Just a little. Please."

Grey ground his teeth. Dead or alive, Christophe Duclaux stood between them.

"A little time, Tori, damned little. I won't wait much longer. Perhaps Christophe was a saint. But I'm only a man!"

He stalked off and settled himself to sleep uncomfortably and angrily on the hard, narrow settee.

It was left to Tori to snuff out the last candle. She felt confused as she pulled up the quilts beneath her chin. She loved Grey—she did. But it would take time for her to get over Christophe's death, to get used to the reality that she was no longer any man's wife. She no longer belonged to a man and was free to give her love and herself to the man she'd loved for so long—the man who declared that he loved her as she'd always dreamed he would.

36

Tori felt a quiver of foreboding in the pit of her stomach as the fairy-tale château of Saint-Rémy came into view.

"Do we really have to stay here again?" she asked Grey, who sat beside her holding the reins of the team drawing the carriage he had engaged at the inn where they had spent the past night.

He cocked a teasing brow. "Why shouldn't we? It is a beautiful place and Gabrielle's hospitality is first-rate. Besides, I have a few loose ends to tie up here."

Tori compressed her lips, piqued. "Then at least promise me we only have to stay overnight. I don't want to be Gabrielle's guest any longer than strictly necessary."

"Don't you like Gabrielle, *chérie*?" he asked innocently.

"I like Gabrielle very much," she told him sharply, chin raised, face deliberately averted. "What I don't like is the way you behave around Gabrielle."

Grey struggled to keep his face a mask of cool indifference, but inside he was delighted with her all-too-obvious jealousy of the beautiful Duchesse.

"I don't know what you mean, Tori," he insisted. "Gabrielle is my little *cousine*. My affection for her only goes as far as a familial—"

"Hah!" Tori broke in. "Your affection for Gabrielle only goes as far as your—"

"Be nice, sweetheart," he interrupted, seeing where her disdainful glare was aimed. "We will leave in the morning, barring any unforeseen obstacles."

"Unforeseen obstacles! There hadn't better be any unforeseen obstacles. I don't want to stay here, Grey. I mean it!"

"Ah, you're turning into a regular little shrew, aren't you? Be careful. Men don't like nagging women."

Tori opened her mouth to argue but by then they were passing into the courtyard of the château and Gabrielle herself stood at the door waiting for them.

"How did she know we were here?" Tori groused. "Have you been in contact—?"

"Don't be so suspicious," he told her. "Likely someone saw us from one of the windows."

There was an edge of amusement to his voice that grated on her nerves, for she knew he thought she was jealous of Gabrielle. The most infuriating part of it all was that he was right!

"Victoria," the Duchesse cooed as Grey lifted her down from the carriage. "How wonderful to see you again. I've been so worried about you since Grey told me you had been taken from the Château de Lurneaux.''

In the face of such a welcome, Tori felt singularly ungrateful and disgracefully petty in her grievances against the Duchesse de Saint-Rémy.

"I'm all right now," she said, trying to keep the sharp edge from her voice. "All I want is to go back home."

"She's not quite all right," Grey disagreed as they entered the château. "She has a cut that needs attention. Is there someone in the château who can see to it?"

"We'll send someone to the village for the doctor," Gabrielle assured him.

"It's not necessary," Tori disagreed.

"It is," Grey insisted. He held up a silencing finger as she was about to argue. "It is!"

"Oh, all right. As long as it can be done quickly, so that we can leave in the morning."

"In the morning?" Gabrielle looked up at Grey, eyes wide and distressed. "Can you not stay a little longer?"

"Well," Grey said thoughtfully. He felt the sharp poke of Tori's finger in his back. "No, I'm sorry, Gabrielle, but we really must leave in the morning."

The Duchesse made a pretty moue. "How sad. But we will simply have to make the most of tonight, then, no?"

Grey cast an amused glance at Tori and bit back a laugh when she screwed up her face and stuck her tongue out at him.

"I'm sorry, Gabrielle," she said, "but I am utterly exhausted. I'm sure you will understand if I remain in my room."

"If that is what you wish," the Duchesse agreed, all too readily for Tori's liking. "I will order your dinner sent up."

"Fine." She glared at Grey who met her look with an infuriating smirk. "I'm sure you and your cousin can find nice, familial, things to occupy you."

"Familial?" Gabrielle repeated, obviously puzzled.

"Never mind, *ma chère*," Grey told her. "A small jest."

"Ah, well then . . ." The Duchesse summoned one of her handsome footmen and ordered Tori shown to her room. "I will send to the village for the doctor."

"As you wish," Tori called back, too tired to argue that she really didn't need a doctor's attention.

She thanked the footman who showed her to her room and requested that a bath be drawn for her. She felt grimy, caked with dust from the drive to Saint-Rémy, and all she wanted was a bath and a change of clothes.

Her trunks stood in the sitting room that adjoined her bedchamber and she rummaged through them until she found what she sought. The gown was of black silk with a high neck trimmed with a tiny, white lace collar. The sleeves were full, gathered at the elbow and wrist, and the billowing skirt was trimmed with three ruffles, the center one of black velvet. The buttons that fastened the modestly fitted bodice were of faceted jet and the sash that tied about the waist was edged with black velvet.

As promised, her bath was drawn. Tori soaked in the warm, scented water, delighting in the soothing caress of the Duchesse's bath oils against her skin.

"Madame?" A maid had appeared in the room, sent by Gabrielle to announce the arrival of Doctor Barbier.

"Very well, I'm coming," Tori promised.

Climbing out of the tub she pulled on her underclothes and a dressing gown. The doctor had been shown into her sitting room and there he examined her wound and replaced the bandages.

"The stitches will have to come out," he told her.

"Now?"

He shook his head. "No. Not for some days yet."

"I am leaving for America in the morning."

"Is there someone who could take them out when the time is right?"

"I suppose Grey could—"

"*Bon*. I will entrust the task to you. You are healing nicely, madame. I will leave you to dress."

"Thank you, doctor. Good night."

The doctor left and the maid who had come to announce his arrival helped Tori into her black gown. Her hair was confined in a fine black net and her only jewelry was a pair of pendant jet earrings and her wedding band.

"Will you have your dinner now, madame?" the maid asked.

A masculine voice answered her question from the doorway. "No, madame will be coming down to dinner."

"No, madame will not," Tori disagreed. She smiled reassuringly at the maid. "Madame will dine in her room. I'll call for my dinner in a little while."

The maid made her escape before any more contradictory orders could be issued. As the door shut behind her, Tori glared at Grey, whose silver eyes slid over her with sardonic amusement.

"Why," he drawled, "if it isn't the Widow Duclaux."

"If you've come here to be obnoxious . . ."

"I came here to ask you to come down to dinner. But I see you'd rather stay up here and mourn."

"Did it ever occur to you, Monsieur Verreaux, that I am now the 'Widow Duclaux' as you put it? I was Christophe's wife for seven years. Don't you think I have a right to wear mourning? Don't you think Christophe deserves to be mourned?"

He rolled his eyes, puffing out his cheeks in exasperation. "You have every right to wear it, just as any woman who has lost her husband has a right to wear it. But I think it's hypocritical."

"Hypocritical! Are you suggesting that I am happy Christophe is dead?"

"I'm not suggesting anything of the kind, Tori." He ran a hand through his hair. "Oh, hell! Look, just tell me this. Do you intend to keep this up for long?"

"Keep this up!" Her blue eyes blazed like ice on fire. "You seem to think this is some sort of pose I'm affecting."

His face was stony, his eyes cold. "I'm not so certain it's not."

"How dare you! Damn you! God damn you!"

He let her fury roll off him with no apparent effect. "I can see it coming," he sneered, circling her, his eyes running over her with obvious disdain. "For seven years you hid behind Christophe, letting him treat you like a child—letting his overprotectiveness keep you from having to grow up. You hid behind your wedding band in order to remain a child."

"That's a lie!" she hissed.

"It's the truth, and you know it! How much of life did you see while you were Christophe's wife, Tori? How much more do you know of living, of people, of human nature than you knew when you left your father's house seven years ago?"

"What are you talking about?" she demanded.

"You don't even know that, do you?" He sighed. "And what's more, you don't want to know. You don't want to know about life and love and passion. No, you'd rather live in your pampered little girl's world. I'll bet you were really terrified when you found out Christophe had been killed and you would have to face life on your own without a protector. But then, you discovered the means by which you could hide on your own, without Christophe."

"You're mad!" she hissed.

"No, I know exactly what I'm talking about." He snapped at the black silk of her gown with his fingers. "Now, with Christophe dead, you can hide behind your widow's weeds. You can retire into your mourning and keep the world at bay out of respect for your loss."

"I'm doing nothing of the kind!"

"You're doing exactly that!" he disagreed. "Anything—anything at all!—to keep from having to grow up and be a woman!"

Furious, Tori brought her hand slashing through the air. Grey's head snapped back as she connected and the room resounded with the sound of flesh against flesh.

"How dare you!" she hissed. "How dare you speak to me—"

In a flash, Grey had her by the arms, his face a mask of fury as he shook her savagely. "I'll do anything I damn well please, you spoiled little hellcat!''

"Take your hands off me!''

"My hands are exactly what you need on you, you high-nosed little prig. My hands, my lips, and more—much, much more!''

Tori shivered, her anger fading into confusion and then fear. That he could do as he pleased with her she had no doubt. He was so much larger, so much stronger than she. She would be powerless to stop him should he decide he wanted her. But that was not what frightened her most. What terrified her—shook her to the very depths of her heart—was the frisson of excitement, the flicker of desire that his words and actions aroused in her. Had he taken her into the bedchamber then at that moment, she knew she would make only a token resistance. She wanted him—God help her—as she could not remember ever having wanted Christophe. And it was that knowledge—the realization that Grey could arouse those emotions, those desires, those passions that Christophe had never been able to touch—that terrified her.

She stood like a statue in his grasp, her face chalk white and her eyes huge and haunted.

"Let me go,'' she whispered. "Grey, let me go!''

His eyes glowed silver beneath his lush black lashes. "Never,'' he murmured, his voice firm and commanding. "Try and escape me, Tori. Just try.''

She gazed up into his eyes, fascinated. Time seemed to have stopped; the world whirled around them, not touching them, leaving them alone in their own private universe.

"Grey . . .'' Tori whispered. "Grey, no . . .''

"Shhh,'' he breathed. "Don't say a word. Not

one word."

The rapping that shattered the heart-stopping tension in the room was like a blow to the soul. A little cry tore itself free from Tori's throat as she wrenched herself out of Grey's grasp.

"Who is it?" she called, turning away from him and grasping the back of a chair for support, for her knees seemed limp and totally unable to support her.

The door opened and Gabrielle appeared. Her smile seemed to fade momentarily as she unerringly sensed the tension that still hung like a thick, dark mist in the dimly lighted room.

She looked from Grey to Tori, perplexed. "Is anything wrong?" she asked uncertainly.

Grey mumbled something unintelligible and left the room. Gabrielle, after stepping quickly out of his way, turned back to Tori, more curious than ever.

Tori toyed with the end of her sash, studiously avoiding meeting the Duchesse's wondering gaze.

"Grey just came to say good-night," she told Gabrielle. "We were discussing our plans to leave in the morning."

The Duchesse nodded. "He told me you wished to go right away. Are you sure you would not like to stay? After all, the war still rages in your country. New Orleans, so they say, will be occupied by Union forces at any moment. Surely you do not wish to return to a city under seige by the enemy."

"Enemy or not," Tori told her, "New Orleans is my home and where I wish to be."

"And Grey? Is that where he wishes to be?"

Tori turned away to hide the flush that crept up into her cheeks. "Grey must do what he pleases. He is free to go where he wants and do what he wants."

"Victoria," Gabrielle said, her tone conciliatory as she moved to the door and closed it. "Victoria, are you certain nothing is wrong between the two of you?''

Tori longed to tell the beautiful Duchesse to mind her own business, but her position as Victoria's hostess entitled her to respect and cordiality.

"No, nothing is wrong. We have been through a great deal in these past few months, Gabrielle, that's all."

"Victoria . . ." The Duchesse moved closer and her tone became confiding, like an intimate friend inviting her to share the secrets of her heart. "Despite what you say, I know what is wrong between you and Grey. I know that the two of you are . . . how shall I say it? The two of you are enamoured of each other. But I also know that you are not the sort of woman who would take lovers while her husband lived. And now—tell me if I am wrong—now you feel you owe Monsieur Duclaux a period of mourning. I think Grey understands this, but it is hard for him. After all, he is only a man with a man's wishes and desires."

Tori thought she was speaking of his trying to make love to her and was astonished that the Duchesse, hostess or not, should attempt to insinuate herself into such a delicate situation.

"I assure you, dear Gabrielle," she replied, her tone and her patience strained, "that as far as Grey's wishes and desires are concerned, I leave him to exercise them at his own discretion."

"Ah!" The Duchesse seemed pleased. "You are very understanding. I had thought American women more . . . more puritanical. I had not thought you would take such an open-minded view of these earthy matters."

Tori frowned, wondering what in the world Gabrielle was alluding to, and said, "What precisely do you mean, Gabrielle?"

"Oh, merely that a man, deprived of the woman he loves, will occasionally seek his pleasure elsewhere."

Tori was thankful she had turned away so that the Duchesse did not see her sudden pallor.

"And Grey? Are you saying he has 'sought his pleasure' with someone here in France?"

The Duchesse turned coy. "Oh, it is not for me to say, *ma chère*." Inside, she knew what she was saying stemmed from pure jealous malice because she had desired Grey so and he seemed to have eyes only for Tori, but she could not help herself. After all, she did not intend to lie to the *belle americaine*, only to insinuate. What Madame Duclaux made of her insinuations was her problem. "But I know that Carlotta Sayce approached him at Lurneaux."

Tori laughed wanly, feigning indifference. "Ah, Carlotta Sayce. But she is a mere courtesan. Hardly a woman to concern me, would you not agree?"

"Indeed. These women such as Carlotta, these demimondaines, they are little more than whores who cater to princes and kings. Women such as you and I must look the other way and allow the men we adore their peccadilloes. Men are men, after all, and wherever you find a handsome man, there you will also find women of low morals eager to slip into their beds. The only consolation is that such women satisfy only the physical needs of most men. It is left to respectable women to satisfy the emotions. And that, in the final telling, is what is important." She giggled, nudging Tori conspiratorially. "Although most times, it seems men are ruled not by their brains but by, shall we say, other portions of their anatomy. Deep down inside, they recognize a good woman when the time comes to settle down."

"I am certain you are right," Tori assured her. "Now, at the risk of seeming rude, I am very tired."

Noticing the quaver in her voice, Gabrielle bit back a smug smirk. The little *americaine* had taken the bait and, considering how prudish and naive she was, the thought of Grey's wantonly bedding with Carlotta Sayce would be enough to give her a disgust of him.

She smiled sweetly. "Then I will say good-night. But, oh! You have not had your supper yet."

"I am truly more tired than hungry, madame."

"As you wish. Sleep well."

Forcing a smile, Tori saw the Duchesse out, then leaned on the door weakly.

Carlotta Sayce! He had slept with Carlotta Sayce! The bastard! While she was being taken to Paris to that fiend Quaratesi, Grey was rutting with Carlotta Sayce!

How could he! First Monique Bouladoux and now Carlotta Sayce! Did the man know nothing about self-control? And now—now!—he had the nerve to try to get into her bed! Well! She'd see about this! He could keep his distance—content himself with his little trollops—and not try to enslave her senses with his practiced wiles. Why, he was little more than a slut himself!

"That whore!" she hissed.

"Madame?"

She turned and found the maid watching her, her eyes wide with wonderment.

"Oh, not you, Thérèse. Monsieur Verreaux."

"Oh." The girl was utterly nonplussed but she knew better than to question her mistress or her mistress's guests. "As you say, madame."

"Will you help me undress and make ready for bed?"

"Of course, madame," the girl murmured, but her expression as she followed Tori into the bedchamber was one of wary confusion.

In short order, Tori was undressed and redressed in her lace-frothed nightdress. Thérèse tucked her into the high bed, then extinguished all but the single lamp that burned low in the adjoining sitting room to serve as a night-light.

Lying in the night-shrouded bedchamber, Tori tossed and turned restlessly beneath the silken sheets that swathed the ornate four-poster bed, haunted by images of Grey and Carlotta Sayce. After all, the treacherous voice of reason taunted her, Carlotta Sayce was a courtesan—she knew all the tricks for pleasing sophisticated men of varied and exotic tastes. What hope remained for Tori and her limited experience in sensual matters? How could she hope to please Grey in bed when he had been serviced by women like Carlotta who made their living—and a good one, by all accounts—making love. She, and women like her, made a science of their bodies and the many and varied ways of using it to please a man.

As she lay there in the darkness, tormented by jealousy and self-doubt, Tori wished passionately that she had never left New Orleans—that Christophe had never left. Perhaps Grey was right—perhaps she had used her marriage to Christophe to protect her from the world. But if it had protected her from many of life's joys, it had also protected her from many of its sorrows, and she thought she could use a little of that protection just now!

37

The Château de Saint-Rémy was lost in the distance
before Grey ventured to speak to Tori, who had been
unaccountably cool to him since coming down to
breakfast that morning.

He cast a sidelong glance at her as she rode
beside him in the carriage Gabrielle had provided to
take them to Grey's ship, which waited to sail away
from France. Why in hell, he wondered, did she find
it so necessary to garb herself in black? She was a
widow, it was true, and propriety demanded that she
dress in widow's mourning, but why this god-awful
stark black? Wouldn't gray do? Or lilac? No, she had
to have black from the tips of her toes to the top of
her head.

"Where did you get that hat?" he demanded,
scowling at the black straw hat whose rippling veil of
the finest lace was held in place by a spray of peacock

Sandra DuBay

feathers in a jet and diamond clasp.

"Gabrielle gave it to me," Tori replied icily, her eyes fixed firmly on the road before them. "She wore it when she was first in mourning for the Duc. Now that she is in second mourning, she doesn't need it."

Grey rolled his eyes. "I see. I thought perhaps her priest gave her the hat as a penance."

"You would," Tori snapped. "Actually, Gabrielle was most generous to me. She gave me several black gowns, some black underthings, and three black nightdresses."

"Oh, Christ," he muttered. The one bright spot in it all had been that she had only the one black gown and he'd known she would not wear the same gown for the entire voyage back to Jamaica. Now, thanks to Gabrielle, Tori was well supplied with the trappings of a good widow. Sitting beside him there, black-gloved hands folded in her lap, little cleft chin raised, she looked as prim as a schoolmarm. He didn't think he could bear seeing her like this day after day.

"You're not going to wear them aboard ship are you?" he asked.

"Of course," she answered calmly, distantly "I'm going to wear them from now on."

"And just who are you trying to impress?"

Her eyes glittered with anger as she turned from her studied perusal of the countryside for the firs time since their departure from Saint-Rémy.

"I know there is nothing you respect, Greyson Verreaux, not life, not death, not anything! But no all of us are that way! Perhaps you don't care for the proprieties, but some of us do. And I will thank you to respect my feelings in this if in nothing else! You are being paid well to take me home—I'll thank you to treat me with the same consideration you would give any other paying passenger."

"Now, wait just a minute!"

"I have nothing further to say on the subject," she snapped, returning her gaze to the road ahead.

Grey ground his teeth in exasperation. Part of him ached to know just what it was that had annoyed her enough to make her act this way toward him and part of him longed to simply turn her over his knee and spank her like the spoiled, willful child she was.

Ah, well, if she wanted to behave like an irritating little girl, she could go right ahead and do so. If she wanted to stare at the trees with her little nose in the air, so be it. He had better things to do than cater to her whims and moods. And he'd be damned if he would play the fool for her and try to coax her out of whatever snit she'd gotten herself into!

Settling himself comfortably into the carriage seat, the reins held firmly in his hands, he urged the horses to gallop and wished away the miles that separated them from the ocean and the beginning of their voyage to Jamaica and then home.

Stepping onto the deck of the *Nightshade* was like coming home for Grey. His crew greeted him like a long-lost friend, and they sprang into action, as eager as their captain to fire up the twin boilers and steam away toward home.

Below, in the cabin she had occupied on the trip from Jamaica to France, Tori sorted her trunks, telling the crewmen who had carried them down which she wanted left in her cabin and which could be stored in the now-empty cabin Niccolò da l'Armi had occupied.

Grey stepped back against the wall of the narrow passageway as two of his crew passed carrying one of

Tori's trunks. They paused as he reached out and lifted the lid. Inside, carefully folded, lay gowns and petticoats in brilliant colors liberally trimmed with ribbons and laces. He sighed. It certainly looked as though she meant to dress in black alone for the duration of the voyage home.

Tapping at her door, he waited for her to bid him enter. When she did, he swung open the door and found her surrounded by mounds of black silks and moirés and velvets. Black linen nightdresses, devoid of the slightest decoration, lay piled on the bed, and petticoats of black cotton and wool, trimmed with bands of black velvet spilled out of small, leather-bound trunk.

In the center of it all stood Tori, prim as an abbess, in a modestly fitted black velvet gown. Her beautiful hair was streaming down her back, but a black net and a black lace widow's cap lay at the ready.

"Yes?" she asked, as though to a stranger.

Grey ached to take her by the arms and shake some sense into her, but he controlled his temper with more than a little difficulty and merely enquired politely:

"We are about to leave. Would you like to come up on deck and take a last look at France?"

"No, thank you." She opened her traveling case and arranged her brushes and combs on the cabin's built-in dressing table.

"That's all? 'No, thank you?'" he asked.

Turning from her dressing table, she eyed him coldly. "No, thank you—sir?" she amended sarcastically.

Grinding his teeth, Grey turned without another word and stormed out of the cabin, slamming the door behind him.

Tori trembled, torn between self-righteous anger and heartrending sorrow, but could not bring herself to call him back.

It was much later when he returned. Darkness had fallen about the ship, concealing the empty horizon where all traces of land had long since disappeared.

Tori had extinguished all but a single lamp. Dressed in one of Gabrielle's black lawn night-dresses, she had pulled back the quilts on the bunk in preparation for retiring. She was not really tired. The tensions and excitements of the past weeks had filled her with a nervous energy that had yet to dissipate, but she did not want to leave her cabin for fear of meeting Grey in the passage or on the deck.

Grey. How was it possible that her feelings for him had gotten so muddled? She loved him. That fact, that single maddening fact had not changed since she was fifteen, and it would never change. But she could not let herself go to him. Perhaps it was pride—perhaps, as he insisted, it was fear. It may have been that she was afraid of passion—afraid of being a woman with a woman's desires and emotions. She had been a wife to Christophe in every sense of the word, but their lovemaking had been more for him than with him. She had allowed him to take her, as she had been taught a good wife should, but it had not been an experience she had shared in equal measure. Perhaps it was that she was afraid to give herself over to passion. But then, a comforting little voice whispered inside her, soothing her injured pride, perhaps it was only women such as Carlotta Sayce who ever wholly devoted themselves to the pleasures of the flesh.

Lost in her thoughts, she did not at first notice her cabin door opening behind her. It was only after

Grey had stepped inside and closed the door behind him that the clicking of the latch caught her attention.

Pushing away from the dressing table, she spun around to face him. His blue-black hair gleamed in the lamplight and his eyes glittered like fine, tempered steel.

"What do you want?" she demanded, feeling trapped.

He moved closer and she backed away. "I want to know what the hell is wrong with you!"

"I don't know what you're talking—"

"You damned well do know!" he interrupted. "And you are going to tell me!"

Feigning a coldness she did not feel and praying he would not notice her trembling, she turned her back on him.

"Get out of here," she ordered. "This may be your ship, but this is my cabin. Now get out!"

He moved not an inch. "Not until you tell me!"

Turning back to him, she was still trembling, but this time with fury rather than fear. "As you wish," she hissed. "Gabrielle told me about Carlotta Sayce."

"What about her?" he asked, perplexed.

"What about—?" Tori took a deep breath, trying in vain to calm herself. "About you and Carlotta, together."

"I don't know what you're talking about," he insisted, truly bewildered.

"At least be man enough to admit the truth, Grey!"

"I would, if there was any truth to it. I don't know what Gabrielle told you, Tori, but nothing happened between Carlotta and myself. I suspect Gabrielle was merely being malicious because I turned down her invitations to her bedchamber."

The ghost of a smile played about the corners of his mouth. So this was what it all amounted to—a fit of jealousy because she thought he had bedded Carlotta Sayce and, by the look on her face, she had suspected him of taking advantage of not only Gabrielle's board but her bed as well. His eyes glittered with devilry. "Not that I wasn't tempted, of course. It's been a long time since I was with a woman." That part, at least, was achingly true, he thought ruefully.

Tori stared at him, wanting desperately to believe him but not quite daring to. At least he had admitted to having been tempted. "But you thought about bedding them both, didn't you?"

"Of course I thought about it. They are both exceedingly beautiful women."

She lifted her chin disdainfully. "You're nothing but a slut!"

His silver eyes widened and the corners of his mouth quivered. "I'm a what?"

"You heard me," she said priggishly. "You're nothing but a slut!"

His laughter started out as a low rumbling deep in his chest but, much as he tried, he could not keep it from bursting forth. It filled the room with its rich, echoing tones.

Tori scowled at him, feeling foolish. "Don't laugh at me, damn you! You have the morals of an alley cat. You want to bed every woman you see."

Her self-righteous tones only fueled Grey's merriment and he gasped for air between bursts of laughter. "I'm sorry, sweet," he rasped. "But what can I say to defend myself? After all, I'm nothing but . . . but . . ." He drew a deep, painful breath. "A slut!"

She tapped her foot impatiently as he sank into an armchair wiping the tears from his eyes. "Are you quite finished now?" she asked.

He nodded. "I didn't mean to laugh at you, sweet, but I've never heard anything like that. I'm sorry. Come here."

Taking her wrist, he drew her down onto his lap, and for once Tori did not protest. She sat there, her head lying in the warm hollow of his shoulder, his arms around her.

"You truly didn't make love to Carlotta or the Duchesse?" she asked.

"I truly didn't," he vowed.

"But you wanted to make love with them?"

"Not the way I want to make love with you," he whispered.

She drew away and gazed down at him with troubled eyes. "I can't. You mustn't ask me."

"Because of Christophe?" he asked wearily.

She hesitated then plunged on. "No, not because of Christophe."

"Then why?"

She stared into his eyes for a long, silent moment, then, with a shudder, buried her face in his shoulder.

"I'm afraid," she breathed. "You frighten me."

Grey let out the breath he had held inside his burning lungs. There it was—at last—the truth. Now all that was left for him was to overcome it, slowly, carefully, restraining the desire that ate at him like some ravenous predator. She was his for the taking, but only if he proceeded with caution and patience, hard as that would be for him.

"Tori, do you remember that night—the night of the engagement party at Barton's Landing?" He felt her nod. "You weren't afraid that night, were you?"

"I didn't think about being afraid," she admitted, blushing.

382

"Do you remember what it was like—how it felt—when I touched you?"

She shivered in his arms. "I remember," she whispered.

His hand slid up from her waist and cupped her breast, his thumb sliding over the taut, aching crest. He heard her soft, mewing cry against his neck. "It can be like that again, Tori. It can be like that always."

She sat up and gazed at him with wide, wondering eyes, but beneath her wonderment, beneath the glimmer of desire he saw there, the fear still lurked.

"I know you're frightened," he told her. "And I won't ask you for more—not now, not yet. But you must promise me, Tori, that you will allow yourself to feel—let yourself be open to the possibility of passion."

Trembling, she nodded. "I can only promise to try," she breathed.

"That's all I ask. And now, you'd better let me get up and leave."

Rising, Tori stood aside as Grey rose from the chair. A long, yearning look passed between them and he lifted his hand and laid it against her cheek. Turning her head, Tori pressed a kiss into his palm and heard him draw a deep, sharp breath.

He moved quickly toward the door before he could bear it no longer and broke his word.

"Good-night, Tori," he said softly, opening the door. "And don't be afraid."

She bit her lip as he left the cabin, yearning to call him back but shaken by the feelings he aroused in her. 'Don't be afraid,' he said, but as Tori extinguished the last lamp and climbed into her bunk, she knew it was easier said than done.

38

Wrapped in a black velvet cloak, her netted hair concealed by a black leghorn bonnet, Tori stood at the railing of the *Nightshade* straining her eyes into the distance, watching for some sight of Jamaica, which Grey had told her they would reach within twenty-four hours.

She was torn between longing to be back in Jamaica and then in New Orleans and a desire to sail the endless oceans forever with Grey at her side.

In the weeks it had taken them to reach the Caribbean from France, Grey had fulfilled his promise to her. He had slowly, patiently, gently brought her newly awakened senses to a fever pitch. He had only to look at her beneath the lowered lids of his heated eyes, touch her with a soft caress as they passed in the companionway, and she came alive with such aching, raw desire that she longed for him to take her then, there, wherever they were. She was ready—more than ready—to throw caution to the winds, but by unspoken agreement they had decided it would be Grey who would decide when the time was right.

She trembled as a gust of wind made the ostrich plumes on her hat quiver against the side of her throat. She knew it would be tonight—this was their last night out of port. He would not, she believed, wait until they reached Jamaica.

At last—at long last—night fell. Tori sat swathed in a frilly, lace-frothed nightdress of diaphanous mauve silk, before her dressing table. The dim lamplight glistened on the chased silver hairbrush as it rose and fell, stroking the shining golden waves of her hair.

She heard the click of the latch and the brush hung poised in mid air. In the mirror she saw the cabin door swing wide as Grey entered the room. She lay the brush aside and rose.

For a long, silent moment they stood there, gazing at each other, the air charged with the tension of their mutual desire. Tori quivered; her lips moved trying to form words that would not come.

"Grey," she whispered at last. "Please."

And then they were in each other's arms, straining together, and the longing, the need, the ravening desire that raged in them both robbed them of the last vestiges of self-control.

Her face clasped between his big, powerful hands, he kissed her, a hot, searing kiss that stunned her and taught her in the breadth of an instant the difference between childhood and womanhood—the difference between merely submitting to a man's desires and wanting him, aching for him in equal measure.

It seemed that only a moment passed before they lay amidst the tangled sheets of the narrow bunk, the dark, burnished flesh of Grey's body pressed to the soft, ivory skin of Tori's.

Beyond doubt, beyond guilt, beyond shame, Tori opened herself to him, heart, body, and soul. She wanted him as she had never wanted Christophe. Her yearning for his possession was a sweet desperation made all the sweeter by the sight of the longing in his eyes, the slight trembling of his body as her hands caressed him.

When at last—at long last!—he took her, the sweet desperation became a delicious rapture that grew with the push and pull of each thrust until she knew nothing beyond the warmth of him, the smell of him, the taste of him as they kissed.

And the parting, when it came, was like nothing she could have imagined. She clung to him, weak, trembling, utterly his to command, even after the glorious peak had passed and they lay side by side, still quivering, their skins aglow in the light of the guttering lamp.

He was gone when she awoke the next morning. Tori lay alone in the bunk they had shared the night before. She felt reborn, filled with the realization of what she had hidden from for so long. Grey was right—she had used Christophe to keep from growing up, from becoming a woman. But now all that had passed. She felt as if her life as a woman had begun last night.

Filled with hope for the future, Tori rode in the carriage Grey had engaged to take her to Stockton

Hall. Close behind, a wagon came with her trunks.

From without, Stockton Hall looked much the same as it had when last Tori had seen it. But once inside, she could see the work Monique had devoted to the old mansion. The rooms sparkled. Gone was the oppressive atmosphere of gloom and evil. In its place was an airy elegance that owed as much to fresh paint and paper as to refinished and renewed pieces of period furniture rescued from unused chambers and attics. Monique had found them, seen them cleaned, painted, in some cases reupholstered, and then had arranged them attractively and harmoniously. She had brought Stockton Hall into a new era of grace and elegance and Tori felt she had much to thank her for.

"Missis?"

Tori turned and found Persephone standing in the doorway of the front parlor. She was dressed in a gown of black cotton and her ruffled apron and cap were snowy white and crisply starched.

"Why, Persephone! I wouldn't have known you if you hadn't spoken."

"I be de housekeeper now, missis. Mam'zelle done made me de housekeeper."

"Congratulations. I must say, you make an impressive housekeeper at that." Tori looked around. "Is Monique here?"

"No, missis. Mam'zelle be at Marse Lytton's. She stay wid Marse Lytton mos' nights."

Tori blushed at the girl's candor. "I see."

"Will you be stayin' here, missis?"

"What? Oh, yes. My trunks are being unloaded."

While Tori removed her bonnet and cloak, Persephone quickly and efficiently went about directing the delivery of Tori's belongings to the room she had occupied during her previous stay at Stockton Hall. She set two maids she herself had handpicked and trained from among the field hands to unpacking for their mistress, then rejoined Tori in one of the downstairs parlors.

"So," Tori said as she bade the housekeeper sit opposite her on the floral cushions of a magnificent Louis Quatorze sofa. "Tell me, Persephone, what is Monique's gentleman like?"

"Marse Lytton be handsome and rich. He be de massa of Woodbridge. Mam'zelle Monique be in love wid him and Marse Lytton be in love with her. He ask her to marry him."

Tori's eyes widened. "He's asked her to marry him? Truly, Persephone?" She remembered Grey's telling her in France that no gentleman would ever, under any circumstances, marry a woman of color.

Persephone nodded. "Many, many times."

"Has she accepted his proposal?"

"Oh, no, missis."

"But whyever not? If they love one another?"

"Marse Lytton—he doan know."

"He doesn't know what?" Sudden realization dawned on Tori. "Oh! I see. He doesn't know she's a quadroon?"

"Tori?" Monique was in the doorway, looking ravishingly beautiful in a riding habit of scarlet cloth. A scarlet felt hat perched rakishly atop her flame-colored curls, and a black feather floated out above a rippling chiffon veil that hung down her back. "Tori! It is you!"

Rising, Tori accepted the perfumed embrace in which Monique enfolded her. "You look absolutely beautiful," Tori told her. "Jamaica agrees with you."

"Not only Jamaica," Monique said, flushing.

She turned and beckoned to the man who stood in the doorway. "Edward, come here. I want you to meet Victoria Duclaux."

Tori smiled, delighted, as Monique's lover strode into the room. He was tall and handsome, his blond hair seemingly touched by sunshine. His smile was brilliant, his air one of contentment. Here was a man happily, utterly, completely in love. How sad it seemed that the issue of Monique's blood should keep them apart, should doom them to the half-world of lovers and mistresses rather than the far more permanent relationship of husband and wife.

"Monique speaks of you often, Madame Duclaux," Edward said, bending over Tori's hand. Then his smile faded and the light in his eyes dimmed. "Please accept my condolences on the death of your husband."

"Thank you," Tori murmured. "Will you come to dinner with us tonight, Mr. Lytton?" She glanced at Monique. "Unless the two of you already have plans?"

"I'd be delighted," Edward accepted. "And now, I must take my leave. Madame Duclaux? Monique? Until this evening."

With a courtly little bow for Tori and a kiss on the cheek for Monique, Edward excused himself and left. As soon as the front door closed behind him, Tori gave Monique a nudge and a grin.

"He's glorious, Monique! Absolutely glorious!"

While Persephone discreetly left the room, Monique sat down with Tori on the sofa.

"Yes, he is," she agreed. "And I love him more than I ever thought I could love anyone."

"Persephone told me he's proposed to you several times."

Monique nodded. "He has."

"But you haven't accepted him?"

A sigh welled in Monique that seemed torn from her very soul. "How can I?" she asked. "I am not what he thinks I am."

"Why don't you tell him? If he loves you—"

"You don't know how many times I've wanted to tell him. But I don't know what he would do. I'm so afraid he would leave me—shun me. I've been so happy these past weeks—happier than I ever thought I could be. If he left me—" A shudder ran through her. "I couldn't go on. I couldn't go back to the way I was before. I couldn't go back to being the plaything of some rich man."

Tori's cheeks pinkened, remembering who the last rich man was who had kept Monique as his private plaything.

"But you cannot live like this forever, either," she reasoned.

Monique nodded. "I know. But I cannot give it up until I absolutely have to. I cannot bear the thought of seeing love turn to hatred in Edward's eyes when I tell him." She stroked her forehead with a trembling hand. "It's been a nightmare, Tori. Ghosts from the past . . . Melanie Stockton . . ." She pressed her fingers to her lips.

"Melanie Stockton? Ghosts? Monique, what are you talking about?"

"She was here. At Stockton Hall. She came to me, more than once, through passages only she knew—the same passages through which she escaped the night she disappeared all those years ago."

Tori stared at her, utterly bewildered. "Monique? What are you talking about? Melanie Stockton is dead!"

"No . . . oh, no . . . she's not. She's alive.

Sandra DuBay

When she left all those years ago, she went to America. She ended up in New Orleans. She killed my father and destroyed my mother. And now she wants to destroy me.''

"I'm sorry." Tori shook her head. "I don't understand any of this.''

Monique sighed, trying to compose herself. "She goes by the name of Dorothée Arnault now. She is the widow of Vincent Arnault. My father.''

"Your father?" Tori was astonished. "I don't understand.''

"My mother was a *placée*. Vincent Arnault was her lover. And my father. He died in her bed and Dorothée Arnault saw that my mother was blamed for his death. She ruined my mother—drove her to such despair and degradation that she died of it.''

"And you think she means to ruin you as well?''

Monique shrugged. "That is what I don't understand. Everyone knows Edward wishes to marry me. I can't imagine her being anything other than outraged at the thought of a respected white planter marrying a quadroon. And yet apparently she has said nothing. There has not been the slightest breath of scandal.''

"Perhaps she has had a change of heart?" Tori suggested hopefully.

"Oh, I'm certain she hasn't. I simply don't understand it.''

"All I can say is, you should not worry about it until it happens.''

"I am haunted by the thought of Edward's love turning to hatred. But I can't live with this fear much longer. I want him to know—I want to know what he feels, what he thinks about it all. But I cannot be the one to tell him." Impulsively she took Tori's hands in her own. "Will you tell him, Tori? Will you?''

392

"Are you certain you want me to tell him?" Tori asked. "Are you absolutely certain you want to take this step?"

"Yes. Yes! Absolutely. Will you tell him?"

Reluctantly, Tori nodded. "When the time comes, if you still want me to, I will."

Monique's relief was liberally mixed with worry. But she seemed determined. "Thank you," she breathed, "I know I will want you to tell him."

Seeming brighter, happier now that this decision had been made, she smiled a brilliant smile. "Now! You tell me all about France!"

Tori wrinkled her nose. "Please! I don't even want to think about France! Trust me when I tell you that I was delighted to see the shores of that country disappearing over the horizon!"

"Really? To hear the matrons talk, one would think that Europe was the most beautiful, most cultured, most genteel place and Paris its crown jewel."

"Oh, Paris is beautiful. And it is sophisticated. And there is culture—wonderful music, masterworks of art, history. But it is like a rotten egg. It looks fine until you crack it open and then it stinks to the high heavens!"

"Well, then, what about Grey? How is he? And where, by the way, is the handsome Monsieur Verreaux?"

Tori sighed. "He's still in Montego Bay seeing to the mooring of the *Nightshade*, and he said he had some business there, although I can't imagine what it would be. In any case, he did say he would try to be here in time for dinner."

"How are the two of you getting along?" Monique asked. She chuckled, delighted, as a hot flush rose into Tori's cheeks. "Never mind, you don't have to answer that. I can see the answer in your face.''

"I love him so, Monique," Tori whispered.

"And he loves you. So at least one of us will live happily ever after!"

"I hope so! Oh, lord, Monique, I hope so."

When he arrived from Montego Bay, Grey was directed to the sitting room by Persephone. She had offered to announce his arrival, but he told her it was not necessary. Now, standing just outside the sitting room door, he heard Tori's fervent wish for their future happiness. His heart ached for them both. How could he tell her that he had but a brief time to spend with her before he had to leave for New Orleans and the Confederate cause, which needed both his skills and his ship? How could he tell her that, having won his hard-fought campaign for the mastery of her heart and her senses, he was leaving her for the danger and uncertainty of life aboard a man-of-war? How could he tell her that their newly born love could turn out to be like the dayflower that blooms from sunrise to sunset—its beauty but a brief phenomenon to be savored for a moment then lost forever.

39

Tori marveled at the changes Monique had wrought on the gardens of Stockton Hall in the months since Tori and Grey had left for Europe. Edward had lent her the gardeners from Woodbridge and they had swiftly and skillfully rescued the rare and beautiful plants from the tangle of tropical growth that was rapidly choking them into oblivion.

She sighed as she walked there at dusk, hand in hand with Grey. The past week had been pure bliss for her. In his arms, awakened to passion, she had discovered within herself a woman she had never known existed. Or rather, Grey had discovered her, encouraged her, nurtured her, shown her how to abandon the inhibitions and fears of a lifetime and open herself to the wonders of love.

"It's so beautiful here now," she breathed, casting Grey a sidelong look. "Not too uncomfortable a place to wait out the war, would you say?'

Grey gazed off into the distance over her head
"Not at all," he replied, strangely reserved, a
though knowing a storm was about to break over hi
head. "I'm certain you'll be quite safe here."

"We'll be quite safe here," she correcte
happily.

He frowned, troubled. "Tori . . ."

All at once, she knew what was bothering him
she knew what it was he was loath to say to her.

"Oh, Grey, no. Please, don't say you're goin
back . . ."

He took both her hands in his and gazed dow
into her eyes, pleading for understanding. "I must."

She shook her head. "No!"

"Listen to me. Listen! New Orleans is no plac
for you now. It would be different if I thought
could stay near you, protect you. But I'll be goin
back to my blockade running. It's dangerou
work—more so now than ever. I'll be away a grea
deal of the time. I don't want you there alone an
unprotected."

"I can take care of myself," she vowed. "I'v
changed."

"No one can take care of themselves in a tow
under siege, Tori. Believe me, there isn't a man in tł
South who doesn't wish he could send his loved on
to a safe haven like this. I'm lucky—the woman
love is safe, among people who will care for her.
you were in New Orleans, I should do nothing b
worry about you. For my peace of mind, if nothir
else, please, Tori—stay here in Jamaica."

Unshed tears glittered in Tori's eyes. "You'll sa
away—you'll sail away and I'll never see you again.

"Yes, you will," he promised. "I'll come bac
for you."

"No. You'll go away, just like Christophe. They'll kill you—those damned Yankees!"

Taking her by the shoulders, Grey shook her gently. "I'll come back! I swear it!"

Defeated, Tori drew her hands from his and turned away, wiping her cheeks with the backs of her hands.

"When do you intend to sail?" she whispered, her words barely audible over the gentle night breeze playing in the greenery.

There was a pause before Grey replied, "Tomorrow."

A cry of despair wrenched itself out of Tori's throat and, taking up her purple moiré d'antique skirts, she ran back through the gardens toward the house, leaving Grey to gaze after her helplessly.

She met Monique in the upstairs hall as they nearly collided.

"Tori! What's wrong?" Monique asked, seeing the anguish in Tori's face.

"It's Grey," Tori told her. "He's decided to go back to New Orleans."

Monique sighed. "I was afraid he might. You know he isn't the kind of man to sit here in Jamaica sipping rum when he could be in New Orleans helping fight the war."

"I know he isn't," Tori admitted. "But he says I must stay here."

"And so you should. You'd be in danger there. Grey wouldn't be able to protect you and you know he'd only worry about you when he was away."

Tori pouted. "You sound just like him!"

"I'm sorry," Monique said smiling. "But it is true. Make the most of the time you have left before he leaves. It may be a long time before he can come back."

"We haven't much time before he leaves. He wants to sail tomorrow." Tori clasped her hands in her skirts. "I'm so frightened, Monique. What if he doesn't come back?"

"None of that!" Monique ordered sternly. "He will come back! You must refuse to even consider any other possibility!"

Drawing a deep breath, Tori nodded. "You're right, I know. It's only that we've only begun . . . I can't bear the thought . . ."

She looked helplessly at Monique, who slid an arm about her waist and drew her to the window seat in an alcove of the corridor.

"You'll have the rest of your lives together once this dreadful war is over," she told Tori. "And you know that part of what you love about Grey is that he is not the kind of man to sit in Jamaica while his country is being torn apart. He'll never take the coward's way out. Can you say you'd want him to?"

"No." Tori laughed. "How have you managed to make me feel selfish for wanting Grey to stay with me?"

"You're not selfish," Monique assured her. "You're only a woman in love."

They fell silent, and Monique toyed with the skirts of her emerald glacé silk gown.

"With all you have on your mind just now, I hesitate to ask the favor I was going to ask of you tonight."

"No, please! Take my mind off Grey's departure!"

"Edward is coming to dinner tonight," Monique told her, her fingers working nervously at the gilded silver sticks of her antique French fan. "I cannot go on with this masquerade any longer. I think it must be tonight that he learns the truth."

She touched Tori's arm. "And if he . . ." she drew a deep breath. "If the worst happens, I will not have to face it alone."

The two women clasped hands, comforting each other, giving each other support and courage, joined as two women in love who each saw a threat to their loves. Rising from the window seat, they went down the stairs together, the stiff silk of their gowns whispering on the carpet.

As they circled the first landing, they saw Grey standing at the foot of the stairs. Resplendent in his evening dress, he looked devastatingly, dangerously, handsome.

"Why, Monsieur Verreaux," Monique purred. "I do declare, you are absolutely the most indecently handsome man I ever did see."

Grey laughed. "How kind of you, mademoiselle. Allow me to return the compliment." The easy smile faded from his eyes as he reached up to take Tori's hand when the two women reached the foot of the stairs.

"Are you all right?" he asked her.

She nodded. "I'm fine."

"And you understand?"

Again, she nodded. "I understand why you must go. But that doesn't stop me from wishing you didn't have to."

Monique swept into the parlor, leaving them alone in the hall. In the light of the crystal chandelier they gazed at each other, each willing this moment to last forever, each knowing they would be parted, perhaps for ever, within hours.

"Marse Lytton be heah," Persephone appeared to announce, having seen Edward's carriage from one of the dining room windows.

The spell broken, they joined Monique in the

parlor while Persephone went to show Edward Lytton in.

The conversation was light, charming, and entertaining, but throughout dinner Monique and Tori exchanged surreptitious glances. Both had reason to be on edge. In the morning, the man Tori loved would be lost to her, perhaps for ever. Tonight, Monique felt she was in similar danger.

Neither was unhappy when it was time for the ladies to retire while Grey and Edward enjoyed their port and cigars.

"He's charming," Tori told Monique as they stood before a tall pier glass tidying their hair and smoothing their skirts. "And it's obvious that he loves you."

Monique sighed, turning away from the glass. "And I love him." Balling her fists, she turned her face heavenward. "Oh, God! Why couldn't you have made me pure-blooded anything? White, black—anything but this limbo I live in! I can't bear it any longer, Tori. As soon as the men have finished their cigars, I shall take Grey walking out on the terrace. While we are gone, will you take Edward into one of the parlors and tell him the truth?"

"Are you certain you want me to?" Tori asked. She did not relish the prospect of being the instrument by which Monique's hopes and dreams could be forever shattered. "What if I make a muddle of everything?"

"You won't. I know it. Just tell him the truth."

"But Monique, wouldn't it be better if you did it yourself?"

Monique shook her head, setting her cascading curls to bouncing. "I can't. If I were ever going to be able to, I would have by now. But it's impossible. Please, Tori, say you will help me."

SCARLET SURRENDER

Still wondering if she could undertake such a
delicate task without doing more harm than good,
Tori agreed reluctantly.

As she'd proposed, Monique slipped her hand
through Grey's arm and enticed him out onto the
terrace overlooking the gardens.

"Would you like to stroll on the terrace as well,
Madame Duclaux?" Edward asked, his blue eyes
sparkling, the lamplight playing in his golden hair.

Tori was struck by his good looks. They were of
a completely different type from Grey's, but were
just as striking in their own way.

"Thank you, Mister Lytton," she replied. "But
no. Actually," she smiled uncertainly. "To tell you
the truth, Monique took Grey out onto the terrace so
that I might have an opportunity to speak to you on a
private, and somewhat delicate, matter."

There was no dawning of surprise in his eyes. "I
thought as much," he said. "Shall we go into one of
the parlors?"

Together they retired to a small parlor that
Monique had had decorated in shades of rose and
cream. Edward sat down, amazingly relaxed, while
Tori, nervous as a cat, perched on the edge of a sofa.

"First of all, Mr. Lytton—" she began.

"Edward," he corrected, smiling.

"Edward," she repeated. "And you must call
me Tori."

"As you wish," he agreed.

"Good. Well, then . . ." She clasped and
unclasped her hands in her lap. "As I was saying."

"Monique asked you to speak to me," he
prompted her.

"Yes." She took a deep breath. "Monique loves
you very much, Edward."

"As I love her."

"Yes. You must remember that above all else. She wants very much to be your wife."

"I have asked her many times to marry me."

"I know. And she wants to. But she hesitates because there is something about her that you do not know. Something she thinks you must know before you commit yourself to marrying her."

"That she is of mixed blood?" he asked.

"It is that she is of—" Tori broke off, eyes wide, as she suddenly realized what it was he had said. "You already know!"

He smiled. "Yes, I already know. I had long suspected something of the kind, but I was not certain until the ball at Faircrest."

"Dorothée Arnault told you?" Tori asked.

He nodded. "She accosted me at the ball. She could not wait to expose Monique's secret. She is a very bitter, mentally unbalanced woman. She could not bear to see Monique happy. She could not stand by while the daughter of her husband's union with a woman of color became the mistress of a great plantation."

"But why did you say nothing? Why didn't you tell Monique you knew her secret?"

"I wanted Monique to come to me—to trust me enough to tell me the truth. I wanted her to believe that my love was strong enough to overcome any obstacle."

"And now that you know about Monique's parentage, you have not changed your mind about wishing to marry her?"

"Not at all. You see, I have a secret of my own. I know more of how Monique feels about this than she imagines."

"You cannot mean . . ."

His smile was positively beatific. "A great-grandmother on my mother's side was an octoroon. You see, there was no heir to inherit my great-grandfather's estates, so he adopted his son by his octoroon mistress. That is why Monique's blood is not a consideration to me. But I wanted her to trust me enough to tell me the truth herself."

"She wanted to. You must believe that, Edward. It was only that she was afraid you would turn against her. She loves you so—she could not have borne seeing the love fade from your eyes to be replaced by loathing."

"That would never have happened," Edward assured her. He rose and offered Tori his arm. "Shall we go and tell Monique? Or would you rather leave her in suspense a little longer?"

"Oh, no. That would be cruel."

Together they left the parlor and went to find Monique and Grey. It took but a single glance at Tori's smiling face to tell Monique that all was well.

In a moment, they had changed partners and Monique and Edward had disappeared into the scented moonlight of the terrace, leaving Tori and Grey alone.

"How wonderful for them," Tori sighed, watching their silhouettes disappear.

"I take it Edward did not mind about Monique's heritage," Grey commented.

Tori shook her head, but told him nothing. It was for Monique and Edward to confide Edward's true reason for so readily accepting Monique exactly as she was.

"Everything will be fine now. I know they are going to be very happy."

"And what about us?" Grey began.

Before he could finish, Monique and Edward re-appeared. Edward was smiling, his air already proud and proprietary. Monique was so radiant she seemed to glow with a new confidence, an inner contentment that showed in her face, in her stance, in the very air that surrounded her.

"We're getting married," she told them, bursting with her news. "As soon as possible. The arrangements have to be made. Edward would like it to be at Woodbridge. Tori, I want you to be my attendant." Reaching out, she took Grey's hand. "We wish you could be there."

"So do I," he assured her. "But I do plan to leave for New Orleans sometime tomorrow."

Monique cooed her disappointment and Edward expressed his regret, but it was Tori who felt desolate and abandoned. Monique's happiness seemed to accentuate the melancholy of her own situation.

As soon as she possibly could, Tori excused herself and retired to her room. She was not jealous of Monique—on the contrary, she was pleased for her and delighted that she had been able to play a part in it all. But she envied Grey's former mistress. She had fallen in love with a handsome, gentle man who loved her in return and the fickle fates had been kind enough to allow them their happiness.

She sat on the window seat gazing out into the darkness. Her silver-backed hairbrush was clasped loosely in one hand as she brushed her hair absently, paying scant attention to what she was doing as her thoughts raced.

Lost in her thoughts, she did not at first hear Grey let himself into her room.

"Tori?" he said softly.

Gasping, she dropped the brush. She stared as he crossed the room, picked up the brush, and handed it to her as he sat on the opposite end of the window seat.

She sighed, leaning her head back against the wall. In the shadows of the dimly lighted room, Grey discarded his jacket and unfastened his waistcoat. He looked as gloriously handsome as she could ever remember. How could she stand by and let him steam away in the morning? He was going to New Orleans—going to risk his life in that cursed, bloody war that raged there. After tomorrow, she might never see him again.

She frowned, biting her lip. No! Monique was right. She could not think such thoughts. Grey would come back—he would! No Union bullet would harm him. No Yankee ship could outrun the *Nightshade*. The day would come when Grey would return to Jamaica, to Stockton Hall, to her, and this nightmare would fade away the way Monique and Edward's problems had faded in the blaze of their love. It was what she had to believe, what she needed to believe, in order to have the courage to go on.

"Monique looked so happy, didn't she?" she murmured. "I just know she and Edward are going to be perfect together."

"I'm sure they are," Grey agreed. "But I did not come here to talk about Monique and Edward."

"Oh?" she glanced at him and then, unable to trust herself to maintain her composure, turned her gaze back to the window. "Have you decided to stay for the wedding?"

"No, I am still determined to go to New Orleans as soon as I can. Tomorrow, if possible. The next day at the latest."

"Have you come to ask me to go with you?" She struggled to keep the hope from her voice.

"No," he answered, dashing her hopes before they were fully formed. He hesitated, seeming to ponder the best way to say what he'd come to say.

"I've come," he said at last, "to ask you to marry me."

Tori stared at him, speechless, as the minutes ticked by. "Marry you?" she said at last, breathless, astonished.

He gazed out the window toward the moonlit night. "I want you to be my wife, Tori. I want to sail away from here knowing you're mine in every sense of the word."

"I am already that," she told him, pulse pounding.

"I know. But I want you to be Madame Verreaux. And there is another reason, although I've already told you the main one."

"What is the other reason?" Tori asked.

"If we've created a child together—and I pray that we have—I want our child to be born a Verreaux, not a Duclaux."

She gazed into his face and saw there a genuine glimmer of anxiety. As if he could imagine she did not wish passionately to be Victoria Verreaux.

"How can we be married" she asked, "if you are to sail tomorrow?"

"I'll see to the ring and the minister first thing in the morning. Ask Monique to be your witness. I'll ask Lytton to be mine."

"And then you will leave me to go to New Orleans?" Tori whispered.

A devilish grin spread over his face. "Well, perhaps the day after. After all, tomorrow night will be our wedding night, won't it?"

Tori nodded, flushing. "I love you, Grey," she whispered, sliding across the window seat and into his arms.

Kissing her gently, tenderly, he lifted her in his

arms and carried her to the four-poster bed that, on
the morrow, would become their marriage bed.

Flanked by Edward Lytton and Monique
Bouladoux, in the presence of Persephone, Grey and
Tori were married. A minister had been summoned
from Montego Bay and Grey had procured a simple
gold wedding band, which he slipped on Tori's finger
while repeating the vows that would bind them
together forever.

Afterwards, they drank a toast to the future and
Monique and Edward slipped away to Woodbridge
to allow Grey and Tori a day and night of privacy
before Grey's departure.

Though they had intended to return in time to
see Grey off, they entered the parlor the following
day to find Tori all alone.

"Where's the lucky groom?" Edward asked, his
tone lightly teasing.

Tori nodded toward the window. There, in the
distance, only the plumes of smoke rising from its
twin smokestacks marked its outward bound course
as the *Nightshade* steamed away toward the open
Caribbean.

"That's not . . ." Monique murmured. "It
can't be . . ."

"It's Grey," Tori breathed. "He's going home
to New Orleans."

"Oh, Tori . . ."

Excusing herself, Tori fled to her room. She
threw herself across the high bed in which she and
Grey had spent the past twenty-four hours alternately
making love and falling asleep entwined in each
other's arms. Somehow the fact that he was her
husband and she his wife made their separation all

the more painful. But she had promised him she would be brave, and she would—if it killed her. Right now she felt as if her breaking heart would do just that.

40

The winter passed in a monotonous melding of days into weeks into months. Surrounded by the luxury of the restored Stockton Hall, Tori felt like the proverbial bird in the gilded cage. She lived in comfort, cared for by Persephone and the staff she had assembled and trained with astonishing efficiency for one so young and inexperienced. Overseers saw to the running of the Hall's cane fields with such clockwork precision that Tori scarcely knew that the business of a great plantation was being conducted all around her.

Not that she had become a hermit. Monique saw to it that Tori spent at least one evening a week at Woodbridge and Tori was obliged to return the invitation. She spent Christmas with the newly-wedded Lyttons only weeks after serving as Monique's attendant at her wedding to Edward.

Their happiness seemed complete. Dorothée Arnault seemed to have disappeared after Edward confronted her with his knowledge of her true identity. There were too many in Jamaica who remembered Melanie Stockton and her barbaric cruelties for her to ever imagine that she could return and settle there.

But if their days were idyllic, Tori's were a perpetual torment. Though Monique tried her best, and Persephone worked hard to keep her mistress's days from falling into too dull a routine, Tori could not help brooding.

There had been no word from Grey since the day after their wedding—the day he had gone from his bride's bedchamber to the deck of his ship and steamed away leaving her to gaze after him. She knew nothing about where he might be or what he might be doing. Had he returned to the life of a blockade runner? Surely the Union Navy had closed off the port of New Orleans by now. Or had he been captured or, heaven help her, had the *Nightshade* been sunk? News reached Jamaica in a trickle, and what did arrive usually came to Kingston or Port Royal and took forever to reach Montego Bay.

Standing beneath the pillared roof that covered part of the terrace, Tori gazed out at the gardens that were soaking, glistening with the moisture of a cool spring rain. It was May—May!—and Grey had been gone for months. Tori rested a hand on her tightly laced abdomen. Had she become pregnant during those truly glorious days just after their arrival in Jamaica, her time would have been drawing near. How she wished it had happened! At least she would have Grey's child to hold, to love.

"Oh, Grey . . ." She sighed. "Where are you? Why don't you come to me? Why don't you at least send me some word that you are alive and well?"

"Tori?" Monique appeared in the doorway, having been directed to Tori by Persephone, who had confided that the mistress was more disheartened than usual today.

"Ah, Monique." Tori reentered the house. "It's good of you to visit. How is Edward?"

"Edward is delightful, as always, thank you," Monique relied, following Tori into a small, intimate parlor that was decorated, not in the delicate, gilded French fashion as were most of the others, but more in the way of an English country house. She sank into an armchair as Tori poured tea from the silver service Persephone had brought to her. "He sends you his love."

"Give him mine," Tori said, handing Monique her tea.

"How are you feeling today?"

Tori shrugged. "Oh, I'm all right. You really mustn't worry about me, Monique. Although you know I do appreciate your concern."

"You don't get out enough. If you went to some of the dinners and soirées you're invited to—"

"I know," Tori interrupted her wearily. "No doubt you are quite right. But somehow I simply can't convince myself to face all those people."

"Well, that, in part, is why I am here. I want you to come to Woodbridge for dinner on Thursday night. We are having a special guest and I think you may be interested in meeting him."

"Him? Now, Monique, don't tell me you are trying to play matchmaker. Grey may have left one day after our wedding, but I am still his—"

"Tori, Tori, slow down! Let me explain. A Union ship, the *U.S.S. Ironton,* has anchored in Montego Bay."

"A Union ship? But what is a Union ship doing in Jamaica?"

"Apparently it has been chasing Confederate cruisers in the Caribbean. They've been wreaking havoc on shipping."

"Have you spoken to any men from the ship, Monique?" Tori demanded, perching on the edge of her chair. "Have they mentioned any specific Confederate ships?"

"Such as the *Nightshade*, for example?" Monique inquired, smiling. "Actually, I haven't met anyone from the ship yet. They've spoken to Edward, though, and he invited the captain, Zachary McWhirter, to dinner."

"And you thought I would want to meet him? Monique, he is the enemy."

"But it is not such a bad thing to get to know your enemy, is it? In any case, it may be of interest to you to hear the latest news from New Orleans."

"He has been to New Orleans?" Tori asked eagerly.

"He is bound for New Orleans. He has been ordered to join Admiral Farragut's fleet." Taking a deep breath, Monique reached across the table and took Tori's hand. "New Orleans has been taken, Tori. Farragut's fleet broke through their defenses three weeks ago. A man named Butler—Major-General Benjamin Butler—garrisoned the town the first of May."

"Garrisoned . . ." Tori felt faint. The thought of New Orleans—beautiful New Orleans—occupied by enemy troops sickened her. She thought of her friends there—of Clairesse and Etienne Candé, of Elizabeth and Valentine Phipps, of Louise, her maid, and of Grey. Grey! Where was he now that their home was in the hands of the enemy?

"So you see why it is important that you come to Woodbridge and meet this captain—"

"Monique! I have to get back to New Orleans! I have to find Grey!"

"Don't be foolish! The war has come to New Orleans. It's no place for you. Grey would not want you there and you know it."

"But Grey might be hurt! He might be a prisoner! For God's sake, Monique, he might be dea—"

"Don't say that! You stop that right now! Do you hear me? I won't have you saying such things!"

"I'm sorry, Monique. But I'm so worried about him. It's been so long with no word at all. Sometimes I'm so frightened."

"I know. We all are. Come to Woodbridge. Meet Captain McWhirter and see what he has to say. You might learn something that will be of comfort to you."

"I will," Tori agreed. "I will!"

"Oh, and Tori? Just in case Grey has been up to his old tricks, it might be better if you were not introduced to the captain as Mrs. Greyson Verreaux. I think it might be wiser for you to be Madame Christophe Duclaux—respectable widow. Do you agree?"

"Perhaps you're right. Oh, Monique, I want to be with Grey so badly! I'd do anything to be with him, anything!"

Garbed in a gown of black silk, over which floated a flounced overdress of black lace whose bertha collar left her shoulders bare, Tori wore about her neck a black velvet ribbon from which depended a locket containing a miniature of Christophe. Long jet earrings swung from her lobes and her hair was dressed in long, shining ringlets held in place by a spray of jet and black lace.

Monique, gorgeous in a gown of violet and purple moiré, met her at the door and led her into a small parlor off the foyer.

"Captain McWhirter arrived a few minutes ago," she said, her voice hushed and confidential. "We've told him you are a widow. That your husband, Christophe Duclaux, was a prominent Creole gentleman of New Orleans. We have made certain he believes that Christophe's death was in no way connected to the war."

"So he would not count me among the enemy?" Tori asked ironically.

"Something like that. Oh, come along. Let's face the enemy. He isn't really so formidable."

Edward and Zachary McWhirter stood as Monique and Tori entered the room. As Monique had promised, the Union captain was no ogre, but merely a man of middle height with a pleasant face that was made more attractive by the impressive cut and decoration of his gold-trimmed blue uniform. His hat, gloves, and beribboned sword lay across a chair.

"Captain McWhirter," Monique said softly, in that gentle, melodious voice that seemed to touch men's souls—the voice she had learned at her mother's knee while being instructed in the fine art of pleasing a man. "Permit me to introduce Madame Christophe Duclaux."

The captain came forward and took Tori's gloved hand. With all the grace of a Southern gentleman, he lifted it to his lips.

"Ma'am," he said, his Northern accent sounding strange to Tori's ears. "How do you do."

"Captain," Tori murmured. "How do you find Jamaica?"

"A paradise, ma'am. A veritable paradise. I am told you are mistress of a sugar plantation."

"Yes. Stockton Hall. You must have Edward and Monique bring you to visit."

"I'd be obliged for your hospitality, ma'am."

The captain's brown eyes were warm with admiration for the beautiful widow of the Creole gentleman. As with so many Northerners, Southern women had a special allure for the Yankee captain. Their beauty—not in actuality any more spectacular than their Northern sisters—seemed brighter. They seemed somehow more feminine with their flirtatious ways. They were seductive and yet demure. It was a powerful combination.

Monique led them in to dinner, throughout which it seemed that Captain McWhirter could not take his eyes off Tori long enough to enjoy his meal.

When after they had eaten, Monique and Tori retired to Monique's boudoir, they could not stifle their giggles.

"Good Lord!" Monique marveled. "Don't they have women in New York?"

"Is that where he is from?" Tori asked. "I thought about asking him, but I could not seem to get him to stop talking about me long enough!"

"I think, Tori, that if you were actually what you purport to be, you would find you have a serious suitor on your hands."

Tori made a face. "I can think of nothing I need less. Still, I should like to talk at length with the captain. I think I may be able to get some interesting information out of him."

In the days that followed, Captain Zachary
McWhirter became a frequent visitor to Stockton
Hall. Though there was never the suggestion of
impropriety—Monique accompanied him on days
when Edward could not—it was clear that the kindly,
gallant—if somewhat less than dashing—Captain
McWhirter had definitely taken a fancy to the
Widow Duclaux.

Regardless of who accompanied the captain, it
seemed that he and Tori found themselves alone on
the terrace or in the gardens with increasing
regularity.

"Monique tells me," Tori said one day just over
a week after her first meeting with the captain, "that
your ship is due to sail soon."

"Unfortunately, that is true," the captain told
her. "We are due in New Orleans shortly. I daresay
we should have been on our way some days ago. But
trouble with one of our boilers prevented our
departure."

"Ah, one must exercise the utmost care with
boilers," Tori told him gravely. "That is how my
husband, Monsieur Duclaux, was killed."

"Was it?" The captain seemed interested.
"How long—that is, when did—?"

"It is nearly a year now," Tori told him, though
that was stretching the truth.

"I see. Do you think . . . what I mean to say
is . . . a lovely woman such as yourself should not
wait too long before she resumes living life fully. You
mean, of course, to remarry at some point?"

"Perhaps," she agreed demurely. "If I should
happen to fall in love with some kind, gentle man."

"Madame Duclaux," the captain said, working
a finger into the standing collar of his double-
breasted uniform tunic. "Please, do not think me

forward, but these times are so uncertain. Desperate measures are sometimes called for.''

"Desperate? Goodness!" Tori breathed.

"It is only that I find myself drawn to you, ma'am. I do believe I am becoming attached to you. I should like your permission to pay my addresses to you in hopes of something more serious—more, if I may dare to say it, permanent.''

Tori turned her face away, feigning confusion, trying to mask her astonishment. Permanent! Good Lord! These Northern men were an impulsive lot!

"I have offended you, ma'am. Forgive me.''

"Oh, no, captain," she assured him quickly. "I am not offended. It is only that your declaration takes me so by surprise." She saw his disappointment and gave him a quick little smile. "It is only that I had not thought of even entertaining such notions until . . .''

"I understand. You are still in mourning." Staring down at his boots, he looked less like the captain of a powerful warship than a shy little boy. "But, perhaps, in time . . .''

Tori gazed out over the gardens. It was a dangerous charade she was playing. No precautions had been taken to keep her marriage to Grey a secret. Surely the minister who had married them had spoken of it to someone. Surely there were those in Montego Bay who knew she was no longer Tori Duclaux but Tori Verreaux. If Grey had gone back to blockade running, or had joined the Confederates in some other way to fight the Yankees, it was possible that he was wanted—that there was some reward for his capture. Should she be exposed to this captain as Grey's wife, it was just possible that he would decide to try to use her as the bait to lure Grey into the Union's trap. Still, as the captain himself had said, the times were uncertain. Desperate measures were sometimes called for.

"Perhaps," she murmured, allowing herself a flirtatious glance from the corner of her eye. "But it's impossible, of course."

"Impossible?" He seemed distressed. "But why?"

"Because you are leaving, are you not, captain? I was certain that Monique Lytton told me you were."

"It is true, ma'am," he acknowledged. "The *Ironton* must sail, and soon."

"Something was mentioned about New Orleans, I believe?"

"The city is garrisoned. We are to join Admiral Farragut's fleet there."

"New Orleans . . ." Tori sighed. "How I miss it. How I long to be there."

"You are far safer and no doubt more comfortable here," the captain told her.

"You may be right, sir," she said demurely. "Of course, if a lady has a strong, gallant gentleman to protect her, she has nothing to fear. I'm certain that the soldiers garrisoned in the city are not common marauders who would harm a respectable lady. Certainly they are not if you are any example, captain."

The captain's chest swelled with pride. "You are most kind, ma'am. You make me wish you were returning to New Orleans as well. If you were, you would find me your most devoted admirer."

"Please, sir," she said softly, "you will turn my head. If you do not stop, I do not know how I shall ever bear your departure."

Taking her hand, the captain lifted it to his lips.

Tori drew a little, gasping breath and lay her other hand on her bosom.

"Sir, I must insist that you do not toy with my affections any longer. I—"

"Tori?" Monique stood in the doorway. "Tori, may I speak with you for a moment?"

Irritated that such a delicate moment had been destroyed, Tori nonetheless smiled politely and excused herself.

"Are you mad?" Monique demanded the moment they were alone. "What do you think you're doing?"

"I am trying to convince Captain McWhirter to take me back to New Orleans with him!"

"You're what? Now I know you've lost your mind! You want to go back to New Orleans when it's full of Yankees! And if that isn't bad enough, you want to sail into New Orleans aboard a Union ship!"

Tori shrugged. "Can you think of a safer way? I don't think any passenger steamers are going there just now."

"Tori, think of what you're doing! You are leading this man—a Yankee officer!—on! He thinks he is courting you! He wishes to be your beau!"

"Actually," Tori said blithely, "he has all but proposed."

"Pro—" Monique paled as she sank into a chair. "You haven't encouraged him, have you?"

"Certainly not! He is going to board his ship and sail away, isn't he? It would be foolish of me to encourage him when he is going to leave. Now, if we were both going to New Orleans, things might be different."

"You haven't told him that, have you?"

"Oh," Tori hedged, "I might have mentioned

that I could not—''

"I see what you're doing! Oh, Tori, you can't be trying to convince the captain to take you to New Orleans by letting him think you would welcome his advances once you got there! What will you do? How would you get rid of him? What if Grey is in the city? How do you think he will feel when you arrive in New Orleans with a Yankee captain as a suitor?"

"You're taking all this too seriously. I've no intention of allowing the captain any liberties. It is entirely his fault if he reads more into this little flirtation than is actually there. Certainly no Southern gentleman would begrudge a lady a bit of flirting.''

"Tori, we're not talking about a Southern gentleman. We are talking about a Yankee and you don't know any more about what they think and feel about women than I do. They're a different breed from our men. I'm certain the captain believes that you welcome his advances. No doubt he thinks you are as serious about him as he, apparently, is about you.''

"I can handle Captain McWhirter," Tori assured her. "I intend to go to New Orleans, Monique. I've got to find Grey, no matter what. And if I have to charm this Yankee captain into taking me, so be it. After all, it is not as if I intend to let it go too far."

"It has already gone too far," Monique said gloomily. "I wish I had never suggested that you meet the captain. If anything should happen to you as a result of this bit of foolishness—"

"Nothing is going to happen. Now I've almost convinced him to take me. If you leave me to my own devices, I believe I *can* convince him."

"Well, you'd better hurry. Edward tells me the

Ironton is sailing tomorrow."

"Tomorrow! Then I haven't much time, have I?"

Excusing herself, Tori left the parlor, leaving Monique to stare after her, her beautiful face set in an expression of grave concern.

"All is well?" the captain asked as Tori rejoined him on the terrace. "I hope nothing is amiss. Ma'am, what is wrong? Are you—? You're crying, my dear!"

Tori dabbed at her eyes. "I am highly disappointed in you, sir. I must ask you to leave my house."

The captain's distress was touchingly real. "But dear lady! What have I done?"

"Mrs. Lytton has just informed me that you are to sail tomorrow! You were merely going to slip away and leave me to pine, weren't you? You were simply toying with my affections after all, you wretched man! How could I have believed that you held me in the slightest regard?"

"Oh, my dear! But I do! You must believe me."

"I've been a fool. And you, sir, you have been a cad!"

"Never say so! Please, ma'am, I entreat you—"

"I assure you, sir, no Southern gentleman would treat a lady with such callous disregard! If all of your compatriots are like you, I despair for the poor ladies of the North!"

"I am not! Ma'am, I must protest!"

"No, sir, I will listen to no more of your fabrications! And to think I had begun to give my heart to you! To think that I nearly accompanied you to New Orleans! Had I, I shudder to think of the folly into which I might unwittingly have stumbled. Oh, there is no more defenseless creature than a woman in love!"

Sandra DuBay

Lifting her chin, she fixed him with a long, cool stare. "Well, I assure you, sir, I shall listen to no more of your tender lies. I would not go with you to New Orleans if you were the last—the very last—man on this earth!"

"My dear, Madame Duclaux. Victoria, say you do not mean any of these cruel words. I love you, my dear, I swear I do! Say you will come to New Orleans. I could not bear to leave you here. Say you will come!"

"I don't know. I could not bear to have my heart broken. Perhaps it would be better to say goodbye now."

"No, please, I beg of you . . ."

Sighing, Tori gazed pensively out over the gardens. And then, fixing the captain with a brilliant smile, she nodded.

"Very well, then, Captain—Zachary—I will accede to your wishes. I will accompany you to New Orleans. But I must insist you be a perfect gentleman. After all, I am still in mourning for my dear Christophe."

"I will ma'am, you will see. I will!"

"Good. Then you must excuse me, for I have a great deal of packing to do."

Turning with a swish of her skirts, she swept into the house, leaving the captain to stare after her dazed, with the air of one who has just been run down by a stampede.

He had, it seemed, gained a pretty passenger for the trip to New Orleans, but just how it had happened he was not precisely certain. And just how he was going to explain to his fellow officers and crewmen, he had not the slightest glimmering of an idea.

422

41

The *U.S.S. Ironton* sailed up the Mississippi past the sad spectacle of the star-shaped Fort Jackson, which had been bombarded with mortar shells during Farragut's assault. On the opposite bank, Fort St. Philip lay in similar condition.

Belowdecks, in the cabin Captain McWhirter had given up for her use, Tori gazed at the forts, a sick feeling of regret in the pit of her stomach. So many dead, so many more wounded—gentlemen, not raised to be soldiers, pressed into service to the land that had bred them, fighting for their honor, their very way of life.

They passed Union ships, the pride of the mighty Federal navy, anchored along the river. So much power—the resources of the North far outstripped those of the South. And so many of the Southern efforts seemed to come to naught. The

Confederate ironclad. *C.S.S. Louisianna* had not been finished when Farragut had launched his attack on the city's defenses. It had lain helpless and immobile at its mooring at Fort St. Philip, unable to do more than blast away at the Union ships running the forts.

From the safe vantage point of Montego Bay, Tori had imagined the brave men of the Confederacy battling to save the Southern way of life. From this closer look, she could see that it was nothing like the gallant duel of gentlemen she had pictured. It was just a dirty, ugly, bloody conflict and death, when it came, was not noble or gentle. It came in the blink of an eye with the impact of a bullet or the sharp stab of a bayonet. It came after a long, agonizing bout with the doctor's saw or gangrene.

And somewhere in the middle of it all was Grey. She could not bear to think of him there, risking his life day after day, living with danger and the threat of capture or imprisonment, even execution.

She looked up from her dismal reverie as someone knocked at her cabin door. "Come in?" she called.

Zachary McWhirter entered. "We're nearly there," he told her. "I won't be able to escort you to your home myself, but I will see that you have an escort."

"You've been kindness itself, Captain," she murmured, and it was true. She had been worried upon their departure from Jamaica about how she would manage to ward off his advances during their voyage. But either he had determined to show her that Northern men could be as gallant as Southerners, or he had decided that her mere presence on the ship had caused enough dissension, for he had scarcely come near her throughout the entire voyage.

He seemed uneasy now. "I hope you will under-
tand if I cannot come calling on you immediately.
Please, do not think my affections have wavered, but
have duties to attend to and—".

"Zachary." She laid a hand on his arm. "I
understand completely. After all, I am the enemy."

"Victoria! I did not mean—"

"Hush, now. We are at war. Sacrifices must be
made. I am certain you will come to me when you
can."

Amid promises and protestations of affections,
Tori was escorted off the ship. A carriage had been
summoned and a wagon commandeered for her
trunks. Her escort, as it turned out, was a young
lieutenant, Cameron Ainsworth, a rabid Yankee who
not only resented her presence aboard a Federal
cruiser, but resented what he saw as a Rebel woman
using her wiles to divert a fine officer from the
proper performance of his duties.

"You must be pleased to be back in New
Orleans," he snarled, his blue eyes cold and hard as
they rested on her face. "Among your own kind."

"New Orleans is my home, Lieutenant," she
replied coolly. "I am pleased to return to it just as
you would be pleased to return to your home."

"I would not try to hoodwink the enemy into
taking me home," he snapped.

"I did not 'hoodwink' anyone, as you say.
Captain McWhirter—"

"Was taken in by a pretty face and syrupy
charm."

"How dare you! I did not ask you to escort me
to my home, sir. As far as I am concerned, you may
leave now."

"I take my orders from my captain, madame,
not from you. However, you may be certain that I

will see to it that Captain McWhirter's breach of propriety will not go unreported. The idea of bringing a woman—and a Reb—aboard a Union cruiser is appalling!''

"He was only being kind, Lieutenant."

"We are at war, ma'am. You are a Southerner. You are the enemy."

"I must ask you not to cause trouble for the captain."

"Understand my position, ma'am. If the captain is going to be fraternizing with the enemy—''

"Lieutenant Ainsworth, if I give you my word that I will have no more to do with the captain, will you forgive his momentary folly?''

"I might. But I warn you, if I discover that you have not kept your word . . .''

"I will keep my word, Lieutenant," she promised, only too pleased to have a reason to discourage the captain's romantic overtures. "And incidentally, I am not a spy, if that is what worries you.''

"I have not said that, ma'am," he reminded her, but he was visibly relieved that she had agreed so readily to his terms.

They entered the Vieux Carré and Tori was aware of the wave of hostility that followed them. It was there in the glares, the epithets, that followed them like the wake of a ship in the ocean.

"You are going to have a difficult time controlling the people of this city, Lieutenant," she told him. "We are a proud, stubborn people. We do not bend easily beneath the yoke of oppression."

The lieutenant cocked a skeptical brow. "I wonder what your slaves would say to that. Perhaps they might enjoy seeing their oppressors cast in the ole of the oppressed for a change."

"So you're an abolitionist." Tori smiled
erenely with all the careful calm of a well-bred
outhern lady. "Well, I shan't debate the subject
vith you. Not only do I feel that you are entitled to
our own opinions whether I agree with them or
ot—we are nearly to my gates."

She directed the lieutenant to the gates of the
ome she had shared with Christophe. From the
epths of one of her trunks, she had retrieved the
ing of keys with which she was prepared to unlock
he gates which the few servants she had kept on to
aaintain the house in her absence—Felix, the butler,
he cook, and Louise, her maid—should have kept
irmly locked against intruders.

To her surprise, the gates not only stood open,
ut the jalousies that had been shut across the open
paces of the courtyard balcony had been thrown
ride and potted plants stood on the railing.

"Who in the world could be in there?" she
sked herself.

A smirk curved the lieutenant's lips. "It may be,
aadam, that Major-General Butler has
ommandeered your home for himself or one of his
taff."

"He couldn't have!" Tori protested.

"Oh, I assure you, he could have." And the
ght shining in Cameron Ainsworth's eyes seemed to
idicate that he would be unashamedly delighted if
aat should prove to be the case. "After all, an
ccupying force must be billeted somewhere."

"Not in my house!"

The lieutenant shrugged. "It must be someone's
ouse. And yours was empty."

They turned into the courtyard, and Tori was

out of the carriage before the lieutenant could ge
out to help her down.

Marching up to the door, Tori yanked on th
bell. The ring of keys dangled in her hand, but sh
was too angry to fumble among them for the righ
one.

She yanked twice—three times—before givin
up and pounding on the panels with her gloved fist

Still, several minutes passed before the kno
jiggled and the door swung inward. Felix eyed her a
though she were an apparition from a child's gho
story. Then his dark eyes filled with tears.

"Madame! Madame, you've come back!"

"Of course, I've come back, Felix. Did yo
think I had disappeared?"

"No, madame, but—"

"Felix!" A voice echoed down the stairs—
voice from the shadowy past that Tori would just a
soon have left there. "Felix! What the devil is all tha
fuss?" Black taffeta hissed on the stairs and hig
heels clicked on the parquet floor of the foye
"Answer me, Felix. Who is it and what do they—

Ice-blue eyes met cat-green. Black taffeta skir
mingled with black peau-de-soie. Tension crackle
back and forth between them. Amanda Hunter wa
the first to speak:

"Why, if it isn't little Victoria! So the prodig
returns." Amanda laughed. "Close your mout
dear, you wouldn't want a mosquito flying in."

"I'll be leaving now, ma'am," the lieutenar
told Tori. "My men will unload your trunks."

Distracted, Tori nodded. "Thank yo
Lieutenant."

Amanda smiled at the young officer, the
pouted when her brilliant charm elicited n
answering grin.

428

"What a perfectly rude young man," she complained. "I shall have to speak with Randall about him. What was his name, Tori?"

Tori shook her head. "It doesn't matter who he is." She marched past Amanda, tugging at the ribbons of her black straw bonnet. "What matters is—what the devil you are doing here?"

Amanda followed her into the grand front parlor, tugging at the bell rope as she passed into the room. Then a maid Tori did not recognize appeared, and her cousin ordered tea and biscuits as though she were the mistress of the house and Tori the unwelcome guest.

When the tea was brought, Amanda poured and served them both.

"Amanda?" Tori prompted. "I'm waiting. What are you doing in my house?"

"Why, Tori, how truly uncharitable you are. It's almost as if you are not happy to see me, but of course that cannot be."

"Of course not," Tori said. "You still haven't told me why you are in New Orleans."

"Well, I should think you could see that for yourself. I am a widow now. My dear Brom—oh, but you never met my Bromfield, did you? No. After that dreadful business with that awful Grey Verreaux, I went to Savannah to stay with my father's cousin, Carson Hunter. While there, I met another cousin, Bromfield Hunter. Oh, such a delightful man. So strong and yet a gentleman to the tips of his fingers. We were so happy together. Oh, my! I loved him so!"

"He was killed in the war?" Tori asked.

"Yes." Amanda drew a lace-edged handkerchief from her sleeve and dabbed at her eyes. "He was killed in the bombardment of Fort Pulaski. Then our home, Hunter's Creek, was burned . . . Oh! It's too dreadful!''

Tori eyed her skeptically. In the letters she'd received from her mother, most of the few references she'd made to Amanda were third-hand accounts of the legendary drinking and womanizing proclivities of Amanda's husband Bromfield, the black sheep of the Savannah Hunters. It was cruel of her, she knew, mean-spirited and petty, but Tori wondered if he died while serving the Confederacy or at the tip of a jealous husband's sword.

"Why didn't you go to your cousin Carson or even to Barton's Landing in Virginia?''

"Tori! You are being unkind. I cannot think what your mother would say! I came to New Orleans because the war is not so severe here as yet.''

"And?'' Tori prompted.

"And?'' Amanda shot her a mutinous glare. "Oh, very well. I am seeing someone here. A gentleman. Colonel Randall Ramsey. Oh, he is such a delicious man! Handsome! Of good family—''

"And a Yankee!'' Tori breathed, feeling the blood draining from her face.

"Well, yes, but—''

"Amanda! Your husband was killed by the Yankees!''

"He wasn't killed by this particular Yankee. Randall is not responsible for every shot fired in this damnable war, you know.''

Amanda's husband hadn't been killed by Randall Ramsey, Tori thought, trembling, but hers had been, or at least on his orders.

"Oh, Amanda,'' she whispered.

Thinking Tori was merely shocked that she had taken up with a Northerner, Amanda assumed a haughty air.

"I don't wish to speak of it any further, if you don't mind." Her eyes swept over Tori. "You are a widow, too, aren't you?"

Tori nodded. "Christophe was killed when a ship he was aboard had an explosion in her boilers."

"What a shame. Well, we can comfort one another, you and I. We will be the best of friends."

"How delightful," Tori murmured with a conspicuous lack of enthusiasm.

"I cannot wait for you to meet Colonel Ramsey. He absolutely adores me! I think it may not be long before I am Mrs. Randall Ramsey instead of merely the Widow Hunter. Then I shall be one of New Orleans' leading hostesses. Randall is General Butler's aide, you know."

"The Yankees won't be occupying New Orleans forever," Tori predicted. "And you may find that you are the object of scorn among the natives. General Butler and his men are hardly popular here, and I should think that Southern women who are seen to be on intimate terms with them would be loathed."

"Oh, pish! Much I care! I will go North with Randall!"

"I shouldn't think Southerners would be popular in the North, either."

"Are you determined to be disagreeable?" Amanda smiled wickedly. "I will tell you something else I happen to find absolutely delicious! Randall has commandeered a beautiful house in the Garden District as his headquarters. And you will never guess who the house belongs to!"

Tori felt the blood draining from her face. "Not—"

"Grey Verreaux!" Amanda was unmistakably triumphant.

"I shouldn't think Grey would have taken that lightly," Tori said, trying not to panic. "He must have put up the devil of a fight over it."

"Oh, he wasn't there at the time. Apparently he hasn't been there for some time—at least that is what the old butler told Randall. And I doubt he will reappear in the near future. He has been running the Union blockade, you know. There's a reward offered for information concerning him. Quite a substantial reward, since there are also rumors he is a spy. I think General Butler wants him very badly, but he seems to have disappeared. Neither he nor his ship has been seen since Farragut ran the city's defenses."

"If he hasn't been seen since the city was garrisoned, why does Butler want him?"

"Past offenses against the Union. I think Butler wants to hang him." Amanda leaned closer. "I suspect that Randall chose Grey's house deliberately. After all, if Grey comes to New Orleans, it is only natural that he should wish to go home. And why shouldn't Randall have the reward money if he can get it? And think of what a feather in his cap it would be! He may well be promoted to Brigadier General! He might be transferred to Washington!"

Tori rose, disgusted that Amanda should be so willing, eager even, to see Grey captured and hanged if it would further Colonel Ramsey's military career and, in turn, Amanda's social climb.

"Is there no one you would not sacrifice to further your own ambitions?" she demanded. "I dread to think what might happen should you decide I have done something the Yankees might think worthwhile to know about."

"Why, Tori, what a cruel thing to say! As if I would ever betray you!"

432

"I can think of once when you did."

"Surely you don't mean—Tori! You do! I'm sure it is not my fault if Grey preferred me to you! You can't hold that against me!"

"I don't, Amanda. That was a long time ago. But if you are going to cause trouble, I will have to ask you to leave."

"Trouble! Don't be silly. I did wonder, though, when I discovered that Grey lived here in New Orleans as well, if you and he had seen each other."

Tori felt the cool gold of her wedding band biting into her finger. "Yes, I've seen him. Christophe hired him to deliver some goods to Jamaica. The sugar plantation is there, you know. He came to dinner to discuss business with Christophe once or twice."

"Has he changed?"

"Not really. He looked the same, sounded the same, acted the same. Grey will never change, you know that."

"Well, the Yankees want him and they want him badly. If he knows what's good for him, he'll stay well away from New Orleans."

Tori excused herself and went to see if Louise was putting her belongings away. She was afraid—desperately afraid. She prayed Grey would not hear that she had returned to New Orleans. He was all too likely to try to come to her, and Amanda was all too likely to alert Randall Ramsey of his presence.

She had to warn him. But how? Who was likely to know if he was in New Orleans and if he would come into the city with Butler's men occupying it? There must be someone who would know. There must be someone in the city he would trust. But who?

"Tori?" Amanda had appeared in the bedroom doorway. "Here you are!" She caught a glimpse of the elegant black straw hat Louise was just placing on a block on a shelf in the armoire. "How exquisite! Did you get this from a milliner here in New Orleans?"

"No," Tori replied absently. Was the woman going to allow her no privacy whatsoever? "I got it in France. A duchesse gave it to me."

"France! When did you go to France?"

"Does it matter just now? I'm tired, Amanda. I should like to take a nap. Was there something you wanted?"

"I just remembered that I am going to dine with Randall tonight. I could ask if he would mind your joining us, or I could invite him here instead."

"No, please go. I doubt I will be awake in time for dinner."

Amanda did not seem displeased. "Are you certain?"

"Quite. Enjoy yourself, dear."

Whirling, Amanda made as if to flounce out of the room. In the doorway, she stopped and turned back.

"Tori, darling, if you're not going to be using that hat . . ."

"Give it to her, Louise," Tori ordered wearily.

The maid handed the hat to Amanda, who disappeared, almost running to her room in a flurry of excitement to try the hat on. Behind her, in the bedroom, Tori exchanged resigned glances with Louise.

"Welcome home, Madame Duclaux," the maid said.

"Thank you, Louise. It is good to be here, even if we must have a houseguest for a while."

The maid shrugged. "It will not be forever, I am sure."

"No," Tori agreed, sighing. "After all, how long can the war last?"

42

The perils of Tori's position were brought home to her the next day when Amanda appeared in the doorway of Christophe's study.

"Here you are, Tori. I went up to your room, but Louise said you were already up and about. You are an early bird, aren't you?"

Tori cast a wry glance toward the clock in the corner. In a very few minutes, both hands would be straight up.

"I've never thought of noon as the crack of dawn before, Amanda."

"Well, I was out rather late last night." She rolled her eyes and sank into an armchair. "I can't tell you what a delight that man is!"

"Colonel Ramsey?" Tori asked skeptically.

"Of course Colonel Ramsey!" Amanda shot her an irritated glance. "Whom else might I mean! He is such an angel! And guess what he said last night?"

"I can't imagine."

"He said he wants to see you! He's quite eager
to do so, in fact. I think he may wish to ask you
about Grey."

Tori prayed the carefully indifferent expression
she kept on her face masked the terrified quivering
inside her.

"About Grey? I told you, Amanda, Grey did
business with Christophe."

"Well, according to Randall, you spent most of
last summer gallivanting all over the Caribbean, the
Atlantic, and France with him."

"I can see that I won't be allowed a moment's
peace until your Colonel Ramsey knows every bit of
my business. As you wish. Christophe engaged
Grey's ship to sail him to Jamaica on business for
Stockton Hall, our sugar plantation there.
Christophe sent the ship back and remained behind
in Jamaica. When, after a reasonable time had
passed, there was no word from him, I engaged Grey
to sail me to Jamaica.

"By the time we reached the island, Christophe
had gone on to France. We followed. We were in
Paris when word reached us that the ship Christophe
had taken to France had exploded. One of the
boilers, apparently. After that, Grey brought me
back to Jamaica and left me there. I've neither seen
nor heard from him since. For all I know, he left
Montego Bay and set sail for China."

"Oh," Amanda murmured. "So you truly don't
know anything about where he might be?"

Tori ground her teeth. "Are you really that
eager to see Grey in a Union prison?"

"Why should I be loyal to him?" her cousin
demanded. "After what he did to me! He was in

438

another woman's bed the night of our engagement party!"

"And so you would turn him over to his enemies? You're inconsistent, Amanda. After all, I was the other woman he was in bed with that night, but you're willing to live in my house."

"That's different. You're family. And besides, you were only a child then. It was a small matter for Grey to seduce you."

It was on the tip of Tori's tongue to tell Amanda the truth—that it was Gussie who had lured Grey into her room—but that was in the distant past and she saw no sense in raking up old feuds and risking antagonizing her cousin any more than she already had. Amanda was a threat to her and to Grey. She was dangerous as a rattlesnake, and it seemed the wisest course to simply steer a wide course around her and avoid her fangs and venom.

"In any case, that was a long time ago. Grey and I went our separate ways just as you and Grey did. As I have told you, I have neither seen nor heard from him since he left me in Jamaica early last autumn. Where he is and what he is doing I cannot tell you."

"It doesn't matter, I suppose. If he is in New Orleans, Randall will find him." Rising, she examined her face in the mirror. "Tori? Do I look old to you? After all, I am nearly twenty-five."

Tori bit her lip to keep from laughing. When Amanda had come to Barton's Landing, she had been eighteen to Tori's fifteen. Now, all of a sudden, she was twenty-four to Tori's twenty-three.

"Of course you don't look old," she said dutifully. "What makes you ask such a thing?"

"Oh, it is just that I want to look lovely for Randall. There are so many beautiful women in this city. I wonder what I should wear tonight. Did I tell you I've invited Randall to dinner here tonight?''

"Here? How kind of you to inform me."

"I told you he wants to see you. Now, come upstairs. We can decide what to wear so our colors do not clash."

"How can black clash?"

"You're not actually going to wear black, are you? Tori! How dull!"

"Widows are expected to wear mourning, Amanda. It is a tradition."

"Pooh! Much I care about silly old traditions. You may be content to be a little black crow for the rest of your life, but I'm not! Black is not my color and I mean to look my best for—"

"For a Yankee!" Rising, Tori circled the desk. "I'm sick of watching you preen for the enemy, Amanda! These men are killing men, women, and children! For God's sake, they killed your husband! We are at war with them and all you can worry about is attracting one—capturing him! Trapping a new husband!"

"Victoria! What has gotten into you?"

"I wish all the damned Yankees would get out of New Orleans! Everytime I see one I want to kick him!"

"You'd better not! Or haven't you heard about General Butler's proclamation?"

"What proclamation?"

"Randall told me about it. It's caused quite a stir among the people of the city. Apparently, the general is sick and tired of the insults the women of New Orleans have heaped upon his men. It seems the Yankee soldiers cannot go abroad in the city without being insulted, abused, spat upon, pelted with rotten vegetables . . . Why, some so-called ladies have resorted to dumping chamber pots on their heads as they pass!''

"Good for them!" Tori said.

"That's easy for you to say, but they had better mend their ways. According to General Butler's proclamation—wait, I have a copy of the order that Randall gave me—" Leaving the room, she rummaged in the pocket of her cloak, which hung in the hall. In a few moments she returned with a folded paper. "And I quote," she went on: " 'When any Female shall, by word, gesture, or movement, insult or show contempt for any officer or soldier of the United States, she shall be regarded and held liable to be treated as a woman of the town plying her avocation.' " Amanda eyed Tori defiantly. "Well? What do you think of that?"

"I think it's barbarous. And I resent your defending these people to me."

"But you will allow Randall to come to dinner tonight, won't you?"

Tori scowled. She did not want any of the Yankees in her house, if it came to that. But it might be a good idea to see Colonel Ramsey, if only to try and discover how much, if anything, he knew about Grey's present whereabouts.

"Yes, I will allow Colonel Ramsey to come to dinner, and I will be cordial to him. But I don't like it, Amanda. Let us get that clear from the outset. Whatever your leanings in this conflict, mine are firmly on the side of the South and you'd best remember that."

Amanda said nothing, but from the angry glimmer in her eyes, Tori got the impression that she would have much preferred it had Tori not returned. Then she could have turned Tori's house into a salon

where she could hold court, entertaining the officers
of General Butler's staff and, perhaps even the
General himself!

By eight that evening, Amanda was pacing the
front parlor, her fingers working agitatedly in the
lace flounces that encircled the billowing skirt of her
yellow silk evening gown.

"Where is he?" she demanded of no one in
particular. "He was supposed to be here an hour
ago!"

Tori, in her black taffeta, a white lace cap
pinned to her simply upswept hair, glanced up from
her book.

"Perhaps he was delayed. He may be out somewhere treating some poor woman like a—what was
it? A 'Female of the town'?"

"Oh, don't be so critical. It is not easy for a
soldier to be so far away from home."

"Well, dear, I'm certain they are grateful for
women like you who strive to make them feel at
home."

"What a mean thing to say!" Amanda cried. "I
don't remember your being so hard! When did you
become so cynical?"

"I'd say about seven or eight years ago," Tori
replied archly.

Amanda stopped in her tracks and gave her
cousin a curious look. "Don't tell me you're still
holding a grudge because I stole your beau! How
silly! In any case, neither of us got him!"

Tori fingered the wide gold band Grey had
slipped on her finger at that brief ceremony in Jamaica.
It seemed like a hundred years ago and a million
miles away. Though she dared not tell Amanda or,
indeed, anyone in New Orleans for the sake of her

442

safety and Grey's, she was still, and would always be, Mrs. Greyson Verreaux.

There was a commotion in the courtyard outside and Amanda flew to the mirror to examine her hair, her gown, the subtle dusting of powder that colored her cheeks.

"He's here! Oh, Tori! Come, tell me if my skirts are mussed. Lord! I don't know what possessed me to wear this yellow gown. It wrinkles like I don't know what! I'll just be mortified if Randall notices."

"Colonel Ramsey," Felix announced dispassionately.

The aged butler was replaced in the doorway by the man Tori remembered from the Opera House here in New Orleans and from Quaratesi's garden outside Paris—the man who had engineered her first husband's death and was now on the prowl for her second.

He was a handsome man, even Tori had to admit as much, and the elegance of his dashing uniform only enhanced his suave good looks.

The dark-blue frock coat with its golden epaulettes was tailored to his body so that the wide belt to which his dress sword was attached showed off his narrow waist.

He smiled, bowing slightly to Tori as he unbuckled his sword and handed it, along with his white gloves and plumed hat, to Felix.

"I was worried about you, Randall," Amanda cooed, moving to stand beside him and laying a proprietary hand on his sleeve. "You're quite late."

"My apologies, my dear. There was some unpleasant business down near the docks. You may find it of interest, but first, I insist you introduce me to this lovely lady."

"Of course! Wherever did I leave my manners!"

Tori struggled to maintain her calm. So he was going to pretend he had never heard of her. That was fine with her, but she was determined to be on her guard against this sly, murdering agent of the enemy.

Amanda was going on, "Randall Ramsey, my cousin, Victoria Duclaux. Tori, Colonel Randall Ramsey."

"Madame Duclaux. Charmed to meet you. And I thank you for allowing me into your home. I assure you there are not many homes in New Orleans where a Union officer is welcomed."

"Surely you can understand that, sir," Tori said sweetly. "Nearly everyone has lost a loved one. How could a woman look with favor upon a soldier who had killed her husband, for example?"

Randall's brown eyes met and held Tori's blue ones and for a long, tense moment Amanda ceased to exist for either of them.

"She should understand," Randall broke the spell to say, "that these unfortunate occurrences are merely the fortunes of war."

"The fortunes of war will not fill her empty arms," Tori said softly. "Nor comfort her when she is frightened."

"*Touché*," he murmured, as he turned to Amanda. "I am expecting a messenger. Could you tell the butler?"

"But of course. Excuse me."

Amanda left the room and Colonel Ramsey accepted Tori's invitation to sit down.

"Tell me, madame," he said when they were alone. "Have you heard from Grey Verreaux since you parted company in Montego Bay?"

"Did we part company in Montego Bay, Colonel?" she countered.

"You must have, since you left France aboard

his ship and his ship returned to New Orleans without you. The logical assumption is that he left you at Stockton Hall.''

"That much is correct, sir," Tori admitted. 'Monsieur Verreaux did leave me at my home in Jamaica where I would be safe. But you will be disappointed to know that I have heard nary a word from him since he sailed away.''

"You should have remained in Jamaica, madame. You should have been safer and certainly far more comfortable there.''

"New Orleans is my home, Colonel. I have friends here. My conscience would not allow me to hide in Jamaica while people I loved suffered in our country's cause.''

"By 'our country,' I presume you refer to the Confederacy?''

"I do.''

"And yet you returned to New Orleans aboard a Federal cruiser?''

Tori shrugged. "I wished to reach my home safely, sir. Can you think of a more secure way to enter New Orleans just now than aboard a Federal warship?''

In spite of himself, Ramsey chuckled. "No, I suppose I cannot. You are a resourceful woman, Madame Duclaux. But then, I knew that the moment I heard that you had escaped da l'Armi and Quaratesi's clutches.''

"About the captain of the *Ironton*. He has not suffered for his kindness to a lady in distress, I trust?''

"He has been reprimanded and reassigned to another ship. His command has been given to one of his junior officers, who was promoted from lieutenant.''

"Not Lieutenant Cameron Ainsworth, by any chance?" she asked, remembering the young officer who had conducted her home from the docks.

"Why, yes. Do you know the lieutenant?"

"We've met. Briefly."

"I see. Well, in any case, you must know that we are quite interested in you."

"I have told you, I know nothing of Grey Verreaux—"

"No, no. I have not come to ask you any questions, dear lady. I have merely come to enjoy a pleasant evening with two charming and lovely ladies."

His reply confused Tori. How could he not wish to ask her about Grey? Amanda had been so sure that every officer in the Union army was positively panting to get his hands on Grey. Either Amanda had exaggerated or . . . no, it didn't bear thinking of.

"I've notified Felix that your messenger is to be brought to you the very moment he arrives, Randall," Amanda said, returning just then. "Now, what was this 'unpleasant business' you thought we might find interesting?"

"It will keep until after the messenger arrives, my dear," he told her. "I should not like to tell you only half the story."

Amanda launched into some inane gossip then, which Tori scarcely heard, for she was filled with the nagging suspicion that something had happened to keep the Yankees from continuing their search for Grey. Something was wrong, of that she was sure. But what? What had happened to Grey?

"Your pardon, Colonel Ramsey?" Felix was in the doorway. "A Private O'Neil to see you."

"Thank you, Felix." Ramsey rose and left the room.

Tori and Amanda fell silent. But though they both strained their ears, they could not hear more than mere snippets of the conversation. They were forced to wait for Randall to return to hear the urgent news the private had delivered.

"Bad news, Randall?" Amanda asked.

"In a manner of speaking," he replied, but the feral gleam in his eyes suggested that he was far from disappointed. "You know that we have been trying to capture Grey Verreaux so that we could question him concerning the blockade-running activities of seemingly respectable shippers in this area. Well, he was seen this afternoon on the docks. Of course, we rushed to the area. The situation got rather out of hand and shots were fired." He fastened his piercing gaze on Tori. "Both Verreaux and another gentleman—most unfortunately—were shot."

Tori gripped the arms of her chair, her face starkly white. Time—and her heart—seemed to have stopped.

Callously ignoring the effect his words were having on at least one member of his audience, Colonel Ramsey went on:

"The men were taken to the hospital. I was waiting for a report, which is what Private O'Neil has just brought to me."

"What did he say?" Tori breathed.

Ramsey seemed to take perverse pleasure in uttering his next words. "According to O'Neil, Grey Verreaux died a few hours ago."

Rising from her chair, Tori mumbled an excuse and walked slowly, as if in a dream, from the room. Brushing past Felix, she went to the stairs intending to go up to her room.

She had almost reached the first landing when she fainted.

43

It was morning before Tori had recovered sufficiently to think coherently. Her first visitor, and the person she wanted least to see, was Amanda.

"Tori! You're awake! Goodness! I had almost decided to send for the doctor."

Pale and listless, Tori lay curled beneath the coverlet of her bed. "Leave me alone, Amanda. I don't need a doctor. I only need to be left alone."

"What I don't understand," Amanda said, ignoring Tori and pulling a chair closer to the foot of the bed, "is why you had such an extreme reaction to the news of Grey's death."

"Amanda—" Tori warned.

"I mean, after all, if you hadn't seen him since last summer, and then it was only a matter of business, what do you care if he is alive or dead?"

"Amanda—!"

"The man was little more than a criminal! He was constantly—"

"Get out!" Tori's voice was high and quivering. "Just get out of here! Leave me alone, for God's sake! Go entertain your damned, murdering Yankee colonel. Entertain the whole damned Union army for all I care! Just leave me alone!"

Sniffing with disdain, Amanda rose. "Very well, I'll leave, since you're going to be so rude. But if I do, you won't hear the rest of the news Randall told me about Grey."

Tori watched her cousin stalk toward the door. Amanda's hand was on the latch when Tori pushed herself up onto one elbow.

"Amanda? Wait. What are you talking about? What did Ramsey tell you?"

"Oh! So you are interested, after all. Well, I shouldn't tell you since you were so rude to me. But I suppose I will."

Returning to her chair, she sat down and Tori feared she was settling in for a long talk.

"Randall told me that they've just learned that Grey sold his ship some time ago. Apparently, it was all perfectly legal, and there is nothing the Federal authorities can do about it. I understand they are quite upset over it. They do so enjoy confiscating former blockade runners and converting them into Union ships. They could have done so with Grey's ship if it had still belonged to him."

"Well, I'm glad he sold the ship. I'm glad your precious Yankees won't get it!"

"Really, Tori, you needn't be insulting. After all, I'm only trying to give you information that you asked for."

"Thank you, Amanda. Now go away and leave me alone, if you don't mind."

"I will. Only too gladly! Heavens above, Tori, the way you're carrying on, one would think you'd been married to Grey Verreaux!"

Amanda slammed out of the room and Tori fell back against the pillows torn between grief and shock.

Grey had sold *Nightshade!* He had sold his ship! He had never meant to sail back to Jamaica! Had he abandoned her? She couldn't believe that. He loved her as much as she loved him. There had to be more to this tale. But what? And how could she find out?

She sighed, her anxiety giving way to resigned melancholy. What difference did it make now? Whatever his reasons for selling his ship, it meant nothing now. He was lost to her forever.

"Damn you, Grey Verreaux!" she sobbed into her pillow. "Damn you! I hate you! I hate you! I—oh, God, Grey, how could you go and get yourself killed!"

She hated him and loved him—hated him for leaving Jamaica when he didn't have to, hated him for putting himself in danger, and loved him as she'd always loved him, even in the darkest days of their relationship—loved him as she would always love him—even now that those evil, hell-spawned Yankees had murdered him.

Exhausted from a night during which she had alternately wept brokenly and lain staring up at the tasselled lambrequins above her bed in stunned silence, Tori fell asleep.

It was later—much later—in the day when she convinced herself to rise from her bed. She bathed, dressed, even allowed Louise to dress her hair in long plaits which were then rolled into a black net.

"Where is Mrs. Hunter?" she asked the maid.

451

"She's gone out, madame," Louise replied.

"Good." In the mirror, she noticed Louise's half-smile. "You are not at all fond of my cousin, are you, Louise?"

"It is not for me to say, madame," the maid hedged. "But I am glad you've come back to New Orleans."

Tori gazed into the mirror. The trip seemed futile now, useless. All the scheming, all the deception it had taken to get here, and for what? To learn that the man she loved had been murdered before she'd even gotten the chance to see him, speak to him, love him . . .

"I may not stay here," she told Louise. "If I could get out of the city, I would go back to Jamaica. There is nothing for me here—not any more." She drew a deep, shuddering breath. "If I leave—if I go back to Montego Bay—I should be delighted if you would go with me, Louise."

"To Jamaica, madame?" The prospect seemed to dazzle the maid. "What is it like there?"

"It is a paradise. Beautiful. Warm. The sun shines all the time and the ocean is as blue as the summer sky."

There was a knock at the door. Lulu, the downstairs maid, who had returned to Tori's employ from the home of a New Orleans matron who had fled to Natchez, appeared to announce that a lady was downstairs asking to see Madame Duclaux.

"Who is it, Lulu?"

"Her name is Phipps, madame. Elizabeth Phipps."

"Elizabeth Phipps," Tori repeated. "Of course! Valentine Phipps!" She remembered the night at the Opera House when Grey had confronted her. She had fainted. When she'd awakened, she was in bed in

452

strange house. Elizabeth Phipps had come in and
comforted her. Then, when she'd been ready to go
home, Elizabeth and her husband, Grey's best
friend, Valentine, had taken her home. Both had
shown her the utmost kindness and she'd been
grateful to them for their comfort in her time of
indecision and confusion.

And now, Elizabeth had come to her again. Tori
wondered why. Had Grey confided in her? Had he
told her about their marriage? Had he told her how
he felt about his wife and his reasons for selling his
ship and depriving himself of a means to return to
her?

She had mixed emotions about going downstairs. Half of her wanted desperately to hear what
Elizabeth had to say. The other half was terrified,
that Elizabeth would tell her something that would
plunge her deeper into the well of loneliness, the
bottomless pit of despair onto whose slippery side she
was already clinging by the tips of her fingers.

She hesitated, rolling her fears about in her
mind. But then, steeling herself, determined to learn
as many of the facts of Grey's death as possible, she
left her dressing table and went down to the small,
family parlor where Elizabeth Phipps waited.

The petite, pretty brunette smiled wanly as Tori
entered the room. She was dressed in a plain, high-
necked gown of purple silk banded with black velvet.
Her glossy dark hair was caught up in a net and
covered with a black leghorn hat with wide, purple
silk ribbons. She looked pale and drawn, as though
the life was slowly being drained from her, leaving
her merely a ghost of the lively, lovely woman Tori
had met less than a year before.

"Madame," Elizabeth said, her eyes wide in her
small, white face. "Forgive me for coming to you

uninvited. But I felt I must.''

"You are welcome, madame," Tori said. "Le
me order something for you . . ."

"No, nothing, please. The reason I have come t
you—''

"I know," Tori breathed. "I know why yo
have come. Because of Grey."

"Yes. Because of Grey. And because c
Valentine."

"Valentine—oh, Lord! Your husband! H
wasn't— That is, I understood another man ha
been wounded at the same time Grey was—tha
Grey—''

"Yes." Elizabeth answered the question To
could not put into words. "It was Valentine."

"I'm so sorry. I know that Grey and Valentin
were the best of friends. I remember how kind yo
both were to me last summer at the opera. I . . .
She broke off, pressing her fingertips to her lip
"I'm sorry. I'm babbling. It's only that . . ."

"Victoria," Elizabeth interrupted. "Please cal
yourself. You must not be hysterical. I need you to b
rational. I need you to help me."

Trying without much success to pull herse
together, Tori sat down. She watched Elizabet
curiously as the other woman rose and went to shi
the door.

"How can I help you?" she asked. "What can
do?"

"Come with me. Come to my home. I need yo
help."

Relieved to have her mind occupied, To
nodded readily. Summoning Felix, she asked for hi
cloak and bonnet.

"Should Mrs. Hunter return, where should I sa
you have gone, madame?"

"Tell Mrs. Hunter I have gone—"

She felt Elizabeth's restraining hand on her arm. She did not venture a glance toward the other woman, but she understood her meaning all the same.

"Tell Mrs. Hunter," she amended, "that I have gone out. More than that she needn't know."

"As you say, madame," the butler acquiesced.

Outside, Tori and Elizabeth climbed into the Phippses' closed carriage. As it rolled out of the courtyard and into the street, Tori debated whether or not to ask Elizabeth for the answers she longed to have to the questions that plagued her.

"Elizabeth," she said softly, shyly, "did you see much of Grey after he returned from Jamaica?"

"Quite a bit," she confirmed. "There were only a handful of people he trusted in New Orleans, you see. And no one, I think, as much as Valentine. He stayed with us part of the time. Of course, he could not go to his own home. The Yankees were after him from the moment he returned. That is why he had to sell his ship. It was too well known. He couldn't go near it. He knew he could never sail her out of New Orleans again. He meant to get a new ship. But that was before . . ."

The two women fell silent and several tense moments passed before Tori summoned the courage to ask:

"Did Grey say anything to you about me, Elizabeth?"

"A great deal. He missed you. He hoped you were with child." Elizabeth's eyes stole stealthily to Tori's middle.

"Unfortunately not," Tori admitted. "I hoped was so, too. Did Grey ever tell you that he and . . . that we had . . ?"

"Married? Yes, he told me he had convinced you to marry him. He said he was glad he had married you before he left Jamaica because he didn't know when he'd get back, but at least he knew you were his and you would be waiting for him."

"I would have waited for him in any case," Tori told her. "I loved him so, Elizabeth. It seems I always have. When I think of the wasted time . . . I would give anything to have Grey back. Anything!"

Elizabeth said nothing as the carriage turned into the courtyard of the Phippses' home. A servant opened the door and handed them down. Tori followed Elizabeth into the house.

"Come with me," Elizabeth ordered, starting up the stairs.

Tori followed and Elizabeth led her to the door of the same bedroom Tori had occupied when Grey had brought her to this house. The green-and-white striped silk draperies were drawn at the windows and the chamber's only illumination came from a lamp burning on a marble-topped table at some distance from the bed.

"You must take care to be quiet," Elizabeth cautioned. "You must not make any loud noises or any sudden movements. The doctor has said he must be kept calm and quiet. It is essential that he not be frightened or shaken."

Tori glanced at her curiously, wondering why Elizabeth was behaving so curiously. Was Valentine supposed to tell her something? Had Grey entrusted him with some message for her before he died?

It was apparent that Elizabeth was going to say no more, so Tori approached the bed, determined to listen with respect to whatever Valentine Phipps had to tell her.

She walked on tiptoe to the bed, careful to make

no sound that could disturb the sick man. Reaching the foot of the bed, she drew back the draperies that had been partially closed to seal out any drafts that might enter the bedroom.

"Monsieur Phipps," she said softly, "I—"

The words froze in her throat as her heart seemed to thud to a halt in her chest. A shudder ran through her, shaking her to the tips of her toes.

There in the bed before her, his dark head lying on the pillows, his naturally swarthy skin pale and waxy, and his lush black lashes lying in feathery crescents on his cool cheeks, lay a ghost out of Tori's dreams. There, in the bed Tori herself had once occupied, his shallow, irregular breathing scarcely lifting the coverlet, lay Grey Verreaux.

Tori turned her pale, shocked countenance toward Elizabeth. "But how? How!"

Laying a finger to her lips, Elizabeth led her from the room and into her boudoir on the opposite side of the hall.

"Sit down," she told Tori as she poured her a snifter of brandy. "Drink this and I will tell you everything."

44

'ori lifted her glass with shaking hands as Elizabeth at down beside her.

"I'm so sorry I had to keep you in suspense, but couldn't say anything at your home. I didn't know your servants could be trusted." Her cheeks inkened. "Pardon me for speaking so frankly, but our cousin, Mrs. Hunter, is known to be keeping ompany with Beast Butler's aide-de-camp."

"Randall Ramsey. Believe me, he is far more angerous than merely as Butler's aide. But what I on't understand is how in the world you managed to pirit Grey out from under the Yankees' noses."

"I volunteered at the hospital—it makes me feel hat I am helping with the war effort, you see. In any ase, while I was helping in the ward, there was a reat commotion. A troop of Yankee soldiers rought in two men. I heard someone shouting that

Sandra DuBay

they had 'gotten' Grey Verreaux.'' She paused,
closing her eyes. Sighing, she went on. "I knew
Valentine was to meet Grey on the docks. I just had a
feeling that the second man was my husband.'' A
shudder shook her petite frame. "I heard someone
asking which was Verreaux so I went in. I told them
who I was and that I thought one of the men might be
my husband. They asked if I knew Grey. I said yes.
They asked if I would identify him.''

"How horrible for you,'' Tori murmured.

Elizabeth nodded. "Still, it was fortunate that I
was there. I went into the room where they had been
taken—it was an anteroom just off the morgue. I
looked at them, lying there. Valentine was
already . . . there was nothing that could be done.
Grey was still alive. His wounds were not fatal if
properly and quickly treated. He had lost a great deal
of blood, but there was a chance he would live.'' She
passed a shaking hand over her brow. "I knew it was
Grey they wanted. And I knew that if he lived, the
Yankees would hang him or, at the very least, send
him to one of their atrocious military prisons where
he would not be treated—where he was certain to die
of hunger or exposure, if not gangrene.''

Tori gasped and her eyes met Elizabeth's in a
mutually horrified glance. Licking her lips, Elizabeth
went on:

"I knew Valentine was dead—I could not help
him. And I knew he would want me to help Grey.
They—the Yankees—did not know which man was
which. So I identified Val as Grey and told them
Grey was my husband.''

"And they let you take him home?''

Elizabeth shrugged. "They had no proof that
Valentine was involved in Grey's blockade running.
There was no reason for them to keep him there once

460

his wounds had been treated."

"Thank God none of the Yankees there knew him," Tori breathed, thinking of Randall Ramsey. "I don't know how I can ever repay you."

"It's not over yet. We must get him out of New Orleans. I'm terrified someone will discover the truth. Everytime there's a knock on the door, I nearly die."

"But how can we get him away? He sold *Nightshade*, and even if he hadn't, how could we run the blockade?"

"Obviously we can't," Elizabeth agreed. "And there aren't so many blockade runners left since Farragut's fleet arrived. But of the few that are left, most were friends of Grey's, or at least men who knew and admired him. We should be able to find someone to take him out."

"Where do we look?" Tori asked, knowing not the first thing about such matters.

Elizabeth shook her head. "Unfortunately, neither Grey nor Valentine was the kind of man who thought a woman should be involved in such matters. They did not include me in their discussions."

"Nor me," Tori admitted. "Grey thought the less I knew about such things, the safer I would be."

Elizabeth nodded and the two women fell silent. They felt helpless. They could not allow Elizabeth's sacrifice to go for naught—the heartbreak of walking out of that makeshift morgue and leaving the body of her beloved Valentine alone and unclaimed could not go unrewarded.

And yet their task seemed impossible. The brotherhood of blockade runners was a tightly-knit one, out of necessity. It would not be easy for anyone, let alone a woman who was known to allow Butler's notorious aide-de-camp into her home, to

461

penetrate their ranks.

"We'll find a way," Tori vowed. "Grey is in danger every moment he remains in New Orleans. I mean to get him out, Elizabeth! I mean to get him out of here and away to the safety of Jamaica!"

That night Tori excused herself from a dinner with Amanda, Randall, and several of Randall's staff at Grey's house in the Garden District. She had too much on her mind to be able to maintain a charade of genteel hospitality while sitting at table with her husband's would-be murderers.

Alone for once in the stillness of her house, she sat in Christophe's great leather chair in the study he had so loved. But her thoughts were not on her first husband, but her second—Grey, lying in that wide tester bed, so pale, so still, so weak. She remembered him as he had been in those glorious days in Jamaica. So strong and virile. He could be that way again—healthy, magnificent as ever. But it would take time, and care, and a safe haven away from his enemies.

But how—how!—could she get him away? How could she spirit him out of New Orleans and across the sea to Jamaica when Farragut's fleet lay like a snarling pack of dogs in the Mississippi?

Rising, she crossed the shadowy room. Her silken gown rippled behind her, swishing on the rich pile of Christophe's prize Aubusson carpets. There had to be a way—there had to! God would not have spared Grey's life on the docks—would not have allowed Elizabeth to rescue him from his enemies—if he were not meant to survive.

Her arms wrapped around her, Tori bowed her head and prayed for help, prayed to be shown the way out of her deadly dilemma, prayed to be given help to deliver Grey out of his terrible peril.

"Oh, please," she whispered. "Please, help me."

A knock at the door brought her to startled attention.

"Yes?" she breathed.

The door swung open and Felix appeared.

"Your pardon, madame, a gentleman has arrived. He says he was directed here by Colonel Ramsey and Mrs. Hunter."

"I cannot see anyone," she insisted.

"That is what I told him, madame. I also told him there was no one here by the name of the person for whom he is searching. But he is most insistent."

Tori sighed. The last thing she needed was to be distracted by misplaced visitors. "Well, who is he looking for? Perhaps Amanda or Colonel Ramsey gave him the wrong address."

"He is asking," Felix revealed, "for Madame Greyson Verreaux. He specifically asked for Victoria Verreaux, madame."

"Verreaux," Tori breathed, feeling the floor tremble beneath her feet. "Victoria . . ."

From behind Felix a ghost appeared out of Tori's past—a phantom from a real-life nightmare.

"Good-evening, Victoria," Niccolò da l'Armi said.

Pale and trembling, Tori backed across the dark room. "No, no, it can't be," she whispered. "You're—you're dead!"

"As you can see, I am alive." A rueful smile flitted across his face. "More or less."

For the first time Tori realized that while he wore a gray kid glove on one hand, his left sleeve hung empty from the shoulder. He limped slightly as he entered the room and, as he came closer, she could see scars marring the swarthy smoothness of his face and neck.

"I don't understand this, Niccolò," she said. "I don't understand this at all."

He glanced silently toward Felix, and Tori dismissed the butler. When they were alone in the study, he gestured with his gloved hand toward a silk-covered armchair.

"May I?" he asked. "I find it uncomfortable to stand for long."

"Oh, yes. Please sit down." Tori drew up a chair and sat opposite him. "Tell me, what happened? I thought Grey had killed you in your duel."

"I wish he had. But I moved at the last moment and the bullet merely pierced my shoulder."

Tori's eyes darted to his empty sleeve. Niccolò, seeing her glance, shook his head.

"No, the other shoulder. This"—he held up his gloved hand—"And this"—he touched his empty sleeve—"And this"—he moved his feet slowly, painfully. "And this"—with his gloved fingers, he touched the scars on his face—"are from the fire."

"Fire? What—"

"Mérimée. Quaratesi came just after you escaped with Grey Verreaux. He was very angry that I'd taken you away after that night in the Tuileries. I had betrayed him by saving your life, you see. And he was determined not to give me a second chance. He had his men take me back into the château. Then he locked the doors and set the château afire."

"My God," Tori breathed.

"The room was blazing by the time I managed to rouse myself enough to try to escape. Some of the beams fell—I was trapped. But Madame Rodolphe and her husband, Timothé, broke into the château and dragged me to safety.

"They carried me to their cottage in the forest. The doctor came. I lost my arm and very nearly my legs because of the burning beams that had fallen upon them. But I lived. Thanks to Olivie and her husband, I lived."

"And when you recovered from your injuries, you fled from France?"

"That is correct. I followed you to Jamaica."

"To Jamaica," Tori murmured, wishing neither she nor Grey had ever left Stockton Hall.

"So you are now Grey Verreaux's wife," Niccolò murmured.

"How did you—?"

"I made inquiries in Montego Bay. I found the cleric who married you. It was not difficult. I also learned that Grey had sailed away the day after your wedding to help the Confederacy and that you had gone after him only recently." A curious smile curved his lips. "I heard—aboard a Northern ship?"

"It arrived in Jamaica just when I needed a way to New Orleans. The captain was kind enough to bring me home."

"In return for which you broke his heart?" Niccolò chided gently.

"I did not want to hurt anyone, Niccolò, but I had to get here. You know what they say—All's fair in war—"

"And love," he finished for her. "Which brings us back to your husband, Monsieur Verreaux. Where is he, Victoria?"

A trembling seized her, and the blood drained from her already pale face. "He . . . he . . . is dead."

Niccolò ignored her words. "I knew he would not be here. Your cousin, Amanda Hunter, is too pleased over his fall for you to risk bringing him here. And Ramsey is elated—if he were to suspect that he had not seen the end of Greyson Verreaux after all—"

"But he has," Tori insisted. "Grey was murdered, on the docks, yester—"

"I've been to the hospital, Victoria," he said simply. "I've been to the morgue there."

Tori sagged in her chair. She could not speak. If Niccolò knew the truth, it was only a matter of time before others did.

"Have you told Ramsey?" she whispered.

He shook his head. "Nor have I told him that you and Grey are married. He still thinks you are merely the widow of Christophe Duclaux." He watched her as she rose and crossed to stare out of the window. "I'll ask you again. Where is Grey?"

"Why should I tell you? Is it the reward that Butler has offered for—"

"The reward be damned! I am trying to help you, Victoria! I am trying to help you and Grey!"

"Why would you want to help me? Why would you want to help Grey? The last time you met, you tried to kill each other!"

"We were adversaries then."

"And now what has changed?"

"Did he not tell you? Grey advised the Duchesse de Saint-Rémy of Quaratesi's treasonous activities. The Duchesse has connections at court, and Quaratesi has been arrested. I blame my condition on him and Ramsey. Grey got rid of Quaratesi for me. Now I will get my revenge on Ramsey by rescuing Grey. He wants to destroy your husband, *cara*, and he thinks he has. But you know, the chances of his never discovering the truth are extremely small."

"But he hasn't discovered—"

"Not yet," Niccolò interrupted. "But only because Ramsey has been too busy enforcing General Butler's proclamation to go to the morgue to view the body. And no one else in the garrison knew Grey well enough to recognize him. But it is only a matter of time. I know your husband is alive, Victoria. He must be gotten away. I can help."

"How?"

"I have a safe conduct from Ramsey. If I tell him I wish to leave New Orleans, it will allow me to go with no interference."

"And Grey?"

"We could take him away. It is not impossible."

Tori trembled. She felt a glimmering of hope inside her but could not allow herself to believe that there might be a way out of her nightmare.

"I don't know, Niccolò," she whispered. "I'm afraid to trust you. I simply don't know if I can afford to."

"Can you afford not to trust me?" Niccolò challenged her. "Have you another way to get Grey out of New Orleans? Have you time to find another way?"

Sighing, Tori sank onto a sofa near the windows. "No, I haven't time, you know that. I shall have to trust you, Niccolò. I shall have to place my life and Grey's in your hands." She shivered, terrified. "Please, please, help me," she whispered. Then, covering her face with her hands, she wept.

45

"He is coming this afternoon," Tori told Elizabeth the next day. "He is definitely going to take us; the only question is when." She took Elizabeth's hand. "Come with us, Elizabeth. Come away from the war."

Elizabeth shook her head. "I have family in Natchez. I will go to them." She laid a finger on her lips. "And I want to try to arrange a funeral for Grey' if the authorities will release his body to me. After all, Grey had no family that they know of here, had he?"

"No." Tori felt almost guilty to be sailing away leaving this gentle, generous creature to her sorrow. "Elizabeth," she persisted. "Please come. We'll wait."

"You will not! The danger increases with every moment you stay." Elizabeth smiled faintly. "But thank you. Perhaps someday I will come to Jamaica and see you and Grey and your children."

Tears filled Tori's eyes. "Yes, you must. You must meet your namesake." She smiled. "Our first daughter will be named Elizabeth."

The two women embraced silently and then Tori went up to see Grey.

Holding her breath, Tori let herself into Grey's room. He lay sleeping quietly, peacefully, in the middle of the big bed. With Tori's acquiescence, he had been kept sedated, for the wounds in his legs and chest were painful and the stitches that held them might easily tear if he were to thrash in his bed against the agony of his injuries. In this way, she thought, he would be easier to move to whatever ship Niccolò managed to secure for their departure for Jamaica.

Gently, tenderly, Tori brushed back the thick jet-black waves of his hair. Bending, she kissed his forehead, his cheeks, his lips. She took his hand in both of hers and clasped it to her bosom.

"Tori?" Elizabeth was peering around the half opened door. "Count da l'Armi is here."

Leaving Grey's bedside, Tori went down to the parlor where Niccolò sat.

He rose as she entered the room. "Victoria. have made the arrangements. But we have not much time."

"Tell me," she asked, sitting opposite him.

"It must be tonight. There is too much risk to wait. I will be waiting on the ship. You must bring Grey."

Tori's mind raced. Amanda had said she was going to some reception or other with Randal tonight. If she were careful, she could get her belongings out of the house after Amanda had left

470

y the time her cousin returned, she and Grey would
e well on their way to safety.

"I will manage," she assured him. "Somehow, I
ill manage."

Darkness had fallen over the city by the time
manda and Randall Ramsey rode through the rain-
wept streets in Colonel Ramsey's closed carriage.

"I haven't seen much of your lovely cousin
cently," the colonel commented. "I hope she is
ell."

Amanda shot him a sharp glance, not at all
king his tone. "Tori's quite well," she assured him.
She's been spending a great deal of time with Mrs.
hipps—the wife of the man wounded when Grey
erreaux was killed."

"Has she?" Randall asked thoughtfully.
Interesting. It was reported this afternoon that
iccolò da l'Armi's carriage was seen outside
alentine Phipps' home."

"Well, the Count knows Tori, doesn't he?
erhaps he took her to visit Mrs. Phipps. Perhaps
ey are courting."

"I doubt Madame Duclaux would welcome da
Armi's attentions. Hmmm. I think this Valentine
hipps might bear watching."

"Should I ask Tori about him?"

Randall shook his head. "No. Don't say
nything to her." He turned the carriage into a side
reet. "If you don't mind, my dear, I must stop at
e hospital for a moment. You needn't come in if
ou don't wish to."

The carriage stopped before the hospital and
andall got out. He disappeared into the building for
hat he told her would be a brief meeting.

When the minutes turned to a quarter hour, then

a half hour, Amanda chafed at the delay. Climbing down from the carriage, she wandered into the hospital.

It was the smell that nearly drove her back out into the rain-washed night. The smell of blood and disinfectant and death. Unsure of where Randall might have gone, she wandered the corridor—silent in the night but for the moaning of the wounded in the wards.

She tried the latch of a closed door. It gave and she walked into the world of nightmares.

Randall stood silently among the tables on which sheeted corpses lay silent, anonymous, deprived of the life that might have been theirs but for the war. And on his face was a look of demonic rage.

"He's escaped me again," he hissed.

"Who has?" Amanda breathed, wanting desperately to be away from that horrible, nightmarish place.

"Grey Verreaux." Randall turned and pointed at the corpse he'd been viewing. "That is not his body."

"But Elizabeth Phipps—" Amanda began.

"Deliberately lied to us." Randall's voice was quiet, deadly.

"Then who did Elizabeth Phipps take home?" Amanda asked, bewildered.

"Who do you think, you fool? Damn! Damn! She took him right out from under our noses!" His mind raced. "She must have him at her home! She must be nursing him—" A new, even more infuriating thought struck him. "Da l'Armi!" he hissed. "She's taking him out on the ship Niccolò da l'Armi hired! And I gave him the safe conduct! We've got to stop them! Now!"

472

With Amanda running in his wake, Randall Ramsey fled the hospital and went to get help in searching Elizabeth Phipps' house.

In spite of his pain, Grey grasped Elizabeth's hand as two of Elizabeth's manservants carried him downstairs.

"I don't like leaving you here," he told her softly. "Val would want you to come with us. He would wish for you to be safe."

"I have to stay," she told him. "But I have told Tori that I may come to Jamaica to see you."

"You'd better. Or I may come back and get you!"

"Goodness! You're getting awfully dictatorial, aren't you?" she teased.

Grey smiled wanly. The pain in his chest and legs was unbearable, but he had refused any further sedation.

"I can never repay you for what you've done," he told her seriously. "If you ever need any-thing—anything!—you let me know. And if you ever need me, send for me. I will come to you. I owe you my life."

"I shall remember that," Elizabeth assured him. "And I know we will see each other again." Taking Tori's hand as well, she smiled at them both. "If you truly wish to repay me, you must promise me to love each other always."

Eyes misted with tears, Tori hugged Elizabeth as Grey was laid on the floor of Tori's carriage. She climbed in after him and, hoping to conceal him should they be stopped for any reason by Union troops, Louise and Tori settled themselves on opposite sides of the carriage and covered him with their billowing satin skirts.

473

"Good-bye, Elizabeth," Tori breathed, reaching toward her from the carriage window. "Are you certain—?"

"Quite certain," Elizabeth told her. "God speed to you, Tori. And all happiness."

The carriage rolled off and Tori waved wistfully to Elizabeth, who stood in the street and watched until it was out of sight.

"Please, let us get away safely," Tori prayed, murmuring it over and over like a litany. She did not stop until they had reached the docks and Grey was aboard, settled comfortably in a spacious cabin. Tori's trunks were brought aboard and stowed below decks.

"Ready, Victoria?" Niccolò asked as she tucked the quilts around Grey who, exhausted, had fallen asleep.

"Yes—oh lord, yes! The sooner we get under way, the better!"

Niccolò's black eyes softened as he watched her fuss over Grey. "He is a fortunate man, Victoria," he murmured wistfully. "A most fortunate man."

Before Tori could reply, he left the cabin and went up on deck to give the orders for the sleek, white ship to slip its moorings and move out into the black, churning water of the Mississippi.

The great twin paddlewheels of the ship began to turn, thrashing the water as she moved out past the dark, hulking shapes of other ships. She was passing the first of the Union cruisers left behind when Farragut's fleet had left to take Baton Rouge, when Randall Ramsey and a troop of Union soldiers arrived at Elizabeth Phipps' home.

EPILOGUE

Later, when she thought of their escape from New Orleans, it seemed to Tori that she held her breath every inch of the way down the Mississippi, past the looming threat of the Union Navy. But since Niccolò had been given a safe conduct and permission to leave port by Randall Ramsey himself, they went unmolested.

During the five-day voyage to Jamaica, Niccolò and Tori cemented their friendship—based for her on gratitude for Niccolò's saving Grey from almost certain death once the Yankees had discovered Elizabeth's trickery, and for him on the genuine and deep admiration and love he had for her and had had since their voyage from Jamaica to France the year before.

Even Grey became resigned to the Count's presence once he accepted the fact that it had been

475

Niccolò who had in effect saved his life. When Niccolò expressed a desire to remain in Jamaica for a few weeks, Grey offered him the hospitality of Stockton Hall.

Niccolò's few weeks in Jamaica turned into a month and then two. The longer he stayed, the more loath he seemed to leave. And if he cut a swath through the ranks of the ladies of Montego Bay—and Monique, now carrying her first child, assured Tori he did—Tori scarcely noticed. She was too caught up in caring for Grey, in nursing him through the difficult early days and in rejoicing to see him growing well again, strong and handsome, with only a slight—a very slight—limp that the doctors assured him would disappear with time.

It was a sweltering morning in mid-July when Niccolò stopped Tori as she passed across the foyer of Stockton Hall.

"Victoria?" he called.

She turned and saw him there. His scars had faded and his limp was almost gone. Even with the pathetically empty sleeve of his coat dangling, he was an undeniably handsome and dashing figure of a man.

"What?" she asked, mocking. "Up already? It's not even noon!"

His smile was teasing, almost sheepish. "Actually, I was just coming in. I met a lady at soirée in Montego Bay last night . . ."

"Spare me the details," she insisted.

He laughed. "I wanted to tell you that I am leaving today—returning to Italy. It is my home and I miss it."

Tori's smile faded. "Oh, Niccolò. Won't you be in danger from Cavour?"

His smile was boyish, almost shy. He seemed touched that she should have a care for his safety.

"Once I am in the midst of my family, even he cannot harm me," he promised her.

He held out his arm to her and she stepped into his embrace. It was warm, caring, a friend's embrace. Tori felt his lips against her hair and pulled him closer.

"Oh, Niccolò," she whispered, feeling the tears of worry welling into her eyes.

"So this is the way it is!" Grey's voice boomed across the foyer. "No wonder you've been so happy to remain with us, da l'Armi! I would have expected no more of you, knowing you as I do!"

His face was dark, his silver eyes stormy as he came toward him. Tori, knowing it for the charade it was, noticed only that he looked tanned, fit, and healthy, and that the limp that was so marked when first he had left his sickbed was scarcely noticeable now.

But Niccolò, not knowing Grey as well as Tori did, was truly concerned.

"Grey, I . . . you must know . . . surely you . . ," he stuttered.

"I am at your service, da l'Armi," Grey growled. "I should have taken more careful aim the last time!"

Niccolò's onyx eyes were filled with a very real alarm. "Grey! You do not honestly think I would try to seduce—surely you do not believe—"

Grey, unable to maintain the ruse any longer, began to laugh and Niccolò, filled with a mixture of embarrassment and relief, eyed him curiously.

"That was unkind of you," he chided. "You made me worry."

Tori, both arms wrapped around one of Grey's

477

arms, reached out and tapped Niccolò's chest.

"Leave him alone, Niccolò. It's such a novelty for Grey to be cast in the role of the outraged husband, you know." She smiled blissfully up at Grey. "Niccolò is leaving today for Italy, darling."

Grey's silvery eyes glinted with deviltry. "And high time, I should say! When do you leave?"

"My trunks are already aboard. I've told my crew to be ready to leave on my arrival."

"I'll drive you down."

With a kiss for Tori, Grey left her side and walked toward the door with Niccolò. As they left, she overheard him say:

"I wish to God I were sailing! I'm driven mad with the lack of news of the war! Every word that reaches us is weeks, if not months, old."

By the time Grey returned, Tori was in one of the rear parlors staring out at the sunbathed gardens.

"Niccolò has left?" she asked as she heard him enter the room.

"Yes," Grey replied. Coming to her, he drew her into his arms.

Tori leaned against him, grateful for his strength, soothed by his caressing hands, his teasing lips, but she was troubled by what she'd heard him say to Niccolò.

"You're going to go back, aren't you?" she asked softly.

Holding her face in both hands, he gazed into her eyes. "I have to. You know that. I can't stay here and play the gentleman farmer while America is being torn apart."

She closed her eyes and he felt her tremble. "I can't bear to think of it," she whispered. "I can't let you go again."

His eyes were warm, reflecting the love he felt for her—the love he saw in her eyes whenever she looked at him.

"Well, then," he said gently, his voice low and caressing. "Perhaps you'd better come with me. I've discovered it's downright dangerous for a man to leave you behind."

Together they sank to the thick, yielding carpet, bathed in a pool of hot, Jamaican sunshine and certain in their love for each other. The war, the perils of the future and the world outside the parlor door ceased to exist for either of them.